BLESS HER HEART

OR

MY LOVE NELLY

FROM E.J. BRETT'S WEDDING BELLS

LONDON:

KELLY AND CO,,

15, GATE STREET, LINCOLN'S INN FIELDS.

CONTENTS.

———◆———

CHAPTER I.

CHAPTER II.

CHAPTER III.

CHAPTER IV.

CHAPTER V.

CHAPTER VI.

CHAPTER VII.

CHAPTER VIII.

CHAPTER IX.

CHAPTER X.

CHAPTER XI.

CHAPTER XII.

CHAPTER XIII.

CHAPTER XIV.

CHAPTER XV.

CHAPTER XVI.

CHAPTER XVII.

CHAPTER XXVII.

CHAPTER XXVIII.

CHAPTER XXIX.

CHAPTER XXX.

CHAPTER XXXI.

CHAPTER XXXII.

ILLUSTRATIONS.

BLESS HER HEART;

OR, MY LOVE NELLY.

"'BE BRAVE AND STRONG, JOHN, AS I AM,' CRIED NELLY."—(See page 17.)

BLESS HER HEART;

OR,

MY LOVE NELLY.

CHAPTER I.

AN ILL WIND BLOWS TOWARDS BLISSET'S MILL—MR. PHANTOM SCORES ANOTHER "NOTCH."

S it is by no means a pleasant day to loiter on the road, let us at once make a skip to the point and place at which our story begins.

Gazzard's Lane, in the parish of Monkshood, Kent; as cosy and comfortable a lane as Kentish lanes not uncommonly are.

A lane with a fragrant hedge on either side of it; as thoroughgoing a sweethearting a lane as though Cupid himself had planned it.

A lane with a perpetual summer odour of something ripening or ripe about it, commencing in May with strawberries and hawthorn blossom, and renewing its nosegay month by month, until it winds up with a glorious bouquet of luscious plums and newly-cut wheat about September.

A lane with such artful windings in it that any separate twenty yards of it may be safely regarded as utterly and completely shut out from the view of any one who might happen to be perambulating any other part.

No end of meadows branch out from Gazzard's Lane.

At the mouth of each, screened on either side by a thick hedge, there is a stile, the low, broad top bar of which calls out " Rest here a little while," as plainly as though it possessed a voice.

At the end of Gazzard's Lane—which is half a mile long, at least—is a hill, and at the top of the hill a mill, with its sails or hands perpetually raised above its head, as though it were a highly moral mill, and was mightily shocked at the billing and cooing not unfrequently on view below, and which, from its commanding position, it could well discern.

The mill was known as Blisset's Mill; it should have been Blisset's Hill as well, if many generations of simple tenancy could have made it so.

But Blisset—old Bob Blisset—was only a renter, as many generations of his name had been before him, and the land all about there belonged to the Viperts, the reigning member of which just now was Squire Reginald.

But, on this gloomy, breezy September afternoon, Blisset's Mill, supposing it to have no better employment (which it has, and is spinning round at a merry rate), may look from one end to the other of Gazzard's Lane, and find nothing in the least calculated to shock its excessive modesty.

Nothing more objectionable than the presence of three men.

Two of them shabbily-dressed, commonplace looking individuals; the other, if the term be allowable, about as uncommonplace-looking a being as it is possible to conceive.

An individual, whose height exceeded that of his companions by six inches at least, but whose breadth was so slender that, had he been doubled over, and welded so, his robustness would have been by no means remarkable.

A person singularly devoid of personal attractions.

A man with high cheek-bones, and with such deep pits for his sickly, pale blue eyes, that they looked like dungeon prisoners, over which his coarse sandy eyebrows kept vigilant guard; while with his pinched nose and hungry, hollow cheeks, and his wide, thin-lipped mouth, he might have sat for a picture of Famine.

His attire was sombre and sad as himself.

It was evident that his clothes, though of bygone excellent quality, were never made to his measure, a considerable tract of dingy white stocking appearing between his low tie-shoes and the hem of his black inexpressibles.

A corresponding space appeared between his wristband and his elbows, and his big bony hands were covered with rusty black cotton gloves, the period of the creation of which must have been coeval with that of the aldermanic, whalebone-ribbed umbrella he carried under his arm.

The trio paused as they came to that part of the lane from which Blisset's Mill was visible.

"There you are; d'ye see it?" exclaimed the lanky, unprepossessing personage just described.

"Yes, master."

"Well, you can't miss coming to it if you keep to this lane. When you reach the end of it, you'll arrive at the mill path that winds up the hill. You won't make any blunder?"

"'Tain't likely, master."

"Don't hesitate or loiter about asking questions. Don't mind the dog. Keep close by the barn, and the brute's chain is so short that he can't reach you by a yard."

"It mightn't be able to reach *you*, master," one of the shabby, bulky men ventured to remark, with a glance at the other's skeleton proportions; " but we're just a *leet*le stouter than you are, and——"

" Are you a yard stouter, you dolt? Are you half a yard?" interrupted the tall, cadaverous man, with a snap of his big teeth that might have well become Blisset's dog itself. " There's no danger, I tell you. If you want to earn the extra guinea I've promised you, you'll just march straight into the cottage, and make your capture."

" Straight into the parlour, I think you said, master?"

" The parlour on the left-hand side of the porch as you enter; yes, there you'll find him."

" He's sure to be there, master?"

" Yes, sure!" and the shadow of a grin that for a moment flitted over the gaunt face of the speaker by no means enhanced its beauty; " not a doubt of it. You'll find 'em quite jolly, I reckon, all of 'em, including dainty Nelly. Such good news! Such happy tidings! Such a blissful future! and then— whew! down comes the thunderbolt! Why, you dull rogues, you ought to give *me* a guinea instead of me giving you one, for providing you with such a treat."

But the men seemed slow at regarding the business in hand in the amiable light in which the tall man put it.

" He's a big chap, this John Gauntlet, I think you said, master? It won't be much of a treat if he turns rusty," one of them remarked.

" But he won't. He'll be so thunderstruck that he'll come away with you like a lamb. There'll be some squall-ing, p'r'aps—women's squalling, I mean; but you won't mind that."

The fellows shrugged their shoulders impatiently, as though that were sufficient answer to so preposterous a question.

" And, d'ye hear? you'll remember what I've been impressing on you all along?"

" About your having no hand in the affair? Yes, master; we'll remember."

" No hand, no voice, no anything; you won't breathe a word about me," continued the wearer of the black cotton gloves. " When I come in the midst of it, you won't, by word or sign, lead them to suppose that you have seen me before?"

" Trust us, master; we ain't fresh from the school where we was edicated," responded the fellow.

And so they went their way, while the gaunt man betook himself to one of the stiles before mentioned, and, withdrawing from his right hand the black cotton glove, commenced nibbling at his finger nails as though they possessed some peculiar refreshing virtue for which his hungry soul yearned.

Decidedly the attraction did not lie in their beauty.

If anything could excuse the wearing of such hideous gloves it was the shape and fashion of the finger-nails they covered.

Odd nails!

One or two preposterously long, as yellow and as hard-looking as the bill of a sparrow.

One or two gnawed down almost to the quick.

One—the forefinger this—long and

jagged, in tiny jags, like the teeth of a fine saw.

And yet, repulsive as were the finger-nails of this extraordinary person, the look with which he regarded them as he laid the lovely row on the begloved palm of his other hand, was one full of satisfaction, affection almost.

And this was the secret; they constituted his private note-book !

They were the tablets on which, with his teeth, he inscribed his designs against his fellow creatures.

When you once had the cue, you might judge of the depth of any particular " grudge " he held against any-one by the ugliness of the nail-notch that was scored to his account.

From this simple instance of Mr. Phantom's eccentricity, it will be seen that he was a person of no common character.

Mr. Joseph Phantom, house steward, confidential servant, business negotiator, man-of-all-work (including dirty work), in the service of Squire Reginald Vipert.

Could you have seen him in the presence of his handsome, unscrupulous master, you might well have supposed him to be some newly-hired drudge, who was anxious, by a display of extreme, nay, abject meekness and humility, to ingratiate himself in his good graces.

Whereas Joseph Phantom was an old servant of the family, and knew as much of its curious history as would have served a different man as a good solid foundation for at least an independent demeanour.

Mr. Phantom, at the age of twenty-seven, or thereabouts, had started as valet to old Squire Reginald, for the reception of whose highly respectable remains the grim vault of old Monks-hood church had opened some six years since.

Certain old folks of Monkshood affected to remember that Mr. Phantom came to be regarded as a person of some importance about the time when Squire Reginald's young wife, the present Squire's mother, was found dead in her dressing room, still grasping the fatal phial, some of the contents of which had trickled over and burnt its terrible brand on the bosom of the gay ball dress her ladyship was at the time wearing.

Temporary insanity and suicide was the verdict of the coroner's jury ; Joseph Phantom being the principal witness.

That was many years ago, but, whether the sad circumstance has any bearing on this narrative, or whether it had passed clean out of Mr. Phantom's memory, nothing but the disentangling of this story can show.

Suffice it that it not in the least interfered with the value of his services as a faithful and discreet servant.

He had served the young squire as devotedly as the old ; nay, while the former was engaged in the delectable process of sowing his wild oats, and was in terrible straits for money, and the father and son were constantly at loggerheads, it was whispered by those who should have known, that Joseph Phantom found a friend somewhere in London who was not averse, at the rate of sixty per cent. interest, to help the young gentleman in his distress, until such times as death laid old Squire Reginald by the heels and his son might step into his shoes.

Not that Mr. Phantom himself ever gave countenance to such stories.

On the contrary, he would meekly shrug his angular shoulders at mention of the absurd rumour, and inquire was it likely that he dare presume to meddle with his master's monetary affairs—a poor old curmudgeon like him, who, any time, was glad of a suit of Mr. Vipert's cast-off clothes !

And when anyone joked him on his influence at the Hall (for Mr. Phantom was an affable man, and would talk freely of his affairs), and hinted at the comfortable emoluments it must afford him, he would shake his head gravely, and reply, that it was altogether a delusion.

If anyone wished to learn exactly the sort of person that young Squire Vipert was, they should take service with him, he declared.

" You should know him as I know him," sanctimonious Joseph would exclaim, clasping his black cotton gloves, and casting his eyes skyward. " I don't say that he is a bad man. As a humble dependent, it would not be right in me to do so. No one can ever say that I was ever heard to utter a word against his father. May the Lord forgive him his unjust treatment of me ! Well, sir, the son is a harder man. He treats me like a dog. Only that I have grown to look on the old place as my home, and am a poor old fellow whom no one else would employ, I would leave to-morrow morning, I would indeed."

Joseph attended regularly at the lit-

tle Baptist chapel at Monkshood, and usually selected such times to enlighten his neighbours as to his master's true character, and, as he commonly wound up his complaint by betaking himself to his knees to pray for the reprobate, he contrived to pass generally as a soft-hearted, addle-pated old innocent, a mere tool in 'Squire Vipert's hands, and very much to be pitied.

And difficult indeed was it for anyone to discover anything to the contrary.

Never did Mr. Joseph Phantom permit the mask he wore to shift so much as an inch, except when closeted with his master and when he was alone.

Alone as he was, when sitting on the stile in Gazzard's Lane, after he had dismissed the two rough, ill-conditioned fellows on their ominous errand to Blisset's Mill.

As soon as the men turned away, and were out of earshot, his countenance changed miraculously.

His thin lip, usually so demurely set, expanded in a cat-like grin that exposed his teeth, that were yet curiously white and even for so old a man, and his pale blue eyes lit up as though the devil within him was breathing flame behind them.

He could see the sails of the mill from his perch, and he clenched and shook towards them his bony fist, with the bitten, jagged nails.

" Make the most of your time ; make the most of it," he snarled, spitefully. " There's an ill wind coming—a biting, blasting wind, that will go hard with you, and all the hateful brood that live in your shadow. This for *you*, bully John Gauntlet."

And he straightened his forefinger, the nail of which was more savagely bitten than any other.

"You will win her, eh? You will make her your wife, in spite of both the lion and the white-livered old jackal who will eat dirt to serve you or him! You make that your boast. Eh, brave John Gauntlet, you would use me to that end, too, and all the while spurn me and spit on me. You will marry her, the proud, saint-faced, little fool! the living image of that *other* Nelly of more than twenty years ago.

"Nelly, the daughter! Nelly, the mother! Nelly, the miller's wife, that should have been mine!

"Nelly, the miller's daughter, that shall be my worthy master's! his to hold, his to lose, at his sweet pleasure, and so I'll sting 'em," he continued, again apostrophising his jagged forefinger nail. "So I'll sting you, John Gauntlet, my handsome Anak! I'll bring you down with all your size and strength, and I'll sit on your neck with your face in the dust. I've notches for 'em all, but yours is the hardest to heal."

And as he spoke, he snapped at the nail as though it had been his enemy's throat, and bit out of it so savage and deep a notch that the quick was touched, and the blood started.

Then he wiped his white face on his handkerchief, and drawing on his black cotton gloves, and recovering his umbrella, that, in his insane fury, had been swept off the stile into the road, he bent his steps towards Blisset's mill, the meek, long-suffering Joseph Phantom that the world knew.

CHAPTER II.

THE DESCENT OF THE THUNDERBOLT—ARREST OF JOHN GAUNTLET.

EANWHILE the ill wind that Mr. Joseph Phantom had predicted had taken Blisset's Mill by storm. Never yet did hurricane or simoom bring about in so short a space of time such blight and wreckage.

Take the evidence of the thoroughly reliable old case clock that stood in a snug corner of the Blissets' best parlour, as regarding the appalling unexpectedness of the calamity.

Its hand was on the stroke of three, when the quick click of the hoofs of John Gauntlet's strong cob came to a dead halt at the gate of the mill-house.

As long, perhaps, as a second and a quarter elapsed, and John's great, glad hands are clasped about, and entirely conceal two other hands, that are many sizes smaller, and more delicate, and a voice, so tremulous with emotion that no one but John could possibly understand it, exclaims—

"It is good news, John; you need

not tell me, I can read it in your eyes. Oh, thank God! thank God!"

And then some one's face is cuddled down so close to the shoulder of John's shaggy riding coat, that nothing of some one's head is visible but a wealth of chesnut curls, and in a rapture, tall John lowers his face and kisses them, and whispers, with his lips right close to the little pink ear—

"Yes, my dear little frightened birdie, good news it is. I'm not to be hanged, drawn, and quartered yet awhile."

By the tick of the sober clock, this is all over in the further space of five seconds, and then some one (who is no other than Nelly Blisset), still holding John by the sleeve, hurries up the garden path, and through the green-coated porch into the parlour, where, ready for him with a joyous greeting, are Dame Blisset and Nelly's sister Nan.

Before the former could reach him, Nan, the bold and buxom, has clapped John's whiskers between her plump hands, and given him such a sounding, sisterly kiss on the cheek that it was impossible that Nelly could take offence at.

They needed no telling that he brought good news.

How could bad news be reconciled with John's radiant visage and bright eyes—John who, only yesterday morning, had started for London with a face as long almost as that of the miller's white horse?

"That's for you, brother-in-law Jack that is to be," cries Nan, "and I'd give you another for half a pin, if it were only to spite that little goose for

making us all so miserable since your lordship's departure yesterday."

"Ah! but it was so dreadful to think of," responded Nelly, with a little shudder, and with her bright brown eyes again filling with tears at the bare recollection. "A prison! my John in a prison!"

"In a dungeon, with fetters on his wrists and ankles, and a chain round his waist, and a big padlock to fasten into a staple in the cold stone wall!" exclaimed her incorrigible elder sister, playfully mimicking Nelly's doleful voice; "with a pitcher of water and one slice of mouldy bread per diem, and a fight with the rats for that! Ha, ha! poor fellow! I wonder his whiskers haven't turned grey with fright at the mere thought of it all."

"Oh, Nan!"

"There, for goodness gracious sake, don't start afresh," continued Nan, as the frightful picture she had drawn caused the bright brown eyes to brim over. "I don't mean it. I'd do the crying for you as well as the laughing if I might, you know that I would. But there need be no more crying for anyone; eh, John?"

"I should hope not. It will not be my fault if there is," replied John Gauntlet, cheerily.

And then, all white and floury, from his shoes to his cap, and looking not unlike a gigantic and jolly character from off a twelfth-cake, in comes father, and the tremendous hand-shaking that takes place between him and John speaks as forcibly for the strength of their respective muscles as for their friendship.

"So things weren't as black as you pictured 'em, eh, lad?" exclaimed the stout old miller, delightedly.

"Thank Heaven! no," returned John Gauntlet, with a big sigh of relief. "I'm luckier a deal than I could have hoped for."

"All a mistake, eh? A try on of Mr. Lawyer's! Danged if I didn't think so! Well, well; let us have a jug of ale, dame. It isn't often I rinse my mouth before tea-time, but John's good luck shall excuse it. And you had nothing at all to pay, eh, lad?"

But at this John Gauntlet smiled, and shook his head.

"Nay, the luck isn't quite of that quality, miller," said he. "There'll be a bit of interest to pay, and I'm allowed two years to settle the debt."

Old Blisset looked a little blank.

"To settle the debt?"

"Ay, the sum I made myself responsible for."

"Oh! so they have saddled you with the debt, have they, John?" said he, with an expression about his mouth as though he had bitten a sour apple.

"Not a bit of it," returned the young farmer, with a straight look at the miller out of his handsome, manly eyes; "nobody saddled me, Mr. Blisset. 'Twas my own doing, my own foolish doing; maybe it's only right that I should bear it till I can honestly cast it off."

"It is a heavy saddle to travel up hill with, John," returned old Robert Blisset, gravely, but kindly. "I'm sorry, very sorry."

"Sorry that I am bound to bear it? So am I; but please Providence, and Nelly, we'll pull through; what say, birdie?"

What could Birdie say, but look her acquiescence, and give his hand the loving squeeze it deserved?

The fact was, this debt with which John Gauntlet was "saddled" was none of his own seeking.

He had been surety for a cousin who had set up in business in London, a man of good credit, and who "wanted some money merely to tide over a crisis. It would be all right, perfectly safe, safe as the Bank of England!"

But just as the bond fell due, the unlucky linendraper took the misfortunes of business so much to heart that he died, leaving several little children to bewail his loss.

Then, after some parleying, a terribly official-looking document came, addressed to "John Gauntlet, Farmer, Monkshood, Kent," apprising that amazed person that the sum of five hundred and odd pounds were immediately due from him, and that, unless prompt payment was made, disagreeable consequences would certainly ensue!

Dreadful was the consternation at the house of old Blisset, the miller, of whom John Gauntlet sought immediate advice.

John was not a man of means.

For a young beginner he was thriving, but of freehold acres he owned none as yet.

All the land he farmed he rented, and this year blight had thinned his wheat.

He had not five hundred pounds!

In ready money he had bare one hundred, and this was Tuesday, and the money to meet the terrible bill must be found by Thursday, at latest.

No wonder that he hurried up to London with such a haggard, anxious face.

Less wonder that poor Nelly Blisset, who, come Christmas time, was to be his wife, seeing him return with a face with so much of hope and sunshine on it, should have greeted him as she did.

"It will be tight work, to be sure," said John, cheerfully, "but that doesn't daunt me. It is fairly my debt, and I'd rather pay it. It's a costly bit of experience, there's no denying; but never mind, I shall treasure it the more carefully, and make a profit out of it one day, if I have good luck."

And as he spoke his eyes sought Nelly's, and if love may be regarded as synonymous with luck, he might have discovered at a glance that he might make sure of a well's depth of it in one direction at least.

"Spoken like a brave lad!" exclaimed old Blisset, from whose face the little cloud of disappointment had vanished. "I like you the better for it, and I shall be proud to call you my son-in-law."

And really, could you have seen that happy little family circle, you might have supposed that the hero of it had been recently bequeathed a legacy of five hundred pounds rather than that he was that sum to the bad.

Half-past three—only one little half-hour since happy Nelly Blisset had so joyously greeted her betrothed—and then there was heard without certain sounds that were indicative of the approach of strangers.

Not the click of a horse's hoofs this time, but the savage barking of Nero, the canine guardian of the mill-house.

"That's a stranger, I'll wager—a tramp, I should say," exclaimed old Blisset. "Nero has a bark he keeps o' purpose for beggars, and that's it. Go and see, Nan."

Nan went to the door and presently returned.

"It isn't tramps, it's two men," said she.

"Two men! What sort of men?" the miller asked. "Gentlemen, are they?"

"They are very well disguised if they are," replied Nan, with a curl of her lip that indicated the unfavourable impression the approaching strangers had made on her.

"Well, well, show 'em in. Oh, there *are* the gentlemen!" continued the miller, with a bit of a frown, as the two individuals in question unceremoniously pushed their way into the parlour. "Pray, what may your business be with me, sirs?"

"No business at all, unless your name happens to be Gauntlet," spoke one of the men, roughly.

"*My* name is Gauntlet," John exclaimed, rising in wonder from his chair.

"Is it John Gauntlet?" inquired the man, fumbling at the breast pocket of his coat.

"The same," said John, with some resentment in his voice at the stranger's particularly free and easy manner; "and pray what may be *your* name?"

"My name is Clipshore, officer of the sheriffs of Middlesex, and I arrest you in the Queen's name for the sum of five hundred and twenty-three pounds, seven, ten!"

If ever there were five aghast faces, they were to be seen at that moment in the miller's parlour.

John Gauntlet was the first to recover.

"Ay, I see how it is," said he, with a reassuring nod to the others; "these men had their orders before yesterday, and they don't know that I have seen the lawyer, and arranged with him. That's the fact, my men; you need not waste time in waiting here; you will find it all right when you get back to London."

"No doubt we should find it particularly right when we got back to London emptyhanded, Tozer."

"We'd be permoted, I shouldn't wonder," growled hoarse Mr. Tozer, with a grin.

The colour mounted to John Gauntlet's face, and the fingers of his right hand twitched, as though they would like to make close acquaintance with Mr. Clipshore's offensively prominent nose.

"Look here, fellow," he began, "you have heard what I have to say——"

"Quite so," interrupted the officer, "and if you will be so kind as to return the compliment, it may tend to expedite

"MY LOVE NELLY."

our little business. Have you got such a thing as a almanack handy?"

"An almanack!"

"You'll find on consulting that useful article that this is Saturday, the seventeenth, if I am not mistaken, and now, if you'll be so good as to cast your eye on this little slip of paper, you'll find that the date of it exactly corresponds."

And he showed his warrant, which John Gauntlet, with white-faced Nelly clinging to his arm, bent eagerly forward to read.

The angry flush had all faded from John Gauntlet's face by this time.

"It is more than I can understand, my friends," he exclaimed, looking from one to the other with a bewildered air. "I told you what was simply, honestly true. I can answer for no more."

"But somebody will have to answer," cried the blusterous old miller. "What do you mean, you scoundrel? D'ye suppose that you are going to pounce down on him like a couple of vultures, and that you——"

"Tozer!" exclaimed Mr. Clipshore, significantly.

Whereon Tozer grunted intelligently, and produced from his pocket his constable's staff, and spat in his hand with

"IN AFTER YEARS, LET HIM REMEMBER THIS." —(See page 31.)

a relish, as though delighted at the prospect of using it.

Observing these symptoms of warfare, plucky old Bob Blisset slipped off his floury jacket in a twinkling.

And, in the midst of this exciting picture just completed—upright John Gauntlet, with his arms folded tight over his chest, as though to keep down the strong emotions that stirred him, and with his face ashy pale; with poor Nelly with her arms fairly round his neck, and sobbing on his shoulder; with Mr. Clipshore's hand on his other shoulder; with Dame Blisset dolefully weeping, and refusing comfort from Nan; with Mr. Tozer, staff in hand, and scowling; with old Bob Blisset in his shirtsleeves, and half a mind to commence the attack—the door was pushed open, and there stood Mr. Joseph Phantom.

It was quite affecting to witness the effect of this distressful spectacle on that good man.

His umbrella dropped from beneath his arm, as he at once raised his astonished eyes and his big, bony hands with the black cotton gloves on them.

" Why—why ! my dear friends— my good Blisset ! What has happened ? Why this consternation—these strange men, and Mr. Gauntlet looking so shocking bad? Oh, dear ! Do tell me —as an old friend of the family, you may, you know—do tell me what has happened."

And pending an answer, the tenderhearted Mr. Phantom withdrew his spotted pocket-handkerchief and buried his face in it.

John Gauntlet bit his lip, and much

more colour than was natural returned to his face.

" You are very good," said he, addressing Mr. Phantom, " but as a friend to the family" (John laid a somewhat bitter stress on these words) " I may appeal to you not just now to press for more than a brief explanation of that of which you have so unexpectedly become a witness. Bear up, Nelly darling; Mr. Blisset, dame ! no good can come of fighting against the law. Come, men, I'm ready to go with you."

" To go with 'em ! Where ?" inquired Mr. Phantom, with a voice choked with grief, and not daring to show more than one tearful eye from behind the spotted handkerchief.

" To quod," replied brutal Mr. Tozer, pocketing his staff and buttoning his coat. " Come on, young sir; our shay is down the other end of the lane."

" To quod !" repeated Phantom, showing all his cadaverous face this time. " What, to prison, do you mean ? Do I really hear that John Gauntlet— honest John Gauntlet—has committed a crime——?".

But at that instant John turned about and faced him with a suddenness that seemed to extinguish the completion of the sentence.

" Crime be hanged ! it's only a debt; that's no crime," explained Mr. Clipshore; and then, as though the mute anguish of Nelly's face had touched even his heart, he added consolingly—

" Lord ! what is it if the worst comes to the worst ? What harm will a few months behind the spikes do a wellbuilt young fellow like he is ? See the constitution he's got to fall back on!"

"Oh, John! my poor John! it will kill him!"

And Nelly hung such a dead weight on John Gauntlet's neck that he knew that she had fainted.

"Thank God for that at least!" said he, in a tremulous voice, as he tenderly kissed her, and gave her into Nan's careful hands. "She will be spared the pangs of seeing me go. Now, men, quick! let us be off!"

But, meanwhile, soft-hearted Joseph Phantom had not been idle.

As soon as he was informed that it was only a matter of debt, he heaved such a sigh of relief that all the family must have heard it, had they not been otherwise engaged, and taking a seat at a table, spread his pocket handkerchief out on it.

Then he commenced a hasty rummage of his pockets, and produced therefrom the following.

An old leather purse with six pounds eighteen shillings in it.

An enormous silver hunting watch, with a gold fob-chain and seals.

A silver toothpick.

A pair of old silver-rimmed spectacles.

"Stay!" he exclaimed, collecting the four corners of the handkerchief and handing the treasures to Mr. Clipshore. "Take this, my good sir; 'tis my little all; but my heart, sir, my heart, yearns towards the captive and distressed. Sell my watch—my spectacles—for what they will fetch, and if they should realise a trifle over and above the sum required to meet the claim of my poor friend's creditors, you can remit it to me in a post-office order."

So completely amazed was everybody present at this display of Christian generosity on the part of Mr. Phantom that for several moments there was a perfect silence.

Old Blisset looked his gratitude; and even John Gauntlet appeared as though remorse was twinging him.

But the person who was most affected was Mr. Clipshore.

For several moments he regarded Mr. Phantom's anxious face, so full of earnest sympathy and self-sacrifice, and then he broke into such a loud guffaw as almost roused poor Nelly from her fainting fit.

"Oh, Lord! I can't help it," roared the sheriff's officer; "I can't help it, Tozer! I should bust if I didn't do it! What a hactor he'd make! what a——"

But at that instant there flashed a gleam from Mr. Phantom's deep-set eyes, a sudden gleam, phit! and away again like lightning out of a black cloud, that seemed instantly to stop Mr. Clipshore's glee.

"What is there to laugh at, pray?" asked Mr. Phantom, in his meekest tone.

"Oh, nothing, nothing," replied the officer, at once taking the cue and looking apologetic; "only, my dear sir, it certainly *did* tickle me to see you offering such a rum lot. Lord bless you! it ain't no good at all. Five hundred and twenty-three, seven, ten, the debt is."

"Five — hundred — and — twenty — three—pounds!" repeated Mr. Phantom, pausing long enough almost to take fresh breath between every word. "Nay, then, much as our hearts must bleed, I am afraid that our poor friend——"

John Gauntlet shrugged his shoulders impatiently.

"If you will not take me, you may come after me," said he, and then a hasty shaking of hands all round, and one long, lingering kiss for still half-unconscious Nelly, and he was out at the door, the officers with him, with the sympathetic Mr. Phantom bringing up the rear.

But scarcely had they reached the gate, when Nelly Blisset, roused suddenly to a sense of her cruel bereavement, and with a cry that brought Gauntlet to a standstill, sprang out into the garden, and the next moment she held him fast clasped about, much to the disgust of Mr. Tozer, who retired and took a seat on some palings a few yards in advance.

"My darling! my darling! I can bear anything but this!" John exclaimed, in a choking voice. "It is torture a thousand times refined to see you suffer so!"

But to his amazement, she looked up into his face with an expression that would have been quite bright, only that it was so tearful.

"But I must wish you good-bye, dear," said she. "I want you to see, not what I suffer, but how brave and strong I am, confident in my own boy's lasting love and goodness. It is only for a little while, make sure of *that*, John, and take this assurance with you to comfort you, poor fellow!"

At this point, it was a tough struggle to prevent all that vaunted stock of bravery and strength from turning to tears, and escaping from her eyes.

"Before a week has passed I will see you, dear John, somehow, and with a purpose. And now one kiss, dear—only one, there! Oh, but you must be brave and strong as I am. There, again then; now good-bye!"

And she turned abruptly, and fled into the cottage.

Just a moment only John Gauntlet lingered looking after her.

"Strong and brave!" he murmured, under his breath, "and so she is both, as she is beautiful. Bless her Heart!"

And not one other word did he say during the whole journey from Blisset's Mill to the debtors' prison in London.

Meanwhile, how fared it with Mr. Joseph Phantom?

As before mentioned, while the majority of the miller's family were too overwhelmed with distress to trust themselves to witness John Gauntlet's departure, he had followed the captive and his captors into the front garden.

He did not, however, advance farther than a full-leaved elder-tree that stood about midway between the house door and the garden gate.

There he halted.

Mr. Phantom was not the kind of man to allow his more tender susceptibilities to carry him beyond the bounds of prudence.

When Mr. Clipshore disdained and rejected his money and valuables, he lost no time in replacing them in his various pockets.

This set his pocket-handkerchief at liberty, and distressful, shocked beyond expression, he hid his face in it, as he modestly sought the screen the elder-tree afforded.

But, good Lord! what a revelation for the Blisset family, for John Gauntlet, for poor Nelly, it *would* have been, could they have caught a glimpse of the villanous, treacherous face that lurked behind it.

While he affected to weep, his repulsive features were rendered yet more ugly by the devilish grin that distorted them.

True, there were tears in his deep-set eyes, but they were tears of malicious satisfaction at the success, so far, of his deeply-laid scheme.

He pricked up his ears as he heard Nelly's parting adjuration to her "poor boy."

He heard her boast of how brave and strong she was, and her promise that she would see him "somehow, and to a purpose" before a week had elapsed.

Then the diabolical grin faded for a moment from his face, and he looked puzzled.

"Humph! What does she mean by that?" he muttered to himself. "There's more meaning in her tone than her voice conveys. Aye, aye!" he continued, savagely, as he peeped from his handkerchief, and noticed the flushed face and the bright, confident eyes of the miller's daughter; "I begin to suspect that I have undervalued you, my dainty beauty. Ecod! a woman with a face like that is dangerous. Hang 'em! Women are harder to checkmate than the devil himself when

they get these confounded 'devoted' fits on them. She'll see him somehow and to a purpose within a week, will she?"

And, for several minutes after John Gauntlet had been escorted down the hill, and after Nelly Blisset had carried her aching heart back into her father's house, Mr. Phantom continued to cogitate under the elder-tree, sharpening his wits by nibbling at that last painful notch in his nail he had scored against John Gauntlet.

"Somehow, and to a purpose," he muttered, presently; "there's only one purpose that will avail him, and that is the procuring the sum of five hundred and twenty-three pounds, seven and tenpence. Can she somehow—anyhow—raise the money? Can her father? It is not impossible. He is a free man, and the mill is his own. I verily believe that the dusty old idiot might be persuaded if she set on to him."

Mr. Phantom gnawed his nail awhile longer, all the time casting such looks at the mill and the mill-house as would have blighted them had his power been equal to his will.

But as he scowled and gnawed, satisfaction gradually dawned in his evil eye, and finally he drew on his black cotton gloves and licked his pale thin lips.

"It won't be safe till I have 'em all in my net," he muttered, as he allowed his features to relapse into their accustomed sanctimonious expression. "I will net 'em, and you shall pay for the sport, my worthy master, Mister Reginald Vipert!"

And indulging in one last mocking grin, Mr. Phantom turned his steps towards home.

CHAPTER III.

IN WHICH THE MASTER OF MONKSHOOD IS INTRODUCED—MR. PHANTOM SUGGESTS A CURE FOR THE OLD WOUND THAT TORTURES HIS MASTER SO CRUELLY.

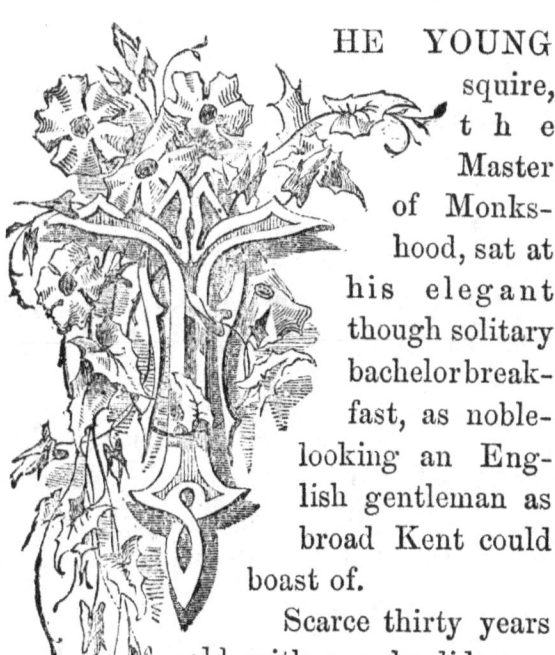

HE YOUNG squire, the Master of Monkshood, sat at his elegant though solitary bachelorbreakfast, as noble-looking an English gentleman as broad Kent could boast of.

Scarce thirty years old, with a splendid constitution, despite the assaults of the many enemies it had encountered; of magnificent proportions, as regards build, and with features of that singularly handsome type for which the Viperts, male and female, had been long renowned; with an estate of five hundred fruitful acres, and a rent-roll that returned him nearly two thousand pounds per annum; it seemed, indeed, that fortune had left him little to care for.

It seemed so, that is to say, to those whose means of judging were merely superficial.

There were undercurrents of the young man's life that some, even of his most intimate friends, knew not of.

Undercurrents, sullen and turbid; dangerous depths, flowing over quicksands and hidden rocks.

Depths in which lurked creatures cruel and voracious as the shark.

Nor was Reginald Vipert unconscious of the peril he incurred in diving down to consort with the animals of prey.

Almost as often as he reappeared again on the fair surface, ruined in pocket as in temper, haggard and exhausted, he would curse his infatuation and vow that for the future he would refrain.

He was cured at last, he would have no more of it.

But as surely as his fit of remorse wore off, would he listen again to the voice of the tempter, the siren whose charmed look was a pack of cards, whose enticing music was the dry-bone rattle of dice.

It was evident at a glance that on the morning in question, Reginald Vipert, the Master of Monkshood, as he was commonly called, was neither happy nor at ease.

The choice viands that adorned the breakfast-table remained untouched, and he sat with his hands plunged deep in the pockets of his elegant dressing-gown, and with his manly face turned towards the fire, in which, judging from the deep and deeper wrinkling of his brow, he was conjuring up pictures that were by no means soothing to contemplate.

Presently his cogitations were disturbed by a soft tapping at the door, and Mr. Joseph Phantom responded to the peevish " Come in " of Squire Reginald.

Meek as ever was Mr. Phantom, with a tread as soft as that of a cat.

His hands were uncovered, and they seemed restless without the black cotton gloves, yet grateful for the warmth their master imparted to them by his constant habit of gently chafing one over the other, thereby producing a sound that was somehow curiously suggestive of purring, and harmonized with the cat-like tread before mentioned.

" I am glad to see you home again, if you will excuse the liberty I take in saying so," remarked Mr. Phantom, timidly ; " the place is sadly dull without you, Master Reginald."

" You surprise me," returned the young gentleman, who had only by the merest nod acknowledged Mr. Phantom's presence ; " I should have imagined that your bright and cheerful countenance would have been equal to enlivening the gloomiest place, a coal mine even."

Mr. Phantom acknowledged this compliment by a bow of deep humility, and by purring with his hands louder than before.

" Are you quite well, may I ask, Master Reginald ?" he presently ventured.

" Do I look well ?" the Master of Monkshood asked, looking up.

" I grieve to tell you, sir, that you are not looking as well as I could wish ; has—has anything gone wrong ?"

" The shortest way to answer that question will be to tell you that nothing has gone right.   It is infernally hard," continued the young man, with a cynical grin distorting his handsome face ; " no fellow can serve the devil more faithfully than I do ; it seems unnatural that he should turn his back on me."

" Do you mean at the gaming-table, Master Reginald?" Mr. Phantom asked, demurely.

" What other table should I mean, you idiot?   Do you think I meant the tea-table?   Ha, ha ! that's more in your line, you born hypocrite and scandal-monger. Come, let's know how matters have been going at cheerful Monkshood during the three days' absence of its master. No news, I suppose?"

"Hoggins has paid last quarter's rent, and sixteen pounds off the old debt."

"I am obliged to Mr. Hoggins."

"Prendergast is a defaulter again; we shall have to get rid of Prendergast, Master Reginald."

"With all my heart," returned Mr. Phantom's master, with a yawn. "Well, put him aside; just now, at all events. Any news from yonder?"

"From——" and Mr Phantom paused inquiringly.

"From the mill; where else?" responded his master, impatiently. "No hopes of a fellow finding consolation in that quarter, I suppose?"

Mr. Phantom licked his lips, and ventured a little further towards that part of the room where his master was lounging.

The expression of his face was curiously altered from that when he was discoursing of the Hoggins and the Prendergasts.

He could scarcely contain the satisfaction he felt that the Master of Monkshood should have so readily broached a subject he had so closely at heart.

"There have been strange doings up at Blisset's since you have been away, Master Reginald."

"Strange doings! In what respect?"

And Squire Vipert's countenance assumed an expression of interest it had not yet worn.

"Unaccountable doings; cruel, cruel doings."

And with a grievous shake of the head Mr. Phantom's hand was seeking the handkerchief that reposed in his coat-tail pocket, when his master, with the toe of his slipper, unceremoniously arrested it.

"Let us have as little humbug as possible, Phantom," he said. "I am aware that you cannot possibly avoid it altogether, and, therefore, I will make some allowance. Speak out, man; what's amiss with Miss Blisset?"

"With Miss Blisset? Oh, nothing, Master Reginald. I am glad to tell you that when I last saw that young lady, she was in good health."

"Then what the devil——"

"You need not feel the least alarm on her account, I assure you, sir," interrupted Phantom, politely; "there is no difference in her except that her grief makes her look more bewitching than ever, if that is possible."

"Her grief, man!"

"Her sorrow for the family misfortune, if I may so designate it," continued Mr. Phantom. "But you may have before remarked it that there are some women who never look so lovely as when they are in tears, as when some real or fancied calamity——"

Reginald Vipert started from his chair.

"Confound you, you accomplished old hypocrite!" he exclaimed, in quite a flurry of excitement. "What about tears? What about her overwhelming grief? Who has caused it?"

"That might be easily guessed," returned Mr. Phantom, "as I need not remind you, Master Reginald, the young man, John Gauntlet——"

"What! has that upstart clodhopper quarrelled with her? Has he caused the poor little thing grief? If he has——"

"But he hasn't, at least not in the way you appear to imagine," Mr. Phantom interrupted; "he has had no quarrel with Miss Blisset that I have heard of; he is put past quarrelling at present with anybody, poor young man."

"How do you mean?"

"He's in prison."

"In prison!" repeated Reginald Vipert, in amazement.

"In a debtors' prison," continued Mr. Phantom, successful this time in securing his pocket-handkerchief from his coat-tail pocket, and applying it to his eyes.

"And who is the creditor that arrested him, may I ask?" Reginald Vipert inquired, with suspicion, a not unpleasant suspicion, if the truth must be told, growing in his eyes.

"That is altogether a mystery," returned Mr. Phantom, looking as solemn as an undertaker, and shaking his head dolefully; "no one knows at whose suit he is arrested."

"And no one is likely to know, eh?" exclaimed the master, with a meaning look.

"It is no one's business in particular to inquire, you see, Master Reginald," said Mr. Phantom, returning the said look with interest. "All I know—all that concerns us, I was about to say, only it sounds so presumptuous—is that the poor young man is in prison for the sum of five hundred and twenty-three pounds, seven and tenpence. A large sum, Master Reginald, for a young beginner, such as he is, to raise. I am afraid that he will lie in prison a long time."

The Master of Monkshood continued to regard his man with increasing astonishment, with which there was blended not a little of what, under different circumstances, might well have passed as awe.

"You pale brother of Satan himself," he presently exclaimed, with a half laugh, "what am I to make of all this? What infernal mischief have you been up to, my faithful friend?"

Nothing could have been more perfect than the look of innocent wonder than the "faithful friend" assumed.

"Mischief! Mischief that I have been up to, Master Reginald?"

"You artful villain!" his master continued; "and this is you who are so poor that you must needs worry me for the few paltry pounds I am indebted to you!"

Mr. Phantom regarded his master with mild reproach in his tearful eyes.

"I am afraid that you do not understand me, Master Reginald," said he; "I did not say——"

"What?"

"That it was through any designs of mine that the young man came to grief. Surely you cannot suppose——"

"That you would do it and confess to it," interrupted his master, now laughing outright; "certainly not, my discreet Phantom; you are the very last man to be suspected of such an act of candour. Let it pass, man; you are a very excellent servant, and I a grateful, and, I trust, not illiberal master. So much for your first item of news; what follows?"

"I should first like to know if you regard the first item as unpleasant, or the reverse," remarked Joseph Phantom, freely regarding his young master from the shadow of his shaggy eyebrows.

"Well I cannot say that it depresses me beyond endurance," returned the young gentleman, lightly, as he drew his chair close to the breakfast-table, and chipped an egg. "I am not so fond of the fellow that I shall expire with sorrow at his misfortune. What I am chiefly anxious to know is, how does my little queen of the mill sustain herself under the calamity?"

"You allude to Miss Blisset, Master Reginald?"

"To Nelly, of course."

"Bravely," Mr. Phantom shortly replied, but with a malicious twitching at the corners of his mouth that his master did not perceive.

"What! she is weaned of her silly love for the clown, is she? Ha, ha! It is only according to the old proverb, Phantom, 'When poverty knocks at the door——' you know the remainder."

"Which reminds me of another proverb, Master Reginald, that one might quote as seasonable, were it not unfeeling to do so."

"What is that?"

"'What is one man's poison is——' but you know the remainder, Master Reginald."

And, carefully regarding him, Joseph Phantom caressed his ugly hands, as though they were twin infants in which his soul rejoiced.

"To be sure," rejoined the Master of Monkshood gaily. "So it is to be capitulation, is it, my blooming maid of the mill? Pshaw! a man is never satisfied, Phantom. I feel now as though I would rather have gone to war with the enemy and made his treasure mine by right of conquest."

Mr. Phantom had turned to stir the fire, and he took the opportunity to indulge in a mocking grin.

There must have been a considerable portion of cat nature in Mr. Phantom's composition.

He loved to torment his dupes as does the animal mentioned that has a mouse at its mercy.

To play fast and loose with it; to rejoice it with a prospect of liberty one moment, and clutch it with its cruel claws the next.

"I said nothing about capitulation, Master Reginald," said he, looking round with a face quite composed and demure. "I am afraid that I have not succeeded in making you exactly comprehend the position of affairs."

"You need not exert yourself in

endeavouring to do so," returned the young man, cheerfully. "You inform me that her turnip-growing swain has abdicated, and that her little ladyship has not cried her lovely eyes out mourning him; beyond that, my prince of stewards, I will not trouble you for either instruction or information."

And Reginald Vipert regarded his handsome face, reflected in an opposite mirror, with serene complacency.

"Judging from appearances, I should say so, most decidedly."

Reginald Vipert's countenance changed ominously.

"You were right," said he, coolly, "you have not succeeded in making me comprehend exactly the situation of affairs. Will you proceed to enlighten me, my cunning, two-edged blade?"

Without the least hesitation, Joseph Phantom proceeded to do so.

JOHN GAUNTLET.

Mr. Phantom bowed reverentially.

"I should not, however, be doing my duty, sir," said he, "were I to refrain from informing you that Miss Blisset's love for this John Gauntlet, so far from diminishing on account of his misfortune, has considerably increased."

"Increased! Why, what the——"

As circumstantially as suited his purpose, he narrated the particulars of John Gauntlet's arrest, together with some details of the woeful parting at the garden-gate, and Nelly's last words to her lover.

The Master of Monkshood had risen from his chair during the recital, and paced the room with a troubled brow.

"WHILE NELLY STOOD BEWILDERED, A STRANGER APPEARED."—(See page 44.)

"And is it merely for the delight of your chattering old tongue," he presently exclaimed, passionately, "that you tell me in a breath, almost, that this fellow, whom I hate with all my heart, is in prison, and that he is presently to be released therefrom? Have you no remedy for this old wound you take such delight in mauling and torturing?"

Mr. Phantom inclined his head, as calmly as though his master had inquired for something that stood already at hand just outside the door.

But he didn't open the door; he merely shot the little bolt under the lock.

"What does that mean?" his master asked.

"Excuse me, Master Reginald; but since you are pleased to honour me with your confidence, I would rather enjoy it with as little chance of interruption as possible. You were speaking of remedies, worthy sir."

"Of the lack of them rather," replied the Master of Monkshood, impatiently.

"I know of one," remarked the cadaverous man, with quiet confidence, "that, skilfully used, must ensure success."

Squire Vipert stopped short in his angry walk, and regarded the strange being before him with an air of comical perplexity.

"Upon my soul, Phantom," he cried, half laughing, "you are the most inexplicable old humbug in existence. What is the remedy, man? Don't fear to mention it because it is a desperate one. If I am to lose the game, it shall certainly not be for the want of bold playing."

"In the first place, then, the remedy I speak of will involve the temporary use of some money," remarked Phantom, gently chafing his jagged forefinger nail against the palm of his other hand, as though thereby seeking some inspiration.

"What do you mean by the 'temporary use?' Why don't you speak out plainly, and say that I shall have to pay so much—so much out of pocket? I might have expected no other since you have a paw in the confounded business."

"I mean exactly what I say, sir," returned Mr. Phantom, smiling blandly. "The temporary use of money is all that will be required. You shall not be a shilling out of pocket, not a penny; nay, the very money, the actual coins that you invest shall be returned to you intact."

Mr. Vipert opened his eyes wide, and softly whistled.

"Proceed, my prince of conjurors," said he.

"I have told you my suspicions, Master Reginald, that Blisset may be induced by his daughter to raise the money required on his property."

"Just so."

"Then we must be beforehand with him."

"What, find the money ourselves and save the miller the trouble?" said Squire Reginald, with a sneering laugh. "But pardon the interruption, my good Phantom. Tell me how we are to be beforehand with them."

"In the manner you yourself just

suggested," replied Mr. Phantom, seriously.

"What!"

"We will find the money to release this unfortunate John Gauntlet from prison," returned Mr. Phantom, with an air that left no doubt as to his sincerity.

"_We_ find it! Why, you have gone mad, man."

And the Master of Monkshood looked pretty much as though he thought so.

"I beg pardon; I said we, I should have said you," returned the undisturbed gentleman. "It would puzzle me, indeed, to find five hundred pounds, or a tenth of the sum."

"By all that's unholy! but it would not puzzle you more than it would me to find five hundred pounds; it is a hopeless case," replied the young squire, laughing; "you should know that if any man should."

"You can borrow it," said the calm Mr. Phantom.

"For a few days I might be able to do so," Mr. Vipert replied, after some moments of reflection; "but first of all I should like to feel much better assured than at present—firstly, that the money will be required but temporarily, and secondly, that it will ensure that amount of success you prognosticate, which at present I regard as considerably more than doubtful. Pray, what is the end you hope to attain by this pretty scheme of yours, my clever Joseph Phantom?"

"In a few words this is it then," replied Joseph, approaching his master closely, and lowering his voice to a whisper; "John Gauntlet's imprisonment made sure and lasting; Blisset's mill—Blisset's land—Blisset himself yours, and then the dainty Nelly."

"How?"

"In this way, my very dear young master."

And still whispering, Mr. Phantom bent over the Master of Monkshood as he sat a wondering, attentive listener, and spoke earnestly.

At the conclusion of the brief discourse, Squire Vipert leaped from his chair and clapped Mr. Phantom on the back, with a heartiness that brought real tears into the deep-set, cold, cruel eyes.

"If you are not the devil himself, you must be his relation by blood, or brimstone, or whatever it is," he exclaimed, with a loud laugh. "Such splendid talents as yours are altogether lost, my handsome Mephistopheles, in the humdrum path of life you have chosen; you should have been a prime minister, at the very least."

"So long as I can prove myself my master's faithful minister, I am content," Joseph replied, meekly, rubbing his great white paws one over the other.

"I can't say, though, that I have much relish for the last act of the tragedy. Ha ha! my respected ancestors little dreamt that there was a taint of Dick Turpin's blood that one day would develop itself in one of their noble race. Seriously though, my good Joseph, I would rather some one else played the delicate part for which you have cast me."

"Who else?"

"Yourself for instance."

But at this Mr. Phantom shook his head decidedly.

"Too tender-hearted, eh?" observed his master, sneeringly.

"I should be exceedingly sorry to deprive you of the pleasure, Master Reginald."

The young Master of Monkshood took a few turns excitedly across the room.

"It shall be done, Phantom," he exclaimed, at last. "Get me writing materials; you shall go to London immediately and get the money we want."

CHAPTER IV.

THE PLOT THICKENS.

OSEPH PHANTOM had come and Joseph Phantom had gone.

Through three dreary days and nights black care had brooded over Blisset's Mill—over the mill-house that was reached by the garden path and the little green gate at which Nelly and poor John Gauntlet had so sadly parted.

Three days, and then came Mr. Joseph in quite a little glow of triumph, and with beads of perspiration bedewing his venerable brow in consequence of his haste up the hill.

It could scarcely be said that he was at all times a welcome visitor at the mill.

As agent of his master, who was Blisset's landlord, business took him there pretty frequently, and no one could say but that his behaviour was invariably polite and civil; but there was that about the man that forbade perfect trust in him as distinctly as though his own voice had proclaimed the warning.

Besides, John's rupture with Squire Vipert was of course well known to the family, and it was equally well known that sly Mr. Phantom was his devoted slave.

Hence John Gauntlet's coolness when Joseph came so suddenly on the scene of the young farmer's arrest, and so pathetically requested, "as a friend of the family," to be told all about it.

Since that memorable miserable afternoon, the event last mentioned had been frequently discussed by the miller and his family, the upshot being a universally-expressed opinion that Mr. Joseph Phantom had hitherto been a misjudged man.

Even the prejudiced Nan had been brought to confess that a certain person was not *always* as black as he is painted.

"And speaking of that same person, here he comes!" exclaimed Nan, who was the first to spy him hurrying up the path. "What on earth can he want here this time of the day? In such a mighty hurry, too!"

Yes, there he came, radiant with the comfort he brought with him, a good Samaritan indeed!

"My good friends, my dear neighbours!" exclaimed Mr. Phantom, bursting into the parlour in which the family had just sat down to their mid-day meal, "you must excuse the abruptness of the visit; you will do so, I am sure, when I make you aware of the cause of it."

"Why, what's the matter?" asked Blisset. "Anything wrong at the hall? Is it burglars? Is it fire? Come, compose yourself, Mr. Phantom."

Nor was this adjuration uncalled for.

Immediately on his entering, Mr. Phantom had flung himself into a chair, so agitated that quite a palsied motion was given to his umbrella, as it stood between his bony knees, and hid his face in his pocket-handkerchief.

"Oh, no, no, it isn't fire, my friends; it is water—healing water from the gourd of mercy that I—that I—don't be alarmed at these tears, my friends, they are emblems of joy, not of sorrow;

the voluntary outpouring of a heart brimming over with gratitude. But it is to *you*, Miss Ellen, that I should specially address myself; to you, to you!"

"To me!" exclaimed the amazed Nelly.

"Aye, to you, my good lass, as his affianced bride. Here, take it. Take from my unworthy hand the key that shall set the prisoner free, and restore him to happiness. Take it, and along with it the blessing of the humble individual who was instrumental in obtaining it."

And as, with a voice choked with emotion, he delivered himself of this affecting little speech, he produced from his breast-pocket a canvas bag of some bulk, and placed it at Nelly's elbow; at the same moment he rose from his chair and hovered his two great paws over her fair head, like two carrion crows hungering for carnage.

There could be no doubt as to the contents of the canvas bag.

The metallic jingling sound that accompanied its setting down announced it money.

Gold!

As much of it as would fill a pint measure at least!

It was all so sudden that hitherto no one had spoken scarce a word or risen from their seat at the dinner-table.

Indeed, old Bob Blisset, who was carving a leg of pork, had become so unexpectedly dumbfounded in the process, that he remained with the carving-knife upraised and a slice of the meat festooning the end of the extended fork.

He was the first to recover the use of his speech, however.

"The key of his prison! Set him free! What, John, do you mean? Our John? And *you* have brought the money; you whom he always suspected—*respected*, I should say," continued the old miller, bolting the slice of pork on the carving-fork to hide his confusion; "you, Mr. Phantom, whom he always *respected* so much and spoke so highly of!"

"Suspected! Aye, curse him, and with good reason."

But it was not aloud that Mr. Phantom made this candid avowal, but within the folds of his pocket-handkerchief, to which he had once again betaken himself.

Removing this convenient cover from his face, he remarked, with humble cheerfulness—

"Within this bag, my friends," and, as he spoke, he laid on it the black glove that covered the notched forefinger nail, "within this bag is the sum of five hundred and twenty-four pounds sterling; it is at your service—at *your* service, Miss Ellen, and his!"

Was it to be wondered at that which followed?

Was it the least bit in the world preposterous or unnatural that Nelly should, for the moment, have her little head turned with joy?

"Oh, bless you, bless you!" she exclaimed. "Forgive us if we have thought hard of you, our noblest, our truest friend!"

And she was down on her knees, almost before she herself knew it; and clasping, in both her own, a hand of his, the hand with the jagged forefinger nail, she kissed it once, twice, thrice!

In after years, let him remember this!

Let him recall it, one day in the future, when still a hale man, his heart is seethed in such torments as only the damned endure, and he curses the hour when the fatal spell was cast for him!

It made but small impression on him at the time, at all events.

Not but that he enjoyed it.

It was part of the little treat he had promised himself.

Coming along all the way up Froggart's Lane he had amused himself by rehearsing the anticipated feast—the grief-stricken family, arrival of the good genius, tears turned to smiles, and a chorus of blessings.

But the hand-kissing he certainly had not reckoned on, and it was all the sweeter on that account.

"It was lucky for her that *I* had my glove on," he chuckled to himself. "It would have been exquisite to have given her a claw for a kiss, to have just nicked her baby-cheek with my nail—the nail notched deeply for her John, and left a mark; quite by accident, of course! It would have been nice to look at afterwards!"

But aloud he remarked—

"Nay, my good girl, it is not to me that thanks are to be given, but to my master."

"To your master! To Squire Reginald! Why, bless us! that's more wonderful still," exclaimed the miller.

"Yes, neighbours, it is the squire who has lent you this money," continued Mr. Phantom, with caution, for the real business he had taken in hand remained to be done.

"May the Lord reward him for the good act," Dame Blisset ejaculated, piously.

"Yes; I think that I managed it pretty cleverly," remarked Mr. Phantom, not heeding the remark of the woman whom he hated to the very core of his sour heart. "He is a hard master; nay, he has faults that I would never attempt to gloss over; but if you know where and when to touch his heart, it is as tender as yours or mine. I resolved on the course I would pursue when I witnessed—for I did witness it; but I am an old man, Nelly, and you won't mind—your parting with John at the gate. I said to myself then—'This must not be—shall not be if I can prevent it.' He—Master Reginald, that is—was away at the time; he only returned last night, and I told him all. Aye, Blisset, with a full knowledge of the unfortunate misunderstanding between him and——Well, well, we won't further mention it. I told him all!"

"And what did he say?" asked the miller.

"Say! I'm proud to tell you what he said, my friends," replied Mr. Phantom, his deep-set eyes sparkling; "he did not say much, but it was to the purpose. He said, 'Phantom, give me my cheque-book, and I will make the poor fellow a present of the amount!'"

"He did?" exclaimed the miller, opening his eyes; "then, all I've got to say is that——"

"He did!" repeated Mr. Phantom, almost beaming with conscious goodness; "but I said 'No.'"

"And you said 'No?'" echoed Blisset, opening his mouth now as wide as his amazement was great.

"I knew you too well to say any other, Mr. Blisset," replied Mr. Phantom, with a glance of admiration towards the miller; "so I said, 'No, no, Master Reginald, much as it would gratify your generous nature to make this precious money a matter of gift, we are bound to consider the feelings of those we would benefit. I know this John Gauntlet is said to be a young man of independent spirit, and one who would be even more grateful for a loan than for a gift.'"

"That's right, quite right. I'm glad that you told him that," said the old miller, heartily.

"I knew that you would be," continued Mr. Phantom, shaking the miller cordially by the hand; "and I went even further than that, Mr. Blisset, knowing you even better than I know your son-in-law."

"You didn't go too far, I hope."

"As far as this. 'The young man,' said I, 'would rather accept a loan than a gift; and as for security, I'll be bound that his future father-in-law, without a moment's hesitation, will give you his mill, his mill-house, and all the rest of it, to hold until the money is repaid.' Said I not right, Mr. Blisset?"

"You spoke as I should, had I been there," replied the miller, quite carried away by Mr. Phantom's eminent opinion of him. "I'd be bound for John Gauntlet to my last pound."

"Exactly; to be sure you would! I knew it; and so, to save time, I thought I might just get the bits of deeds drawn out and bring 'em with me: and here they are, all ready for your signature."

And Mr. Phantom, with the dexterity of a man who is used to such business, spread the papers out on a side table.

"Of course it doesn't matter," he continued, in an easy and confidential manner; "it is not of the slightest consequence the extent of value you place as security in the hands of a generous lender; indeed, it occurred to me, my dear Blisset, that you would rather make a show of confidence for confidence, and give as ample security as possible."

"As you say, it can make no difference," replied the old miller, putting on his spectacles, "all that I should require would be time sufficient for the repayment."

"Exactly; and so I have included everything," said Mr. Phantom, pleasantly, "mill, homestead, mill-house, furniture—all! Pshaw! it's my pains thrown away, I'll be bound! Much more likely than not he'll refuse to take a penny when the time for repayment comes."

"But that I should insist on—John himself would insist on it," answered the miller, gravely.

And then, not wishing to cast a doubt either on the kind-hearted agent's designs or his handiwork, he made a mere pretence of reading the terms of the document, and set his sturdy sign-manual to them.

"That's all regular and proper," remarked Mr. Phantom, folding the papers, and securing them in his fat pocket-book (as he did so, he hung his head to conceal the gleam of malicious satisfaction he felt in his eyes). "Now, the next question is—what are the shortest and most effective steps we can take towards Mr. Gauntlet's liberation?"

And he looked towards Nelly, who was holding fast by the precious bag that contained the price of her lover's ransom as it lay in her lap.

"I brought the money in gold," Phantom continued, with the hesitation of a man who feels that his kindly intentions may be misconstrued into meddlesomeness, "thinking that, perhaps, Miss Ellen herself might——"

"Might what?" asked the miller. "We shall be glad of your advice in the matter, you may be sure, my old friend. Don't be afraid to speak out."

"Pray don't regard it as advice," replied the old friend, with an eagerness that would have surprised them had they been in the least suspicious. "It is merely my idea—a weak one, maybe, emanating from an old nunks like me. I had an idea that Miss Ellen herself would like to be the bearer of the good news—that she would take a pleasure in being the first to——"

"Oh, indeed—indeed, I would!" Nelly exclaimed, clasping her hands, and casting a look of sweetest thanks at Phantom. "I promised him, and he will expect me. Yes, father, I will go alone to London, and I will bring him back with me."

But old Blisset shook his head.

"Alone to London with so large a sum of money with thee? Nay, my lass, it's odd but we'll find a safer way than that."

" But I could go in the chaise, and Peter could drive," urged Nelly, her lovely face aglow with excitement. "Peter can take care of me; he's big enough. Oh, pray, pray, don't refuse me, father."

And, before he could say yea or nay, her arms were round his neck, and his mouth effectually sealed by her rosy lips.

"There would certainly be no danger if Peter went with the young lady," remarked Mr. Phantom. "If she started this evening, she might reach London before ten o'clock, and I should be glad to furnish her with the name and whereabouts of a highly respectable hotel, where she might stay till morning, and then go to the lawyer's office straight, and so bring the matter to a swift conclusion."

And so, to Nelly's great delight, it was finally arranged; and Mr. Phantom, wishing her a pleasant journey, took his departure.

It was quite an event for Peter.

Big enough, certainly, as Nelly had declared.

A slow-going, broad-shouldered, thick-headed man, above middle age, but still sturdy and strong as a Spanish mule.

A man-of-all-work at the mill, carter, labourer, carrier—anything.

Nan discovered him with his braces girding his waist, undergoing extraordinary ablutions at the pump in the back kitchen.

"You'll take care, Peter, of my sister?"

"Care on her! rayther. I should like to see the chap as dare touch her while she's under *my* charge."

And Peter looked fierce and red out of the coarse jack towel on which he was excoriating his countenance.

"You ain't afraid, Peter?"

"Afraid, Miss Nancy! Ha! ha! ha! That's what the clerk at the Tunbridge coach office said; only I don't know as he laughed so valiantly before he started on horseback for London with the money he was robbed of. But that's a good many years ago —twelve years. I was reading the inscription on his tombstone the last time I was in Tunbridge."

Peter essayed another laugh, but got not beyond one feeble note.

"Ah, that was a bad job," said he, still fussing over his toilet to hide his suddenly altered countenance. "That coach office clerk wasn't armed, was he, Miss Nancy?"

"I've heard not; the foolish fellow!" Nan replied quietly, coming to Peter's assistance in the matter of a collar-button, that in his hurry to dress, he had torn from its holding. "Hold up your head, or I shall prick your throat, stupid. Yes, it is awful to think of; those terrible times when you couldn't carry a little money along the road at night without the risk of a bullet through your head, isn't it, Peter?"

"It is enough to make your blood run cold," returned Peter, with a shiver; "but he should have took a pistol with him, you know."

"To be sure he should. Where's the harm of carrying such a safeguard?"

"Where, indeed? That's exactly *my* opinion, Miss Nancy. Not that I'm afraid! Ha, ha! fancy Peter being afraid of going a journey by road at night."

Five minutes after, the chaise bearing Nelly and the valiant driver, Peter, descended the hill into Froggart's Lane.

Nan peeped anxiously into Peter's bedroom.

Customarily a big flint pistol hung over the fireplace.

It was gone, and on the table were untidy evidences that Peter had recently been cleaning it.

"Thank goodness for that!" Nan exclaimed with much satisfaction, though under her breath. It isn't often that I'm afflicted with foolish fancies, but I have thought this evening of that which I would not have the old folks know for a necklace of guineas."

CHAPTER V.

THE GREY MASK—THE MYSTERY—THE SHOT IN THE DARK.

HE dull September day had waned to a duller evening and a pitch dark night.

The twilight was deepening ere the gaunt figure of the miller's white horse was lost sight of from the mill, and ere three miles of the momentous journey that Nelly Blisset had undertaken was accomplished, the road became so dark that Peter was fain to light the lantern that hung in front of the splashboard.

If the truth must be told, Peter was not completely at his ease. As far as bravery went, he had as fair a share of it as any man could desire; but it was of the sort known as daylight bravery.

Nancy's sole object had been to rouse him to a full sense of the responsibility with which he was about to be entrusted; but, unfortunately, she overshot her mark.

True, she had succeeded in inducing him to carry his big old pistol with him, and there, gorged to the muzzle with powder and shot, the butt of it protruded conspicuously from his pocket.

But the seat of his disquiet was the driving-box.

There reposed the precious treasure, the heavy bag of gold that was to set John Gauntlet at liberty!

Nelly at first had insisted on taking charge of it herself, but this was overruled, and Peter had become its custodian.

"There!" exclaimed that valiant

hero, as he brought his cumbrous weight down on to the seat, "if anybody wants to get at that there between this and Lunnon, they'll find it a toughish job; they'll have to slice me down till there ain't enough left of me to keep the box lid fast."

But it was early in the evening then, and Peter was flushed with the novelty of his position.

knowledge, and those, the more highly coloured ones, he had heard his companions tell of.

A half-mile further on (for this was a terrible road in the earlier days of the Dover mail), just where the larch overhung the road, Captain Thunder stopped the coach, and pistolled both guard and coachman, and carried off before him on his coal-black steed the banker's

JOSEPH PHANTOM.

He was flushed now; to that extent, indeed, that tricklets of perspiration rolled from under the broad brim of his hat, but his emotions were of a different nature quite.

Had every guinea in that bag been a thorn it could have hardly caused him, as he sat on it, more uneasiness.

His mind was filled with stories of highwaymen within his own personal

lovely daughter, who was a solitary inside passenger.

"Ah," he exclaimed, involuntarily, and but half aloud, "that was done in Shrouder's Gap, that was !"

"What was done in Shrouder's Gap?" Nelly asked from her nest of shawls and wrappers, quite alarmed at his sepulchral tone; "we haven't got to Shrouder's Gap yet, have we?"

"REGINALD VIPERT REGARDED THEM WITH SPEECHLESS AMAZEMENT."—(See page 67.)

Peter was roused to a sense of the indiscretion he had been guilty of.

"No, miss; it's a good three miles further on. I—I was only just a saying to myself that of all the ugly bits of road, that bit about the Gap is the ugliest; not that anything pertikler ever happened there, eh, miss?"

"Not that I recollect," replied Nelly, innocently. "Dobbin will go faster than this if you whip him, Peter."

"I am saving of his wind till I get to that spot I was speaking of, miss; then he'll go fast enough, I'll wager! So you never heard of anything happening there? Well, now, that's a comfort," and Peter began to whistle a lively air, that was presently cut short in his mouth through an observation he happened to take of the white horse's ears.

The light of the lantern shone full on them, and Peter saw they were cocked suspiciously.

"Hark!" he exclaimed, turning his alarmed face to Nelly, in the chaise; d'ye hear anything, miss? There's summat coming behind or before, that's a certainty!"

Nelly listened.

"It is the click of a horse's hoofs behind us," said she, knowing of old what a hare-hearted old fellow he was in the dark, and rather enjoying than otherwise the fun of seeing him frightened.

"It is some one we know, perhaps. I hope it may be, for company's sake. How dark it is, Peter!"

"Just such a night, you may depend, as when Captain—I mean—I should say, that it is dark, most awfully dark, Miss Ellen."

And hearing the sharp "click, click" of the hoofs of the approaching horse, growing quicker and more distinct, Peter, forgetful of his design to save Dobbin's wind, laid on to him with the whipthong hard and heavy.

But if he had any idea of outstripping the coming horseman, he was disappointed.

At full gallop he overtook the chaise and shot past it.

A silent horseman who took no heed of Peter's quaking "good-night," beyond a curt waving of his riding-whip above his head.

A tall horseman, on a tall horse; a traveller equipped as for a long journey.

A prudent traveller, expecting a rough night, and provided against it, judging from his dark, close-fitting travelling-cap, the lappets and peak of which were pulled down, concealing his face almost entirely.

Not quite entirely.

Peter, quaking on his seat, and keeping a sharp look-out by the aid of his lantern light, was able, in a single flash as it were, to make out something of the stranger's face.

The horse was dark; the cloak and the cap of the horseman were black as the night itself, but that little portion of his face that was visible was of ghastly hue.

The paleness of a pale living face was ruddy compared with it.

It was grey rather than white; the grey of linen unbleached.

But with that flourish of his riding-whip, the ghostly rider rode on at such headlong speed, that his horse's feet spurned back sparks of fire, and he was speedily engulfed in the blackness ahead.

But Nelly had seen nothing of this.

She was only conscious that a person on a horse had passed their vehicle rapidly, and without the customary salute one expects in the country.

"Did—did you ever see the like of that, miss?" Peter gasped, the darkness luckily screening from his young mistress the terror that was depicted on his countenance.

"He might have spoken, certainly," returned Nelly, thinking that Peter alluded to the rider's want of courtesy.

"Might have spoken! The Lord forbid," replied the quaking Peter. "You didn't see his face, miss?"

"No; he was a stranger, no doubt, in a hurry."

Peter was just on the point of declaring his opinion on the matter, but by a tremendous effort he checked himself.

"Aye, to be sure," said he, a happy idea penetrating his thick skull, "he's in a hurry because he doesn't want a wet skin, because his horse is timid of thunder and lightning, just as our old Dobbin is, miss."

"What do you mean, Peter? I see no signs of a storm," Nelly remarked, at once suspecting his design.

"Ah, that's because you've got a wail on," persisted the mendacious Peter, stoutly. "I can see the signs of it up here. Whew! we shall have a buster presently. No, no, Miss Ellen, I know my duty too well to let you face it."

And he checked the horse and commenced to pull him round.

But Nelly Blisset was up from her seat in an instant.

"What are you about to do?" she asked, resolutely.

"Do! I am going to drive you home again, miss. My last words to your own sister was——"

But Nelly cut him short.

"You may go back, Peter," said she, "but you shall walk back. I am ashamed of you, you big booby. I shall go on with or without you. Run home, big Peter, and tell them you left me to make the journey by myself because you were afraid of bogies."

Thus exhorted, big Peter must have been a booby indeed had he persisted in his original intention.

Unintelligibly grumbling something about its being "all for her sake," he sheepishly turned about, and again the white horse jogged along the road with that long swinging trot of his.

On for a further distance of two miles, to the dip that led to Shrouder's Gap.

Here chalk hills rose high on either side of the road, and on the left-hand side a jagged fissure, not more than ten feet wide, extended from top to bottom, from which freak of nature the place derived its name.

It was this dismal, dreadful spot that had haunted Peter from the commencement of the journey, and he took a good grip of the reins with one hand and of the whipstock with the other, determined to make short work of passing it.

At the rate of twelve miles an hour, at least, the chaise rattled down the hill, and the chicken-hearted coachman had just began to congratulate himself that the danger was past.

But he was suddenly convinced of the contrary.

Starting up in the horse's path, sheer before its head, as though by some miracle he had shot out of the ground, a man grasped the bridle and brought the vehicle to an instant standstill, while Dobbin snorted in fright and backed on his haunches.

It was the grey-faced horseman, but without his horse.

Peter recognised him at once, and uttered a yell of horror and affright.

Starting up in the chaise, Nelly saw him.

The lantern that hung in front of the splash-board shone full on his face.

She saw the black travelling-cap, and the mask of grey cloth, and, gleaming like stars, the eyes that twinkled through the eye-holes that were cut in the mask.

She saw, too, that while the hand that held the bridle likewise grasped a heavy riding-whip, in the other hand there was held a pistol, so that she could have no doubt as to the strange horseman's intentions.

He seemed about to speak, but suddenly it appeared to occur to him that the lantern before mentioned performed its office a little too faithfully to suit his purpose.

Still grasping the bridle, he swung aside the horse's head, the better to reach the object of his resentment, and with one vicious blow of the butt-end of his riding-whip, he shivered it in a dozen pieces, and sent it with a clatter to the ground.

Then, in the black darkness that immediately ensued, he exclaimed in a disguised, muffled voice—

" Quick, the money !"

But almost before the words were out of his mouth, the valiant Peter had vacated his seat.

The fact is that that brave personage had slightly misconstrued the highwayman's intentions.

When the latter, swiftly reversing his riding-whip, grasped the thong and swung back the heavy butt for a blow, Peter made sure that his head and not the lantern was the object aimed at.

Simultaneously with the smashing of glass, therefore, he exclaimed—

" Spare me, spare me ! take it ! It is in the driving-box."

And then the abject coward leapt from the chaise ; the pistol with which he had so carefully provided himself tumbling harmlessly out of his pocket.

But Peter did not make a clean jump of it.

Whether his fright spoilt the use of his legs, or whether his foot caught between the fore wheel and the carriage is not certain ; but he came to the ground headlong a tremendous crash, and there lay in a fit of real or assumed unconsciousness.

Probably the latter !

The grey mask was a man prompt of action.

" Take it, it is in the driving-box !" Peter had cried, and next moment what was in the receptacle mentioned was secured and snugly deposited in an inner pocket beneath his cloak.

He made a step or two towards the crevice in the chalk hill before mentioned, and where his horse stood, but promptly turned back again towards the vehicle.

"Why not?" he muttered to himself, with a half laugh that had little of the highwayman's ferocity in it. "It is the custom of the profession to take toll at the lips as well as of the purse of our fair victims."

And he advanced to the chaise, and, raising his cap, peered under the hood where Nelly was crouching.

Appalled with that one benumbing dread that had overcome her when she caught sight of the mask and the pistol —that dread that had now become a sickening reality—she had remained speechless and powerless to move.

To see her lover's ransom snatched out of her hands, as it were, was like seeing him stricken dead, and the anguish she felt was at the moment as crushing as though this latter had been.

The masked horseman, failing to see her under the leather hood, put out his hand and it touched her face, and in the same muffled voice he spoke, in a low tone—

"My pretty one!"

Then the spell that bound her was broken.

With a wild cry of terror, she shrank from him, and leaped out at the further side of the chaise.

More fortunate than Peter, she cleared it without damage, and heedless which way she ran, sped into the darkness.

For some moments the masked horseman seemed to hesitate as to whether he should follow her, as he might easily have done, the white woollen shawl that she wore making her swiftly-retreating figure easily recognisable.

But presently the dim, white figure sank suddenly down, and a sharp cry of pain instantly followed.

"By Heaven!" he muttered in tones of alarm, "she has fallen and hurt herself!"

And with a few rapid strides he reached the spot where she lay.

But it would have been better for that gallant highwayman had he acted faithfully to the end the brutal character he had essayed, and kept his sensitive heart within safe bounds.

His aim was accomplished.

Without the least difficulty he had secured his golden booty, and now he should, like a true knight of the road, have mounted his steed and galloped away.

But with a face, could it have been seen, almost as pale in alarm as the mask that covered it, before two might be counted he was down on his knees by the little white figure by the roadside, with his hands tenderly about her to raise her.

But who was he that she should expect tenderness of him?

Even as she felt his hands on her shoulder, there was a flash and a loud report, and the gallant highwayman, with a cry that was half an oath, half an expression of agony, staggered away from her, and reeled for support against a wayside bank.

Peter's pistol was the weapon that performed the timely service.

In his dastardly flight that ancient implement had tilted out of his pocket into the chaise, and, with a brave woman's instinct of self-defence, Nelly had immediately secured it.

She held it in her hand when she leaped from the chaise.

Scarcely aware of it, she had carried it with her as she fled from the danger that had threatened her.

It was not until she felt, except for the pistol, at his mercy, that she turned it against him.

It was such an unwieldy old thing that one of her little hands was quite unequal to the grasping of it.

She held it in both her hands, and touched the trigger as he was stooping over her.

She heard the cry he gave, and was conscious that he had staggered away from her.

Then a sudden, desperate hope flashed to her mind.

Had she killed him?

Was he so desperately wounded as to be unable to resist her efforts to regain what he had robbed her of?

Peter might help her!

Swift as a fawn, next moment she was speeding back to the spot where Peter was lying.

"Peter! Peter! up! We may yet recover the gold of which we have been robbed! Oh, Peter, for my sake —for John's sake!"

But Peter's swoon stuck to him for its own master's sake, and nothing more than an appalling groan could be wrung from him.

With a desperate resolve to rouse him, she tugged at his hair with both her hands, but immediately recoiled with a cry of horror!

Peter's hair was wet, and she needed not a light to know that what had so awfully moistened her fingers was blood!

But the brave little heart was not quite daunted.

The robber in the grey mask carried, under his cloak, "the key of dear John's prison," as generous Joseph Phantom had called the bag of gold, and she felt strong enough, cruel enough to kill him rather than he should carry it away.

But when she hurried up the lane again, she found that the wounded man had recovered sufficiently to make an effort to reach the spot where his horse was.

She met him dragging himself painfully along, and with his head bowed, so that he had neither seen nor suspected her coming, and, fierce young tigress that she was, she sprang at him.

Sprang at him with such strength and suddenness that the fastenings of his cloak were partly torn away, and, wounded and weak as he was, he was borne to the ground.

"Help! help!" Nelly shrieked. "You shall not take it away! I have hold of you, and you shall kill me or give me back the bag of money!"

But he was a man of great strength, and still had one serviceable arm to use.

He plucked away her hands as easily as though she had been a baby, and muttering savagely, scrambled to his feet, and flung her from him.

As he did so, the sounds of a horse's hoofs were distinctly heard, as yet a long distance off, but rapidly approaching.

Nelly heard them.

"Help! help!" she cried. "He will escape unless you come quickly! Help! help!"

But the masked robber heard the sounds as well, and this seemed to give him desperate strength.

Nelly would have grasped him again, but he pushed her off, this time so roughly that she was thrown to the ground, and before she could recover from the stunning effects of the fall, her assailant had reached the spot where his steed was tethered, and was off and away with the speed of the wind.

Nor was this the only retreat.

Already alarmed almost out of his sober wits by the outcry and the smashing of the lamp, the white horse Dobbin was altogether panic-stricken by the flash and the loud report that accompanied the discharge of the old flint pistol, and with a loud neigh of terror, he turned and fled homewards.

Meanwhile, the sharp click of the horse's hoofs, that had so effectually scared off the robber, drew closer and closer, and a stranger appeared on the scene.

CHAPTER VI.

THE PURSUIT AND THE ESCAPE—"I'LL HUNT YOU DOWN AS SURE AS MY NAME IS LORD LAVERING!"—THE STAINED CROWN PIECE.

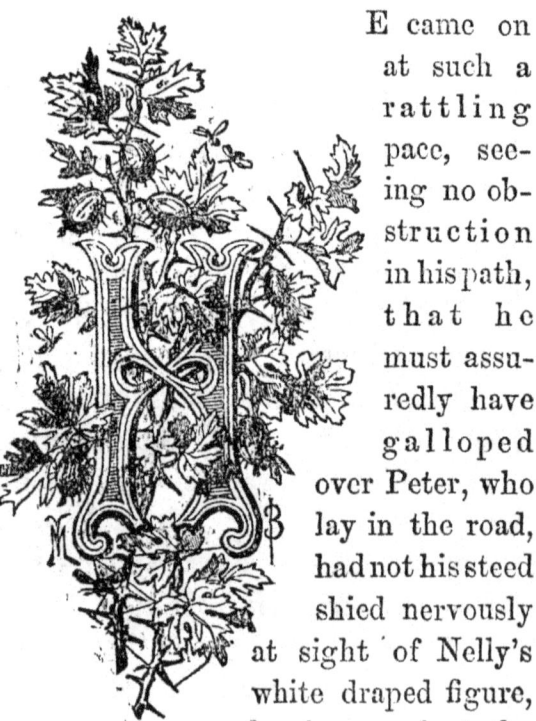

E came on at such a rattling pace, seeing no obstruction in his path, that he must assuredly have galloped over Peter, who lay in the road, had not his steed shied nervously at sight of Nelly's white draped figure, leaning against the bank, and looming like a ghost in the darkness.

By the quickness with which he quieted the creature, and brought him to a standstill, it was evident that the stranger was a thoroughly accomplished rider.

Whether he was young or old, ugly or handsome, was a secret that the darkness at present kept.

All that in the gloom could be made of him was that he was a person of small stature, with thigh boots of polished leather, and glistening silver spurs, and that the steed he rode was an animal exceedingly slender and handsome of build, and of the true breed.

"If I am not mithtaken, I heard a woman'th voith calling for help," the horseman exclaimed hurriedly, and with a decided lisp in his speech. "Wath it your voith? If tho, what'th the matter, my good woman?"

Nelly could not speak.

With one hand pressed over her heart, she with the other pointed in the direction the retreating highwayman had taken.

"Why don't you thpeak?" exclaimed the rider, suspiciously. "If it wath you that hallooed, you can't be dumb, you know. Let'th have a look at you, my lady."

And as he spoke, he advanced still nearer.

Then, observing the shattered lantern lying in the road, its wick still smouldering, he motioned Nelly to hand it to him.

Then, striking a match, a tolerably good light was procured.

Now his shape and figure could be better made out.

A young gentleman, handsomely attired, and with a face that would have been handsome, too, had it not been so wonderfully pretty.

As sweet a face as was ever moulded in wax, with light blue eyes, mild as a baby's in their expression, and now wide open as a baby's are not unfrequently seen, with pink, plump cheeks, adorned with the tiniest mite of downy whiskers, with a perfect little mouth, and teeth as beautifully even and glistening white as those of a shepherd's collie.

Within a dozen feet of his horse's legs, a man lay prone on the flat of his back, and with his hair all bedabbled red!

Blood on the chalky white floor of the road!

Blood besmearing the wayside bank against which the robber had leaned.

Blood on the dress, on the hands, on the face of the young girl, surpassingly beautiful, despite her terror, and the deadly pallor that overspread her face!

Scarcely five seconds were occupied by the stranger in making this amazing survey.

But meanwhile, such a change had come over his pretty face as showed that there was staunch manly stuff in him.

"This is no time for wasting words," said he, quite forgetting his lisp in his downright earnestness. "Tell me, young lady, how can I help you? Is that the ruffian who is accountable for this outrage?"

And with indignation flashing in his blue eyes, he pointed to the prostrate Peter, and prepared to dismount.

"No, no!" Nelly gasped. "He, the robber, has gone that way! A man riding a swift black horse!"

"A robber?—a highwayman?"

And he quickly settled himself in his saddle, and peered eagerly in the direction that Nelly pointed.

"Of what has the rascal robbed you, madam? Tell me, quick!"

"Of what I can never replace!" cried poor Nelly, woefully. "Of that on which depends the liberty—the life, perhaps, of—of a dear friend! Oh! Heaven speed you, good sir, if you will try and overtake him!"

"I envy the ruffian his beast if he beats my Bay Dolphin, even with a minute's start," exclaimed the plucky little cavalier.

And smartly pricking his mettlesome charger, he shot away in pursuit.

But to Nelly Blisset it seemed not one minute, but twenty, since the base robber had galloped away, and she looked after her unknown champion, shaking her head hopelessly.

"He will not overtake him," she exclaimed, half aloud. "It is too late—too late! I did wrong in angering him. I should have informed him of the money's precious worth to me. I should, while I had the opportunity, have endeavoured to make him understand that it was sacred money, and that Heaven's curse must fall on the robber who snatched it from me.

"Oh! let it fall—let it fall!" the poor girl cried, passionately, with clasped hands, and her white face turned to the black night. "Let the dear hope that he has snatched from me turn to blight and desolation in his hands! Alas for my poor, poor boy in prison!"

And then, her marvellously sustained courage suddenly forsaking her, with a great cry of grief, she sank down on the hard road, and there lay still as though stricken dead.

By which time the recreant Peter appeared to take it into his head that he might now recover from his swoon.

His hurts were not mortal.

To be sure, his tumble from off the high-perched driving box was an awkward one, and might have gone hard with anyone possessing a skull of no more than the average thickness.

But Peter's cranium was remarkable for its density, and as the matter stood, the flint stone against which, in his headlong descent, he struck it, was the chief sufferer.

For, whereas his scalp had sustained but a trifling gash, the flint was broken into several pieces.

To say the least, he must have been fairly on the road to recovery at the time of Nelly's passionate outburst; for, simultaneously with her falling faint to the ground, he cautiously raised himself, and looked about him.

Finding the coast clear, except for Nelly's prostrate figure, huddled by the wayside, Peter felt his wound, and shook his head from left to right, as though he suspected that some of its interior furniture had become displaced, and he wished to convince himself by taking note of any unusual rattling noise.

But discovering nothing alarming in this respect, he crawled towards the spot where his young mistress was lying.

Whatever were Peter's vices and wickedness, want of affection for Nelly did not reckon among them.

He had been in his present service since she was a tiny toddling thing no higher than his knee, and all the devotion he was capable of was humbly at her service.

Had it been daylight instead of dark, it wouldn't have been against one man—one *real* man, that is—that broad-shouldered, lumbering Peter would have turned, while standing up in her defence.

But the fact is, Peter hardly believed in the fleshy reality of the recent highwayman's presence.

The lightning swiftness of the black

steed—the sparks of fire that its heels kicked up—the sudden and appalling rising out of the ground, as it were—the ghostly grey face !

As Peter thought of this latter, he gasped again in fright, and could feel all his hair rising on the scalp, except that patch of it that was limp with the sanguineous fluid that sopped it.

By the light of the shattered lantern, as he knelt over her, he had a full view of her pallid face, all smirched red, her half-closed eyes, her dishevelled hair, and believing her to be dying, he blubbered like a schoolboy, and reviling himself in unmeasured terms for his cowardice, busied himself in endeavouring to restore her to consciousness.

Meanwhile, how fared it with the gallant stranger who was so unmercifully putting to the test the speedy powers of Bay Dolphin ?

The odds against the latter were too heavy, and except for a fluke, it was impossible for him to win the race.

Already had the swift little horse carried his master from London, whereas the tall black horse the robber rode was fresh from the stable.

At the commencement of the chase, the masked horseman had a start of more than half a mile, and little of that gap would have been abated till the goal was reached, and the latter had found safe harbourage, but for his crippled shoulder.

On he sped the way he came (which was the way to Monkshood) for a couple of miles or so, almost forgetful of his wound in the excitement of escape.

But suddenly he was aware of a feeling of giddiness, which was at once accounted for by the fact that his coat-sleeve was drenched in blood, that welled so rapidly from the ragged hole that would, if four inches lower, have led a straight path to his heart.

To have continued his headlong flight would have been to ensure a fall from the saddle, and he checked his horse, and spying a little pool of water by the roadside, resolved on a little off-hand surgical relief.

Slipping off his horse, he tore open the coat-sleeve that pressed on the swollen arm with tormenting tenacity, and dipping his handkerchief in the icy cold water, applied it to his wound.

The sensation of relief was delicious, and he dipped and dipped again, his docile black steed standing by.

Precious moments those for the rider of Bay Dolphin !

On he came at rattling speed, until he drew so near that the dull ears of the wounded man could no longer remain unaware of his approach.

With an oath, that was something more than muttered, the grey mask hastily arranged his dress, and painfully climbing into his saddle again, applied both whip and spur.

But it was now too late.

Emerging from a wind of the road, Bay Dolphin's master caught sight of him, and his voice (a voice melodious as that of a woman) came faintly with the wind, proclaiming the rider of the tall black horse a " cowardly thief," and bidding him " stop and face a man."

The grey mask heard the summons, and the words in which it was conveyed, and such a grin of anguish distorted his face as had not appeared there throughout that torturing ride.

"A cowardly thief, am I?" he muttered through his close-set teeth. "Curse you, whoever you are! Did I *dare* face you, my one sound arm should suffice to prove you a liar; but I do *not* dare. On, Fury! Spill out the last drop of my blood with this infernal jolting, since it can't be helped,

He was not more than a hundred yards behind!

"Halt, you villain! You shall not escape me. Halt, I tell you!"

The grey mask ground his teeth in rage, and plunging his hand into a side pocket, drew forth a pistol.

"One of us shall halt presently," he muttered, grimly.

It did not in the least seem as

LORD LAVERING.

so long as you carry my body home safe and unrecognised!"

But the weak and wounded horseman swerved in his saddle, so that Fury hardly knew what to make of it, and was restless rather than swift under the cruel digging of the spurs at its sides.

The stranger horseman was rapidly making way.

though it would be Bay Dolphin's fate to do so.

The chase seemed to have infused new pluck into that game little horse, and he came on at a splendid pace.

In twice as many seconds, the hundred yards were reduced to twenty—to ten!

Then the retreating horseman turned half round in his saddle, pistol in hand.

"LOOK AT YOU, YOU CARELESS GOOSE."—(See page 80.)

"Back, you fool, or you are a dead man!" he exclaimed, furiously.

The pursuer's only reply was a stinging cut at his horse's flanks, that urged it forward at increased speed.

The grey mask, with a muttered oath, fired, and Bay Dolphin uttered a short, quick cry of pain.

Its tremendous speed was arrested, and it staggered and sank to its knees.

It was at the horse, and not at its rider, that the pistol was aimed.

Had it been the other way, however, the latter could scarcely have exhibited more fury.

"You horse-shooting rascal!" he shouted, shaking both his little fists at the rapidly retreating figure. "You ill-looking robber of women, you shall swing for this! You escape this time, but it shall not be for long. I will hunt you down as sure as my name is Lord Lavering!"

Far away, a hundred yards at least, was the grey-masked horseman by the time that the gallant rider of Bay Dolphin concluded his denunciation by announcing his name, but the former heard it.

Heard it, and set his teeth the closer.

"The imps of misfortune are leagued against me to-night, it seems," he muttered, passionately. "I was a fool —a madman to embark in so rash a folly. But I'm in for it, and will fight to the end."

A further ride of ten minutes, and he reached the lane that led to the Monkshood stables.

Snatching the mask from his face, he hastily thrust it into a pocket.

As he reined in his panting steed, a huge, shambling figure emerged from the shade, and with a gruff salute, laid his hand on the bridle.

"Why are you here, fellow?" asked Reginald Vipert, angrily. "Where is Osborne? Was he not told to wait?"

"Master Osborne had a call to the village to see one of his young 'uns what's taken dangerous. But I can manage him, squire. 'Twon't be the fust time that Black Lutterloh groomed a horse. Eyes o' me, squire! he's as wet as a steeplechaser!"

"I have ridden him from London," returned Squire Reginald, with an effort to speak like a man at ease, though all the time he was suffering agonies. "Give him an extra dressing, and here's a crown for you to get drunk on, you poaching rascal."

And so saying, by a private way, he entered the house.

Black Lutterloh led the reeking black horse into the stable.

"From London, eh?" he muttered, in his unpleasant, grumbling voice, which, however, was rendered unusually amiable by the munificent gift that had just been bestowed on him. "Eyes o' me! it's a sign that he ain't been *sweated* as the horse has, or he wouldn't be so free with crown pieces. Ha! I likes the money better than I likes the hand that bestowed it; *that's* sterling, anyhow. That wouldn't send a chap to Maidstone for three months for a bit o' poaching, and his old mother took to the union workhouse in consequence!"

And in his admiration for his friend that was sterling, Black Lutterloh spun the crown piece on his broad thumb, and regarded it lovingly by the light of his stable lantern.

But suddenly he dropped it, as though the lantern light had made it red-hot.

"Eyes o' me! there's blood on it!" he gasped, in amazement.

But it was only for a moment that he permitted his surprise to overcome him.

Black Lutterloh was hardly the man to shy at money because there was blood on it!

With a cunning, curious grin, he stooped and picked up the crown piece, handling it carefully by its rim.

"Thick blood, half dried; the stamp of a finger-end on one side, and a thumb-end on t'other. How came Squire Reginald Vipert with red hands to-night?"

The black horse Fury stood with the sweat chilling on his glossy coat while Black Lutterloh pondered the riddle he had asked himself.

"I'll give it up just for the present," said he. "I'll put it by, and think on it over a pipe. I'll put this by, too. I'll preserve the pooty mark what he set on it!"

And so saying, he opened the door of the lantern, and held the crown piece against the candle-flame until even his horny fingers could not hold it, it was so hot, and the crimson impress of the thumb and finger was well dried.

Then, with a by no means unskilful hand, he proceeded to his job of grooming, and then, still with a puzzled grin on his great swarthy face, he locked the door of the stable, and blew out the lantern light.

"It's a rum go!" he muttered to himself. "If he had only cut his hand by accident, why didn't he bind his handkercher round it? Halloo! why, here is his handkercher."

There, lying on the ground, just where the hasty rider had dismounted.

In the dark, it showed white like a pocket-handkerchief, but it was not.

It was the grey mask.

In his haste, the Master of Monkshood had thrust it but carelessly into his pocket, from where it had fallen in his scrambling descent from the saddle.

Black Lutterloh picked it up, and, with his heavy underjaw agape, stared at it, as he held up the mask with two of his fingers thrust in the eye-holes.

Gradually, however, his features resumed something approaching their ordinary expression.

"'Ere's summat else to put in that there pipe which I'm a-going to smoke presently," he grinned. "P'r'aps nothing will come of it, p'r'aps summat. P'r'aps summat that'll square that Maidstone job, and a bit over by way of interest."

And taking the red-stained crown from his pocket, he wrapped it in the linen mask, and stowed the precious parcel carefully in an inner pocket.

Let us return to Lord Lavering and his wounded steed.

A hurried application to his wax match-box was the means of affording his lordship unspeakable consolation and relief.

Bay Dolphin was neither mortally nor even dangerously wounded.

The pistol bullet had struck a silver ornament (luckily a stout one) that decorated the horse's head furniture, stunning it for a moment, but glancing off, inflicting no more than a mere skin wound.

It was futile, however, to think of continuing the pursuit, so, tenderly binding up Bay Dolphin's wound with his cambric handkerchief, his little lordship remounted, and fuming with rage, till the dainty pink of his complexion was red almost as a peony, he rode slowly back the way he came.

"The desperate rascal! It might have been me instead of you, poor fellow," Lord Lavering muttered, stroking his horse. "I wonder it wasn't, especially as a woman had to do with it! A woman again—it's always a woman. If ever a poor beggar was a martyr to the female sex, it is me. I'm driven out of my senses by women, including my darling mamma-in-law; may Heaven receive her as soon as convenient!

"I fairly run away from the twaps the witches surrounded me with in town," continued his lordship, his lisp returning with his good nature, "and now a woman baulks my journey before it's half way through, sets a sort of womantic twap for me, conjures up a highwayman to knock her esquire on the head, and leave her twembling and wailing in the road till I come to her rescue.

"Of course, this can't be a twap," he continued, suddenly growing serious at the bare possibility of such a thing. "No, I don't think it can be a twap; I should feel more afraid of going back to her if it was so. She seemed very beautiful, though. I'm half afraid of her. By George! here she comes!"

Yes, there came Nelly, still very weak and trembling, and bearing heavily on the arm of the remorseful Peter, who with the wreck of the lantern, lit the way homeward.

As she caught sight of the young horseman, she sprang eagerly forward, and grasping his hand, looked up into his face with such pitiful imploring as caused the same hand to tremble, and a blush, that might have been indicative of the approach of that dreadful sensation of which his lordship went in such mortal dread, overspread his countenance.

"Much as it pains me to tell you so, young lady, I bring you nothing in the way of substantial comfort," said he, nervously.

And in a few words he recounted the result of his pursuit of the robber, as well as his resolve to take immediately such steps as should ensure his capture.

"First of all, however, I shall feel much pleasure in assisting you to reach your home, wherever that may be."

"Blisset's Mill, about five miles from this," put in Peter.

And then he artfully suggested—

"I could hold you on to the gentleman's horse, Miss Nelly, if he would be so kind as to lend him to you for a spell."

Sick and weary, Nelly was but too glad to avail herself of the stranger's ready acquiescence.

Scarcely had they so traversed a mile, when the hurried approach of a vehicle was heard.

It was the chaise and the white horse.

Years of experience on that road had enabled Dobbin, despite his terror, to find his way home as easily as though some one was behind him handling the reins.

Great, indeed, was the consternation of the miller's family, more especially as the effects of his fright were still troubling Dobbin, and his coat reeked with sweat.

Dame Blisset, as soon as she heard that the chaise had returned empty, and with the lantern missing, fainted altogether.

But her daughter Nan was made of more durable stuff.

"Come father," said she, whisking the old miller into his coat and hat almost before he was aware of it, "we will seek her together. I had a pre-sentiment of this."

"What, of old Dobbin taking fright and spilling them and returning by himself?" exclaimed old Blisset, snatching at this poor straw to save himself from drowning in the flood of grief that threatened him. "That's what you mean, Nan, isn't it? You don't think worse has befallen my precious darling?"

"There is bare time for acting just now, father, let alone for thinking," was Nan's equivocal reply; and in five minutes more the white horse was on the road again.

"There they are!" exclaimed old Blisset, leaping to his feet with such violent delight that Dobbin was nearly relapsing into that state of fright from which he was but slowly recovering; "see, Nan! Why—why, what on earth can it all mean?

Something in the way of a fairy story as much as anything.

Beautiful Nelly, drooping on the horse, with her face as white as milk, partly screened by the loosened chesnut curls that hung over it, the said horse (with a white handerchief most comic-ally bound about its brow) being led on the one side by Peter, all towzled and chalky as to his dress, and with his Sunday beaver hat crushed into a shape indescribable, and on the other side by a handsome young gentleman, who was a stranger.

Little time, however, was wasted in contemplating the romantic picture.

Ten seconds after beholding it, thank-ful old Bob Blisset broke it up by running and snatching Nelly from the saddle and folding her in his arms.

Then the brief, sad story was told, poor Nelly's sobbing and almost un-intelligible account of it being eked out by Peter, who, finding that a small fib he had ventured on remained uncon-tradicted, boldly launched into such a glaring account of his heroism, as caused both Nan and her father to bestow on him their present hearty thanks, besides liberal promises of future reward.

Meanwhile, the stranger stood modestly aside until the operation of bestowing sorrowful Nelly in the chaise was accomplished, and then, remounting his horse, he politely expressed the plea-sure it had afforded him to have rendered the young lady such trifling assistance as lay in his power, and prepared to take his departure.

But Nelly roused at this.

In a few earnest words she described

to her sister and father how nobly he had come to her aid, and how that, all unarmed as he was, he had risked his life in the desperate hope of restoring to her the precious money she had been robbed of.

"Nay, then," cried the old miller, grasping the young fellow's hand gratefully, and with tears in his honest eyes, "we must not part so soon. For the dame's sake I must beg of you to ride home with us. She would never pardon us, young gentleman, did we not take you to her that she might bless you for the daughter's sake."

"Oh, thank you very much, but I—I—am afraid that—I—my other engagements," stammered Bay Dolphin's master nervously.

But Nan cut him short.

Old Blisset had taken but one of his hands; Nan took them both in her own, and with her handsome face flushed with thankfulness and her bright eyes aglow.

"Ah, you don't know us if you think that we can part with you so," said she, with a glance at him that caused him an instant perspiration. "You cannot realise the gratitude we feel towards you until you learn how much our hearts are bound up in her whom you have so generously befriended. You will not deny us!"

How could he?

To state the honest truth, he willingly would have done so, had it been in his power; but he was under a spell.

He had looked into Nan Blisset's eyes, and he was helpless in her hands.

His great consolation was that he had not experienced that remarkable sensation that warned him of the vicinity of a "twap."

"It is nothing but gwatitude as she says!" he reflected, as he rode with the chaise towards Blisset's mill. "It would be nothing short of bwutal to wefuse to accept their thanks in their own fashion. I don't think that I ever witnessed such a stwiking effect of gwatitude on the human countenance as on the face of that nice-looking, cherry-cheeked party. Such a—such a thwilling effect! Gad! if twaps were set with this sort of thing, I'm afwaid that many a spooney young fellow would be caught in them."

Let us pass over poor Nelly's reception at home.

Let us likewise spare the sensitive feelings of little Lord Lavering by refraining from recounting the prayers and blessings he received from Nelly's mother.

It would be difficult to say which embarrassed him most; this, or the grateful attention of the cherry-cheeked party before mentioned.

All for his own simple sake, too! and that was the best of it.

At present they knew nothing of his "lordship," and could only regard him as an ordinary young gentleman discovered riding in the country for business or pleasure, and whose good luck it had been to render them a trifling service.

The worst of it was that the "nice-looking, cherry-cheeked party," deceived possibly as much by his delicate face as by his diffident manner, persisted in treating him as a very young gentleman—indeed, in a way that was almost motherly, in fact.

Before he himself was hardly aware of it, she had brought him to confess that a night's break in his journey would occasion him no real inconvenience, and, within ten minutes of the admission, it was an understood thing that he would remain a guest at the mill-house till the morning.

It was the "nice-looking, cherry-cheeked party" that so peremptorily insisted on his releasing his feet from his travelling-boots, and who turned a deaf ear to his mild protestations against desecrating with his masculine feet the dainty pair of plush slippers that she brought him from her own room, fitting them on his mites of feet with her own plump hands.

"You musn't mind me, you know," Nan the broad-shouldered and buxom remarked, with sisterly confidence; "I am bigger and older than you. I always thought I should like to have a nice little brother to spoil."

Sitting by the miller's sorrowful fireside, the strange guest listened wonderingly, and for the first time, to the story of the calamity that had befallen John Gauntlet, the borrowed money that the highwayman had stolen, and the purpose to which it was to be applied.

He did not say much, but he took careful heed of what he heard, and when Dame Blisset, comforting poor Nelly, bade her make sure that Heaven would take pity on her, and in some way befriend her, he responded "Amen!" with a heartiness that was remarkable, and which he himself was not a little startled at, judging from the blush that suffused his fair face.

The sudden interest he took in John Gauntlet's case was peculiar.

Did they know the name and address of his creditor?

They only knew the address of the lawyer—the shabby rascal, as old Blisset bitterly stigmatised him—to whom John had applied, and who had deceived him so cruelly.

The miller's guest withdrew his elegant little tablets from his pocket, and made a note of the lawyer's abode, remarking, in some confusion, and as an excuse for doing so—

"That it was as well to know the whereabouts of such a wascal, were it only for the sake of avoiding him."

After that he grew fidgety, and repeatedly consulted his watch.

"It is growing late, my friends, and I am an early riser," said he; "if you will permit me, I will retire."

"Are you an early breakfaster as well as an early riser, young sir?" the nice-looking, cherry-cheeked party inquired, solicitously.

"I—I like to wide a few miles before I bweakfast," he replied, stammering, and blushing guiltily. "It is my intention to do so to-morrow morning; but don't let me put you to trouble on that account. I can find my way to the stable, and it isn't the first time that I've saddled Bay Dolphin without assistance. Good-night to all!"

Nan lit him upstairs.

"You will sleep pretty comfortably here, I think," she remarked, with that motherly way of hers, as she surveyed the exquisitely clean and snug apartment. "By-the-bye, do you wear a nightcap?"

The shy little lord could not have blushed more violently if she had asked did he wear a wig.

"I—I am not accustomed to—to wear such a thing; but if it would be agreeable to—to—"

"Oh! I have no feeling in the matter," interrupted the matronly damsel, with an assuring smile. "I know that curly-haired people sometimes do wear such things. There should have been another pillow here; but these are very large ones and will bear punching up—in this way, see! if you like lying with your head high."

And demurely indenting the ends of the snowy heap at the bed-head with her little white fists, Nan bade him "Good night, and God bless you!" and took her departure.

For several minutes little Lord Lavering sat at his bed-foot, gazing with an odd mixture of delight and displeasure at the door through which the matter-of-fact young lady had passed.

"Well, this is wich!" he presently murmured, his natural good humour rapidly gaining the ascendency. "It would be highly intewesting to know that extwaordinawy young person's pwivate opinion of me. I wonder she didn't wish to know if I took bwead and milk at bweakfast! I never was so completely taken under the female wing in all my life! It's awfully widiculous! but—but, I'm not sure but that it's wather nice!"

He proceeded with his dainty unrobing, and when he came to wind up his watch, he paused in the midst of the delicate operation and looked pensive.

"She often has wished that she had a bwother, has she? Well, I wish I had a sister of her sort. Gad! such a sister would be a blessing to a fellow. He needn't trouble and worry himself about "twaps" with such a wonderful creature as she is to look after him. She'd twap 'em. She never could become a fellow's sister, of course; but it would be jolly to get to know her very well, so that I might take her into my confidence and ask her advice. There's the pillow she punched up! A fellow should be able to sleep on it, I should think, and rise without a headache. Hope I shall. Seventeen miles before bweakfast to-morrow morning will be a tidy spin. But it shall be done, I'm wesolved on that."

And hard indeed would it have been had he not slept sound with that precious resolution of his lulling him off.

Did the other restless sleepers of the mill-house dream of it?

Did poor Nelly, feverishly tossing on her couch and bemoaning her cruel loss, hear the whispering of no gentle angel of promise?

No!

There are tribulations that must be borne to the end, dismal nights that must be endured, and which will not abate one jot from their dark hours, though sunrise is certain.

Little Lord Lavering must indeed have been an early riser.

It was but half-past five when, by prearrangement, the maid knocked at his door, but he was already out riding.

CHAPTER VII.

THREE DAYS AFTER—A SECRET FRIEND—JOHN GAUNTLET AT LIBERTY.

HREE DAYS had gone since the happening of what is described in the last chapter.

Fortunate it was for Reginald Vipert that since his father's death Monkshood Hall had been little better than a shut-up house.

He was seldom at home.

He had no great love for the sombre old place, and much preferred the gaiety and excitement of life in London.

On this account, besides Mr. Phantom and a groom or two, the only servants retained on the establishment were such as were sufficient to minister to the young squire's personal wants.

Otherwise awkward results might have attended the exploits of the leading actor in the recent tragedy of Shrouder's Gap.

The spot where he encountered Lord Lavering was not more than a mile and half from the hall, and, as has been seen, drenched in his own blood, faint and well-nigh helpless, he reached the back entrance to the Monkshood stables.

Mr. Phantom was anxiously awaiting him.

Great, indeed, was that devoted person's consternation at the ghastly spectacle.

"Good Heaven, Master Reginald!" he exclaimed, as the latter reeled past him, "you are hurt, surely."

"Surely I was an ass, an idiot, to take counsel of you, you devil's cousin!" returned his master in a voice hoarse with fury. "Let me pass, and bar the door. Quick! I am a lost man if they trace me here. Give me early notice if they should do so, Phantom, so that I may put a bullet into my unlucky skull before they find me."

And, assisted by his faithful steward, the Master of Monkshood secretly, but with difficulty, reached his bedchamber.

There he had ever since remained.

He was fortunate in more respects than one.

The bullet, large enough to kill an ox, that Nelly had fired at him out of the old flint pistol, had, by a miracle, glanced off the bone, entering the thick fleshy part of the shoulder, and emerging out the other side.

A ragged, ugly wound, but one that necessitated but the simplest treatment.

Mr. Phantom possessed some slight surgical knowledge.

His father, when living, was the most renowned quack doctor of any in the large provincial town in which he resided, and Joseph was his valued assistant.

Indeed, had not an ugly accusation of manslaughter deposed both father and son from their eminent position, it is likely that Joseph Phantom would have succeeded to the business, and never have turned valet, to the great loss of the Vipert family as well as of this story.

To be sure Mr. Phantom's surgery was of the roughest kind, but it was that or none.

It was of all things necessary that Squire Vipert's injury should be kept the profoundest secret, even though a protracted cure and a stiff shoulder were the penalties to be paid for it.

It was easy enough for the steward to make such an excuse as should disarm the suspicions of the servants.

It was by no means an uncommon occurrence for the jovial Master of Monkshood to return suddenly from London in a condition that rendered his immediate presentation to his most fastidious friends not exactly desirable.

It was so, and a little worse, on the present occasion.

"Bad, very bad!" Mr. Phantom intimated to the old housekeeper, with an ominous shrug of his shoulders, and at the same time significantly tapping his forehead with his forefinger. "Swears and raves awfully, and won't hear of anyone waiting on him but myself. But I don't mind; if you will kindly bring anything I ring for, and place it on the sideboard outside his door, I shall manage very well."

And exhaustless indeed must have been the patience—the malice—the hatred—which was it?—of Mr. Vipert's soft-spoken, soft-treading nurse.

A sick panther would have been easier to please than his prostrate master.

It was lucky he had lost so vast a quantity of blood; otherwise, Mr. Phantom would assuredly have had a raving madman to contend against.

As it was, the pain of his wound, and his ungovernable fury against the cause of it, much disturbed his brain during the first day and night.

His one desire was for vengeance !

Vengeance against John Gauntlet, against Nelly Blisset ("that tiger cat" he called her), against the whole family of Blissets.

And his faithful nurse had no better method of pacifying him than producing and holding up for him to see the bag with the money in it.

The money that he had lent and stolen back again.

The money that represented, according to the bond so jealously preserved by Mr. Phantom, the full value of the mill, and the meadow, and the homestead—the sole worldly possessions of Nelly's father.

"It is hard to bear, Phantom," remarked the wounded man, grinning with pain as his man dressed his hurts afresh; "it is infernally hard to be skulking here like a wolf, crippled and driven to his lair; but, at least, I am not baffled. My injury is no victory for my enemy, eh, Joseph? He is no better off because of my misfortune?"

"I hope not, Master Reginald."

And, judging from the expression of his countenance, Mr. Phantom did hope not most devoutly.

"You may make sure not!"

"We need not waste time," continued the ferocious invalid. "I think you

desire it. It shall be done, Phantom. I shall never get well until it is."

"I wish, my dear master, that every other means of curing you was as pleasant handling," returned Joseph, with a snarl that his cheerful tones covered.

"Yes, you shall manage it, my clever Joseph! Curse 'em! We'll rout 'em out like a nest of rats! Ha,

NAN BLISSET.

said, Phantom, that you had so drawn the deed that there need be no delay in enforcing the terms of it?"

"The bond is due this day—this hour, my dear master, if you desire it," returned the faithful servant, meekly.

"That's good! That's sweeter than water and wine to my parched throat, Phantom!" returned the wounded man, grating his teeth in his agony. "I do

ha! we'll burn the mill, Phantom, so that if that gaol-bird, Gauntlet, contrives to make his escape, he may find no lack of ashes to strew on his bereaved head. But he can't escape! Every coin in that bag is a link, a tough and strong link of the chain that confines him in prison, eh, Joseph?"

Mr. Phantom nodded, while a grin of satisfaction flitted over his ca-

"HE HAD NEVER DREAMT HOW CHARMING SHE WAS." —(See page 88.)

daverous countenance, as his master uttered these words.

As he sat by the invalid's bedside listening to his raving, he alternately made purring noises by rubbing his hands together, and sawing his notched nails against his teeth, as though he was thus keeping himself in working order against the coming of the precious time his master spoke of.

His mind, too, was reverting to the origin and mainspring of the deadly animosity that the Master of Monkshood felt towards John Gauntlet.

The rivals had not stepped into the field of contention together.

Even as a schoolboy, Reginald was acquainted with the miller's daughter.

He was aware of her existence, that is to say.

As he grew and she grew, the said knowledge did not escape him.

In his education was included a taste for the beautiful, and Nelly Blisset was beautiful, and he admired her for that quality just as he would any other creature, or shrub, or flower, on the paternal estate.

He noted her charming face, her beautiful hair, her cherry lips; a glance of her bright brown eyes would cause him a pleasant emotion; but his *heart* remained untouched.

It was not for him, a Vipert of Monkshood, to fall in love with the daughter of a miller.

If she chose to fall in love with him, which, of course, was only what was natural, and to be expected, that was a different matter.

He had no objection; he was well used to that sort of thing.

Within a circuit of ten miles, he could count a score, at least, of really eligible damsels who were by no means insensible to his personal attractions, and the advantages that attached to his social position; and, if he wanted a wife, as he one day might, he could any time select one from the number.

But Nelly Blisset came not within this category.

She was a charming little thing, and he liked to chat with her at times.

Liked to encounter her by chance in his summer afternoon's strolling in the sunny lanes of Monkshood, and to kindle a blush on her artless cheek by his pleasant badinage.

It amused his highness to note her scared demeanour, and her pretty confusion whenever he condescended to address her in familiar language.

One day he thought the said amusement might be much enhanced if he made bold to snatch a kiss from her damask cheek.

He essayed the rash attempt, and straightway his eyes were opened to the very serious mistake he had made.

The shrill cry of alarm and indignation that Nelly raised had hardly left her lips, when a pair of nimble feet cleared at a bound the four-foot hedge that skirted the lane, and amazed and angry, John Gauntlet stood before them.

In an instant John's quick eye detected what was amiss; perhaps he previously had a suspicion of it, and, in a moment, he was grasping a big fistful of Squire Reginald's coat collar.

Had it come to a tussling-match, it would have been difficult to bespeak the victor.

Both young men were of an equal height; and the advantage John possessed as regards muscle, was at least equalized by the other's skill as a trained wrestler.

But Reginald Vipert could not forget what was due to "caste."

What would be thought of him in certain quarters if it were told that he so far lost his temper as to brawl with a mere bumpkin?

"How dare you, fellow!" he exclaimed, white with fury. "Unhand me instantly. Do you not know who I am, John Gauntlet?"

"Not well enough, perhaps," replied John through his set teeth. "It is only of late I've took to studying you, Squire Vipert. I know this, however, and I'd have you know it; I've got a dovecote up at my little place, and if I find a bird of prey hovering over it, I never wait to judge its quality—crow or kestrel, down it comes."

"You dare threaten me, John Gauntlet!"

"Nay, that cannot be. *You* are a gentleman, Squire Vipert. I was speaking of birds of prey, those rascally poachers from whose marauding no poor man's preserve is safe unless he keeps his eyes open and his gun loaded."

And so John Gauntlet walked off triumphant, with trembling Nelly Blisset on his arm.

Since that time the Master of Monkshood and John Gauntlet had not once met.

But even had he possessed the inclination, the unpleasant affair was not allowed to die out of his memory.

Joseph Phantom guarded against that.

His heart was set on one devilish end, and he cared not to what lengths he proceeded so that it was attained.

In honest truth, not one word had John Gauntlet uttered, out of the miller's family, respecting the insult to which Nelly Blisset had been subjected, and the manner in which he had resented it.

But Mr. Phantom, in his confidential discourse with his master, gave the matter a very different complexion.

If his word might be taken, John Gauntlet's constant theme of bragging was how that he had taught the doughty squire a lesson he wouldn't be likely to forget.

John, according to the mendacious Joseph, was never tired of roaring out that great laugh of his in derision of the man who pretended to the favour of the handsomest damsel in Kent, and yet had not the courage to resent as smart a shaking as ever terrier gave a stoat, or any member of the vermin tribe.

Squire Vipert affected to shrug his shoulders and laugh in contempt at these petty stories; nevertheless his face reddened with anger.

"I can't very well call out the clod-hopper, Phantom," said he, "but the next time I happen to meet him, it will be bad for him if I happen to have with me my heaviest riding-whip!"

Mr. Phantom smiled sardonically.

"You are more merciful, Master Reginald, than your father would have been," said he.

"Merciful! He must wear a toughish

jacket if my thong does not write me a fair quittance for his insolence in black and blue on his bull shoulders."

"Your father would have cut at his heart, not at his shoulders, Master Reginald."

"At his heart!"

"Aye, and with a less clumsy weapon than a whip's thong. The lying braggart! he deserves it. No, I beg his pardon; it was not all lies that he uttered."

"How do you mean?"

"He brags that she is the loveliest damsel in Kent," replied Mr. Phantom, meekly, "and so she is, without doubt, if my humble opinion may be taken on the matter."

"It may at least be regarded as an impartial opinion, Phantom," returned his handsome master, with a sneering laugh; "but what is her beauty to me, an insolent jade?"

"To be sure; that's just what I thought, Master Reginald, when it came to my ears—quite by accident, as you may depend—that in secret she entertains the idea that her beauty is something to you. That she thinks, perhaps hopes so."

"That she thinks and hopes so! Gad! she has an odd way of showing it then, the little vixen!"

And quite a relenting expression came over the young squire's face as he smiled grimly at the remembrance of that memorable repulse he had experienced.

"Perhaps she is properly conscious of the wide social distinction——"

"Social humbug," interrupted the gay young Master of Monkshood, pleasantly; "she is a bewitching little vixen, there is no denying that, Phantom. And so you think, my worthy old tutor, that the better way to punish this Adonis of the straw-yard will be to cut at his heart instead of his shoulders. Ha, ha! I know which would be the pleasantest revenge. Cut at his heart, eh? Gad! I'll reflect on that."

What came of his reflecting on it, what came of his acting on the result of his reflections, aided and abetted by the sly and desperately cat-like Phantom, has already been shown.

"*This* has come of it!" mused the imperturbable Joseph, as he sat at the foot of Squire Reginald's bed of pain. "Things have gone a little cross, but really there's no harm done. Nay," he continued, as a mocking grin for an instant lit up his fishy eyes, "is it not written that evil is sometimes permitted that good may come of it? And if the wound that this pretty master of mine has received serves to goad him to take heavier revenge on my enemies than he otherwise would, should I repine?

"But I must not reckon my chance prematurely," Mr. Phantom continued, covertly gnawing his forefinger-nail. "His rancour may cool as his wound heals! If I thought it would be so," and his cadaverous face, with a diabolical expression on it, was turned for a moment towards his master, "if I thought it would be so, even my poor knowledge of the doctor's art should suffice to——"

But Joseph Phantom's fears on this score were groundless.

The second and the third day passed,

and still Squire Vipert's vindictive mood continued.

For his satisfaction a regular medical practitioner had been fetched secretly from London, and he had pronounced that, although the treatment the injured limb had received was all that could be desired, the inconvenience would by no means cease with the healing of the wound.

It would be necessary for the Squire to carry his arm in a sling for three— six months perhaps, and even then he would be fortunate if he were not troubled with a stiff shoulder-joint for the remainder of his life.

This dismal intelligence, coupled with the fact his mirror revealed, that he was pale and haggard, and looked at least five years older for his disaster, did not tend to sweeten his temper or lessen his animosity against those he regarded as answerable for these various evils.

It was evening, and master and man were, as usual, alone.

For the first time since his accident, Squire Vipert was up, and seated in an armchair, the loose sleeve of his dressing-gown concealing the cumbersome bandages that supported his wounded shoulder.

The London M.D. had taken his departure not more than an hour, and the young Master of Monkshood was still keenly smarting under the bitter sentence that had been passed on him.

"There shall be no further delay, Phantom!" he exclaimed, savagely. "It will be some consolation to know that I am not the only sufferer by this confounded business. How you will manage it I neither know nor care; but let it be to-morrow."

"The bond will be sufficient warrant, Master Reginald," the crafty Phantom replied. "Still, if you will kindly leave the matter in my hands, I think that I may so contrive to manage it that while the amplest satisfaction is afforded you, your reputation shall not in the least suffer."

"Good; so long as your delicate scheme involves no showing of mercy, I shall not fall out with it; but understand this, Phantom: there must be no holding off, no granting of grace—I won't hear of it. They have fairly earned my hatred, and they shall feel the full weight of it. I'll rid me of the vipers, and I'll purge their nest. Who is that?"

This last remark in reference to a tap at the chamber door.

Phantom rose from his seat.

It was the housekeeper.

"Miss Blisset, of the mill, begs the favour of a few words with the Squire, if he is well enough to see her," said she.

"Miss Blisset! Which one? There are two, you know," remarked Phantom, opening his eyes wide in amazement.

"The younger, Miss Ellen," replied the housekeeper; "there is a person with her; he didn't give his name."

Mr. Phantom returned to his master, who, many shades paler than before, had risen from his chair.

"Will you see her?" Phantom asked, with a sinister grin on his unhandsome visage.

"What can she want here? How dare she come here?"

Mr. Phantom glanced towards the door, outside which the housekeeper was awaiting an answer, and laid a finger on his lip.

"You forget, Master Reginald, that there is nothing daring in it from her point of view," he whispered. She has doubtless come to thank you in person for your noble endeavours to save her betrothed, and to acquaint you with the tremendous misfortune that frustrated it!"

And a flicker of malicious glee played for a few seconds on his villanous face.

"Do you advise that I should see her?" the Master of Monkshood asked, nervously.

"I think so," returned Mr. Phantom, with a sly nibble at his forefinger-nail; "if you were very gracious, Master Reginald, very kind—and—and sympathetic, it would certainly give weight to the crash that to-morrow will follow."

Mr. Vipert nodded his appreciation of the sweet idea.

"But the person who is with her—who is he?"

"Her father, no doubt; she would not come alone as late as it is."

"I will see her, Phantom; him as well, if he wishes it; it will be a pleasant foretaste of what is to follow."

Mr. Phantom licked his lips as though in delicious anticipation of the sport, and conveyed his master's gracious message to the housekeeper.

Ere many seconds had elapsed, eager footsteps—footsteps light and footsteps heavy—were heard ascending the stairs.

"You will stay here, Phantom," remarked Reginald Vipert, with a

beating heart, as he listened to the approach of the girl, his last interview with whom he had so many reasons for remembering.

"Very good, Master Reginald."

And then the door was opened, and there stood revealed—

Nelly Blisset and John Gauntlet!

It was well that the wax lights that illuminated the invalid's chamber were screened with shades.

Well that the fire in the grate burnt with a sullen glow, and not with a bright, light-giving flame!

As Nelly and John Gauntlet entered, expecting no other than a pleasant reception, the Master of Monkshood and Phantom regarded them with a stare of speechless amazement.

Not downcast and suppliant, but happy and radiant, they came in, her hand locked in his, and advanced to the middle of the room.

Not till then did they discover that Squire Reginald was ailing.

A look of concern took the place of the pleasant smile on John Gauntlet's face, and he came a step or two further forward, holding out his hand.

"We were unaware that you were ill, Squire Vipert," said he. "It is nothing serious, I hope?"

The colour rushed to the face of Reginald Vipert, and he hastily rose from his chair, as John Gauntlet thought to take his proffered hand, but really with a threatening gesture.

But loss of blood had weakened him considerably, and his strength was not equal to the sudden excitement.

Scarcely had he gained an upright position—before, indeed, he could utter a word, a faintness like the faintness of death overcame him, and he sank back in his chair again.

Scarcely less moved was Joseph Phantom; but his emotion took another shape.

It seemed to pinch in his hollow cheek and to render still more indistinct the narrow pinky-white line that represented his mouth, while, with his hands clasped together, he nervously rasped his jagged finger-nails one against the other.

It was only on Nelly's sudden and alarmed exclamation—"See, he has fainted!" that he turned to his master's aid.

Even then he seemed scarce able to withdraw his eyes from the wonderful vision; and, with his voice quivering with suppressed rage, he remarked—

"I was afraid of this. My dear master is still so weak from his—his last attack of illness that it was rash, very rash of him to consent to see visitors."

"I am very, very sorry if our coming has caused him any hurt," said John, earnestly, "we thought that he would be glad to see us, didn't us, lass?"

Mr. Phantom opned his eyes in blank bewilderment.

"Glad to see you!" he repeated; but his presence of mind immediately returning, he continued—

"Oh, to be sure, I forgot. Of course you would think so. P'r'aps it was a sudden spasm of delight at beholding you that sent him off."

He was bending over his unconscious master, laving his forehead with a scented water as he spoke, so that neither John Gauntlet nor Nelly saw the diabolical grin that distorted his face as he made this last remark.

"Did—did my master expect you to-night?" he presently asked.

"I can't say that he expected us at all," John replied; "he does his good work so quietly like the true gentleman he is, that I shouldn't wonder if he wouldn't have been better pleased if this last example of his generosity could have been kept a secret even from us."

Mr. Phantom's shaggy brows knitted more and more in the extremity of his amazement, and his hands trembled violently.

What could John Gauntlet mean?

Phantom's hands trembled so that the water in the basin he held was spilled over the edge, saturating the collar of Mr. Vipert's coat.

Nelly Blisset observed this, and, with a woman's natural impulse to succour the helpless, at once came to the rescue.

Promptly withdrawing her gloves from her hands, and before Mr. Phantom could object to the Christian act, she took the vessel from him and tenderly applied herself to the unconscious gentleman's restoration.

John Gauntlet looked on approvingly.

"That's a good lass," said he. "Nay, don't baulk her; she has a lighter hand than you, Mr. Phantom, and will manage better."

"To be sure, to be sure," returned Joseph, hovering about the group and wringing his hands in a terrible frame of mind; "but what I am thinking of is—is the trouble, the inconvenience. Oh, dear, I wish you would leave him to me."

Mr. Phantom did not finish his first sentence as he honourably should.

What he meant was, that he was thinking of the pretty scene that would probably ensue should Reginald suddenly open his eyes and discover who it was that was tending him.

"Man alive! never speak of the inconvenience," said John Gauntlet. "He deserves more of us than we can ever repay him. More than *I* can ever repay him. But it was her desire that we should come before we went home, for I'm straight from prison, you must know, Mr. Phantom, and bless her heart, I couldn't refuse her."

"But wouldn't the—the business you have come on keep till daylight?" Mr. Phantom asked, artfully groping his way to a solution of the mystery.

"Aye; 'twill keep for many and many a year, I trust," John Gauntlet heartily replied; "but I felt such a weight of gratitude pressing on my heart towards yourself as well as the squire" (here John, with his bright eyes brimming, seized Mr. Phantom's damp, white paw in his own big, berry-brown hand, and gave it a grip that made him gasp again), "that it seemed quite impossible for me to sleep once more as a free man without——"

The further John Gauntlet proceeded the more bewildered Joseph Phantom became.

At this point, in a bland voice, though with his very knees trembling with rage, he broke in—

"Exactly; to be sure. Nothing could be more—more natural; but just now, you see——could you make it convenient to call in the morning?"

But before John could consider the suggestion, matters took an unexpected turn.

Nelly Blisset, the better to perform her task, had slipped off her little bonnet, and, with her shawl thrown back from her shoulders, was laving the forehead of the Master of Monkshood as tenderly as a mother tends a sick child, putting back his chestnut curls with her gentle fingers, and chafing his temples.

She, however, was not successful with her ministering, so she put down the basin, and took to chafing his hands.

The hand that came first was the hand that hung from the crippled shoulder; and before the watchful Phantom could interfere, the mischief was done.

With a scream of pain, Reginald Vipert awoke to consciousness.

Leapt back to life with a savage oath on his lips, and eyes glaring, to find bending over him the lovely, pitying face of the girl he had so cruelly used.

The girl whom, an hour since, he had abhorred with all his fathomless depths of turbulent love turned to hate.

Bending over him so closely that he could feel her breath on his cold face; so closely that her rich, clustering ringlets brushed his cheek almost.

"You are better now. I am so glad! Let me make your pillow comfortable. There, that's nicer, isn't it?"

He did not answer yes or no, but lay with his head on the pillow, just as her gentle hands arranged it, regarding her like a man spellbound?

What else was he than spellbound?

How was it possible that his savage anger should live when the light of so much tender regard and solicitude was brought to bear on it ?

He was not a very hardened villain as yet.

"Is there anything more that I can do for you ?" Nelly's soft and musical voice was heard again. "I shall only be too happy. Our kindest, our best friend! How can we sufficiently show our gratitude ?"

She held his hand (the sound one luckily) in her own as she said this, and he felt a pressure about his fingers that sent a thrill to his heart.

But then she had said "we." "How can *we* ever sufficiently show," etc. That damaged the charm.

John Gauntlet's stepping forward and opening his mouth broke it completely.

"Squire Vipert," said John, eager to second the expressions of gratitude his betrothed had given utterance to, "I could not rest before I came to you to thank you with all my heart and soul for your first—no less than your second and more successful—endeavour to restore me to liberty, and to one whom I love more than all the world besides. Nay, I must go beyond that; I must ask your forgiveness for the wrong opinion I held of you. D'ye see, squire, I am so bound up in her " (and his great hand rested lovingly on Nelly's curly head), " that I am jealous almost of the wind that blows on her, and—and I thought that you envied me my little treasure, and would take her from me if you could win her willing. Now I know you, Squire Vipert, and I am sorry that I did you such injustice. Nelly knows how sorry I am ; and, let me tell you, sir, it must be a big sorrow that I can feel just now. It is wonderful, with my heart so full of love for her and thankfulness to you, that there is room in it for aught else."

As a rule, John Gauntlet was a man of few words, and the excitement of speaking at such unwonted length brought the rich colour to his cheeks, and enhanced the manly brightness of his eyes.

His hand still reposed on Nelly's shoulder, and her hand had stolen up to keep it loving company ; and so they stood—as pretty a pair of sweethearts as the devil himself could desire to set before and inflame the heart of a rival.

It can scarcely be said that Squire Reginald Vipert distinctly heard the whole of John Gauntlet's earnest speech.

All the time he was delivering it the Master of Monkshood sat regarding him like a man who is in what he hopes is a dream, but which he momentarily dreads to discover is grim reality.

But if he was incapable of paying due attention to John Gauntlet's words, his jealous, envious eyes were keen to observe his actions.

They noted the loving hands, the look of unutterable happiness that beamed in Nelly's eyes as her betrothed uttered these words, so simple and yet so full of exquisite meaning—

"I am so bound up in her."

He caught a glimpse of his own haggard, sickly face in the opposite mirror, and, in bitterness of spirit, he contrasted it with that of the young farmer, so bright, so immeasurably contented, and he felt baffled—beaten. Worse, he felt despised.

Through the haze of jealousy that sprang up before him, he saw in John Gauntlet the prime cause of all that had befallen him.

Then flashed to his mind Phantom's words, " She thinks, she hopes, that her beauty may be something to you. I have secret reasons for knowing that it is so !"

And as the stalwart young farmer stood before him, he hated him from his heart's bitterest depths.

Well, indeed, for him was it that the sure-thinking, keen-witted Joseph Phantom was there !

In another moment Squire Vipert, resenting and scorning the young farmer's expressions of good will, and in his passion, almost forgetful of Nelly Blisset's presence, would have blurted out that which it would have been impossible to recall; but Phantom, who stood behind Nelly and John Gauntlet, attracted his attention, and rapidly and impressively laid his finger on his firmly-closed lip.

CHAPTER VIII.

MR. PHANTOM MEDITATES A CLEVER MOVE.

MYSTERIOUS as unmistakable was the sign made by Mr. Phantom.

His tongue had, for a few minutes, been still, but his ears, his eyes had been vigilant.

What was the mystery that had directed Nelly and her betrothed on such a mistaken errand remained to be solved. The first essential towards his success was that his master should fall inextricably in love, of some sort, with the miller's beautiful daughter.

Recent events had caused the unscrupulous schemer some uneasiness in this respect.

Now there appeared an opportunity for restoring matters to their original balance, perhaps of improving them.

The look of kind solicitude with which Nelly had regarded the invalid— the glance with which Squire Reginald had returned the look, had not escaped the astute Phantom.

What might not be accomplished if Nelly Blisset, so full of tender pity for the sick man, so grateful to him for his supposed noble benefaction, could be brought, though only temporarily, into close companionship of Reginald Vipert!

Quite private companionship.

With no one to annoy the one and embarrass the other.

Mr. Joseph Phantom was not well versed in the tender science of love culture: but he knew well that romance was in the highest degree favourable to it.

Here was romance!

The scorned and rejected rival, winning the gratitude of the lady by his

Convalescents are proverbially more impressionable than people in health.

With Nelly to tend him, to sit by him, to read to him, just for a few hours every day, and with Mr. Gauntlet's free consent, of course, and the trick would be as good as done!

True; and the alarming thought cost Mr. Phantom a spasm of alarm; the trick might be *overdone*.

REGINALD VIPERT.

manly generosity, and her pity by his misfortune.

Her pity! Who, to look at her hovering over him like an angel of mercy, could doubt that she pitied him? And was not pity, as everybody knew, next of kin to love?

It was an excellent thing to have a good solid foundation of pity to start on at all events.

Thinking thus, he advanced quietly, saying—

"If I might be permitted to speak alone with the young folks, Master Reginald, I am quite sure, sir, that you will understand that I speak solely for your good!"

And, as he uttered these last words, he directed a glance full of meaning at his puzzled master.

"NELLY STRUGGLED TO FREE HER HAND."—(See page 100.)

In a moment it seemed that Squire Vipert was about to resent this daring act of interference.

But he knew Joseph of old, and that he might trust him.

He bowed his head acquiescently, therefore, and bent back languidly, covering his eyes with his hands.

Mr. Phantom politely beckoned both Nelly and John Gauntlet to the further end of the room.

"No doubt, my dear friends," he began in his blandest whisper, "no doubt that you are puzzled to understand my poor master's strange manner —his apparent ignorance of the business that brought you here, and I am really and absolutely in the dark!"

"But, of course, you know—you heard about the cruel miscarriage of the money Squire Vipert—Heaven bless him!—was good enough to lend me to get me out of prison—and of the highwayman, a cowardly scamp? It would be bad for his breathing if I once got his ugly throat in my grip!"

"Aye, to be sure, we heard about the —the heartless robbery; everybody did," Mr. Phantom answered. "Hence my amazement, my joyful amazement, my good John Gauntlet, when you made your appearance here."

"What! you don't know how it came about? *You* don't know?"

"Upon my Christian word and honour, I do not!" replied Mr. Phantom.

"Why, man," said John, plucking the steward by the collar and drawing him closer that he might whisper in his ear, " 'twas the squire!"

Mr. Phantom's face had not worn so natural an expression for many a day.

"The squire!" he repeated. "What, Master Reginald, and I not know it? How—who—how do you know that?"

"I must show you more substantial proof," replied John, spreading his arms to make the most of himself. "Here I am, and you well know that couldn't be if that confounded money was not paid."

"And he paid it; you are sure?"

"I have it from the lawyer's own lips. He sent the money up to London by a messenger," John replied.

Mr. Phantom caught at this.

"Aye, I begin to see matters in a clearer light now," said he. "But it is a mistake about the money being sent. The squire took it to London himself? That accounted for his sudden haste for his horse! That accounts for his late return home. Ah! such charity is its own reward. Yes, my dear friends, it must have been in returning from London on his mission of mercy, that he met with his accident. The roads are anything but good at this time of year, and that high-bred horse of the squire's is very apt to stumble."

"His accident!" exclaimed both Nelly and John in a breath.

"A fall from his horse—a desperately dangerous fall! He pitched on his shoulder and his head, and, in short his brain has been somewhat shaken, and the doctor's orders are that he must be kept from every excitement."

"Then we will take our departure at once, dear John," Nelly said. "Heaven forbid that we should for a moment afflict one to whom we owe so much."

"Your kind heart does you credit, Miss Blisset. You have a treasure,

Mr. Gauntlet, that an emperor might envy you. I trust that my dear master may soon recover."

"Does the doctor say so?" John asked, anxiously.

Mr. Phantom gave a half-glance towards his master.

"The doctor says many things, my good friends, that are not heeded. 'You are not fit to tend him,' says the doctor. 'Your heart is good to do so, Phantom, but you have not the knack; you lack that inborn, indefinable talent for tending a sick man that a woman possesses. He must have a regular nurse, a female,'" said Mr. Phantom, with a troubled sigh; "and there's the difficulty, you see!"

"There are women in the house, are there not?" asked Nelly, compassionately.

"There are two women in the house, only two: Mrs. Mustash, the housekeeper, the elderly party with the hair on her upper lip, who opened the door to you! and there's the cook in the kitchen, and she's got a complaint that causes her to wheeze, so that I am afraid she would be a nuisance rather than a soothing to a nervous invalid," replied Mr. Phantom, plaintively; "that's our unfortunate position, and he won't think of hiring a stranger!"

Nelly's eyes sparkled.

She laid a hand on John Gauntlet's shoulder, and tiptoed to whisper in his ear.

"Surely, my darling, surely," John replied, heartily, "if he will permit it. It is what I myself should have suggested when I had time to think about it."

And then Nelly whispered to Mr. Phantom, and it was worth untold gold to see how that good, grateful old man clasped his hands, and raised his eyes, as his large ears drank in her words.

"Aye, now, if that might be brought about, it would be such a relief, were it only for a single hour a day. You wouldn't mind, Mr. Gauntlet? As you said a little while ago, you know the squire, now."

"Except her own father there is not a man in England I would more freely trust with her," returned simple John, proudly.

"That's what I like to see, that's the confidence that honour begets between men of noble mind," replied Joseph Phantom, casting up his eyes, as though to thank Heaven. "God bless you both! I will mention to him your kind-hearted proposition this very night, and let you know the result in the morning. Good bye! Good bye!"

And he wrung their hands with much affection.

"Devil take you both, I say!" he muttered, as he closed the door. "As for you, Miss Nelly Blisset," he continued, with a satanic grin, "you are as good as snared. The net is spread, my dear, and the bait has lured you. Ha, ha! we will take you even while your numskull lover is standing by, grinning and wagging his head in approval. Ah! there's nothing like the confidence that honour begets between men of noble mind."

And, having thus relieved his mind, Mr. Phantom returned to the chamber where he had left his perplexed and impatient master.

CHAPTER IX.

IN WHICH LORD LAVERING AND MISS NAN BLISSET BECOME BETTER ACQUAINTED—
BREAKERS AHEAD.

O one in the least suspecting his rank or title, young Lord Lavering continued to haunt Blisset's Mill.

After that memorable morning ride to London (by a singular coincidence so swiftly followed by John Gauntlet's release from gaol), his interest in the miller's family seemed hourly to increase.

As has already been stated, the night preceding the aforesaid memorable ride, he had, escorted thereto by that amazing young chamber-maiden, Nan, tasted the sweets of repose in the best bedchamber of the mill-house, and next night saw no alteration of the programme.

The day following, he rode out and returned at noon, to announce, with his fair face blushing the deepest crimson, and with a voice faltering with conscious guilt, that he had been tempted by the lovely situation of a cottage situate about a mile and a quarter from the mill, to become its tenant for a brief period.

He had no idea of making a prolonged stay; he averred it was quite a sudden freak.

He made this statement to the family generally, but it was to Nan that he turned with the apology for the daring act he had committed.

The fascination that that "nice-looking, cherry-cheeked person" possessed for him, seemed to increase on acquaintance, and it was evident at a glance that some sort of confidence had already been established between them.

A shy sort of confidence on his part, much of the same sort as that of a young noviciate who, for the first time, seeks the ghostly confessional.

But handsome, frank-faced Nan resembled a priest—austere, uncompromising—but in one respect; she had no soul for "sentiment."

That is to say, for sentiment of the lackadaisical and spooney order.

It wanted yet fully four months to her birthday, and then she would be twenty; but for clear-sightedness and shrewd discerning, when set beside the little London lord (who, by the bye, was Nan's senior by more than a year), she was, as compared with him, a mother—a grandmother, even.

It was this that perplexed him so.

He stood in mortal dread of women, especially pretty, marriageable women.

This weakness was the result of the judicious education that had been bestowed on him by his amiable stepmother, Lady Pinchbeck.

So Lord Lavering (whose father had died when he was quite a little boy, leaving him a solitary orphan) was kept at home, and tenderly simmered in as much education as the masters Lady Pinchbeck engaged, and her ladyship's medical man decided, would not be injurious to his constitution.

Her ladyship's desire was to save this delicate young man from the tempest-trouble, and possible wreckage and foundering that inevitably attend those daring spirits who essay a voyage to the Bay of Matrimony.

It is scarcely too much to say, speaking in metaphor, of course, that up to the age of twenty the heart of Lord Lavering was as green as a May apple.

How could it possibly ripen with so bleak a wind blowing on it?

He was still fully impressed with the prejudice his stepmother had taught him that women, one and all, were a race of cold, heartless schemers.

He felt nothing of the warning sensation when he first encountered Nan, though to confess the truth, his sensibilities were all alive in expectation of it.

"She is older than she looks," was his private explanation of the mystery. "Her manner certainly is old, and no doubt she is one of those wemarkable persons who go on blooming till their hair is gwey, and then a little dye does the business. Phew! they don't do *me!*" and his wide-awake young lordship winked to himself knowingly.

But when Lord Lavering discovered (that was after the first evening, and her behaviour over the slippers, and her distressing remark concerning nightcaps) that Nan was but a little over twenty, for the moment he felt stunned.

This was on the third day of his appearance.

Nelly, on receipt of an urgent letter from the lawyer, had gone to London, this time sure of bringing John back with her, and Nan and Lord Lavering were picking damsons in the old orchard.

His lordship was on the ladder, and Nan, with her ample apron held out before her, was the recipient of the fruit that fell from above.

Lord Lavering had divested himself of his coat, the better to accomplish his delightful task, though at the expense of his manly appearance.

"There are a prime lot on that bough just out of reach," he said. "I must dismount and shift my ladder."

"Don't trouble to do that. I'll show you. Hold tight."

And so saying, taking the ends of her apron in her white teeth, so as to set her hands at liberty, Nan took the sides of the ladder and turned them about once or twice, and then, in her mirth to see the scared and breathless face of the noble gentleman desperately clinging to the rounds, a corner of the apron slipped, and out rolled the damsons amongst the dead leaves.

Lord Lavering was constrained to laugh too, though he was angry.

"You are awfully strong," said he, maliciously. "I began to think, Miss Blisset, that you were about to serve me as the street conjurors do, and balance me on your chin, or something in that way."

"Well, I might have been tempted, but I was not quite sure that your balancing power was perfect enough," Nan returned, with merry mischief. "It is too bad, though, I must confess, for you might have fallen. By-the-bye, how old are you, Jimmy?"

Now, the reader must not imagine that "Jimmy" was a *nom de plume* adopted by Lord Lavering in lieu of his true baptismal name.

Desiring for the present to preserve his incognito, and finding that he could not get on without a name of some kind, he had chosen that of "Mr. Cecil."

Nan, however, for some reason which she herself would have found difficult to explain, found it easier and more suitable to call him "Jimmy," and there was an end of it.

"By-the-bye, how old are you, Jimmy?"

This was a chance not to be lost.

"If she hitherto has been labouring under a mistaken impression as to my age, she shall now be undeceived," thought Lord Lavering.

"My age, Miss Blisset," said he, solemnly, and at the same time folding his arms over his breast, "my age is twenty-two next birthday."

He would not have been in the least surprised had she looked startled, and attempted some confused apology for the elderly airs she had taken with him, but without the least alteration in her voice, she replied—

"Twenty-two next birthday, eh? There's about a pint of damsons rolled amongst these raspberry canes; mind how you get them, Jimmy, or you will prick your fingers."

"And pray how old may *you* be, Miss Blisset?" he asked, with a redder face than stooping after the damsons warranted.

"Oh, I'm a bit over twenty; but that's different, you know," Nan replied, looking coolly at the damsons in her lap. "I've got enough for this time; will you carry the ladder, or shall I?"

"How is it different, Miss Blisset?" remarked Lord Lavering, returning to the question of age.

"What, the years?" Nan replied, with a laugh; "oh, don't you know? Country years are like country miles as compared with town miles? they're of the same length, but *there's more in 'em.* Of course you wouldn't for a moment pretend that you are as old as I am? *Really* as old, I mean?"

"If you mean that you are wiser than I am——" began Lord Lavering, gallantly.

"That's just what I *do* mean," said Nan, nodding her head gravely. "Ha! ha! there's a way to carry a ladder!"

Lord Lavering had the unwieldy instrument hugged in his arms as Punch hugs his baton.

"How would you have me carry it, miss!"

"Balance it, Jimmy; put it on your shoulder, and balance it; that's the way!"

And all the while, wonder of wonders! not a ghost of that warning sensation had appeared to him.

"Beware of women," Lady Pinchbeck had adjured him. "Beware, my dear Cecil, of all women, but especially of those who are young and handsome."

And was not this one young and handsome?

True, her beauty was not of the hothouse kind to which he was accustomed, but did she lose by the comparison?

What were those fragile, pink-and-white, powdered and polished beauties of the drawing-room contrasted with this charming woman?

This plump and luscious nectarine of Nature's own growing and ripening!

What was the veneer and tinsel with which, under the name of "accomplishments," the shallowness of their minds was hidden, compared with the ready wit and kindly good temper of Mr. Blisset's eldest daughter Nan?

These were the reflections that disturbed Lord Lavering as he came on behind, carrying the ladder still in a very unworkmanlike manner, in spite of the instructions he had received.

"I should get to like her very much—much more than ever I liked Lady Pinchbeck," he mused. "Only she makes so confoundedly little of me. And yet there's a sort of feeling of liking about it. Deuthe take it! there must be thomething! A fellow couldn't take so kindly to cawying a confounded ladder, and to being addwessed as 'Jimmy,' unless he expewenced some thort of compenthation. Would it be any different if she knew who I weally am?

"Is it only because I'm thupposed to be a common-plathe person that this young lady maketh no disguise of her weal, unthophithticated nature? If that is the case, then I am obtaining pleasure under falthe pretenthes! Gwathious Heavens! I never thought of that."

And the appalling discovery brought the honest little lord to a standstill.

"Ah I thought you would find it too heavy," Nan remarked, as she looked back with a laugh that displayed her even, double row of pearly teeth. "Let me take it, and you carry the damsons."

And, in a twinkling, the apron-string was untied and the bulky parcel placed in his lordship's hands.

But the exchange brought his lordship no comfort. Evidently there was that on his mind that put it quite out of his power to pay due attention either to ladders or damsons. A corner of the apron slid out of his fingers and a thick stream of the luscious fruit trickled down to the ground.

"Look at you, you careless goose," laughed Nan; "pick them up this instant, sir, every one of them."

But Lord Lavering bit his thumb nervously.

"Miss Blisset," said he, blushing up to the roots of his curly hair, "I have been deceiving you!"

Nan opened her eyes wide and in feigned alarm.

"Ah," said she, with a tantalizing smile, "you have been eating the damsons after I warned you not; and now you begin to feel the consequence."

"No—no, it ithn't that. Pway be

sewious, Miss Blisset! What I mean is that I am not what I theem!"

"How?"

"I am—I am not a common perthon; shall I tell you who I am?"

"You are Mr. Cecil, and a good-natured young chap, and I like you very much; there is nothing more to tell, is there?" asked Nan.

"Ah! but I'm afraid that you wouldn't tell me that you liked me very much when you know that I have been acting the part of an impostor. I am not Mr. Cecil, Miss Blisset, I am Lord Cecil Lavering!"

Nan displayed about as much emotion as though he had told her that his name was not Mr. Cecil, but Mr. Tomkins.

"Well, where's the harm of that?" said she, coolly.

"The *harm*, Miss Blisset!"

"Aye, can't you be a good-natured little chap and a lord at the same time? You're all right, Jimmy; come along."

And Nan marched off with the ladder.

"But do you mean to say that you don't expewience—that you don't feel——"

"What?" Nan asked, facing round.

"That you don't feel awe-stricken——"

Nan exploded in an irresistible fit of laughter.

"Oh! you are a funny creature!—do I look awe-stricken?" she presently replied, mimicking his lisp, and with her merry eyes twinkling.

But suddenly her mirthful demeanour changed to one of gravity.

"Since you are a lord, you are rich," said she; "tell me what business was it

that carried you to London the morning following your coming here?"

The question came so unexpectedly on his little lordship that he was quite staggered by the force of it, and turned first red and then pale.

"The bithness was pwivate bithness," he stammered guiltily.

"Aye, that I know it was; but its nature? You may tell me, sir."

Little Lord Lavering was in extreme distress.

"Weally, Miss Blisset," said he, "the thaid bithness was so extremely pwivate—to confess it would be to declare myself such a—a meddlesome person that—that unless you most particularly wish it——"

"I do wish it; though now, I think, I can guess without being told," Nan interrupted, looking full into the little lord's face with a look that should have called up that " warning sensation " if anything could. "Tell me, and the secret shall be as safe in my keeping as in your own. I promise you that on my honour."

"But—but, what ith it you thuspect me of?"

"Shall I tell you? Of obtaining the release of John Gauntlet."

Lord Lavering stood aghast at this instance of Nan's extraordinary shrewdness.

"Good Heaventh!" he grasped. "I—I can't deny it; but you will be merthiful, Miss Blisset? You will not expothe me?"

"Heaven bless you, Lord Lavering," was Nan's fervent reply, and next moment the ladder dropped, and a pair of the plumpest arms in Kent were round his neck and her rosy lips sounded on his downy cheek.

Little Lord Lavering blushed so violently that something very like tears welled up into his amiable blue eyes.

"It was the mewest twifle," he stammered. "You spoke the other day about—about wishing you had a brother, Miss Blisset; if you would condescend to regard me as such; or, if you would prefer it, as—as an——"

"An orphan?" put in Nan, her wicked eyes twinkling again.

"Exactly; anything in that way. You would confer on me an obligation it would be my constant endeavour to requite."

And in his confusion he embraced his load of damsons with an ardour that sent the juice gushing through Nan's apron.

"And you wish me to keep the secret of the morning ride to London?"

"Oh, certainly; oh, most decidedly," responded Lord Lavering. "You promise that."

"I promise," Nan replied.

"Whatever happens, you will keep your promise; even as regards your sister?"

"As regards everyone," said Nan, with a face as serious as his own. "I have pledged you my word of honour, and I shall not forfeit it. It is impossible I should regret making such a promise as that," was Nan's reflection, as they made their way to the house.

But in this she was mistaken.

She regretted it—bitterly regretted it—that night before she slept.

For it was that night Nelly returned with John Gauntlet.

And after the kissing and greeting was at an end, and Nan had introduced to John Gauntlet "Mr. Cecil," the young gentleman who had so chivalrously acquitted himself in connection with the highway robbery, and John (who had heard all about it already) had given him a real Kentish hug by way of present thanks, then came the particulars of the lovers' call at the Hall, and their interview with Squire Vipert.

"That's my own good lass," exclaimed old Blisset; "since you could give him no more than your thanks, it was quite right to give them promptly. Heaven prosper him, he is a noble gentleman."

Nan bit her lip.

"There can, of course, be no doubt that it is to Squire Vipert we owe this great obligation?" she ventured.

"Nay; there might have been a doubt before, though but a small one," answered happy John Gauntlet. "But there can be none now, eh, Nelly?"

"Why?" Nan asked.

"Why, lass! Because he—no; if I remember rightly, he did not confess to it, but it was the same thing; when I thanked him for it, he did not deny it."

Nan looked appealingly towards Lord Lavering.

"Oh, there could be no doubt that Squire Vipert was the good Samaritan," the latter struck up stoutly; "as Mr. Blisset says, he is a noble gentleman, a true gentleman; I hope that no one will deny it; I most respectfully beg and entreat that no one will attempt to deny it."

And he cast an imploring glance towards the corner where Nan sat.

"Ha, ha! you'd ride him down as you did that white-muzzled thief, t'other night, if any one dared to deny that Squire Vipert is a true gentleman!" cried jovial John Gauntlet. "Bravo! we shall be friends, my brave little bantam; there is no doubt of that. He is sick at present, poor fellow!"

"Sick!"

"Aye; had a fall from a horse on his return from his mission of mercy," put in Nelly, her brown eyes beaming gratefully; "think of that, mother!"

"The Lord be good to him! if my prayers will help him, he shall not lack them," spoke the good dame.

"He needs help, mother," said Nelly, compassionately. "The doctor says his nursing is not what it should be."

"Who told you that?" Nan asked.

"Mr. Phantom," Nelly replied; "and so, with John's permission, I offered to go up to the Hall every day for an hour or two, just to make things straight and comfortable for him, poor fellow."

"That is only as it should be," remarked Dame Blisset, approvingly. "I myself would go to him most willingly, were it necessary."

"So you should, wife, so you should!" spoke the old miller. "Whoever does a child of mine a kindness, I am his debtor. But Nelly will do better, mother. Let her go, let her go!"

Nan found it hard to dissemble her anxiety.

"It was very strange!"

If it were really true that it was their handsome young guest and not Squire Vipert who had found the money by virtue of which John Gauntlet was finally released from gaol, how did it happen that the Master of Monkshood "had not denied" the generous act when John thanked him for it?

If it was because of this supposed generosity that Nelly was disposed to act the part of nurse to the sick squire, with John's full consent—nay, with his earnest persuasion—and there was no foundation for it?

"Did—did Mr. Vipert accept your offer, Nelly dear?" she asked her sister, hesitatingly, when they had retired for the night.

"Yes."

"Has his sickness altered him so, darling?" and Nan looked hard at her lovely sister.

"Oh! he is handsome enough still, if that is what you mean," answered the girl, laughing. "Indeed, I'm not quite sure but that his pallor does not become him even better than his customary complexion. But it's his temper I'm speaking of now, dear—he who was so courteous, so elegant and polite in his manner towards women—it is a shame to speak so of him, poor fellow, but it is a fact. His accident has made him as surly as a bear. Don't be in the least surprised, Nan, if you hear that he has bitten my head off!"

And, shrugging her round shoulders in pretended terror, she laughingly kissed her sister, and bade her good night.

But Nan lay awake a very long while.

Her sister's last words were playful, trivial enough; but somehow Nan could not get it out of her head that they were ominous—prophetic!

CHAPTER X.

WHEREIN IT IS ON THE CARDS THAT THE MILLER'S MAID SHALL BECOME
MISTRESS OF MONKSHOOD.

HE villanous device conceived by Mr. Phantom had already begun to bear fruit.

Squire Vipert had given his consent that Miss Ellen Blisset might come, and, in his behalf, make herself useful at the Hall.

In the profoundly respectful little note he caused to be conveyed next morning to the mill-house, he thanked Miss Ellen sincerely for her sympathy, and the humane and Christian offer that had sprung out of it.

And he would very gratefully avail himself of any little leisure she might feel disposed to bestow on him.

There was only one drawback, he declared, to the pleasure her kind assistance would afford him, and that arose from the uncomfortable suspicion that a desire to return the trifling obligation it had been his good fortune to confer on her future husband, might, to some extent, have helped towards the benevolent suggestion.

He sincerely hoped that this was not so, and that Miss Blisset and her friends would not magnify beyond its small dimensions that little business in which a temporary loan of money had figured.

"It will be as well to add that, Master Reginald," said Mr. Phantom (who was at his master's elbow when the epistle was being written). "A temporary loan of money! That alludes to the first loan, of course; to the only loan you know anything of. What do we know about other loans? Ha, ha! if folks will run their heads against brick walls, they must."

"There need be nothing more added, Phantom?"

"Unless you think it worth while to throw a sop to the bulldog that presumes to be Miss Blisset's guardian," suggested Phantom, blandly.

"What, to Gauntlet?"

"Aye, Master Reginald; it will cost nothing, and may help to keep him in good humour."

With a disdainful shrug of his shoulders, Squire Vipert took up his pen once more.

"WASP PLANTED HIS BRAVE LITTLE FEET ON THE PROPERTY OF HIS BELOVED MASTER."—(See page 114).

After a feint or two at the paper, he threw it down again.

"I can't write it, Phantom," he cried, passionately; "I have so hot a hatred for the fellow that it parches the ink at my pen's point. Since last night when she was bending over me, and I looked up and saw him, I have had *two* faces haunting me continually—one loving and gentle, and the other grinning in devilish mockery. I have had no sleep for dreaming of them. I have felt like a poor wretch clinging to the threshold of Paradise with Satan hauling him away! One must not throw sops to Satan. We will resist him, and keep our sops for a more worthy object."

"It is for me neither to object nor to order, my dear master," returned the oily man; "but a soft word or so may disarm this Gauntlet. I'd rather, for my part, see his teeth behind a muzzle than bare."

The Master of Monkshood smiled grimly and again betook himself to his pen, and with much contortion of countenance and grinding of his teeth, added as a postcript—

"Nor must I forget the kindness that Mr. John Gauntlet has exhibited in so readily yielding his consent to Miss Blisset's charitable design. Let him rest assured that it will strengthen that love of faith and good-will so happily renewed between Reginald Vipert and his tenant."

Six hours after saw Nelly at the Hall.

The Squire of Monkshood had, at least, not exaggerated when he declared himself in need of nursing.

His wounded shoulder still caused him such intolerable pain that he found it difficult to obtain ease in any one position for many minutes together, and his recent excitement had made him restless and feverish.

Not that, as regards personal appearance, he suffered on this account.

On the contrary, it lent a brilliance to his dark, flashing eyes, and a colour to his handsome face that considerably lessened his invalid aspect, and caused innocent Nelly to congratulate him on his amendment since she had last seen him.

"I verily believe it is my anticipating the good I shall derive from your visits that has worked the change, Miss Blisset," he replied, with a kindling glance.

"Your hand feels a little feverish," said Nelly, shaking her pretty head seriously.

"Oh, that's nothing," he replied, with a smile; "it is enough to flutter a solitary old ogre such as I am, when so kind a ministering angel condescends to cross the threshold of my door."

But Nelly had come to do and not to talk.

Compared with that he had beheld her in when last they met, her costume was most sober and demure.

She wore ornament of no kind; no ring, no brooch.

Even the brilliant little ear-rings were missing from her dainty shell-like ears.

Her already sufficiently high-necked gown bristled chastely with a *chevaux de frise* of starched quilling, that reached to her throat almost, and she wore linen cuffs, and when she withdrew from her little basket a homely matter-of-fact apron, the picture was complete.

So thought Reginald Vipert, as, reclining in his easy chair, he affected to read while he covertly watched her flitting handily about the room, noiselessly arranging the general disorder, comfort and easiness growing perceptibly under the magic of her touch.

He had never dreamt how charming she was.

Her dress, of the plainest cut, developed more than would a more elaborate costume the exquisite symmetry of her figure, the perfectness of her bust, the roundness and tapering delicacy of her arms, the smallness of the white hands that moved so cheerfully busy.

Her magnificent hair was its proper setting, and though at present it was held in bondage, it was so evident that the mere slipping of a knot would send the dancing deluge down that it was as good as done by the mere imagining.

It was better than done, because here at a glance you had, in fact, Nelly the household goddess, prim as a snowdrop, and, in fancy, Nelly the lovely, with all her beauties free for your enchanted eyes to feast on.

It was as a revelation to the ardent young Master of Monkshood.

It had been his wont impatiently to wonder what so solid-headed, matter-of-fact a fellow as John Gauntlet could find, and so to charm his fancy, in this pretty, little, summer butterfly of a woman.

Now his eyes were open to the fact that she was something more than this;

that she combined with the beauty of the butterfly the more substantial qualities of the bee; that, like the sun, she shed around her, as well as dazzling light, that warmth which is the essence of life, and which is to be summed up in two short words — "home happiness."

And day after day she came, her every visit being, to the invalid, gall and honey.

Honey, sweetness inexpressible to see her, to be conscious of her presence, to hear the rustle of her dress, to feel the touch of her gentle hand; gall, a bitterness that dried the moisture of his mouth, and set his heart sickening, to think that this fleeting pleasure was but borrowed, that his enemy had lent it!

That the lovely face was compassionate not for him, but for his ailment; that her hand's gentleness, and the sweet soothing of her voice, was for him only so long as sickness prostrated him.

It was the old, old story of forbidden fruit.

Might it be his own for the choosing, the mere trouble of tip-toeing to reach it, maybe, would have cooled his craving; but, being the pride of another man's garden, the case was different.

Mr. Joseph Phantom remarked the symptoms that betrayed Mr. Vipert's condition of mind.

They could not escape him.

They were bad for the wounded shoulder, that required a temperate condition of blood instead of a hot and fevered.

He found it out, too, in his master's

increased irritability; in his impatience of restraint; in his painful and ill-concealed anxiety for the approach of the hour when Nelly Blisset came; in his despondency as soon as she had taken her departure.

Mr. Phantom noted these signs, and approved of them.

Matters were working to the desired end.

The brewing, towards which he had so liberally furnished ingredients, was approaching boiling-point.

It was nearly ready, and then—look out for scaldings!

"Look out, you bully, John Gauntlet! Look out, you perfidious mistress of the mill, and the addle-pated idiot you chose in place of a better man as your husband! It is long, long ago, but love turned to hate is at molten heat at the core, and doesn't easily cool. Look out, one and all, the mist-brew is bubbling!"

"Phantom!" exclaimed the Master of Monkshood, as on the fifth day the miller's lovely daughter bade him "good-bye till to-morrow," "there must be an end to this; it is driving me mad!"

"An end to the visits of Miss Blisset, Master Reginald?" said Phantom, in feigned surprise. "Certainly, if you desire it. I thought——"

"What did you think?" asked Mr. Vipert, impatiently facing round on him.

"I ventured to think," continued Mr. Phantom, rubbing his hands deferentially, "that you were rapidly arriving at that conclusion; that is all, Master Reginald."

"Why did you?" his master asked, dryly.

"Because it is so difficult to foresee any other. It was a mistake to have the young lady here at all, Master Reginald. We agreed that her presence might amuse you, might beguile the tedium of your confinement, and tend to your rapid recovery. In the latter respect, at least, there can be no doubt that we miscalculated. You are not nearly so cool as you should be, sir!"

"By Heaven! a man with his heart on fire can scarcely be cool!" returned Squire Vipert, fuming, as he paced the room.

Mr. Phantom was so tickled by this promising outburst, that, for his life, he could not forego a toothsome nibble at his notched finger nails.

"As you say, Master Reginald, there had best be an end to it—of her visits here, I mean. They only upset you. The Fates seems to declare for this clodhopper. Miss Blisset, handsome as she is, and quite unsuited to mate with one of his boorish breed, will marry him, and there's an end of it. If I overstep the privilege of an old servant in speaking so plainly, Master Reginald, I am sorry—but I speak from my heart, sir."

Reginald Vipert drew a deep breath as though a long-pending question on his mind was that instant resolved.

"Phantom, I wish to consult you on a matter that, to me, is of great importance," said he, in a low, determined voice.

Mr. Phantom bowed, and covertly licked his lips.

"You imagine it to be my desire that

Miss Blisset should come no more to the Hall? You are mistaken!"

Mr. Phantom tried to look surprised, but the attempt was not a brilliant success.

"I have but one desire," continued Mr. Vipert; "all others are trivial, and subservient to it; and that is—that Miss Blisset should come here, and never go away again."

Mr. Phantom's eyes sparkled.

"Here?" he repeated, with a peculiar look.

Mr. Phantom hesitated.

"I know your indomitable will, Master Reginald, and that you will accomplish what you set your mind on, but think you it would be quite prudent?"

"Pray am I to discuss with you the prudence of such a step?" Mr. Vipert asked coldly.

"You misunderstand me, Master Reginald," Mr. Phantom hastened to explain; "it is not the prudence of the step that I venture to question; it is but a natural step, and one that anybody but this silly fool Gauntlet might have foreseen; it is the—the direction in which it is taken in which I see difficulty. Why not take her to London? The caged bird will ever be restive if it is living near the wood where it was snared."

For an instant the Master of Monkshood glared threateningly on his plastic man-of-all-work.

"You cold-blooded rascal, do you dare——" he began.

But he suddenly altered his tone, and with a brief little laugh, remarked—

"I am sorry to discredit my school-master. I have no doubt, Mr. Phantom, that you have reasons for expecting better things of me; but this time I must disappoint you. It is as my wife that I would welcome Miss Blisset to Monkshood Hall!"

As his wife!

Had a measure of icy cold water been unexpectedly poured down Mr. Phantom's back, he could not have gasped more spasmodically.

"As your *wife*, Master Reginald?" he repeated. "Did I rightly understand you to say as your wife, sir? It—it is impossible."

"You forget the indomitable will you just gave me credit for, my good Joseph; or have you so gracious an opinion of me as to regard it as effective only when exercised in an unworthy direction?"

Joseph Phantom's face was white, and his speech incoherent with the rage that filled him. It was only by a most violent effort that he was enabled to maintain an appearance of composure.

"Pray, has Miss Blisset given you— has she led you to suppose——"

"Nothing, except that she regards her marriage with Gauntlet as certain as the rising of to-morrow's sun. There is the thorn, Phantom. She is so loving, so trusting, so confident that I cannot bear to part with her. Phantom, *I will not* part with her."

"But do you think it probable that she will sacrifice——"

"Her pig-tending swain for *me*;" interrupted the Master of Monkshood, with his lip curled in scorn at his man's audacity. "Upon my soul, Phantom, your ideas of the privileges of an old servant must be tolerably extensive ! Trust me, your fears on that head are groundless. It is *I* who make the sacrifice, man. An alliance of the sort at which you hinted, you miserable old sinner, is one thing—to be the wife of Reginald Vipert of Monkshood Hall, is quite another."

Mr. Phantom, with his face still ghastly pale, had his head turned towards the window.

"It is quite, quite another thing !" he replied, huskily. "And have you quite resolved on this step, Master Reginald ?"

"My heart already beats the marching tune that shall lead to its accomplishment," responded the young Master of Monkshood ; "to-morrow shall set the matter beyond a doubt."

"To-morrow !" repeated Mr. Phantom, eagerly, and with a something in his deep-set eyes it would have been to his master's advantage to have read and interpreted ; "you will ask her consent to-morrow, Master Reginald ?"

"As surely as it comes," returned Reginald Vipert, gaily. "I have *your* consent to the contract, I suppose, Phantom ?"

"I cannot study the interests of my master without, at the same time, studying mine own," responded he, as, with a low obeisance, he left the room.

But, ah ! could the Master of Monkshood have seen that look of malevolence, that shaking of both his clenched fists, in which his faithful servant indulged as the door closed behind him !

CHAPTER XI.

MR. PHANTOM IS STRUNG WITH HIS OWN STRING, AND SEEKS A DESPERATE REMEDY.

HAVING quitted his master's presence, Mr. Phantom's pent-up wrath found slight vent, but it was not till he gained his own room, and double-locked the door, that he ventured to let loose the flood-gates.

He flung himself on his bed, and in his excess of rage, he tore and bit at the pillows as a mad dog might.

"Baffled after all ! after all !" he moaned, "after all my pains, all my patience, all my toil and trouble ! The fool ! the silly moth ! to be dazzled by the glitter of a woman's eyes.

"She will jilt the other, and this lovesick idiot, my master, will make her his wife, and all my plans, all my darling, cherished schemes will be ruined ! Oh ! it is terrible to feel the deadly thrust of the weapons one has sharpened and pointed for others !"

But Joseph Phantom was not the man to lie down and be thrust to death by any weapon whatever, while there was a chance of wriggling out of harm's way.

His paroxysm of passion exhausted, he gradually grew more calm, and betook himself to reviewing the unfavourable aspect matters had so unexpectedly assumed.

Undoubtedly he had been betrayed into making a very grave miscalculation.

He had flattered himself that Squire Reginald Vipert was a man who was altogether superior to the weakness of marrying a woman merely because he was in love with her.

He gave him credit for being a gentleman whose resources for winning an obdurate woman's heart were amply sufficient without resort to marriage.

But now, when his man held it in his hands, he was about to allow himself to be befooled, bewitched!

"To be sure there is a chance that she will reject the offer that this madman will assuredly make to-morrow," mused Joseph Phantom, pallid with anxiety. "A slender chance, indeed. It will never do to rely on it. No. Something must be done. It is a desperate case, and I must not stick at the remedy."

He did little else but muse for an hour or so after this, and until the shades of evening fell, and then he stole out of the house, and made a curious survey of the exterior of the Hall.

Especially that part of it that was immediately contiguous to the windows of Squire Vipert's sitting-room.

There was a balcony before the said windows, with stands for flowers, and several—five or six—flowering shrubs of rare value, and of large size.

They stood in their great pots at equal distances along the front of the balcony; but first making sure that no one was within the sitting-room, Mr. Phantom took a fancy for rearranging the tall, bushy shrubs, and bringing them closer together.

Then, after viewing the singular arrangement with evident satisfaction, he retired into the house, and resumed his customary duties.

Between nine and ten o'clock, however, he might have been observed, had there been any one to watch him, to steal out again with his coat buttoned about his meagre figure and a comforter about his neck (for the autumn night was chilly), and to make his way towards Froggart's Lane.

Up the lane to the hill, on the crown of which Blisset's mill was perched.

But he didn't go up the hill.

He halted at the foot of it, and took his stand under a tree, as though waiting for some one he knew would be sure to come that way presently.

Nor was he mistaken.

Just as the old church bell was chiming ten, the burly figure of a man could be dimly made out descending the hill from the direction of the mill-house.

A blithe and cheery figure softly whistling to himself, as happy men will, and flourishing his oak sapling, gay as a schoolboy.

When he reached the foot of the hill, he was still flourishing the oak sapling, and, not perceiving Mr. Phantom, who stood in the dark, brought it so close to that venerable gentleman's head that, in self-defence, he put up his hand and caught hold of it.

But in an instant it was jerked out of his grasp, and he felt the knuckles of a mighty fist inconveniently encroaching among the inner folds of his comforter.

"Who skulks here at this hour?" rang out John Gauntlet's manly voice. "Open your mouth, man, or you'll feel the weight of the switch you just now took liberties with."

"You, you are throttling me, my good sir," he cried. "Mr. Gauntlet, it is I—Joseph Phantom, your friend. I came out; I was waiting here on purpose for you."

John instantly relaxed his grip on the comforter.

"You, Mr. Phantom! *you* here!" he ejaculated, in wonder, and if it could have been seen, not without a slight change of colour; "you were waiting to see me. Why were you?"

"Because I am your friend, my dear sir," replied Joseph, meekly, as he settled his neck in his ruffled neckcloth; "because I have made a discovery, my good friend, that, as a man with a conscience, I could not keep to myself an hour longer than was possible."

"But if it is so urgent," said John, with an uncomfortable presentiment of "trouble looming," "why didn't you come up to the mill-house? You knew that you would find me there."

"True, Mr. Gauntlet, true; but I knew likewise that *she* would be there, and——"

"She! of whom do you speak?" John asked, with growing alarm.

"Hush! let me take your arm, my poor friend," replied Mr. Phantom, hooking on, with his black-gloved paws; "we need not talk so loud that all the parish shall hear us. It *is* to Miss Nelly Blisset, to your future wife, I alluded when I just now spoke. But you need not tremble so, my good sir; there is nothing *much* the matter."

John Gauntlet suddenly released himself from Mr. Phantom's arm, and faced round on him.

"Look you, my friend," said he, in a husky voice; "I call you so because it is no less that you deserve, and the Lord knows that to my dying day I shall remain obliged to you. But don't beat about the bush *now*. There is something the matter—not much. How much? Tell me as we stand still, because after I have heard what you have come to tell me, there is no knowing which way we may have to walk."

Mr. Phantom was sorely distressed.

Even while John Gauntlet was speaking, his ever-ready pocket-handkerchief was out and on duty.

"For Heaven's sake be calm, young man!" he sobbed, "don't set me off again if you can help it! My heart has been recently wrung but not dry. No, the tear of compassion will flow."

John stamped his foot in disgust and impatience.

"For Heaven's sake speak out, man!" he cried; "tell me quickly and get it over; what is it you have to communicate about Miss Blisset?"

"Respecting Miss Blisset, my good young man, nothing—nothing at all! It is of *him*."

"Of *him!*"

You could see John Gauntlet's face now, it was so white in the darkness.

"Did you say of—of *him?*"

"Ob, Lord!" whined Mr. Phantom, wriggling in his grief, "the cat is out! I had only to say 'him,' and he knew who I meant in a moment! He jumped as suddenly to the conclusion as though he already had his suspicions!"

What a contrast— the blithe young fellow who came whistling down the hill ten minutes since, and the pale, bewildered man who stood confronting Mr. Phantom!

"Suspicions!" he repeated dreamily, passing his hand across his forehead.

"Because if you have, let me hasten to assure you that they are unfounded," continued the cadaverous man, sweetly grinning to himself on account of the pleasant progress of his devilish schemes. "She knows no more of his —of my master's insane designs than a babe unborn. But let us be walking, my good friend; I would not press it, only I am such a martyr to rheumatism. We can talk as we walk just as well."

And John Gauntlet, like a man from whom all self-will had gone, obeyed.

And Mr. Phantom talked, and John listened.

Say that he was wrong in doing so, say that he was weakly credulous—mean even, and I will not defend him.

Did he doubt his Nelly's constancy?

No, no; a thousand times no! But still——

What *was* the matter?

Was it possible that the circumstantial story that the old tattler brought him had no foundation?

For Nelly's sake it was necessary to follow to the end the scent, true or false, he had been set on.

No doubt it was nothing more than idle scandal, but the young farmer would let them know that his affianced wife was no subject for silly gossip, as he would by-and-bye prove to them.

So he listened with all the patience he could muster till Mr. Phantom had quite exhausted his artfully-packed budget, and then with a look of affected indifference, he bade Mr. Phantom make his mind quite easy, at the same time promising to consider the information that had been brought him.

"But you are forgetting," urged Mr. Phantom, "there is not much time for consideration, my good sir, between this and to-morrow."

"To-morrow!" John repeated, biting his lip.

To-morrow morning.

"To be sure, there would be one way of avoiding any—any unpleasantness!"

And, as he uttered the words, as though communing with himself, he darted a rapid glance at John's perplexed face.

"How?" the latter asked.

"You might prevent her coming to the Hall in the morning," returned Mr. Phantom, blandly. "It would be easy to invent some plausible excuse to account for your objection——"

"What!" thundered John, fiercely, for the first time during the interview permitting his temper to master him. "No, Mr. Phantom; I'll have no hand in baulking Squire Vipert. Let him play his game out so that we may see the card he held. No fear that he'll win what you say he's playing for! I cannot believe it, Mr. Phantom; but if he should be so great a villain as you would make him, why, the sooner he ripens, the sooner he'll be ready for plucking."

Mr. Phantom groaned, and held up his hands, as though, as a man of peace, John's words harrowed him to the soul; but there was a sinister light in his deep-set eyes that gave the lie to his gestures.

"Besides," continued John Gauntlet, growing ominously calm, "don't you see, man? It would seem as though I was afraid to trust *her* if I interfered."

"That's true, that's very true, indeed," remarked Mr. Phantom, wagging his head in admiration; "but still——"

"What?"

"Since you are determined that my poor infatuated master shall put his insane purpose into execution, wouldn't it be as well if you were close at hand —somewhere where you might see all, hear all, without being seen or heard?"

John hesitated.

"There's a smack of meanness about your proposition that isn't to my mind," said he; "though, for that matter, I need not in such a case show myself without occasion, eh?"

"That's exactly what I mean," returned Mr. Phantom, rubbing his bony hands together in genuine satisfaction; "that was precisely what I was about to remark when you interrupted me."

"But where's the use of talking?" said John, shaking his head. "How could I be close at hand without being seen?"

Mr. Phantom pretended to reflect, but responded with a promptness that might have provoked the suspicion that he had in his mind previously provided against this difficulty.

"Trust me," said he; "I will arrange that quite to your satisfaction. Meet me to-morrow morning at ten, under the walnut-tree that skirts the garden."

And so they parted.

The sitting-room that the convalescent squire occupied overlooked the lawn, and its windows were sheltered by a balcony, in which stood, in their pots, several fragrant lemon trees, tall and bushy.

Before he retired to rest that night, Mr. Phantom busied himself with these bushy trees, and arranged them to suit his fantastic fancy.

*   *   *   *   *

The French windows of Squire Vipert's sitting-room were somehow unaccountably out of order on the morning following the evening on which occurred the above detailed interview between Mr. Phantom and John Gauntlet.

The one that looked on the part of the balcony on which the bushiest of the lemon trees stood would not quite shut close.

"Why the —— don't that window shut?" Mr. Vipert petulantly asked, as he entered the room.

"There has something gone wrong with a hinge, I believe, sir," meek Joseph replied; "it shall be seen to to-morrow. If you will permit me to turn your chair a little this way—so, you will not feel what little draught there may be."

And as he spoke, the crafty villain (who, at that very moment, had in his pocket the screw-driver with which the hinge had been misplaced) wheeled his master's easy chair into a position that afforded the best view of it from the outside.

Reginald Vipert was nervous, and a shade or so paler than yesterday.

"Did you pass a good night, sir?" Joseph asked solicitously.

"I passed a confounded bad night," his master snapped irritably.

"Is your shoulder still so painful, dear sir? Ah, it was a miracle that the bullet——"

"Who the —— wants to talk about bullets and wounds?" interrupted the invalid gentleman. "I've something else to think of. How am I looking, Phantom? Gad! I needn't inquire!" he continued, as he caught sight of his haggard, though still handsome face in an opposite mirror. "I'm looking as seedy as some poor beggar just discharged from an hospital. Give me some brandy, Phantom."

Joseph bowed demurely, but, as he turned his head to execute the command, he indulged in a grin that showed his back teeth.

"He means it," he inwardly chuckled. "He shies rather at the job before him, but he's a Vipert, and he won't flinch at the last moment. He won't quarrel with me if I give him a heavy dose, I'll be bound."

And, filling a big glass to the brim, Mr. Phantom gave it to Squire Vipert, who swallowed it at a gulp.

"What's the time, Phantom?" he asked, presently.

"Past eleven, sir."

"She should be here by this time, or nearly. What's that, Phantom?"

The question was asked so abruptly and with so much alarm that Joseph Phantom changed colour, and cast a hurried glance towards the lemon tree.

"What—what do you allude to, sir?" he stammered.

"That noise at the window; don't you hear it, you idiot? It's raining, if I am not mistaken."

"To be sure it is, Master Reginald," replied Joseph, heaving a sigh of relief. "Nice seasonable weather, sir, good for the——"

"Good for the ——" interrupted his master, with a wicked word; "it isn't good for me. It is just like my confounded luck! She won't come now!"

"Maybe, Mr. Gauntlet will accompany her with an umbrella, sir," said he, edging so close to the window that any one listening the other side of it must have heard. "He is very careful of her health, I have heard, Master Reginald."

"Confound the dull brute! Why mention his name to me? *His* care, indeed! let him bestow it on his pigs."

"Hush!" whispered Joseph Phantom, with a finger on his lips; "here she comes, sir."

And then came a modest tap at the door, and in came Nelly Blisset.

She had been, as it seemed, caught in the sharp autumn shower, and been running.

Her pretty face was all aglow, and her close-sitting bodice betrayed her quick breath, while her bright brown eyes seemed to have caught and retained the sparkle of the raindrops.

At a sign from his master, Joseph Phantom quitted the room.

Never before had Reginald Vipert seen her looking so lovely.

Who else saw her?

" ' WELL, WELL, NELLY, I WILL CONSIDER, I WILL REFLECT,' SAID MR. PHANTOM."—(See page 137.)

It was still raining.

There must, however, have been wind as well as rain without, or how else was the strange disturbance of the lemon bushes outside in the balcony to be accounted for?

The lemon bushes over which Mr. Phantom had so busied himself on the previous evening after his interview with John Gauntlet.

"A showery morning, Miss Blisset!" the Master of Monkshood remarked for lack of anything more to the purpose.

"It is indeed! I narrowly escaped a wetting," returned Nelly, cheerily, as she prepared to busy herself about the room.

"A very dull and melancholy morning," continued Mr. Vipert, with peculiar emphasis, as he covertly regarded lovely Nelly, and gave vent to a sigh; "a morning, Miss Blisset, that is curiously in harmony with my own feelings."

"I am indeed sorry to hear you say so," Nelly returned; "do you not feel so well this morning, sir?"

And sympathetic Nelly more closely approached him.

"I am afraid," she continued, "that the poor services it is in my power to render you, Mr. Vipert, are very insufficient."

Now for it!

Squire Vipert put out his white and delicate hand, on the fingers of which glistened diamonds of worth, and laid it softly on Nelly's arm.

The wind was increasing evidently.

Within ten feet of the speaker were the windows that overlooked the balcony, on which stood the thickly clustering lemon bushes, and now see how the latter rock and rustle!

"Miss Blisset," began the handsome invalid, his lips twitching nervously, despite the brandy he had swallowed, "you have been very kind to me; you have shown yourself so gentle, so compassionate that I have, even in our short acquaintance, grown to regard your possession of the last named virtue as illimitable. Hence it is that I am armed with courage enough to speak to you as I never before spoke to woman!"

Nelly's face was turned from the speaker.

It was directed blank towards the window.

The window that looked on to the balcony.

The lemon bushes now no longer rustled, but stood still, as though a dead, breathless calm had fallen on them.

The miller's daughter did not make any immediate reply.

Her amazement was too great.

The colour in her face flickered to and fro, and she felt that shrinking and tingling that presages a fit of fainting.

She endeavoured to remove her arm from the jewelled hand that lay on it.

But as she did so, his fingers nervously closed about it.

This startled and roused her.

"Sir!" Nelly began indignantly; but turning to look at him, she discovered his face so ghastly pale and so strange a light kindled in his eyes, that her thoughts at once reverted to that night when she first saw him after his "accident."

The accident that Mr. Phantom had accounted for by explaining that he had fallen from his horse on his return from his hasty journey to London, and that he much feared that his master's brain was in consequence slightly affected.

This, at all events, was the lesser calamity.

It was not Squire Reginald Vipert making villanous love to her; it was merely the irresponsible raving of a madman.

"I must appeal to your compassion, Mr. Vipert," she quietly remarked. "You are breaking my arm. Pray release me!"

But the Master of Monkshood took no heed of her gentle remanstrance, and only regarded her the more passionately.

"You spoke just now, Miss Blisset," he continued, "of the service it is in your power to render me. We will not call it service, we will call it by its proper name—favour. Yes, Miss Blisset; Nelly Blisset! charming, lovely Nelly! It is in your power to confer on me such a favour as shall make me the happiest man in all broad Kent. Say, Nelly, sweet Nelly! will you be my wife?"

The hand that held her arm had slid downwards, and now grasped a hand of hers, as handsome Reginald Vipert, on his knees, looked up into her face with impassioned beseeching.

The wind was rising again!

A sudden gust of it just then almost overtoppled the great lemon bush that faced the window.

The man at Nelly Blisset's feet was no madman.

She did not dare hope so a moment longer.

But she did not faint, or fall to trembling or weeping.

Her indignation held her superior to all such weakness.

She held the honour, the happiness—nay, the very life of her affianced husband in her keeping, and the proud knowledge armed her as with a coat of mail.

"Squire Vipert," she exclaimed, in a firm voice, "dare you address yourself to me, knowing me, knowing *him*, dare you?"

"Nay, look not on me scornfully, my pretty one," replied Vipert, making surer grip on the imprisoned hand. "It is because I love you so that I dare so much. There is but one thing that I—for my life's sake—for my soul's sake—I must not dare. I dare not contemplate my terrible fate should you refuse me.

"Listen, Nelly Blisset. You cannot be unaware that I have long regarded you with feelings for which respect would be too tame a term. In secret long have I borne the pangs of jealousy, of an envy——"

And here he passionately kissed the little hand he held in his own.

But the gallant act put a stop to his love-making.

Once before had the Master of Monkshood seen the lioness in the woman he now knelt to.

That night in the lane when she wrestled with him for the stolen money-bag.

Now he was doomed to a second and a more soul-thrilling witnessing!

Nelly struggled to free her hand, and at length, snatching it from him with a prodigious effort, she smote him on the face, with the single word, "Coward!"

This was the blinding lightning flash, and swiftly followed the thunder.

A crashing of glass, and the great plunging thud of a man of bulk leaping into the room.

John Gauntlet.

The "wind"—the pestilent wind for Reginald Vipert, that all through that exciting interview had been stirring the lemon bushes out on the balcony.

With a wild cry of affright, Nelly sprang towards her betrothed, and clung to him.

But her weight in no way impeded his advance.

With lips ashy white and with eyes flashing, he strode towards Vipert (gasping in rage and dismay, and as yet but half risen from his knees), and grasping him by the collar, swinging him round, flung him to the ground.

The violence of the fall set his wounded arm bleeding afresh, as the sudden crimson patch on his dressing-gown attested.

John saw it, and withheld the avenging fist that was raised above the other's prostrate form.

"Nay, I'll not kill thee," he exclaimed; "you gave me my liberty, I give you your life. So far we are quits, Squire Vipert. Come, Nelly, my brave lass, I'm a prouder man this day than ever before."

Reginald Vipert scrambled to his feet, and, hastening to the shattered window, in a voice that was hoarse with passion, shouted aloud—

"Help! help! Murder! Help!"

And, with singular promptitude, his cry for assistance was responded to. A man sprang from the lawn up on to the balcony.

A tall, lithe man, who, although his hair was streaked with silver, was evidently still possessed of considerable strength.

He was attired in the costume of a gamekeeper, and carried a gun.

The hasty glance he cast on John Gauntlet had even more of malice than amazement in it.

"Here am I, master," he exclaimed, handling his piece ready for action, if need be. "What about murder? Who is the ruffian? Where is he, Squire Vipert?"

"That is he," replied the squire, still panting, and with lips ashy pale; "that is the breaker into honest men's houses —the brave assaulter of the wounded and helpless. Drive him out, Burke; you are strong enough. Pitch him over the balcony, and I'll give you a guinea."

And, for the moment, it seemed as though the gamekeeper had thoughts of obliging his master and earning the coin in question; but a glance at John Gauntlet's herculean proportions and flashing eyes cooled his courage considerably.

"If Joel Burke were as big a fool as he is a knave, he might risk what you ask," exclaimed the strong young farmer, with a scornful laugh. "Not but that he would dare a deal to do me a hurt. I know him of old."

"I thought that I knew you, John Gauntlet," returned the other, maliciously. "I thought that I knew you, and that you were nothing more than a big, bragging bully ; I did not dream that you were a housebreaker."

" A housebreaker !"

And had not Nelly at that instant clasped John's arms about, and implored him to be calm, it would have gone hard with rash Joel Burke ; unless, indeed, he was on the alert, and wished to provoke an excuse for lodging the contents of his gun in his enemy's body.

" I only speak after my master," said the gamekeeper, coolly, " and I have the testimony of my own eyes to bear out what he says. I have been watching you for the half-hour past, Mr. Gauntlet. I saw you climb stealthily up into the balcony here, and sneak in among the bushes for hiding. Thought I to myself, there's a thief ; ah ! another step, and I pull trigger, John Gauntlet."

It was only by a most prodigious effort that the young farmer could restrain himself.

For years past this Joel Burke, who was head gamekeeper on the Vipert estate, had been his most provoking of petty enemies.

An old grievance of John's was the havoc that the squire's game committed among his growing crops ; an injury that Burke stoutly swore was monstrously exaggerated.

In every instance when the young farmer had applied to the master for compensation, he was baulked of it on account of Joel Burke's lying testimony.

Presuming on his master's favour, Joel Burke was insolent ; and this more than once had brought him in collision with John Gauntlet, always to the disadvantage of the former.

" We will stay here no longer, my lass," said John, addressing trembling Nelly, who still clung to him. " I dare not trust myself to do so. Squire Vipert, we shall meet again. As for you, you cringing cur," he continued, shaking his fist savagely at Joel Burke, " beware our next encountering ! I have let you off too easy hitherto. Keep a look-out ahead in future ; and should you see me coming, take another road."

And with the bearing of a proud man, and with his protecting arm still encircling the waist of his now trembling birdie, John Gauntlet took a short cut out of the house of danger by way of the shattered window.

*   *   *   *   *

Black Lutterloh had smoked the pipe he had promised himself.

He had smoked several pipes.

Indeed, since the truth must be told, he had done little besides smoke pipes since the memorable evening on which he had made such singular discoveries, and in which figured a crown piece with blood on it, and a certain something he picked up outside Black Fury's stable door, and which looked like a white handkerchief, but was not.

It was now nearly a week since that memorable event.

To use his own figurative language, he had put the piece of money " in his pipe," and he had put the grey mask in his pipe, and he had encouraged his cogitations with many quarts of beer, and the result was not satisfactory.

It was not at home that Black Lutterloh pursued his narcotic investigations, unless, indeed, by constant usage, the drinking room of the " Pied Pig," the dirtiest little beershop in Monkshood, might claim that distinction.

Ever since his three months' incarceration in Maidstone gaol, Dick, or, as he was more commonly called, on account of his swarthy visage, Black Lutterloh, had no home proper.

As already hinted, during his time of durance, his old mother had been compelled to sell for food the bit of furniture that made comfortable the humble little cottage that, with her son, she occupied; and, that failing, she took to the workhouse, and there died.

Black Lutterloh knew nothing of this till, hastening to see the old woman, whom he had not clapped eyes on for a quarter of a year, a stranger opened the old cottage door he had so hopefully tapped at.

Poacher, rascal as he was, Black Lutterloh was fond of the old woman.

He was the last of seven hale and hearty fellows—all as big rascals as himself—the old woman's sons, and he stuck to her faithfully.

Indeed, it was to tide over a hard-up time, and to get the old lady a pheasant, to tempt her failing appetite, that he had committed the crime which had been the cause of his arrest, and at Squire Vipert's prosecution, his committal to prison.

There was gipsy blood in Lutterloh's veins.

His first impulse on discovering the full extent of the mischief his enemy had wrought him was to lay wait for him and knock his brains out with a hedge stake; but cool reflection showed him the danger that might attend such a summary method of proceeding, and finally said Black Lutterloh, " I'll wait my time.

" I'll play 'possum!

" I'll be 'umble and act the sneak. I'll wriggle my way to the Hall and get a job there. I will, though I crawl through muck and mire to accomplish it. I'll get the devil to give me a pick-a-back to rouse me up a bit, so as I may spy over him and find something about him.

" I'll hunt over his cursed hide, though I do it a hair at a time, and it takes me a year till I discover a ' raw,' then I'll tickle him."

And by dint of sinking the wolf part of his nature and showing only the serpent part, he had made some progress towards the amiable end he aimed at.

He had found employment as " odd man " at the Monkshood stables, though how much his services were appreciated may be guessed by the reception Squire Vipert vouchsafed him that night when he returned with his horse as wet as a steeplechaser, as the humble stable helper remarked.

It was this hungering to find something out that made Black Lutterloh, when he had possessed himself of those two strange bits of evidence, the blood-stained coin and the grey mask, so eager to put them in his pipe and smoke them.

But, as before mentioned, nothing came of the operation, and they only spoilt the flavour of his tobacco.

He had caused so many chalk marks to be scored against him behind the bar door, that the landlady of the " Pied Pig " had declined to add one more to them; and though he had been drinking all day, his throat was as dry as a lime kiln. And all the while he had that crown in his pocket.

The price of ten pots of foaming ale, all to be brought in with smiles of welcome!

It was an awful temptation.

" Hang me, I'll do it !" said Black Lutterloh. " Cuss the thing ! it's good for nothing else."

And he gave the bell a pull.

" Two quarts of beer," he called out, throwing down the crown before the astonished eyes of the landlady, as well as of his mates assembled. " Ah, it's a good un," he continued, with a sinister grin, as the hostess of the " Pied Pig " suspiciously bit the coin. " I hopes that you admires the flavour of it."

" Thought you hadn't no money," the woman remarked.

" More I ain't, none of my own : that's trust money, that is," laughed Black Lutterloh. " Don't you see how ? It's a friend to me when you won't trust me any more. If anybody asks you what trust-money is in future, don't you go for to say you don't know. Hullo ! here's another !" exclaimed the reckless fellow, as the latch was raised. " Ha ! ha ! the chink o' money brings 'em in like the rattle o' barley when it's the chicks' feeding time."

But it was no ordinary customer that raised the latch. It was not a head of the type commonly found in the taproom of the " Pied Pig " that cautiously introduced itself into the room.

" Alack ! alack ! Oh, dear, you—you are very full of smoke here, gentlemen. Is Richard Lutterloh here, pray ?"

Richard Lutterloh recognised both the voice and the man from whose mouth it proceeded.

It was Mr. Joseph Phantom.

The cunning gipsy half-bred had a game to play, and at once dropped his swaggering air and became obsequious, fawning almost.

" Yes, sir ; yes, Mr. Phantom, I'm here, sir ; I'll come out to you this minnit, Mr. Phantom."

And with a wink to his companions that was meant to convey, " You wouldn't wonder at this line of conduct, if you were aware of what I hope to make by it," he joined Mr. Phantom in the street.

The conversation that passed between them was brief.

At its termination Black Lutterloh left Mr. Phantom (they had walked as they talked, and so strolled fully a hundred yards down the street), telling him to wait a little and he would presently rejoin him.

Before his hasty steps had carried him fifty yards, however, he turned back.

" Well, what is it ?" Phantom asked, impatiently.

" Beg your 'umble pardon, sir, but have you got any loose silver about you ?" said Black Lutterloh.

" What for ?—drink ? I thought you told me you wanted to return only for your cap ?"

" 'Tain't much that I want, master ; a matter of—let's see. Ah ! fourteen pence will do it."

"Not now; you shall have ten times the amount, p'r'aps twenty, when you have——"

"I must have it now," interrupted Black Lutterloh, eagerly, "and must have it, or—or I can't come with you, master."

Mr. Phantom angrily drew half-a-crown from his purse, and Lutterloh hurried away with it.

He had to cross the little room where his mates sat, where, on a table, stood temptingly the recently-ordered two pots of beer, but he made no pause till he reached the bar.

"I want that crown piece," said he. "Take wot's due out of this here, and give it me back."

And he made the request so peremptorily, that the landlady handed him the coin without further question.

Black Lutterloh held it up to the light.

"It's the same one," said the woman.

"I know it; I'd swear to it among a thousand," he returned with a grin, and with a bare good-night, and an injunction to his mates to drink up the beer, he was off and away.

"He didn't give you any idea what he wanted with me, master, might I make so bold as to ask?" Black Lutterloh inquired, as he joined Mr. Phantom.

"He said should you ask impertinent questions, I was to tell you to shut your mouth, and to wait until you were spoken to," replied Mr. Phantom, very sourly.

Black Lutterloh grinned in the dark, and felt in a pocket under his smock, and he said not another word till they arrived at the Hall, and at that back way which Reginald had entered on the night of the highway robbery.

They found the Master of Monkshood alone in his sitting-room.

Was it to any improved system of nursing that he owed his amended condition?

Had he already tasted of the healing that a gentle woman always brings to the couch of the ailing?

Anyway, he was better.

Stronger, and less liable to fatigue.

His face was flushed, as though fevered by some sudden resolution.

"You may be seated, Lutterloh," he graciously responded to the gipsy's low salutation, while Mr. Phantom stood aside, watchful as a cat, and making that old purring noise by the chafing together of the white paws.

Mr. Vipert commenced the conversation.

"I believe, Mr. Lutterloh," said he, "I'm not mistaken in thinking you a rascal?"

The gipsy looked up in sudden surprise, and fidgeted nervously with his cap.

"You are very condescending to be so plainspoken, squire," he began, a bit of a scowl mounting to his repulsive visage; but the Master of Monkshood cut him short.

"If I am mistaken, I will not trouble you to stay one minute longer; if you plead guilty, Mr. Phantom will give you a glass of brandy, and we will proceed to business."

There was something so perfectly original in the terms of this preface to "business," that Black Lutterloh, despite his funded stock of self-reliance, felt embarrassed.

"With my best respects to both on you, gentlemen," he answered, licking his lips, in anticipation of the rare treat of a glass of brandy; "I should like first of all to be informed of what it is you are driving at?"

"You will address yourself to but *one* gentleman, if you will be so good," remarked Reginald Vipert, with mock politeness; "this, as you know, is my servant; you can leave us, Phantom" (Mr. Phantom with a low bow left their presence, but retired no further than an ante-room, a nick in the heavy curtain of which gave a fair view of the apartment). "*Are* you a rascal, Mr. Lutterloh?"

"Why?"

"Because I want a rascal to do me a service just now."

Black Lutterloh bit his lip and scowled, but it was in quite a pleasant voice that he answered—

"I ain't got a character from my last place in my pocket, master; but you, who recommended me to it, should know where that was."

Squire Vipert looked up with a startled look, but seeing Lutterloh's face with nothing more serious than a grin on it, he was reassured.

"You have a good memory, my friend," he laughed. "Not a vindictive one, eh?"

Black Lutterloh laughed too, and held out a hand that might have made a toy ball of a Dutch cheese.

It was as dirty as the rind of one, and he covertly spat on it and gave it a rub on his smock.

"Ah! it's too grimy," said he. "I won't ask you to take it, master, but give us the brandy; windictive—ha, ha!"

The master did as requested, substituting a tumbler for a wine-glass, and Lutterloh, having duly filled from the decanter, drank it off without so much as a wink.

"Now, master, what do you want a rascal for?" said he.

"My good fellow," returned Reginald Vipert, pleasantly, "you are much too easily drawn out. I merely spoke of a rascal in the sense that a—a spy is one—I want a spy."

Black Lutterloh nodded his head.

"A spy that, while he keeps his mouth shut, will make up for the inconvenience by keeping his eyes wide open."

"What's the use of a man keeping his eyes open if he keeps his mouth shut, master?" replied Lutterloh, cunningly. "You'll want to be told what he sees, I suppose?"

"It does not of necessity follow; possibly he himself might act on what he saw, and still keep his mouth shut," returned Vipert, meaningly. "You know John Gauntlet, I presume?"

"What, Mr. John as is going to marry Blisset's daughter? Aye, I know him well enough, and nothing bad on him," said Lutterloh, his bluntness for once mastering his discretion.

"That's a pity," returned Vipert, sneeringly.

"Why is it, master?"

"Because if you did know anything bad of him—anything really *very* bad, you know—it might save you some trouble."

A keen rogue would by this time have seen the drift of the Master of Monkshood's discourse; but Black Lutterloh was not a keen rogue; there was much more of the bludgeon than the sword in his roguery.

He shook his great head hopelessly.

"I don't see how it would save me trouble, master," said he.

"I'll tell you," observed Squire Vipert, blandly, but at the same time looking fixedly at Lutterloh. "If you knew something very bad of this Gauntlet, it might be that very something I wish brought home to him— that something that you must spy and spy until you do bring home to him."

Lutterloh's heavy mouth had fallen ajar in his perplexity, but now he brought his jaws together with an intelligent snap.

"Spy and spy, until I do, eh?" he repeated.

"Quite so."

"Is there any clue, master?"

"No clue; but if you are the clever dog I take you to be, you can hunt without a clue."

And Vipert assisted him to brandy again.

"D'ye see, master?" said the villain, smacking his lips, "'tain't cos I'm dull that I don't twig—leastways, cotton, which is perliter, but cos I don't understand the langwidge in which you puts it. It's hazy like; ain't there a plain way of putting it?"

Mr. Vipert shrugged his shoulders.

"Since it is no more than hazy, I should like, first of all, to know what you make out through the haze?" said he.

"A 'plant,'" returned Black Lutterloh, bluntly. "I can't quite explain the workings on it, but what I can make out at t'other end of the haze, is, Mr. Gauntlet in quod."

Mr. Vipert held up his hands deprecatingly, but Lutterloh saw plainly enough that he was on the right scent now.

"I may be wrong, of course, master," he continued; "if so, that's the fault of the haze I was speaking of, but, as far as I can make out, it wouldn't fret some people if this Mr. Gauntlet was sent across the herrin' pond."

"If his evil doings merited a punishment so severe, exactly," responded Mr. Vipert; "but it is quite idle to discuss that at present; it will be time to discuss the deservings of his case when what he is suspected of is brought home to him."

Black Lutterloh nodded intelligently.

"Is the job in a hurry, master?" he asked.

"It should be set about with as much promptitude as is consistent with a certainty of results," returned the Master of Monkshood.

Black Lutterloh fidgeted on the edge of his chair.

Presently he asked in a low voice—

"How much, master?"

"How much what, my friend?" asked Mr. Vipert, innocently.

"What's the screw—the tip—the— the—what'll you stand, if you must have it in perlite English, master?"

"That depends. I'll give the value, you can reckon on that."

"How's walue to be reckoned, master?" asked Mr. Lutterloh, sinking his voice still lower, and looking round, "s'pose now he had a accident?"

As the ruffian spoke his eyes were within a yard of Squire Vipert's.

The words were simple, but the eyes were eloquent of that which made the Master of Monkshood start with a shudder of horror.

"You unscrupulous villain! How dare you——" he began, but Lutterloh interrupted him.

The brandy had made him bold.

"How dare I? Ha! ha! What sort of word's dare?—it's furrin to me. I'll back money agin it any day, master. How much?—don't be afraid—there be only we two here!"

"Exactly so. That's a fact that cannot be too strongly impressed on your mind, my friend," returned Reginald Vipert, who by this time had recovered his serenity; "there are but you and I here; and for your neck's sake, whether or no you prove an adept workman, you will breathe not one word to a living soul of our interview."

Black Lutterloh bit his thick lip reflectively.

"You might tell me one thing, master."

"What is it?"

"You ain't *very* particklar so long as—as the work's well done."

"I am very particular that it should be well done, as I just now told you," returned the Master of Monkshood.

"A good lasting job—a job as won't come to bits and cost a lot of money and trouble to patch and cobble arterwards!"

"There need be no more talk, I think; you appear to be a keen fellow," said Squire Vipert. "You need not stay here a moment longer than you please."

"Only a moment, master; I'm hard up."

"Well."

"It always upsets my mind when I'm hard up. I can't bring my kalkilations to a fine p'int like. Give me a trifle down."

"I have not my purse just now. Look on the sideboard yonder; maybe you will find a guinea lying there."

Black Lutterloh looked as directed, and found what he sought.

"I wish *I* had a sideboard vot guineas growed on," said he, with a grin, as he pocketed the coin, and made ready to take his departure from the room.

"You may, at least, earn the next crop that grows there," returned Reginald Vipert, meaningly. "In three days from this twenty guineas will have grown there. Earn them and come and fetch them."

"I will so," replied the ruffian, with a grin of confidence.

And he bowed himself out of the room.

"REGINALD ALPERT IN THE HUNTING FIELD."

CHAPTER XII.

IN WHICH JOHN GAUNTLET'S DOG DISCOVERS A CLUE TO A TERRIBLE TRAGEDY.

ONSIDERING the handsome inducement offered, Mr. Lutterloh had not been so prompt in his execution of the little job he had undertaken as his employer might have expected.

Two clear days had elapsed since his interview with the Master of Monkshood; the morning of the third day had arrived, and for all that appeared to the contrary, the twenty guineas might grow and rot on the sideboard at the Hall ere he, Black Lutterloh, had a right to gather them.

Had the victim been a little man, his fate would have been decided very quickly.

But, like all ruffians, Lutterloh was a coward at heart ; and, strong as he was, a face to face encounter with the young farmer was by no means to his taste.

His line, to use his own expressive language, was to " ketch him unawares," but fortune had been provokingly against him.

He had lurked about John Gauntlet's homestead with no other result than that he had been able to purloin a handkerchief that was set out to dry.

A silk pocket-handkerchief, with John Gauntlet's name written on a corner of it.

" It ain't much," mused Lutterloh ; " it ain't waluable taken for what it will fetch, but something may turn up as his hanksher might play a useful part in."

But here was the third morning and nothing as yet was done.

Black Lutterloh was desperate.

The guinea " earnest money " he had drawn of his employer was all gone in drink—he had not as much left as would buy him a quart of table-beer to cool his parched, liquor-thirsty throat.

There was villanous determination in his bloodshot eyes as he strode along the lane in which he had ascertained in a little while John Gauntlet might be met.

" I'll be a man or a mouse this morning," muttered Lutterloh, grimly. " I'll yarn that twenty pound afore dinnertime. How's the question ! If I had a gun—no, a gun would make too much noise. A knife ; but where's the good o' this old turnip cutter o' mine ? Pr'aps I might sharpen him."

And at the moment spying by the wayside a handy stone, he sat down on a bank and commenced the operation of sharpening his knife.

The stone that Lutterloh had picked up, was almost round, and about four pounds in weight.

Suddenly he desisted from his sharpening, and eyed the stone admiringly as he poised it in his hand.

"What a sling it'd make!" he muttered under his breath. "If I on'y had something to tie it in now."

And then the silk pocket handkerchief—John Gauntlet's handkerchief—suddenly occurred to him.

"That's the very thing!" said he, with a grin. "One good swinging crack as I creep up behind him, and the trick is done."

And he retired into the plantation close at hand that he might complete his little job of sling-making unobserved.

But, all the while, a keen pair of eyes were watching his every movement.

Joel Burke's eyes!

That astute old watcher knew Master Lutterloh of old. It was he who had taken him red-handed in that affair that terminated in three months' incarceration in the gaol at Maidstone.

"He's up to his tricks again!" muttered to himself the jealous preserver of the Monkshood game. "He's setting snares!"

And, bold in the possession of his loaded gun, Mr. Burke, by stealthy steps, gradually lessened the distance between himself and the huge gipsy.

Suddenly a heavy hand was clapped on his shoulder, and with a big oath, Lutterloh sprang to his feet.

He had just finished his job.

The knotted silk handkerchief, with the heavy stone in it, was in his hand, and the gamekeeper's eyes were fixed on it.

"What sort of plaything do you call that?" Joel Burke asked, jocularly, as he pointed towards it with the barrel of his gun.

With a savage growl, Lutterloh slapped the gun aside with the flat of his hand, and somehow it went off.

In an instant the old man's choleric temper was roused, and he seized Black Lutterloh by the collar.

"You poaching blackguard!" he cried, "I've half a mind to send the contents of t'other barrel through your ugly head!"

They were the last words the poor old fellow ever spoke!

*   *   *   *

That same morning other individuals, besides villanous Mr. Lutterloh, set out from home on an errand of importance.

Nelly Blisset and her faithful sister Nan.

As may be readily understood, that scene at the Hall, in which Squire Vipert and Nelly were the chief actors, had reflected no little commotion at the mill-house.

Not that the whole story had been related, only just enough of it to account for the abrupt termination of Nelly's nursing, and for the excitement —the out gushing of the pent-up flood of tears to which the brave little woman yielded as she reached home, and flung her arms round her mother's neck.

There was something else to be accounted for!

John Gauntlet and Nelly did not go

straight home after they left Monkshood Hall.

Certain explanations had to be made which John would willingly have avoided, and out of which he emerged but sheepishly.

How came he behind the lemon bushes on the balcony?

Then out came the whole story of the meeting with Phantom, and the conversation that had resolved her lover to play the spy.

"Not on you, dear Nell," the handsome young farmer fervently declared, endorsing the declaration with a kiss (the seclusion of the lane they were walking in favouring the pleasant act); "too well I know the sterling love my pretty, brown-eyed birdie has for me for a moment to doubt it, though a thousand slanderous tongues wagged against you."

"But has any slanderous tongue spoken ill of me?" Nelly asked, the colour returning to her pale cheeks; "did Mr. Phantom——"

"Nay, my darling," John hastened to assure her; "Mr. Phantom is too fast a friend of yours to breathe a word against you. Ha, ha! he grew quite enthusiastic in your praise, Nell, lest I might draw a false inference from what he had to tell me. He's a warm-hearted old chap for all his queer ways; a true friend. I'm content to regard him so because of his age; but I tell you, miss, were he a twenty years younger man, I might grow jealous of him."

And so, with his blood still tingling, did honest John contrive to soothe his frightened "birdie;" and the walk back to the mill-house was consequently protracted.

And so, before that venerable homestead was reached, it was finally argued, with much fervour and ingenuity, by John Gauntlet, and ultimately agreed to by the miller's daughter, that, considering the lowering clouds, and the cross currents that somehow seemed determined to impede their steady voyaging to the regions of bliss at the period originally planned and designed, it would be better to 'bout ship—courtship, that is—and, for safety sake, to run with all convenient speed into the harbour of matrimony.

Or, to put it in language simpler though less poetic, John and Nelly agreed to marry as soon as the third "asking" in Monkshood church might be consummated.

It was in connection with this noble resolution that Nelly Blisset and her sister were bound on a visit to Tunbridge on that morning when Black Lutterloh took a stroll through the lanes, determined on working out "somehow" the villanous problem that weighed with the weight of twenty guineas on his mind.

Nelly's mission that bright morning was of a nature to stamp itself on her memory, since it was unlikely to occur more than once in her lifetime—the choice of her wedding dress.

John was to meet the sisters on their return home.

And the dress was selected, and, lighter of heart than she had felt for many a day, happy Nelly tripped along, looking out for John, for now it was time that he met them.

Tripped along, chatting gaily, the little dog that was with them—John's dog—running on before, and in and out the plantation that skirted the road on either side, as though he enjoyed the fun of the fine morning as much as anyone.

Tripped along, until a shrill and startling sound brought them both to an appalled standstill.

John's dog, howling piteously!

They could not see the little animal, for he had not entered the plantation, but he was not far off.

"He has got one of his poor little legs in one of Master Burke's cruel traps!" cried Nan, indignantly.

And, leaving her sister's side, she ran forward in defiance of the game laws, to render poor Wasp assistance.

She had not many yards to run, and was but for five seconds at most lost to view; then she appeared on the path again with her hands raised, and her face like the face of a dead woman.

"Keep back! keep back!" she cried, in a hard, dry voice, as she hastened towards Nelly; "you must not see it. It is—oh, poor John!—poor John!"

And she leant against the bank, merciful tears coming to her aid, and saving her from fainting.

She still held Nelly, but only until she uttered the words "Poor John!"

Then, with a wild cry, she broke away, and at a bound almost discovered the dreadful truth.

Blood!

Thorns and briars trampled and torn, and stained with it! Blood in a pool on the ground!

But it is not over these that Wasp is so pitifully moaning, but over a man's coat!

A man's coat with the sleeve half pulled through, and hastily abandoned, evidently.

It was John Gauntlet's coat that lay there.

She knew it at once by its colour—by the pattern of the buttons, two of which were torn away at the throat, leaving the button-holes frayed and ragged.

Blood on the coat too!

From the front of it to the skirt the garment was sprinkled with crimson.

She would have raised it from the ground, but Wasp prevented her, planting his brave little feet on the property of his beloved master, and showing all his teeth savagely when a hand was laid on it.

Then, scarce knowing what they did, the two women went shrieking down the road, crying, "Help! Help!" distractedly.

The hurried thought that filled their minds was—John Gauntlet murdered!

"Help! help!"

And then a cry was heard.

Heard and answered by John himself!

"This way, this way! I can't come to you!"

Why not? neither Nelly nor her sister paused to ask themselves.

It was *his* voice, hale and hearty, albeit eager and strangely excited, but he was not dead, not hurt; and with an ejaculation of thanksgiving, the sisters joined hands and ran the faster.

Ran until the turning of a sudden bend in the lane brought them so close on John that they nearly ran against him.

Against him, and what!

Horror of horrors! a man stark and bleeding!

A man whose hands hung like dead hands by his side, and whose head and face were covered with a handkerchief, as though it was too terrible a sight to be looked on.

Seen by itself, the awful thing was enough to send the sisters frantic with fright, but the antidote to that was John alive and well—John, in whose strong arms the poor body rested.

"Don't be alarmed, Nelly, darling; don't let her stay here, please, Nan. It is an accident, a dreadful accident, I am afraid. Hurry forward and send on assistance."

"Who is it?" Nellie asked, tremblingly.

"Poor old Joel Burke, the man ——"

"The man whom you threatened for his rudeness that day at the Hall. Is it that man John, dear?"

The words were uttered unthinkingly, but their effect on Gauntlet was unmistakable.

"Those were foolish words of mine, my girl," said he, his lips quivering with emotion. "Poor fellow—poor fellow!"

"John," asked Nan, in a voice terrified—"John, how came your coat torn and bloody?"

"My coat torn and bloody!" repeated John, bewilderedly; "nay, that is a mistake."

"Both bloody and torn," repeated Nan, with a manner suddenly and strangely altered; "the dog found it so. Nelly saw it; I saw it. There it lies for all to see. My God, John Gauntlet! Is it true that this man was your enemy?"

Had her words been great stones vengefully hurled at him, John Gauntlet could not have more unmistakably winced from them.

His colour went and came, deserting his lips finally, and leaving them white, and his arms seemed to grow so weak as to compel him to set down his terrible burden.

"I have been rash—terribly rash!" he spoke, in a troubled voice. "I should have known that my unlucky star was in the ascendant, and——"

"What!" almost screamed Nan. "Do you confess it? Is it indeed true, then, that——"

"No, no, woman! a thousand times no!" cried John, desperately. "Great Heaven! has it come to this? Can you think me capable of a deed so infamous? My darling, can you?"

No; though a hundred witnesses had stepped forth to swear it, his darling could not.

Ere the words had left his lips, her arms were about his neck—her arms that trembled so—and she kissed him passionately.

"No, no, my almost husband," she cried; "it is but a seeming mystery that may be simply explained. Poor Nan! she had no meaning in what she said; this terrible scene has so upset her that—that—oh, dear John, speak! speak the simple words that shall convince my sister how cruelly hard she has spoken against you."

And brief and simple, indeed, were the words that John Gauntlet had to speak; and, with her pale face close to his, with her eyes that knew his so well looking into them to their depths of truth, she heard him, and never doubted.

He had set out to meet them as he promised.

He had proceeded as far as a certain spot—they knew the spot—when he suddenly came on the body of the old gamekeeper, lying on his face by a pool of blood.

Thinking it possible, although it was not perceptible, that there might still remain a little life in the poor fellow, he had thought that the shortest way would be to carry him to some place where assistance might be rendered him.

That he had found it difficult to do so while wearing his heavy overcoat, and that he had divested himself of it and laid it aside.

There was no more to tell, except that he was now carrying poor Joel Burke into the village.

"As for there being blood on my coat—the overcoat, I mean," said John, sadly, "I did not notice it; but, even if it should be there, sister Nan, I hope that you won't hang me as a murderer, considering how easy is the solution how the garment came so."

"But torn as well as bloody," urged Nan, covering her eyes and shuddering. "God forbid that I should think wrong of you, John, but so it is, believe me. Torn at the sleeve, torn at the collar, with buttons dragged away as though —as though a man in his death strug-gle had grappled the wearer. Come with me, John; for your own sake, see it."

And, with trembling Nelly still clinging to him, Nan took his arm and hurried him back in the direction they had recently come, while the dead and still body of Joel Burke lay extended on the grass.

It was not a great distance to the spot.

Not more than a hundred yards.

Faithful Wasp was still on mournful guard by the bespattered coat, and great indeed was the little animal's frantic delight to see his dear master unharmed.

"Down, Wasp! down, good dog!" exclaimed John Gauntlet. "I reckon if there is a rent in the strong broad cloth, your sharp teeth are responsible for it."

But when John raised the garment, and the bright sunlight revealed its condition, great beads of sweat stood on his brow, and he shook like a man who is palsy stricken.

"My God!" he cried, "is this some devil's trick to snare me, or am I mad, and did this horrid thing, not knowing it?"

"What is it in the pocket?" exclaimed Nan.

And as she spoke she drew forth, all hideously stained as the coat was, a silk handkerchief—a yellow handkerchief with white spots, and, knotted in the handkerchief (at a hanging corner of which appeared initials, unmistakably showing John Gauntlet to be its owner), a great round stone.

With a cry of horror, Nan dropped

the terrible weapon, clearly that which had assisted at the gamekeeper's murder, and turned from Gauntlet.

"Now who can doubt it?" she cried, in a harsh voice. "Stand from him, sister; his hands are wet with the blood of a fellow creature! Fly, wretched man. Escape while you may—quick!"

But John Gauntlet, with all this array of damning evidence against him, this evidence, the connecting links of which were so perfect and impossible to refute, looked about as capable of flying as the image of a man carved in stone.

He picked up the handkerchief, weighted with the stone that Nan had thrown down, and, with a mazed, bewildered air, made out that it was his, and a dizziness seemed to fall on him, so that he was fain to lay his hand on Nelly's shoulder to save himself from falling.

In an instant, however, he withdrew it quickly.

"I—I had forgotten," said he, with a ghastly smile. "It is a hand wet with blood! She believes it, and so it is, according to all that may be seen and judged. My God! what have I done that I should be tortured so?"

And with a groan of agony the strong man flung both his hands before his face, and hot tears trickled through his fingers.

And what did Nelly Blisset?

Did she—his Nelly—too shrink from his touch?

Did she, weighing all this terrible array of evidence that pointed so fatally to her beloved, making him a murderer—did she there and then recoil from him and shut him out of her heart?

No.

He had nestled there too long to be so unceremoniously turned out into the cold.

Besides, she *knew* him—knew him as completely as she knew herself, and when she looked at him, scared, haggard, weeping as a weak child might, she saw not a murderer, but a poor fellow on whom an affliction more terrible than death itself had undeservedly fallen, and who, excepting her, might in a little time find himself without a friend in the world to believe in his innocence.

Like a weak child was the man so tall and strong, sobbing and gasping; like a child she treated him, flinging her arms round his neck, and pulling down his white sorrowing face lower and lower, kissing it as it came until it rested against her bosom, and there she pressed it, and with every word of fond endearment at her command, caressed and consoled him, and bade him, for her sake, to take courage and trust himself to the keeping of Him in whose sight the blackest and most subtle plots that man can invent are plain as the white rocks at blazing noon.

And just then poor Wasp, who by his pitiful whining was showing his sympathy with his master's distress, pricked up his ears, and, by a short, sharp bark, announced approaching footsteps.

Nan was the first to heed the warning.

"What is to be done must be done

at once," she exclaimed hurriedly. "Quick! let us get further into the wood; or will it be better to face the danger and——"

But, before she could finish the sentence, without, at that terrible crisis, a moment's time for deliberation, the long, lazy strides of a man's footsteps were heard quite close, and Black Lutterloh appeared.

CHAPTER XIII.

IN WHICH BLACK LUTTERLOH FIGURES MYSTERIOUSLY.

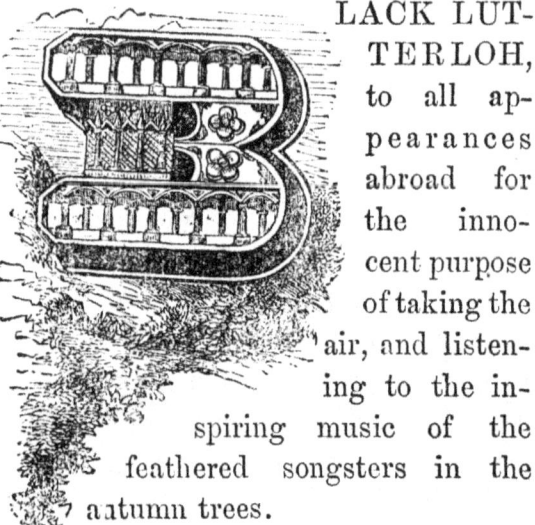

LACK LUT-TERLOH, to all appearances abroad for the innocent purpose of taking the air, and listening to the inspiring music of the feathered songsters in the autumn trees.

The reader will bear in mind when he was last seen and how he was engaged.

At that time the swarthy ruffian had business of importance on hand, and his furrowed countenance was indicative of the fact.

But now Black Lutterloh was quite serene and comfortable.

Both his hands were plunged into his pockets, and his stumpy black pipe (which, as the reader will please bear in mind, was furnished with a brass rim and a little lid), was at full blast.

He came along, humming the burden of a stave he had heard at his last drinking bout.

It was wonderful the natural way in which the gipsy started, and in his amazement, let his cherished pipe fall from his gaping jaws and break, and scatter the sparks and ashes on the ground.

"Good morning, Mister Gauntlet and ladies—I—eh?—why, what's the matter?"

It was decidedly a natural question for a peaceful wayfarer to ask.

What *was* the matter?

John Gauntlet—frank and honest John, who had ever a kind word and a cheery greeting for young and old—with a face white and haggard, and with his head bowed and turned from the speaker—the two aghast women, the blood on the ground.

What else?

Something that to Mr. Lutterloh—providing always that he was as innocent as he assumed to be—must have appeared stranger than all.

A man's coat tumbled in a heap, and Nelly Blisset—rash, heroic Nelly!—

thinking but of *his* safety, craftily, busily engaged the while she faced and looked at him, in dragging with her feet the heaped-up fallen leaves over it, to conceal it.

"It seems to me," remarked Mr. Lutterloh, scratching his head, "that I had better ha' gone another road; it goes agin my natur' to be pokin' and pryin' into what don't concern me. But since I *am* here, and with two eyes in my head, I can't help repeating my question. What *is* the matter? Whose blood is that what's on the ground?"

John Gauntlet raised his face with a fierce look on it, but Nelly stepped before him.

"Lutterloh," said she, and her sweet, trembling voice contrasted strangely with that of the coarse ruffian she was addressing, "you—you are not obliged to tell all that you see!"

"I'm not obliged to do anything agin my will, mum, or agin my conscience, which is a harder master than t'other," Lutterloh virtuously replied.

"But you can keep a secret?"

"I've kept a many in my time, but I never found 'em werry profitable," replied the gipsy, with a grin.

"Will you keep one for us—for me?" Nelly asked, laying her little hand entreatingly on his arm.

"Wot's the colour of it?"

"The colour?"

"Aye; is *that* the colour?"

And, as he spoke, Black Lutterloh pointed at the crimson patch on the earth.

Then John interposed.

"This must not be, my darling; it is guilt, not innocence, that makes secret compacts with—with men such as this."

Lutterloh shrugged his shoulders, broad as John's own.

"It's a queer sort of innocence that tries to bury a coat that's good enough for wearing, among the leaves and grass!" said he. "I wonder how much innocence is wrapped up in this 'ere?"

And, as he spoke, he stooped and picked up the knotted handkerchief, so sickenly stained, and in which the heavy stone was slung.

"Don't talk no more to me about 'secrets!'" cried Black Lutterloh, dropping the handkerchief with a shiver of well-affected horror. "I hain't a hangel, and I knows wot the inside of a prison is like, but I can't have nothing to do with jobs of *this* kind. Phew! there's a smell o' murder about it. I shall regard it as my dooty, if you'll 'scuse the liberty, to keep my eye on the whole lot on yer, till this 'ere matter is seen about."

And, as a man of tender heart, who finds himself compelled to a painful task, Lutterloh folded his arms and looked severe.

Well would it have been for John Gauntlet had she whom he loved dearer than life been absent at that moment.

Then, maybe, he would have indignantly scorned forbearance or favour from any man, and, of his own accord, sought the aid of the law to unravel the terrible mystery in the meshes of which he was involved.

But Nelly's terror for her lover's

immediate safety surmounted even her trust in the righteous ending of all things.

She, from the bottom of her heart, knew that her John was innocent, but how would the world regard the matter?

Here was an instance of how.

This man, Lutterloh, who at present knew not the worst, had not hesitated to pronounce in his blunt way that "it smelt o' murder."

Had it never happened that an innocent man had been prosecuted—nay, hanged even—his guiltlessness not appearing for years afterwards?

The bare thought was madness.

Plucking Lutterloh by the sleeve, and beseeching his attention, Nelly eagerly and briefly related the brief, cruel story, as John Gauntlet narrated it to her, showing him from the road where the dead body of the unfortunate gamekeeper was still lying.

There was some sign of relenting on Lutterloh's swarthy visage as he listened to the strange tale, but at the end of it, he shook his head doubtingly.

"It's a ugly business, anyhow," said he. "I ain't a judge and a jury, nor a coroner's 'quest to sit on the body, or you might 'spect me to give my werdict on the evidence. I only knows one thing; if *I* was in such a mess, I should make haste to put as many miles as conwenient between myself and Monkshood."

"But why should I, man?" John exclaimed, wildly. "Who dare say that I am not innocent?"

"Not me," Black Lutterloh replied, significantly. "I don't say nothing, not being called on as a witness—as yet. I am only telling you what I should do—of course s'posing there was no one to hinder me."

"And you would not hinder him?" cried Nelly, clasping her hands imploringly. "You would not prevent his going? You are right; it would be better for him to get away to a place of safety. With your friends' help, my dear John, you will be better able, if still at liberty, to discover and expose the author of this cruel wrong."

Black Lutterloh applied the cuff of his smock to his eyes.

"Oh, you will not hinder him going! I beg—I pray of you—do not hinder him!"

The gentleman appealed to, turned his face away, as though not desirous that they should witness the struggle between his stern sense of duty and the merciful promptings of his generous nature that were afflicting him.

"Hang it all," said he at last, "if there is anything that touches my tender heart, it is the tears of a female. 'Sides," he continued, with a meaning look at his open empty palm, "blood money was never to my liking; I'd sooner yarn a honest pound in helpin' a feller creeter out of a scrape anytime."

Nelly Blisset took the hint at once, and emptied the contents of her little purse (containing between three and four pounds) into his big hand.

"All I say is," said Lutterloh, "if he is going, let him be off as soon as— this instant."

"Yes, yes, dear!" Nelly urged, "do go! Go to London, go anywhere to a place of safety until this terrible mystery is cleared up. He had better go, don't you think, sister?"

"NELLY STOOD AT THE PORCH UNTIL HE VANISHED FROM SIGHT."—(See page 152.)

"As an innocent man he is free to do as he pleases," replied Nan, turning away her head.

"I will go if you think it best," replied John Gauntlet, speaking like a man lost in the mazes of a dream. "I have no mind of my own; I feel as though my brain was frozen. Yes, my darling! my poor little unlucky dearie! I will go."

"Lutterloh, I may have an opportunity one day of rewarding you for your kindness," exclaimed John Gauntlet, hurriedly. "You will say nothing?"

"I'm mum as a milestone," returned Mr. Lutterloh. "I've give my word, and I'll keep it. Now be off, sir."

"You'll see these ladies through the plantation. They must not go by the lane," and John shudderingly glanced towards the spot where the gamekeeper was lying.

One lingering kiss, and he was gone.

Nelly looked after him distractedly, and as though she already half repented the counsel she had given him.

"You think that it is for the best, Mr. Lutterloh?" she exclaimed. "You think that it is better that he should go than stay?"

"Much better," replied that person, emphatically; "much better for all on us. And now," he continued, "I think I'll be off, too. He spoke of me seeing you through the plantation, but I'd rather not, if you've no objection. You'll come out t'other side all right, if you keep well to the left. Of course, misses, the understandin' is, that I hain't clapped eyes on you, nor you on me, this blessed morning."

Nelly dumbly assented.

"Stop a minute!" said Lutterloh, as though a bright idea had suddenly struck him. "What about the coat?"

"The coat?"

"Aye; you won't leave it laying there, will you? It's a orful bit of evidence, don't you know; there's many a man been hanged on a lesser."

"What should we—what should you——" Nelly began.

"What would I adwise you was going to say," interrupted Black Lutterloh. "I adwise nothing—'taint my business to adwise. All that I knows is this; that stone in his hankysher 'ud be better in the coat pocket than where it is; that there's a deep pool further through the wood; and further, that a few more stones clapt in the tother pocket would keep it from rising in judgment. That's all. Good morning, ladies."

It sounded like friendly advice, this hiding of the tell-tale coat; it sounded so, at least, to the two desperately anxious and deluded women who listened to it.

The pool was found, and the torn and stained garment made into a small parcel, and duly weighted, was cast in.

Black Lutterloh, from the friendly shelter of a neighbouring tree, witnessed the rash act.

He was still smoking his short pipe, but he put it down by his side, so that the smoke of it might not betray him.

"That's a werry comfortable clincher to my morning's work," muttered the ruffian, chuckling with devilish glee, as he saw the sinking of the coat.

And then he walked off, clinking the gold and silver in his pocket.

CHAPTER XIV.

IN WHICH THE GREY MASK AGAIN APPEARS.

"ILL Lutterloh keep his appointment?" This was the question so anxiously discussed between Reginald Vipert and his plastic agent, Joseph Phantom.

Twenty-four hours at least had elapsed since the discovery of the terrible murder of Joel Burke, the gamekeeper; since the finding of the damning evidence that seemed to fix the hideous crime unmistakably on John Gauntlet.

If any further proof was required, it was furnished by the fact that the young farmer had vanished.

Many hours since, matters assuming so serious an aspect against him, the constables had been at his house, and he was not to be found.

"He had slept away from home," his housekeeper said.

The next likely place to discover him was at the mill-house.

But the sorrow-stricken folks there were, according to their own showing, equally ignorant of his whereabouts.

John Gauntlet had absconded!

This was the startling news current at Monkshood, and no less in the humblest cottage than at the great hall did it provoke amazement.

Where was Black Lutterloh?

He had not absconded!

He had been seen a dozen times since.

From the moment when the sickening and horrifying intelligence had reached Squire Vipert, he had caused inquiry, stealthy and careful, to be made after the gipsy, relative to his behaviour.

But the result only increased the painful puzzle.

Mr. Lutterloh had not altered in the least.

He was no more drunk than ever—no more sober; which would have been an equally significant indication of something wrong.

He was no more inquisitive than his neighbours, no more greedy for the latest news.

He still haunted the tap-room of the "Pied Pig," and swigged beer, and smoked his short black pipe, and listened with his heavy jaws innocently agape, to the startling bit of gossip the last customer brought in.

Mr. Phantom himself had observed this, and knew not what to make of it.

Was John Gauntlet really guilty?

To the initiated it seemed beyond doubt.

The known ill-feeling that existed between the men, the blood-stained coat, the stone in the handkerchief—the absconding, all pointed undeniably to his guilt; but those behind the scenes saw much that was inexplicable.

To set the matter in its simplest light, Lutterloh had been hired to work a mischief against John Gauntlet.

He had accepted earnest money in the service.

He himself had broadly hinted that, if needs be, he would have no objection to strike down once and for ever the object of his employer's animosity.

To be sure, the sanguinary villain's offer had not met with any encouragement.

Bitter as was Reginald Vipert's spite, reckless as was his malice, his conscience was not as yet so utterly tainted as to enable him to countenance a murder.

But here was murder done, and, apparently, instead of the murdered, John Gauntlet was the murderer!

But will Lutterloh keep his appointment?

That was the momentous query that tortured the minds of master and man, as they sat in the dim autumn twilight in the same room where was the sideboard on which it was promised twenty guineas should grow all ready to be gathered by a certain villanous hand, should the work it had done give it claim.

Master and man had discussed the matter with guilty interest, and the guineas had *not* grown on the sideboard!

Under any conditions it was considered best that they should not grow there.

If the ruffianly Lutterloh had been baulked of his bargain by the strange intervention of the hand of fate, if Lutterloh was really *absolutely* innocent, then Gauntlet was guilty, and the gipsy had done nothing that he could dare claim payment for.

If by some miraculous stroke of luck and cunning, his was the blood-guilty hand, and he had contrived to shift the crime on to innocent shoulders, then he dare not for his neck's sake acknowledge the deed.

But even as they were comforting themselves, the subject of their miserable discussion was announced, and with as much cool assurance as though he had recently completed a job of gardening, or something equally innocent, and would be glad of his wages, he came in.

There was confidence, insolence even, in his unabashed bearing, in the easy familiarity of his nod, and his " Evenin', squire," in the coolness with which, unasked, he took a seat on one of the splendid brocaded chairs.

" Good evenin', squire, and you too, Mr. Whatsoname. Good evenin' to you both."

It was Mr. Phantom whom the free and easy gentleman addressed as " Mr. Whatsoname," a compliment which that person acknowledged by the stiffest of bows.

There was a lengthy pause.

" Well?" at last was the squire's questioning ejaculation.

" Well it is," returned Mr. Lutterloh, encouragingly. " Hope I find *you* well, master?"

" Pray what may be the business that

brings you here?" the Master of Monks-hood coolly asked.

"What business!" Black Lutterloh grinned, in assumed amazement. "Why, *the* business, to be sure. What other, master? And since it ain't the most cheerful, 'spose you lights up, Mr. What-soname. I can't stand twilight inside a house."

It was beyond twilight, it was almost dark; but Mr. Vipert discouraged the other's hint about lighting up.

"Thank you, you are sufficiently visible to me," said he, "but you have not answered my question. What do you want here?"

"My earnings," replied Black Lutter-loh, with a growl that betrayed his rising ill-humour.

"Your earnings!" and master and man glanced at each other in the dusk.

"Ah! twenty guineas wot was to be already growed on this here sideboard," said he, approaching the article of furni-ture in question. "You promised that they should be here. Where are they?"

In crder to accomplish the last move-ment, Black Lutterloh approached with-in two yards of the person he was addressing.

The latter shrank back as though he feared the contagion of blood with which the cool ruffian as good as confessed himself stained.

"Return to yon seat, fellow," said he, still with an effort to speak calmly, "and listen to me."

"I'm a listenin'."

"You are sober enough, I presume, to understand what you are saying?"

"Likewise what *you* are saying," said Lutterloh, with a nod and a grin.

"You remember our last conversation in this room?"

"It's a ringing in my ears at this werry minnit, Squire Vipert; it's that wot gives such a relish to my comin' here. You ses, ses you, 'We are here alone, remember, and if in doing my bidding—if in sendin' your soul to the devil, that you may pocket the twenty guineas I tempt you with'—them warn't quite your words, but that was your meanin'—'if you dare attempt to drag *me* into the mess, I'll set my gentlemanly oath against your black-guardly word, and you shall get it all the hotter.' You see I am sober enough, squire!"

"What has since transpired——" began Reginald Vipert.

"Likewise you said," continued Black Lutterloh, unceremoniously interrupting him—"Likewise you said, at least, you insinuated that although you thought me good enough to do your dirty work, you would bo careful not to place in my hands so much as a rag of substantial evidence that there had been dealings betwixt us. Please bear that part in mind, because it's rayther important."

And Mr. Lutterloh chuckled and slapped his leg, as though he had said a good thing.

Mr. Phantom whispered to Squire Vipert.

"Precisely so," said the Master of Monkshood aloud, and approvingly; whereon Mr. Phantom advanced towards the bell.

"What's that for?" Lutterloh asked, suspiciously.

"That I may give instructions for the summoning of the constables," replied Mr. Vipert, severely. "Unless I am mistaken, they are at present on the wrong scent for the murderer of poor Burke."

Lutterloh laughed his great, rough laugh.

"So you would double on me already, would you?" cried he. "Curse you! but I'm a great mind to let you do it! Or is it that you think to scare me with the threat? Look here, comrade. See how scared I am. You have rung for your constables; there's the window, and who's to hinder me taking a jump through it and making off? Why don't I do it? Because I ain't a least afeard of you—because I hold the whip-hand of you—because you are a doomed man, you and your feller here— if I so much as hold up my finger!"

It had grown dark and still darker, and the gipsy had risen from his chair and spoke in a dangerously hard voice.

Vipert was white with rage, and Joseph Phantom paced the room, chafing his hands in a state of bewilderment.

"We must wash our hands of this villain!" said the Master of Monkshood, in a low voice. "He has more of the devil in him than I reckoned on."

But softly as he spoke, Lutterloh heard him.

"I told you so," he laughed defiantly. "Let us have lights, not constables, and talk as chums should. What's the use of being cantankerous? We're in one boat; he who knocks a hole in it, may drown his shipmates, but he'll go to the bottom himself as sure as death's grip can clutch him. Let's float, and

be jolly, then—eh, my masters? Let's have a taste of brandy?"

"Look you, Lutterloh," spoke Vipert, nervously, "I promised you money."

"Aye, so you did—twenty pounds," replied the ruffian.

"Will you promise to go away— right away—if I give you the sum promised?"

But Black Lutterloh chuckled, and shook his shock head knowingly.

"What, right away, as Mister Gauntlet has done? I couldn't do it, squire," he replied. "Who knows what false tales might be told of me behind my back?"

"What then, will you do?"

"I'd rather tell you what I won't do. I won't go away, and I won't take twenty pounds," replied Lutterloh, coolly.

"You won't?" cried Mr. Vipert, furiously.

"You may take a rascal's word for it," grinned Mr. Lutterloh.

"Then abide by the consequences. Phantom, you understand?"

And this time Mr. Phantom tugged at the bell-pull with energy.

Lutterloh started to his feet.

"I'll answer the door," said he.

The room was a large one.

It was at least a dozen paces to the said door.

The moon had by this time risen, and its pale light dimly illuminated the apartment.

Lutterloh carried his cap with him, and as his back was towards master and man he appeared to be at some pains to place it carefully on his head.

By the time he reached the door, a tap was heard at the outer side of it.

"Come in!" cried Mr. Vipert, desperately.

But Lutterloh held his heavy hand against the panel.

"How many constables shall we order?" said he. "Suppose we say two for the murderer, *and two for the highwayman!*"

He turned suddenly round as he spoke, and the pale moonlight revealed his face covered with a grey mask!

The sudden cry of affright and amazement that the Master of Monkshood gave utterance to was the signal for Lutterloh to snatch off the mask, and thrust it into his pocket.

"The squire says—will you bring up the candles?" said Lutterloh blandly, as he opened the door just a little way.

CHAPTER XV.

IN WHICH NELLY BLISSET PLAYS A CONSPICUOUS PART, AND MR. PHANTOM IS BEWITCHED.

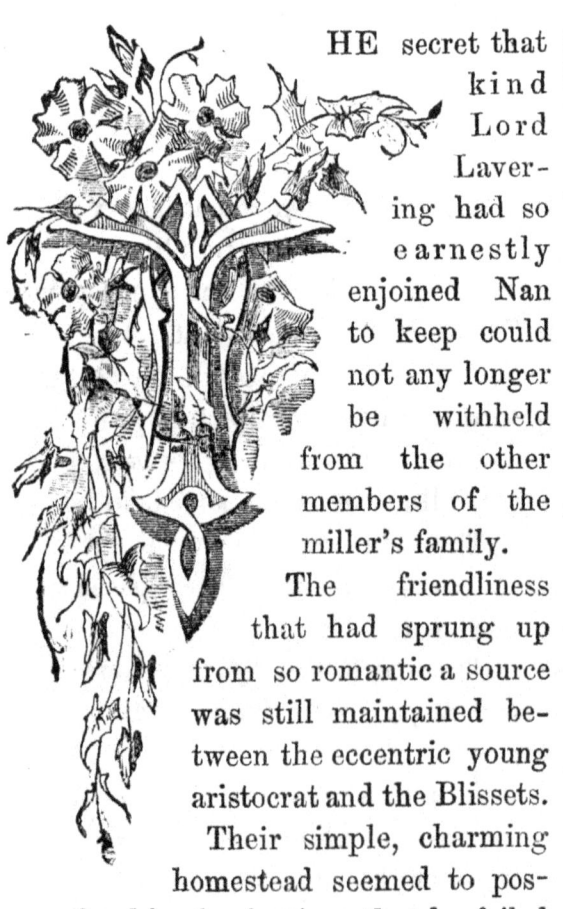

HE secret that kind Lord Lavering had so earnestly enjoined Nan to keep could not any longer be withheld from the other members of the miller's family.

The friendliness that had sprung up from so romantic a source was still maintained between the eccentric young aristocrat and the Blissets. Their simple, charming homestead seemed to possess for him fascinations that he failed to discover at his newly-hired and expensive villa residence, and scarce a day passed that did not find him haunting the mill-house or the mill.

Lord Lavering (of whose rank his newly-found friends were still as ignorant as on the first day of his arrival) was in a terrible frame of mind when he became acquainted with the disaster that threatened to complete the wreck that, through some mysterious agency, had of late been hovering over the innocent homestead.

He was not, as a rule, remarkable for his power of discernment, but he at once perceived how serious a mistake had been made when John Gauntlet was persuaded to take flight.

Was he guilty?

As a calm, unprejudiced judge, it is not unlikely that Lord Lavering might have been inclined, on the strength of the overwhelming evidence, to have given an opinion in the affirmative.

But he had consulted Nan on the subject.

Every succeeding day found him more and more convinced of Nan's sound and impartial judgment on matters generally, and, if the truth must be told, more and more solicitous to submit to her consideration matters so trivial as to give rise to a suspicion that the pleasure of listening to her wise remarks exceeded his lordship's interest in her decisions.

Nan was firmly convinced of John Gauntlet's innocence.

At first, it must be admitted, that her mind, so suddenly shocked and exposed to terrible doubt, had been inclined to condemn her sister's lover; but mature reflection, backed doubtless by poor Nelly's persuasive and confident eloquence, had quite converted her, and she now expressed her entire belief in the young farmer's innocence, and straightway Lord Lavering was as firmly convinced as anyone.

But still there remained the damning facts—the discovery of the bloodstained coat in the pool, the finding of the implement with which the murder was done in the pocket of that coat, the knowledge that there existed between the owner of the garment and the murdered man considerable ill-feeling; that the farmer had vaguely threatened the latter, and bade him "beware when they next met;" and, to crown all, the sudden and unexplained disappearance of the man against whom the finger of guilt so plainly pointed.

It had not transpired at the coroner's inquest that John Gauntlet had been persuaded to take flight.

It was not even known that Nelly Blisset and her sister were cognizant of the crime a moment before it was accidentally discovered and generally known.

Black Lutterloh had kept his promise.

He had declared that he would remain "mum," and mum he had remained.

No one had thought of asking him to stand before the coroner as a witness, and, with characteristic modesty, he had not volunteered his services.

All that he had done was to casually inquire among his cronies assembled in the taproom of the "Pied Pig"—was it true, as somebody had told him, as they had heard somebody else say, that the weapon that the murder had been done with had been found in a pond, or some other piece of water in the wood?

It was a mere remark, but it was artfully worded and cunningly timed.

There are always to be found in times of panic any number of benevolent people eager to adopt the lying children of rumour.

Half-a-dozen chawbacons in the room had heard the same thing, and in the talk that followed, the situation of the pool, its steep sides and black depths, and its marvellous aptitude for the murderer's purpose, the original promulgator of the rumour was altogether forgotten.

The upshot of it was that the pool was dragged, and there, on the coroner's table, lay the grim, incontestible proof of John Gauntlet's atrocity.

Verdict, wilful murder against John Gauntlet, farmer, of Monkshood, with a recommendation to the jury that the Home Secretary should be solicited to offer a reward of fifty or a hundred pounds for the apprehension of the suspected absconder.

Then, as before mentioned, came out at the mill-house the secret that it was their generous guest, and not Squire Reginald Vipert, who had supplied the money that had eventually released John Gauntlet from prison, and the previous mystery became tenfold mystified.

To be sure there remained the fact that the Master of Monkshood had furnished the money that the rascally highwayman had stolen, but how was it to be accounted for that he had pretended to the second generous act that had elicited from John Gauntlet such expressions of gratitude and contrition for his wrongful ideas previously entertained towards the squire?

That had induced poor Nelly to conquer all her old foolish prejudice against the gay, handsome gentleman, and to trust herself with him as his nurse!

Was the fabric on which that brief season of floating happiness was built utterly delusive and false at the foundation?

Was it really certain that Squire Vipert deserved any credit at all?

Supposing that Joseph Phantom, out of the same distaste for ostentatious benevolence that instigated "Mr. Cecil," had, out of his own honest hoardings, provided that five hundred pounds the Grey Mask had so basely plundered them of.

It was not impossible!

Mr. Phantom's behaviour, at least, was beyond suspicion.

Who but that good old man was it—who, on the occasion of poor John's arrest, had offered his little all, even to his watch and his gold-rimmed spectacles, in the innocent hope that it would suffice to effect the captive's release?

Who but the humble, sensitive old gentleman in question was it who risked his master's displeasure, and almost certain dismissal, so that he might warn Nelly's lover of the danger that threatened her?

John believed in Mr. Phantom.

He had emphatically stated as much.

Such was the current of Nelly Blisset's thoughts through all that time of dismay and affliction intervening between John Gauntlet's flight and the verdict of the coroner's jury.

Lord Lavering was one of the sorrowing family council; but he was as helpless to advise as the rest.

It was too late now, it seemed, to take any step that was in the least hopeful.

The fatal mistake—the flight of John Gauntlet—had been committed, and could not be recalled.

To add to the trouble nothing had been heard of John.

He had promised to communicate immediately his place of hiding, and now four days had elapsed and not a word!

Then it was that, out of the depths of her dire distress, Nelly Blisset resolved on a course of action.

She would seek an interview with Joseph Phantom!

Without an atom of proof or a thread of clue, as substantial as the gossamer of a spider's web, distracted Nelly was ever haunted by the suspicion that her lover's awful peril dated back to the scene in the sitting-room.

All day long she thought of it; all night long it was before her sleepless eyes.

The picture of Reginald Vipert prostrate—baffled—on the ground, where John Gauntlet had thrown him, rising therefrom the deadly implacable enemy, quite unscrupulous in his blind rage as to the means of vengeance he adopted.

If it really were so, if her tormenting suspicions had the least foundation, would Joseph Phantom know aught of it?

He was in his master's confidence; that was undoubted, but, already following the dictates of his nature, he had shown that in a good cause he might be induced to betray that confidence.

Again, had not John—dear, fugitive John, declared (though, to be sure, it was half in fun) that Mr. Phantom had evinced so friendly a disposition towards her that, were he twenty years younger, he would be quite jealous?

It brought a fresh flood of tears to her eyes as she remembered the time, but yesterday, as it were, but which seemed so long ago, when the said words were spoken, but she checked her grief with stern resolution.

Such material as she had to work on was meagre indeed, but for her poor boy's sake, she would not leave a stone unturned, though the turning of it cost a foot-sore journey of a hundred miles.

If she could see Joseph Phantom privately, she might learn something, though never so little, that might set other and cleverer heads than hers to work, to show the innocence of her betrothed.

Was it true that Joseph Phantom admired her?

Then he would the more readily listen to her pleading—to her persuasion, if it came to that.

Ah! the rugged steeps a brave woman will set her tender foot to, the dens and lairs she will dauntlessly enter, smiling bewitchingly, singing gaily, even, when her poor heart is drowned and dead in woe, so that she may charm the monster who holds her darling captive, and who, by her daring manœuvring, may be helped to escape.

And so the note soliciting an interview with Mr. Joseph Phantom was secretly written, and as secretly dispatched and duly delivered.

The man with the notched nails was uncertain what to do.

Should he disclose its contents to his master?

Such was the question that perplexed Mr. Joseph Phantom, as his evil, twinkling eyes devoured the purport of Nelly's missive.

It was a humble note—an imploring note.

It appealed to the man of the notched finger-nails as " dear Mr. Phantom," and " as one of the few true friends that sympathise with us in our overwhelming distress."

The writer of the touching little epistle begged excuse for the liberty she was taking, on the ground that the unfortunate man to whom her heart—her life—was devoted, had informed her of the genuine and utterly unselfish nature of Mr. Phantom's friendship.

Mr. Phantom grinned and winked one of his fishy eyes as he read this last passage.

Should he acquaint Mr. Vipert of the reception of this letter?

Under existing circumstances, it was his duty perhaps.

On the other hand, why should he?

Where was the use of riding down one's enemies, except for the pleasure of seeing them writhe and wriggle in the dust?

Such a treat was scarce.

Why divide it with any man?

No, he had been very hard-worked of late, and worried, and put about, and he would enjoy the offered luxury without assistance.

Nelly was very confiding.

"When and where he might choose to appoint" were the terms of the solicited interview.

What place better than the Hall?

Mr. Vipert was away in London.

It was his intention to remain there until the unpleasantness of Monkshood had subsided, or to return earlier if Mr. Phantom found it necessary to summon him.

It was in his own little sanctum—made more than usually cosy for the occasion—that Joseph prepared for his visitor, and wherein he awaited her coming with impatience.

He sat by the comfortable fire, for the evening was chilly, ruminating on the past, as he gently sawed with his front teeth against his left thumb-nail,

on which there was a notch that the edge of a shilling might have sunk in.

This was his "spite notch" against Nelly the mother.

Years had not softened Joseph Phantom's hatred against the woman who rejected him to marry Blisset, the miller.

"I'll humiliate her!" he snarled. "I'll bring her to her knees! I'll hold out little meaningless baits of promise that shall send tears of gratitude coursing down her cheeks, and I'll make believe to condole with the pretty-faced little fool, all the while that my heart that thirsts, as the sands of the desert thirst, for vengeance, is drinking in her grief and fattening on it! I'll fancy that it is *my* Nelly over again—the likeness between them will favour the delicious deception—she shall pay something off the old account!"

So he thought when she was announced and entered his room, with her face so white, and her anxious, feverish eyes twinkling in the lamp light, like two restless stars, behind the thick veil that screened them.

So he thought when, at sight of him, her strong resolution broke down, and she covered her face with her hands, and, before she had spoken a word, fell to sobbing and crying as though her heart would break.

As Mr. Phantom bowed low, and mumbled a few words of condolence, he thought to himself—

"It will be a richer treat than I thought! Her heart is in so deliciously tender a condition that it will not miss a single one of the stings with which I will presently torture it."

"'WANTED!' CRIED LUTTERLOH, WITH A SAVAGE SCOWL, 'WHO WANTS ME?'"—(See page 160.)

But he was not long to enjoy the relishing spectacle of seeing beautiful Nelly Blisset in tears.

As sudden as the outburst was the recovery, and she put her veil back, and seated herself on the chair he had placed for her.

"Mr. Phantom!" said she, her low, sweet voice trembling with emotion, despite her determination, "I thank you from the bottom of my heart for this your last act of kindness. Only that I—that we have experienced your self-sacrificing—your noble generosity, I should have hesitated ere I ventured on an errand so delicate."

She laid her hand on his as she spoke, and with her lovely eyes so full of entreaty, looked deep into his own fishy optics.

And not only her eyes, her every beauty, the heightened colour, the excitement brought to her pallid cheek, the little forced smile of beseeching that parted her lips, and revealed the glistening pearly teeth, her quick breath, that betokened her struggling hopes and fears, the trembling of the little hand against his own, one and all seemed to give point and potency to her innocent pleading, and combined, at the very outset, to spoil Mr. Phantom's appetite for the "treat" he had promised himself.

"I shall be happy, only too happy to be of service to you, if it be in my power, Miss Blisset," he remarked. "Pray be so kind as to explain to what I owe the pleasure of your visit."

"I will endeavour to do so as briefly as I may, dear sir," Nelly replied. "But, first of all, let me bespeak your forgiveness if my errand shall offend you. Pity me, Mr. Phantom. You are an old man now, but years do not pass so tediously but that you must remember when you were young as he— my John! When your life, your soul, your every desire and wish on earth was bound up in———"

But here Nelly paused.

As she proceeded, she had taken Mr. Phantom's hand between both her own, and she spoke more and more eagerly, and the brightness of her eyes became more and more intensified.

But in her simplicity she had struck on a chord, the holdfasts of which were fixed in a wound that still rankled.

Mr. Phantom almost gasped as he drew his hand away.

"Ah!" cried poor Nelly, "I have already offended you. I had no intention of doing so, dear sir. Pray—pray forgive me!"

And the little hands that he had so cruelly repulsed were now clasped together, and the brightness of the glorious eyes was again dimmed in tears.

Mr. Phantom felt more, and still more, uncomfortable.

A dread fascination was on the man, a fascination that he willingly would have battled against and defeated, but that his powers of resistance were spellbound, benumbed.

With an anguish that seemed to shatter and threaten with dissolution the casket of ice in which his heart had long been frozen, he muttered to himself—

"I never thought her half so beautiful! I should not have dared to face her had I known how much witchery there is in eyes such as hers. I will make short work of the interview, and beware for the future."

His evident embarrassment was not lost on Nelly, and she saw, too, that it was not altogether the embarrassment that springs from anger.

"Tell me," said she, in a voice so low that it was almost a whisper, and still regarding him with more of the "witch" than ever in her eyes, their brilliance being, as it were, mellowed and ripened by the soft tears that brimmed them; "tell me, my dear, true friend, that you are still inclined to listen mercifully to the question I have come to ask you."

As before mentioned, a cosy fire burnt in the grate, but the heat it projected into the room would scarcely be held accountable for the gathering beads of sweat that bedewed Mr. Phantom's retreating, cat-like forehead.

"It is you who are merciless; you, I should say, Miss Blisset, who are such an object of—of compassion that it is impossible that I should feel offended. To be sure, by accident, your words recalled—but let that pass; we are friends again—dear, true friends, as you say. There, let us shake hands. And now for your question."

But he did not let go her hand after he had shaken it; and she, cunning little diplomatist, did not scarcely insist that he should.

"Tell me," said she, regarding him so that not a quiver of the tiniest muscle of his face could escape her, "tell me, can you inform me of anything that shall yield me the least ray of hope,

the least gleam of comfort, as regards my—as regards John Gauntlet?"

And did aught come of her close scrutiny?

Of that crucial test on which she relied infinitely more than on his spoken words.

Little or nothing.

As the reader is already aware, Mr. Phantom professed no more *certain* knowledge on the subject than did the coroner who held the inquest on poor Joel Burke's body.

Undoubtedly he had his suspicions, but they were unsupported by a single substantial fact, the revelation of which would not compromise his master.

He shook his head pityingly.

"At least I can give you this consolation, my poor girl," said he, with a squeeze of her imprisoned hand that sent the blood tingling and coursing through his dull veins.

"What?" Nelly interrupted, eagerly.

"I can assure you that I share with you the belief that the unfortunate young man is guiltless of the crime imputed to him."

"Thank you at least for that, Mr. Phantom !" replied Nelly, with heartfelt earnestness.

"As you say," continued the hideous Phantom, growing more and more entranced with the surpassing beauty on which his eyes were feasting; "as you just now said, I am an old man, but well can I understand the ardent, fervent love you feel for this young man. Nay, never blush to hear such words from an old man's lips ! The ardent, the inexpressible love, I repeat, that agitates your tender bosom.

I can understand your feelings, Miss Nelly, and, strange though it may seem (for, as you say, I am an old man), I can even comprehend the sweet content, the immeasurable rapture that knowledge affords the husband of your choice. I—I will help you if I can; I will, as true as I stand before you a living man."

And he uttered the words with sudden vehemence and accompanied by such a look that Nelly started, terrified as though he had suddenly been transformed into some dangerous beast of prey.

But she was courageous in her virtuous cause, valiant in her steadfast purpose.

"And you can give me no immediate hope?" said she, winningly. "Ah, my dear friend, if you could but disclose to me but the most distant glimmer—the merest spark of promise—that, steadfastly followed, would grow into that broad light that should make manifest my poor John's innocence! If you could do so, I would, through all my life, love you——"

It was almost terrible to see Joseph Phantom's face now.

"Yes, yes, you would love me——"

"As your own daughter."

Mr. Phantom groaned, and turned to hide his face in his pocket handkerchief.

"Well, well, Nelly. I—I am an old man, and you will pardon the familiarity," he gasped, "but I will consider—I will reflect. It is not impossible—mind, I make no promise—but it is not impossible that I may be able to help you. If anything on earth would urge me on to do so, it is your charming eloquence. You will love me as a daughter if I am able to do so? Let me claim, just to strengthen my resolution, an earnest of the love you speak of. And now, good-bye till you hear again from me."

And as he, in a strange, quivering voice, uttered these words, his colourless lips, that burnt with a white heat, pressed her forehead.

"It will not be very long before I hear from you?" said Nelly, bearing up bravely against the distasteful assault. "Promise that it shall not be very long, dear sir."

"Yes, yes; I promise that, if you will love me—well—well—as a daughter," returned Phantom, making an ugly gulp at the last uttered words. "Say again, Nelly Blisset, that you—you——"

"I will keep my promise as you keep yours," said Nelly, with her sweetest smile, and tripped away, while Mr. Phantom, bewildered, giddy with the strange "glamour" that had fallen on him, remained staring at the door through which she had passed.

CHAPTER XVI.

IN WHICH, FOR JOSEPH PHANTOM, CUPID'S DARTS BECOME SCORPIONS' STINGS.

WEEK of terrible suspense.

No news of John Gauntlet.

Not a hint; not the smallest clue as to his hiding-place or his safety.

No news, although the terribly matter of fact placard that described his height, his breadth, the colour of his eyes, his "complexion florid, teeth white and even;" and offering the sum of one hundred pounds to anyone who would apprehend the said John Gauntlet, and safely lodge him in any one of her majesty's gaols.

Through seven long days had the degrading announcement adorned the doors of the Monkshood lock-up, and disfigured sundry walls and palings of the village, and still the delinquent was "wanting."

There are hours, days that may not be measured by "mean time;" hours that sixty common minutes are ridiculously inadequate to represent; days in which are concentrated the pain and anxiety of ordinary years.

Such were these seven days to Nelly Blisset.

She felt that she had sent him away; that, but for her, he would have stood his ground bravely, and, despite the terrible accumulation of evidence pointing to him and branding him guilty, have proved his innocence.

No one had told her that she had done wrong in urging her betrothed to escape, "for the present," from the threatening danger.

Neither her parents nor kind Lord Lavering (who, wavering between duty to himself and charity to his friends, had not yet made up his mind to abate his frequent visits to the mill-house) could find it in their hearts so to add to the poor girl's affliction, but she read their thoughts in their dismayed and sorrowing faces, and acknowledged her error in bitter, silent self-reproach.

But why did not John by some means contrive to let *her* know where he was?

Did he mistrust her?

Should he not, by this time, be aware that she loved him more than all the world besides—that she would leave parents, home, everything, to join him and share his trouble?

Why, then, did he deny her the privilege?

"He need not risk his liberty by coming," sobbed poor Nelly; "but surely—surely he might write!"

But, thank Heaven! John Gauntlet, while his heart glowed with love for her as warmly as did her own for him, possessed a cooler head.

Who shall tell, during that sickening week of hiding and misery, what the brave fellow endured—what he would have sacrificed—providing that the risk might be all his own, only for a little minute to hold those dear hands in his own, and to hear her repeat those blessed words, the remembrance of which, indeed, was all he had to cheer him in his wretched solitude: " I know that you are innocent, dear John; were the whole world to declare otherwise, I would die constant in my belief."

" I know that she still thinks it," groaned poor John; " I know that she says it to herself times enough all through the day, bless her heart! and I should be no better than a brute were I to jeopardise her fair name by privately seeking an interview with her while this terrible accusation is hanging over me; but I can't help longing to see her. My very soul seems starving for her dear company. Lord send that I may be able to hold up awhile longer!"

Mr. Phantom had pledged his word that he would privately use every endeavour to discover a clue to the whereabouts of the fugitive, and he had kept his word.

No man than he could have been more vigilant in making inquiry.

Poor tormented old man !

That casket of cold ashes, his heart, had been strangely translated since the witchery of Nelly Blisset's eyes had kindled in it scorching fire.

The news of John Gauntlet that he yearned for was, however, not precisely of the sort that would have gratified the public in general, and the police authorities in particular.

John Gauntlet alive and in safety would have been no consolation to the man of the notched finger nails.

John Gauntlet arrested, and, according to the terms of the placard, lodged in one of her majesty's gaols, would have brought him no comfort.

In the latter case there was a possibility of the suspected man's acquittal as the result of his trial.

This would have been " hope deferred " to an extent that must have caused Mr. Phantom's monstrously afflicted heart to sicken and give up its pulsing at once.

No. The news that Joseph Phantom hungered for was that John Gauntlet was dead !

The law offered a hundred pounds for his living body.

Mr. Phantom would cheerfully have given twice the money, had he possessed it, for a sight of him in a six-foot elm box.

He would not scrupulously stipulate as to the manner of his death either.

He might come by his death by poison, bullet, or razor—anything, so long as he was bereft of breath by fair means or foul.

Mr. Phantom would have been delighted to have drawn on his private hoard to the extent of two hundred golden sovereigns by way of reward to the man who brought him the blissful assurance.

Morning after morning his greedy, bloodshot eyes scanned the newspaper, and especially those columns in which commonly were inserted accounts of coroners' inquests and "bodies found."

"A skulking coward!" exclaimed the miserable old wretch, possessed by a demon disguised with the mask of Cupid. "A chicken-hearted poltroon! Why, innocent or guilty, he should have made away with his life by this time. If he be really guilty, he should be glad to escape the gallows, and if he be innocent, how can he dare face a world that has proclaimed his guilt, and set a price on his head as a murderer? How can he retain audacity enough to yet hope, with his hand that has been adjudged blood-stained, to place on that pretty tapering finger the token that makes her his? If he had one spark of manhood left in his vile breast, he certainly would commit suicide!"

And then, with increased vigilance, and in quite a perspiration of virtuous indignation, Mr. Phantom would hunt the newspaper for the details of John Gauntlet's self-murder.

Twice he thought that his faithful diligence was about to be rewarded, and he made swift and secret journeys to London to view "bodies found," the description of which in some measure tallied with that of the fugitive on the police placard.

Twice he returned, bitterly disappointed, sourer in heart and poorer in pocket.

So passed day after day, and he had no information to give Nelly Blisset, but somehow he contrived, between sunrise and sunset, to see and speak with her once at least.

Since that fatal hour when he sent for her to mock her, to find devilish pastime in her grievous sobs and her woeful tears, to feast his pent-up spite, his heart of malice, on her lovelorn face, her breaking heart; since the fatal hour when he bargained for this feast, and found each and every one of his choice weapons turn and stab him, he had been a miserable man indeed.

The infatuation grew on him.

It was like the progress of some terrible disease, the course of which is inexorable.

Every day since that fatal evening when, with the witchery of her eyes, she had enchanted him, had he sought an interview with her.

Truly he had nothing to communicate.

Nothing but lies, at best!

But what was the sin of telling a lie—a dozen lies—to the bitter sweet, the bliss that was at the same time torture, of hearing her speak, of gazing on her lovely face with no one near, of looking into those eyes that were most marvellously beautiful when they were tearful, of noting the trembling of those sad little lips, pale as pink coral?

Of pressing her hand; perhaps of repeating, at parting, the kiss on the forehead—the chaste salute—such as, in all ages, and in all countries, it has been the privilege of patriarchs to bestow on the youthful of either sex, especially on the distressed and sorrowstricken!

"It is pleasant to renew the innocent pledge of friendship that sealed our mutual promise, when your deep affliction led you first to seek my counsel!" meek and sleek Joseph would remark, with an application of his handkerchief to his eyes, not to dry his tears, but lest she should see the devil lurking in them. "It is like a renewal of our compact, poor little one! It brings me peace and strength. 'She is as my own daughter,' I say to myself; and I pray for you, my dear child, ere I close my eyes in slumber, and I wake in the morning hopeful that I may have good news for you ere the day closes."

Lies, all lies, like the rest.

"Peace! Poor self-tortured wretch!

If *his* was peace, so is the bottomless pit a haven of rest; so is the stinging of venomous snakes desirable.

Truly, he had dug a pit, and had fallen into it.

A single week had altered the man strangely.

His whole time—his nights as well as his days, were spent in alternately cursing his mad infatuation, and in yielding to the tormenting bliss it afforded him.

He begged of her that she would regard him, and give him her confidence, as an old man, whose only remaining object in life was to succour the afflicted, all the time that he was cursing his age, and blasphemously reviling his gaunt shape and repulsive features.

"Could I but show her my heart!" groaned cadaverous Joseph. "Could she see *that* as plainly as she can see my hideous face (and he felt inclined to tear it for its ugliness), then, if those wretches were out of the way—this Gauntlet, and the rascal who calls himself my master—then I might dare

speak; then I might avow to her the tormenting anguish that is consuming me, and beg of her, pray of her, cringe and crawl in the dust at her feet, and implore her to—to spare me!"

By which he meant, in his heart, "love me."

He did not dare say it, though he was alone in his chamber, and the door was locked.

He caught a glimpse of his reflected self in the hateful, honest looking-glass, of his pinched cheeks and nose, of his high cheek bones and retreating forehead, looking like the polished skull of a skeleton; of his deep-set little treacherous eyes, of his scant white hair, and with a piteous moan he turned away his head, and substituted the word "spare" me, for "love."

He could not rest in his bed.

The kiss of peace he had imprinted on Nelly's innocent brow seemed to infect him with a fever that spread through him—body, heart, brain!

He took to stealing out of the house at night to walk in the cool air.

Poor, miserable old dotard!

He skulked out into the night, and he made his way, trembling and quaking lest he might be seen, up the lane that led to the mill-house, for the poor pleasure of being near her.

For the meagre satisfaction of covertly watching the lights in the mill-house windows, and speculating which was *her* window.

He found it out at last.

It was the one just over the porch.

Once he had seen her shadow unmistakably reflected on the blind, and ever after no idol worshipper of savage lands could have been more devout.

Night after night, half crazed with the torturing dream that possessed him, Phantom would seek a safe post of observation, and feast his eyes on the window above the porch, until the sudden extinguishing of the light told him that his goddess had sought her couch.

Then, while poor, unsuspecting Nelly laid her throbbing head on her pillow, and ere she closed her eyes, offered up a prayer for the safety of "dear John," Mr. Phantom, gnashing his teeth in impotent rage, crept home disconsolate.

"It is some infernal enchantment; it is not natural," he groaned. "What is she to me that I should make myself so wretched? Why should my head be tortured with racking pains because hers can boast of—of—a wealth of brown curls such as an empress might envy? Why should my heart ache till its strings are like to crack, because *her* heart is closed to all save my enemy? Oh, curse him! curse him! He will get her at last! Some tantalizing devil within me seems to whisper to me that it will be so, and laughs at and mocks me. If she were dead I should not so much care; then she would be out of *his* reach as well as mine. If he were dead, it would be something! Curse him!"

On the seventh night, as on all the others of the week that followed John Gauntlet's mysterious disappearance, did Joseph Phantom indulge in his insane pilgrimage.

A boisterous night, with a cold, cutting wind and rain that assaulted one's unprotected face and ears like a shower of fine needle-points.

But Mr. Phantom was defiant of wind and rain; indeed it is doubtful if he was aware of either.

It was dark, too; pitch dark, but he rejoiced at this.

It would enable him to perform his pilgrimage to the shrine of his idol the better screened from observation.

The shrill blast piped through the dismantled trees, and sent the crisp, brown leaves whirling in a shower about his ears.

But his faculties of observation were otherwise employed, and he heeded no more than though a summer breeze was blowing.

His only anxiety was "to be in time."

He dared not quite closely approach the house.

The watch dog in his kennel forbade the rash act.

The best that he could do was to stealthily make his way to a hawthorn bush, distant from the garden gate about twenty yards, and there crouch with his eyes fixed on the window, and his tortured heart bowed in hopeless worship of the woman whom he knew to be in the room beyond.

His haste had not been in vain.

He was in good time.

All the rest of the house was in darkness; but *her* light still shone for him as the faraway beacon shines to mock the wrecked mariner who clings for life to the frail spar.

And there he crouched under his bush, hungrily regarding it.

The church bells chimed ten, eleven, and still the beacon twinkled in the window.

The storm increased.

The wind blew almost a hurricane, and the rain pelted down more fiercely than ever.

But what of that?

Nay, the storm did him a good turn!

It came with a swoop at her window, and she heard it!

With her mind filled with dismal forebodings for the dear absent one, she heard it, poor girl! and woefully wondering, was *he* exposed to the fury of such a night?—she came to the casement, and raising the blind just a little, looked out into the blackness.

She held in her hand a book that the watcher at once recognized—the little bible that she invariably carried to church with her.

Now he knew why the light was kept burning till so late an hour.

And was Mr. Phantom touched by this simple evidence of Nelly Blisset's trust and piety?

Did he slink away ashamed?

Not he!

The good book could rouse no feeling of contrition in a heart such as beat in his bosom. He did not bestow a second glance at it.

Time was precious, and he could not afford to do so.

He grudged even the moment that was wasted in that involuntary wink of amazement in which he perforce indulged, because it, for that brief space of time, shut out the lovely vision.

Judging from Nelly's appearance, she had retired to her couch, and risen therefrom in order, by reading, to banish the terrible forebodings that assailed her pillow.

She wore a prim little frilled cap, beneath which (except one or two which, in her sorrowful neglect, had escaped), her wealth of brown curls was snugly tucked, while her snowy gown, demurely buttoned at her throat, draped her exquisite maiden figure.

All unconscious of the hideous watcher that lurked beneath the hawthorn bush, there, at the dimly-lighted window, stood sad Nelly, her eyes red with weeping, her wan lips moving as though imploring the fierce elements, that perchance were beating on her lost lover, to abate their violence.

Then, as though in mockery and derision, a heavy gust of wind swept a deluge of rain against the window. Nelly Blisset shook her head mournfully, and let fall the curtains, and the lovely vision vanished.

It is said that angels shed tears of pity on the lost ones of the pit that is fathomless.

Could the miller's daughter have beheld that terrible face peering from the black shadow of the hawthorn bush; could she but for a moment have contemplated its agonized working, that told the man's torment, she must have pitied Joseph Phantom while she loathed him.

"She's gone!" he croaked, as he craned forward on all fours, and with his spread fingers resting in the mire. "She's gone! my enchantress, my lovely little charmer! Just now it was dazzling bright, now it is black night again. Ugh! it is like the end of all things, when the stars and the sun shall be no more!"

Would she come to the window again?

Would a fiercer blast of wind than hitherto, rattling the casement of her chamber, cause her again to look out?

Mr. Phantom was cold now—chilled to his bones, but at that moment he would gleefully have welcomed a hurricane strong enough to blow the few remaining grey hairs off his head.

It was fortunate, however, that his words were but muttered under his breath, and that he had not as yet altered his position.

When at length, finding that the light appeared not again, he essayed to struggle to his benumbed feet, he immediately shrank down again, his heart beating with dismay.

He was observed!

Not by the girl at the window, the contemplation of whose surpassing loveliness had caused his eager eyes to burn hot in their orbits.

It was a man who seemed watching him!

A crouching figure, whose approaching footsteps were so stealthy that they were not heard.

It came up the path that Mr. Phantom had so recently trod; it came up, as it seemed, straight towards the hawthorn bush that concealed his aghast and quaking form.

Should he run? Should he cry out?

No! Desperation made the man with the notched nails bold. He grasped his umbrella in his bony fist with a venomous clutch, and held in his breath.

In another moment his fright gave way to amazement.

The figure—he could see now that it was that of a tall man of considerable breadth and bulk—passed within three yards of him without perceiving him.

Passed him and crept straight towards the garden gate, and without the least noise, raised the latch and walked in!

"'MR. REGINALD VIPERT, I BELIEVE?' SAID LORD LAVERING, ADVANCING."—(See page 175.)

CHAPTER XVII.

A PERILOUS RETURN.

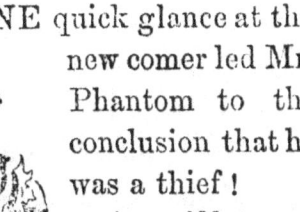

NE quick glance at the new comer led Mr. Phantom to the conclusion that he was a thief!

A villanous burglar, who had selected this tempestuous night as a good one on which to rob the mill-house!

Screening his eyes with his hands, Mr. Phantom peered anxiously through the darkness, watching every movement of the mysterious figure.

He might have run away now, had he so chosen, but a spirit of chivalry restrained him; at least, he flattered himself that it was chivalry.

Who knew what might happen?

These burglars were invariably terrible fellows, who, in pursuit of their purpose, stuck at nothing.

What if he dare invade that sacred room in which the light just now burnt?

What if there should by-and-bye arise a scream for help, and he should be there to render it! There to clasp in his arms—though only for a moment —the trembling, fleeing Nelly, in her snowy gown!

He would have swum the river—icy cold as the water was—for a privilege so blissful! He would have fought his way through fire for a single sip of such divine ambrosia!

But the tactics of the stealthy figure were scarcely those of an experienced housebreaker. He must have seen the dog-kennel fair in his path, but he took no step aside to avoid it.

"There's the dog," Mr. Phantom whispered to himself, as he heard the animal's chain rattle; "he doesn't know that there is a dog; he'll know it presently, the villain. Nero will pin him."

But the villain seemed to carry with him a charm against the attacks of watch-dogs.

More, he appeared to possess a wonderful faculty of guessing, at the very first try, the name of any strange dog he might encounter in the course of marauding.

As the crouching, creeping figure approached the kennel, Nero scented him, and uttered a preliminary growl; but the mysterious stranger softly exclaimed, "Quiet, Nero, quiet!" and the animal was instantly pacified.

The angry growl gave place to a whine, and to the sound of impatient scraping of the dog's feet, as though it were anxious to reach the intruder to fondle him.

Still straining his vision, to see all

that was to be seen, Mr. Phantom could not fail to note this last-mentioned circumstance, and as he did so, his demeanour altered considerably.

The bony hands that had been shading his eyes were now clenched vengefully — clenched so that the notched finger nails dug into his palms, while his heavy brows lowered passionately, and his upper teeth grated against the lower.

"Now I know you, curse you !" he muttered. "You are not drowned then ; you are not dead and gone to the devil, John Gauntlet, as I hoped you were ? You are alive, and you dare to come here !"

And well was it for our hero that the weapon that Mr. Phantom grasped was nothing more deadly than a gingham umbrella ! Had it been a loaded pistol there would have been murder done ; Mr. Phantom could not have helped it.

Still jealously watching him, he saw him bending low, and cautiously approaching the house.

Saw him pause at the door, and take from his breast a something small and white that looked like a letter, and then he stooped down still lower, and the white thing had gone out of his hands.

"He has pushed his letter in at the bottom of the door !" said Mr. Phantom.

He saw John raise himself again to his full height, with his face upturned to *the* window, and his hands clasped together ; noted the agony of the white face and the dumb movement of the lips ; heard a moan that was not the moaning of the wind, and there he was, with his face resting against a pillar of the porch, as though some mighty spasm of pain had seized him, rendering him helpless.

This new and unexpected change in the strange scene was not lost on Mr. Phantom.

From his lurking place, his face white with fury indescribable, looked out and saw it all.

The man of the notched nails was amazed, bewildered.

What did it all mean ?

"Curse him ! curse him !" he muttered through his close clenched teeth. "What can he want here ? He, a man with a price on his head ! A fellow, the sight of whom would be as good as a hundred pounds down to any country booby who chanced to set eyes on him ! He must be an idiot—a madman ! What is his object ?"

Not to see Nelly Blisset.

Had it been, he would not have been at the pains to prepare a letter to convey so stealthily into the house.

He might easily make her aware of his being there if he had a mind to.

The window over the porch—*her* window—was not more than eight or ten feet from the ground ; with a switch broken from a bush, a tall fellow like John Gauntlet might have reached it easily.

He might have thrown a pebble at the lattice ; there were a dozen ways of rousing her had such been his desire.

But he availed himself of not one of them.

He still stood against the pillar of the porch ; his great frame convulsed with the great grief that was wringing him, helpless to do aught else.

"There's a pretty specimen of a man !" snarled white-faced Mr. Phantom, crouching in the mire. "This is your high-spirited John Gauntlet, the fellow who once said that I was no better than a faithful mongrel who did his master's bidding. This is the noble fellow, and he comes here snivelling and whining like a wayside cadger! This is the man that stands in *my* way."

And cadaverous Joseph, blinded by jealousy to his own ridiculous appearance, cast up his eyes under the brim of his limp and saturated hat, and indulged in a haughty sneer that made him appear more old and wrinkled than ever.

"There is one thing," said he to himself, "I'll have that letter as soon as——"

But there his speech failed him.

The curtain of the little window over the porch was swiftly drawn aside, and there again was Nelly Blisset.

She had heard "the moaning that was not the moaning of the wind," and her quick eyes piercing the darkness, she saw the form that leant against the pillar.

An instant to fling a gown and shawl about her, and then, ere he had time to escape, she sprang down the stairs, and opening the outer door swiftly and noiselessly, clasped his drenched and haggard figure in her arms.

"My darling! my darling! my poor outcast love!"

"Oh, Nell! My dear, true little angel. It was not for this I came! I did not dare hope——"

But his drooping head was hugged so closely to her bosom that his speech failed him and gave place to half stifled, heart-wrung sobs, while still holding him close, she kissed and kissed him, and softly said—

"Hush, hush! my poor dear boy, hush!"

Although her own voice faltered and was well-nigh melted to speechless bliss in her rapture at seeing him, holding him once again.

Mr. Phantom, crouching down to the wet grass like a venomous toad, witnessed all this.

Low as were these spoken words of endearment his madly jealous ears were quick to hear them, and he ground his teeth in impotent fury.

"Curse them! curse them both!" he muttered under his breath as, in his insane rage, he grasped in his bony hands clods of earth and wet grass as though to hurl them at the objects of his hatred; but in an instant he altered his tone, and his growl became a pitiful whine as he continued—

"No, no; I can't curse her. I could not, even though she spurned me, spat on me. No, no; I can't curse you, Nelly, my idol, my torment, my terrible enchantress; but him I can. He shall not triumph. I'll bring him down; I have the power, and I will do it! Yes, and all the while I will pretend to be so good a friend that when he is gone, you shall come to me, and for consolation lay your darling head—your pretty curly head, sweet Nell, on my breast, my fatherly breast, he, he! and we will mingle our tears and——"

It was the sound of John Gauntlet's

whispering voice that roused him from his delirious rhapsody.

"Nay, my darling, you ask me what I no more dare consent to than kill you here as you stand," said he, evidently in reply to some softly spoken entreaty of hers. "It could do no good, poor birdie. It could do nothing but harm to you and all those we hold so dear."

"But I shall die if you again go away from me," wailed poor Nelly, still clasping him about the neck and passionately kissing his cold cheek (the sound sent a cold thrill through Mr. Phantom's veins); "my heart grows so cold, my darling, as I lay awake through the long night in doubt and dread, that it seems it must presently stand still !"

"That is my great trouble !" returned John, earnestly. "For myself, dear Nell, so that I could clear my name of the terrible stain that my enemies have cast on it, I care nothing at all; it is of you I am always thinking. I say to myself 'Bless her heart, she is so brave and true, she will be so jealous of a word or hint even against me that she will become a common topic in the mouths of malicious gossips and sneerers,' and I picture you, my sweet Nell, so cruelly served, and all for my sake, and I feel at times that it would be better if I——"

"What, John ?" Nelly asked, eagerly, as the poor fugitive gulped back a word he was about rashly to give utterance to.

"That it would be better if we had never met, my love," said he.

"Aye, but that is not what my poor boy was about to say," returned Nelly, her unsteady voice suddenly growing firm. "I don't ask you to repeat the terrible words ; my quaking heart tells me what they would have been but too plainly. John, you are not so brave as I thought you; not so strong. Your burden is too heavy for you to bear, my dear, persecuted, innocent love. You must let me share it with you."

"How, share it, Nelly ? Do you not already——"

"Aye, but that is not enough. You yourself just now said that your anxiety for me so far away from you was your great trouble. This must no longer be, my betrothed, my darling, who, in heart and soul, are already my husband. You will retrace your steps to your place of hiding, dear John, but you must take me with you !"

"The devil !" muttered Phantom ; "that would indeed be a nice turn for affairs to take !"

John Gauntlet, too, was not a little taken aback by her sudden demand.

"My noble little woman !" said he, folding her more closely to his bosom ; "it should not in the least astonish me to hear you talk so, but it is quite impossible. We must not be selfish in our love, my darling ; there are aching hearts besides ours in this unhappy business—hearts that are as one with your own as in mine—hearts that would break if you were to do as you suggest. Your father, my Nelly ; your mother ! Think of them, dear lass !"

"I do—I do," Nelly replied, mournfully ; "I think of them as much as I can, but *you* are my one thought, John.

It may be selfish; it may be wicked, but pray, pray, forgive me; for I cannot, cannot help it!"

And she sobbingly clung to him, as though her poor little heart would break.

"It is I who need forgiveness of you," he returned distressfully; "it is cruel of me to stay a moment longer. It was rash, more than rash, for me to venture here, but I dare not send by any other hand the few poor words of comfort I wish to convey to you. Now you have them in my letter, and from my own lips as well, and I will return as I came."

"Without me?" and she looked beseechingly up into his face.

"It must be so, my darling."

"Ah! you are afraid that I should embarrass you; but I wouldn't, dear. I wouldn't. I only want to be near you, John. I would creep into your hiding place, and lie as still as a little mouse. I'd sit by the door, darling, all the night through, and keep watch while you slept!"

"Good bye! Good bye! I cannot— dare not. God bless you, Nell! Now let me go, and pray for my next safe coming."

"You are quite resolved?" she whispered, after a pause.

"It can be no other, darling."

"Why, then I must part with you," she continued in a strangely altered voice, a voice with so much of desperation in it that Mr. Phantom, shrewd man of the world as he was, shrugged his wet shoulders, and grinned a ghastly grin. "Shall you walk straight back to London, John?"

"I shall walk back as far as Deptford, and to a little inn there where I halted on my way here, and rest for a few hours," he replied. "It isn't a grand place, Nelly," he continued, with some sort of bitterness in his tone; "a common lodging for tramps and that sort of folks, so I shall have no difficulty in obtaining admittance, late as it will be."

"And what, dear, is the sign of the little inn?" she asked.

Mr. Phantom raised his saturated hat well clear of his ear, and craned eagerly forward.

"Why do you ask, Nelly?" John Gauntlet asked.

"Because—because I should like to think of it, since its roof will for one night at least give my dear love shelter."

"But for one night? Yes, but for one night," returned John, as though that fact gave him impunity to tell her what she asked. "It is a strange sign, my darling; the 'Willow Weavers.'"

"The 'Willow Weavers,'" repeated Nelly, slowly. "I shall bear it well in mind."

"The 'Willow Weavers,'" muttered Mr. Phantom, under his breath. "I've no great memory for tavern signs, but I shall recollect that, never fear!"

"You will keep a brave heart, dearest," said John, making a desperate effort to speak cheerfully, but not succeeding very well.

"I will most earnestly pray for one, dear John, for I shall need it very much."

Again that mysterious tone of determination, that seemingly was lost on

John Gauntlet, but in which Mr. Phantom read such deep, significant meaning.

"And we will meet again soon, Nelly !"

"Aye, that we will !"

And she uttered the words with such perfect confidence, that, as though afraid of arousing her lover's suspicions, she hastily added—

"I have a presentiment that we shall meet again, dear John, soon—very soon. It is that which makes me so courageous to bid you farewell."

"Farewell then, dear Nell !"

And then one close embrace, one long, lingering kiss (that was long-drawn torture for the enemy crouching under the hedge), and then the lovers parted.

The hapless fugitive passed within a few yards of Mr. Phantom's quaking, skulking figure, and luckily for the latter, without observing him.

With his head drooping on his breast, and without once daring to look back, he hurried away into the wind and the rain and the darkness; but Nelly Blisset, all so scantily clad, stood there at the porch, until he had quite vanished from sight.

"Now God give me strength, and assist me in my desperate venture !"

Very softly she uttered these words, and with her hands clasped and her eyes raised to Heaven.

But Joseph Phantom both saw and heard, and he rubbed his icy cold hands together in satisfaction, while the germ of some new devilish design shone in his deep-set eyes.

"She won't start for half-an-hour yet, that's certain. She would be afraid of overtaking him else," he muttered. "That will give me time to get back to the Hall and shift my wet clothes. Ugh ! they stick to my bones like the skin to a snake ! But there's warmth ahead, warmth and lasting, loving comfort, if I'm careful ; if I'm prudent as well as daring. Good-bye, beauty, for a little time. Good-bye, cherry-lipped sweetheart !"

And the poor old dotard rapturously kissed and waved towards the chamber, in which the light once again appeared, his great white paws with the notched nails.

CHAPTER XVIII.

AT THE OLD INN.

THAT ancient and not highly respectable hostelry, the "Willow Weavers" was situated on the Kent Road, as Woolwich was approached.

A huge, rambling pile of building, in more prosperous times a flourishing posting-house, but now little better than a common lodging house for tramps and wayfarers.

The "Willow Weavers" was not a public house that was supervised by the police with undue severity.

There are scores of such houses in and about London.

So long as the publican does not too glaringly defy the law, its officers are content to see and say nothing, on condition that no obstacle is thrown in their way should it be necessary to require the arrest of a lodger.

Dilapidated, however, as was his establishment, the proprietor of the "Willow Weavers" had no reason to be dissatisfied with his business, and on the night when John Gauntlet paid his melancholy visit to Blisset's mill, the "large room" was well filled.

Sunday night though it was (or rather the early hours of Monday morning), the company assembled were hilarious, and song-singing the order of the hour.

And well enough could the motley assemblage afford to be jolly, and empty their glasses and rap loudly on the battered table for them to be instantly replenished.

The orgie cost them nothing.

A gentleman present was generously standing a night's treat to all comers.

The gentleman "in the chair," to whom the landlord was so humbly attentive, was a gorgeously-attired personage.

He wore a shooting coat of plum-coloured velveteen, with gilt buttons that glistened in the gaslight; a crimson plush waistcoat, about the front of which were displayed the hanks of a resplendent silver watch chain; while on his head, elegantly adorned with oily "side locks," as black as jet, was jauntily stuck a white hat of costly texture.

It was the reader's old acquaintance —Black Lutterloh!

The gipsy half-breed was faithful to his old instincts in the days of his prosperity.

At a single stroke—a stroke that

involved the sudden covering up of his repulsive countenance with a *grey mask* at a sort of drawing-room entertainment, to use his own words—he had " made a fortune."

Reginald Vipert was his banker.

On the memorable occasion indicated, Mr. Lutterloh had demanded a hundred pounds as being " enough just at present," and his request had been complied with without a murmur.

Ever since he had been " enjoying himself" to his heart's content.

He had been to London, where, in certain shady parts, he had many friends, and had made the money fly to the amazement of all of them.

Now, he was returning to his " native parts," and, having a shrewd idea that he should find at the " Willow Weavers" a considerable number of his bosom friends and old acquaintances, he had made it his halting place.

With what result the reader had already seen.

He was a gentleman now.

Could afford to do the handsome thing by 'em, and might something dreadful happen to his eyes and limbs if he wouldn't do it.

He had done it.

Since nine o'clock a score or so of choice spirits, after his own heart, had, at his expense, sat indulging in ardent spirits and in singing jolly lays of rogues and highwaymen, and all was as merry as Wedding Bells.

Mr. Lutterloh, too drunk to be any longer ferocious, was becoming sentimental.

With the hat jerked over his right eye further than ever, he had contrived to balance himself on his legs to make a speech, in which, with tears in his eyes, he thanked the gentlemen present for the honour they had done him in drinking his health about five and twenty times each all round on that auspicious occasion.

" It goes to my 'art, it do," continued Mr. Lutterloh, plunging his great hairy hand in at the bosom of the scarlet plush waistcoat, " and I feel at this 'ere moment as if I had a enemy wot was as savage agin me as a mad dawg, I could say—' Give us yer paw, my brother, and I'll forgive yer.' But I hain't got no enemies. I never does nothing wot'll make 'em ; I'm that soft-'arted———"

But at this moment there was a commotion at the room door.

" I would rather not go in—I'm wet, tired ; I would much rather go to bed, if you will allow me."

" You may go as soon as you like, when you have had a glass. It's all free, you fool. I wouldn't show a cross-breed among 'em, if I was you."

And then a man was pushed in, and the door slammed to.

A man ghastly pale, and with his wet hair hanging about his face.

A man, from whose saturated clothes the rain ran in tiny rivulets, and who looked forlorn and miserable indeed.

The Willow Weavers were in a mood to be hospitable, and the fire was at Black Lutterloh's end of the room.

" Why, you are like a drowned rat, man," bawled one of the company. " Come this way and dry your jacket and wet your in'ards."

But something affected the worthy chairman.

Since the entrance of the stranger, he had not once taken his eyes off him, and the longer he looked, the faster the liquor he had imbibed seemed to evaporate.

"I've had enough of it for one night," he growled, as he slunk out of the chair of honour. "I shall be off; I—I didn't know how drunk I was."

"But you must drink the last comer's good health, brave captain! It wouldn't be manners to leave him out. You surely won't have it said now, for the first time, that Black Lutterloh shirked his liquor!"

The landlord was at the other side of the room as he spoke, but Lutterloh made him a swift sign, which the other was not slow to comprehend.

"The worthy captain's had enough," said he, suddenly altering his tone. "Our noble president, gentlemen, has got his skin full and desires to go to his roost. He leaves orders, however, that you may all have an hour's more drinking, as hard as you like."

And, pretending to be completely intoxicated, Lutterloh, hanging his head so that the new-comer might not see his features, staggered out of the room, the landlord accompanying him.

The latter led the way to a side room that was still dirtier than the one in which the half-drunken company was assembled.

It was a small room, with a window partly shaded by a blind of red stuff, and lit by a dim gas jet.

The only occupants of the room before Lutterloh and the landlord entered it were a tramp, who, having rolled, intoxicated, off his seat in the adjoining apartment, had been dragged in here and flung on the floor to sleep himself sober, and a woman.

A beggar woman, who, bundled on a seat in a corner, with her arms resting on the table before her, and her face hidden, appeared to be out-wearied and asleep after a long journey.

"What's amiss, old fellow?" the landlord asked, curiously. "Your having had enough is all a sham, you know; a child might see that. You look as scared as a scouted rabbit, man."

"Well, the fact is I do feel a bit queer," returned the gipsy. "I'll be off, I think."

"Off! Off to bed you mean, of course."

"No, I don't. I mean off and away from this place. I—I don't like your company, man."

The landlord opened his eyes, and whistled softly.

"You don't like the company, old boy? Shall I tell you the member of it you don't like?"

"If your tongue wants exercise, you may," replied the other surlily; "we ain't quite alone, remember."

"We're as good as as alone. I'll answer for Barney here, and as for the woman, she's sound asleep, anyone may see. Now, between friends, what's up, Lutterloh?"

The beggar woman must have been dreaming, surely.

How else could the sudden start she

at that moment made be accounted for?

But the two men had their backs to her, and did not perceive it.

The gipsy faced the landlord with one of his eyes screwed close, and his broad finger laid against the side of his nose.

"Did ever you go to school?" he asked.

"Certainly; why?"

"Do you recollect 'em ever setting you a writin' copy, 'Mind yer own business?'"

"Can't say I do; they was civil people where I went to school," returned the landlord, with a scowl.

"So am I civil till I'm riled," returned Lutterloh, "and there's nothing riles me so soon as any one poking their nose into my business. Take the reckoning, my friend, out of this fi' pun' note, and I'll bid you good-night."

"Good mornin', you mean; d'ye know the time, man? It's nearly half-past one."

"When I want to know the time of you, I'll ask it," returned Lutterloh, impatiently, as he buttoned his coat. "Hang you, give me my change and let me go, I tell you!"

And, growling and shrugging his shoulders discontentedly (for he had made sure of detaining his profitable customer many hours yet), the landlord took the note and left the room.

CHAPTER XIX.

A FRESH PLOT.

AS the landlord left the room, Lutterloh took his handkerchief from his pocket, and with it wiped his forehead that was reeking with perspiration. "Curse him! What the devil brought him here?" he muttered. "Is it chance, or is there a meanin' it it? I'll be off anyhow. It gives me a queer feeling of tightening of the shirt-collar to be within sight and sound of him!"

The beggar woman was *not* asleep.

Lutterloh's back was to her, and she had raised her face, which was hidden by a thick old veil, as though she had an interest in his words.

"Is it still raining, I wonder?" said Lutterloh; and, to see, he approached the window and raised the red curtain.

As he did so, he uttered a cry that caused the beggar woman to raise her head entirely.

No wonder that Black Lutterloh uttered that cry!

A miracle had happened.

As he lifted the curtain, he thrust his face close to the window pane, and there, at the other side of the glass, within an inch of his own, was another face!

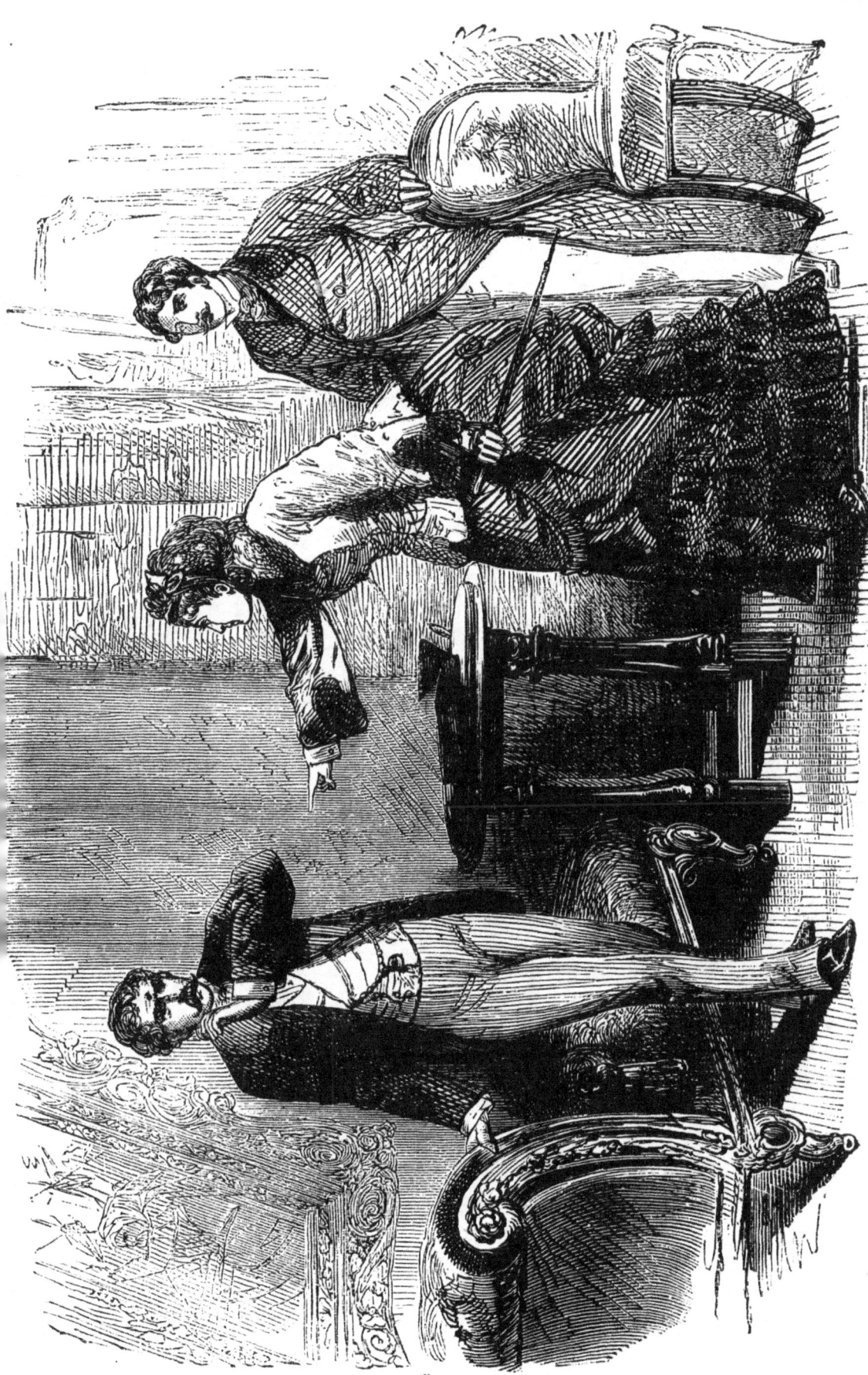

"'MISERABLE COWARD,' CRIED NAN."—(See page 189.)

A man's face !

A face he knew well and dreaded.

It vanished the moment he saw it, but the recognition was mutual and unmistakable.

The landlord returning at that instant found his generous customer deadly pale and trembling.

But he suddenly recovered his presence of mind and ferocity as the host of the " Willow Weavers " entered the room.

He made a spring at him, and had him by the throat before three might be counted.

" What's this ?" he exclaimed, in a voice hoarse with passion. "Is it a plant? Is it a trap? D'ye think to nab me, and I won't have a fight for it? Call 'em in ! Call 'em all in, and see !"

" Call 'em in ! Call who in? Leave go my throat, you drunken madman," gasped the landlord; "you're choking me ! Help !"

Lutterloh's passion was but momentary.

Nobody came, and he presently released the affrighted landlord.

" I—I'm better now," he growled. " It'll be the death o' me one day—the cursed drink ! I felt the fit comin' on me while I was in t'other room. Keep the change, master, for the squeezing I gave your throttle. Now I'll be off; the cold rain and the wind'll do me good."

And, without farther parley, he hurried out of the house, muttering as he went—

" It was only my fancy; it couldn't be him."

Outside, and as far as the darkness would permit him to see, the coast was clear.

" Ha ! ha ! it's all right ; but, my eyes ! what a scaring it gave me ! I'd as soon just now meet the devil himself as——Hallo !"

Had it been his Satanic majesty in person who suddenly rose before him, Mr. Lutterloh could not have started more guiltily.

It was Mr. Joseph Phantom.

Disguised to a miracle, but still unmistakably the wily steward of Monkshood Hall.

Instead of his customary tall hat, he wore a slouched countryman's cap, and a stout waterproof coat, and leather leggings. He carried a walking stick, too—stout, and of peculiar make.

Not less astonished than the gipsy was he, when he peeped through the window and saw that ferocious swarthy face so close on the other side.

The fact was, Mr. Joseph Phantom was off the scent somewhat.

As the reader has already been made aware, shrewdly suspecting Nelly Blisset's determination to follow her betrothed, he had hurried back to Monkshood Hall, to shift his wet clothes, and assume a disguise.

But he had miscalculated the time.

He could not believe that, in the little time it had taken him to equip himself for the journey, Nelly could have reached and passed the cross roads, and there he loitered half an hour at least.

At last he was driven to the conclusion that she must have passed before he came up ; and he set out on his long, miry tramp.

The "Willow Weavers" was easy enough to find; but Mr. Phantom knew the character of the house, and he prudently paused ere he ventured in to make a few inquiries.

It was while he was thus reconnoitring that he chanced to spy through the window and made the discovery already indicated.

"Don't be alarmed, my friend; there's no cause, unless you yourself make it," remarked Mr. Phantom, taking care to keep the width of the horse-trough between himself and the gipsy.

It was several seconds ere Black Lutterloh could recover his speech.

"What's the meaning o' this, master?" he said at last.

"Hush! walls have ears, they say, and why not horse-troughs and sign posts?" returned Mr. Phantom, with a grin that showed his teeth. "You are wanted, Mr. Lutterloh, that is all."

"Wanted!" returned the gipsy, with a startled look round and a savage scowl. "Who wants me?"

He looked so threatening that Mr. Phantom started back, and as he did so the end of his walking-stick struck the ground, and out sprang a gleaming little sword-blade of six inches long or so.

"I want you, my friend," said he, blandly. "I've come many miles to find you, and I took the precaution to bring this little instrument with me, knowing what an uncertain tempered man you are."

"I'd twist it out of your hand and spit you with it like a herrin' if you forced me to it," growled Lutterloh, contemptuously; "and mind yer, I'll do it, too, if you are after playin' tricks. Let's have it out, quick, now. What do you want with me?"

"You'll be more civil when you hear I've come to do you a service."

"You!"

"Aye. I've come to warn you."

"Of what?"

"Danger. Those who are hunting after John Gauntlet, as the murderer of Joel Burke, are on the wrong track."

Black Lutterloh started, but in a moment answered, with his accustomed dogged insolence—

"Put 'em on the right track, then, and bag the hundred pounds they are offering as a reward."

"That is my intention, my friend," returned Mr. Phantom, coolly, and with his finger on the spring of the sword-stick.

Black Lutterloh again glanced about him, as though finding it difficult to believe that this mere pipe-stem of a man would have the daring to approach him on so dangerous an errand, unless he had assistance close at hand.

But he did not lose his coolness.

"Well, what's it to do with me?" he asked. "What sort of 'service' do you do me by a comin' and a consultin' me about what don't concern me?"

Mr. Phantom nodded his head complacently.

"So that's the ground you mean to take, eh?" said he.

"Why not?"

"You mean to fight it out to the last, in spite of all the evidence that may be brought against you—I beg your pardon—against the man who murdered Joel Burke!"

At the word "evidence," Lutterloh turned a shade paler.

"Evidence !" said he. "What d'ye mean ?"

"Not much. Do you always smoke over your work, my man ?"

"Smoke over my work ?"

"Aye; you must be a cool customer to smoke over a job like that. *How came you to drop your pipe ?*"

Lutterloh turned paler still, and grasped the edge of the horse trough for support.

He *had* lost his pipe.

As the reader will perhaps remember, at that time when he advised the sinking of John Gauntlet's bloodstained coat in the pool in the wood, he had, from the screen of a bush close at hand, beheld the deed accomplished, and in order that his tobacco smoke might not betray his place of hiding, he had taken his pipe from his lips, and laid it by his side.

His favourite little black pipe with the metal lid, and on the inner side of which his name was scratched.

Only a day or so before, Mr. Phantom, in his restless searching after a clue to the murder mystery, had taken a walk through the wood, and discovered the pipe.

There was not much in the discovery, but Mr. Phantom had thought it worth while to treasure it.

"Let's be reasonable !" spoke Black Lutterloh, presently, in a conciliatory tone; "let's take a walk down the road, where nobody can overhear us !"

"And where nobody can see us—where nobody can see you put into execution the ugly threat you just now used towards me, eh ? No, thank you, my friend, I prefer staying where I am. I've business here."

"What, here at the 'Weavers ?'" asked Lutterloh, in amazement. "Why, what can a gen'leman like wot you are want with anybody what uses the 'Weavers ?'—unless——"

"What ?" asked Mr. Phantom, as Black Lutterloh paused, with strange meaning in his eyes. "Out with it, man—unless what ?"

"Unless you got business with *him ?*"

Mr. Phantom nodded.

"With them both," said he, in a whisper.

"Both !"

"Aye, with Gauntlet and the poor girl whose wretched infatuation has led her to follow him," and Mr. Phantom cast up his eyes, and endeavoured to look virtuous.

"You needn't pretend to look astonished," he presently remarked, sharply, to Mr. Lutterloh. "You confess to knowing that he is here."

"Aye, but t'other," replied the gipsy.

"She's here, too."

Lutterloh opened his eyes wider than ever.

"No !"

"I say she is, and you know it."

"That's a lie !" said blunt Lutterloh; "and, if she is, why, good luck to her then, I say ! Good luck to anybody as she sticks up so staunch for !" And the ruffian clenched his expressed approval of courage and devotion in womankind by an oath of tremendous force and power.

But Mr. Phantom did not entirely approve of Black Lutterloh's sentiments.

"You wish good luck to John Gauntlet then?" said he sourly. "That being the case, our interview may at once come to an end. You are a more gallant fellow than I took you for, my friend; you appear to forget that luck for him means a halter for *you!*"

A vindictive scowl that the other did not perceive crossed Lutterloh's face, and after a few moments he drew Mr. Phantom to the shadow of the wall.

"I begin to see my way a bit clearer now, master," said he; "let us have no more beating about the bush. The bad luck wot's overtook him ain't bad enough; you'd have it worse!"

"My good Lutterloh," returned the man with the notched nails, brightening up considerably; "so far we understand each other. Go on!"

"No, *you* go on," returned the other, bluntly. "How much of bad luck, and what quality of it, would you like to fall on him, master?"

"What is the worst luck that can befall a man, my friend?"

"Being knocked on the head by another man, who he thinks is going to betray him," replied Mr. Lutterloh, meaningly. "I don't know a wusser fate than that."

"Except it is hanging," suggested Mr. Phantom, pleasantly.

"Aye; hanging ain't a good end," growled the gipsy. "Don't let's talk about it."

"It wasn't *your* hanging I alluded to, my good fellow," replied Mr. Phantom, "but John Gauntlet's."

"Who's to hang him?"

"You."

"Me?"

"Yes. I don't mean that you are to put the noose round his cursed neck with your own fingers, my friend. I don't think I should like to trust you; your nerves might fail you at the last moment. No; what I mean is, for your own sake—for all our sakes—you must put him in that road, the last stage of which is the hangman and the gallows!"

Black Lutterloh's brow lowered.

"You mean to say that I must peach on him!"

"That, I believe, is the correct term, according to your polite vocabulary," sniggered Mr. Phantom, rubbing his hands.

"Give him over to the police, for—for——"

"For the murder of Joel Burke, the gamekeeper!"

It would have dismayed Mr. Phantom not a little, could he have read Mr. Lutterloh's thoughts at that instant.

"I should be a hundred pounds in pocket by it, shouldn't I?" said he, in a low voice.

"To be sure you would," replied Mr. Phantom, delightedly; "you might claim it as surely as asking change for a bank note."

"And, I dessay, *you* would stand a summat handsome?"

"I am not a rich man, my friend; and, really, the affair would benefit you much more than anyone else, but—well, I daresay that I might find you a twenty pound note or so. Lord bless me! a hundred and twenty pounds, and all to be earned by five minutes' talk with a policeman! What do you say, my friend?"

"I say that I'll see you —— first."

Mr. Phantom stood aghast.

"And why not, pray?"

"For private reasons; don't you ask questions," replied the gipsy, cunningly.

"You'd rather he did a similar kindness for you, eh?" answered Mr. Phantom.

"No fear of that."

"Don't be so certain. What took him to Monkshood to-night?"

"What, John Gauntlet—to Monkshood!" and Lutterloh stood still, incredulous.

"Aye, to Blisset's mill, to seek a private interview with the good folks there. To what end do you think, my friend?"

"It's all a lie," said Lutterloh. "I don't believe he's been there at all."

"Shall I describe to you his disguise? You have seen him, and will judge if I am right or wrong."

And he accurately enumerated the articles of attire in which the fugitive was dressed.

Black Lutterloh preserved a moody silence.

"He wouldn't have ventured there if he didn't think that things was brightening for him," said he presently.

"You may rely on that," returned Mr. Phantom, emphatically.

"And there ain't no question, that wot's bright for him is black for me."

"You are growing to be quite a philosopher, my friend," and Mr. Phantom rubbed his hands. "You say that you saw him; did he speak to you?"

"Never saw me; never raised his eyes to look at nobody."

And Black Lutterloh narrated the way in which Gauntlet had been forced into the drinking room.

Mr. Phantom reflected for a few moments.

"If you didn't possess such ridiculous respect for the fellow, the way would be easy enough," said he.

Black Lutterloh laughed.

"I've got my likes and my dislikes," said he, "but this is the party wot I've got most respect for."

And he slapped his broad chest with his hand.

"It might be done that quiet and easy," continued Mr. Phantom, as though not heeding what the other said, "that, taking all the circumstances into consideration—all of 'em, mind you—there's not a coroner's jury in the whole kingdom but would bring it in suicide."

"What! the giving of him up? How the——could they bring that in suicide?"

"Pshaw! for a bold man, you are very short-sighted," returned Mr. Phantom, with good-natured pity; "a wise hunter never starts for the chase with but a single arrow in his quiver; if one misses its mark, he has another remaining."

And Mr. Phantom thrust his hand in at the breast of his coat, as though there and then he intended to produce the arrow he had been speaking of.

But it was not a steel-tipped and feathered instrument that he drew forth.

It was only a tiny screw of blue paper, no bigger than the top of a man's thumb.

"What's that?" Lutterloh asked.

"A sleeping powder, my friend," replied Joseph Phantom, with a devilish grin.

"It's p'ison, ain't it?"

"Deadly poison, my dear sir. This little dose dropped into his beer, into his coffee, or anything else he may be drinking, and there's a certain end to his being able to tell tales!"

Mr. Phantom held out the tiny paper, but Lutterloh hesitated to take it.

"What can be more natural?" urged the man of the notched nails. "Here is a man hard driven and desperate; rather than endure the torture that an evil conscience brings to every one, he chooses to make an end of it with a dose of poison!"

"I'll do it!" said Lutterloh, with an oath. "Give it here!"

"When will you do it, my friend?"

"When? Soon as I find a chance. P'r'aps to-night."

"It would be best done to-night. How shall I know?"

Black Lutterloh reflected.

"If it is done to-night, it will be within half an hour," said he; "and I'll stick a little bit of the blue paper wot it's wrapped in on one of the panes of that there window that you looked through. If you don't see the sign in the time that I say, you may know that the job is unavoidably put off till the morning."

"Yes, yes; I understand. Anything else?"

"No—yes; s'pose we change hats. He'll be less likely to know me with that old slouch of yours pulled over my eyes. That's the ticket; now I'm off."

Mr. Phantom still lingered.

"You are quite sure that she is not there?" he asked.

"Who? Miss Blisset? No; she ain't there, that I'll swear."

"You think that you must have seen her had she been?"

"Certain sure of it."

Mr. Phantom nodded his head contentedly.

"That's as well, under the circumstances," he muttered, and then aloud he wished Black Lutterloh good luck, and assured him that he should be on the watch.

"She hasn't come, that's evident," said he, as he walked briskly down the road. "I made a mistake; a lucky one though, by Satan and all his angels, a lucky one!"

But there was somebody else on the watch besides Mr. Phantom.

The beggar woman who was sitting in the little room that overlooked the road when Black Lutterloh and the landlord held their interesting conversation.

CHAPTER XX.

THE PLOT WORKS.

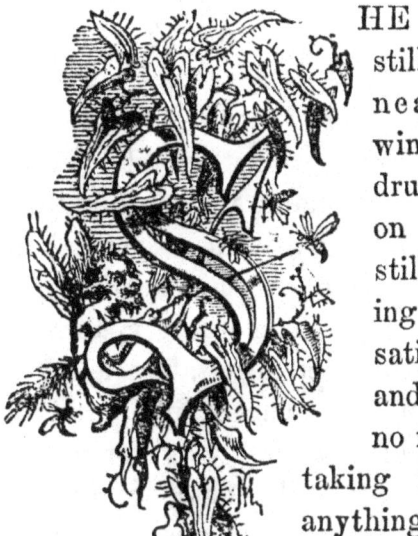

HE sat there still, though nearer the window. The drunken man on the floor still lay snoring like a satisfied hog, and there was no fear of his taking notice of anything that happened.

In the adjoining room, the great room, the noise of tipsy revelry was each moment increasing, and it was that room that had peculiar fascinations for the beggar woman. More than once since Black Lutterloh had staggered out, she crept to the battered, ill-hung door and peeped through the chink.

The individual she sought sat by the fire at the further end.

It was the man who so unwillingly allowed himself to be induced to enter.

She had heard him decline to drink, and under her shabby thick old veil her white lips had moved in thankfulness.

"Staunch and true, as he ever is!" she muttered. "Aye, they may tempt him, but he has that in his heart that makes him strong to say 'Nay.' That he will not falter I will pray."

And pray she did, the seeming beggar woman, as she leant with her face on her hands on the grimy table.

A little while after, and she stole to the door and again peeped, and there, to her horror, she saw him her eyes so eagerly sought with a steaming glass in his hand, sipping it as though, starved and wet with cold, he had tasted and found it too hard to resist.

There was a flush on his cheek, now, that before was so pale, and he held his head more upright and looked not nearly so downcast.

A terrible sight this for the beggar woman.

She almost reeled from the door and back to her corner in the adjoining room, and there she sat, pale and trembling.

She dare not look again.

She dare not enter the hideous place.

"Oh, Lord, give him strength!" she sobbed. "Let him not, who has stood up so bravely, fall so miserably!"

Then in came Mr. Lutterloh, who, by this time, had finished with Joseph Phantom that little conference of which the reader has already been made aware.

She knew him at once, despite the alteration in his appearance.

The capacious dark felt hat he had obtained of Mr. Phantom was pulled down as low as his eyes almost, and his velveteen coat, buttoned tight up under his chin, quite concealed Mr. Lutterloh's gorgeous waistcoat, but, with a kind of instinctive dread of the man, the beggar woman could not mistake him.

He looked cautiously into the room, but to all appearance everything was as he had left it.

There lay the drunken man on the ground.

There sat the beggar woman sleeping in the corner.

Then Black Lutterloh crept stealthily to the door of the room where the motley company were carousing, and applied his eye to the crevice.

He stepped back into the room where the beggar woman was, his villanous face beaming with satisfaction.

"Drunk as a fiddler," he whispered, with a grin; "making a speech, or singing a song, or summat, I think he is. He'll be quieter arter he has took his physic."

And as he spoke he took out the tiny screw of blue paper, and examined it by the gas light.

But as the beggar woman, with her face resting on her folded arms, fearfully regarded him, she observed a sudden change come over his swarthy countenance.

"I'm a fool, a regler stoopid fool," he muttered. "How do I know what he may chatter about now the liquor's in him? The sooner I get my little job over the better. I'll wheedle him to come in here if I can."

And he replaced the screw of blue paper in a handy pocket.

Then with the air of a man determined on some desperate business, he again left the room.

His doing so was the signal for the beggar woman to raise her head, and thick as was the veil she wore, the whiteness of her face was such that it seemed to shine through the close meshes of it.

"In danger!" she murmured, wringing her hands; "in terrible, deadly danger, and I unable to help him."

She cast a hurried, despairing glance round the room, and by the dim gas-light discovered something in the fire-place that attracted her attention.

A stout, short bar of iron that did duty as poker, as well as a pot rest.

This she hastily snatched up, and, concealing it in the folds of her cloak, resumed her seat in the corner.

Barely in time, however.

At the same moment she heard the door of the next chamber slammed open, and the voice of the ruffian she had seen and listened to but a few minutes previously.

Another voice, too!

A voice, the sounds of which were wont to fill her heart with pride and joy, but which now made her shiver and hold her breath.

"Come along, old pal! It ain't wot you've had that's overcome you. Why, you ain't had a thimbleful! It's the smoking; that's wot it is. This way. You'll get a mouthful of fresh air out here."

She heard their unsteady footsteps in the passage, and the next moment the villain and his victim stood in the doorway.

Black Lutterloh the one—the other John Gauntlet.

But how altered!

As the beggar woman furtively glanced at him, she felt as though her heart was setting fast and pulseless in ice.

His gait was unsteady, and his eyes, usually so clear and bright and fearless, were dull and bloodshot.

It was evident that the drink had been forced on him and overcome him, but not so entirely as that he still possessed a consciousness of his condition—a bitter, remorseful consciousness.

"I am a fool!" she heard him mutter; "a weak, self-confident fool. I should have known better."

"Known better!" repeated Lutterloh, so disguising his voice that the listener scarcely recognised it as his; "what a fuss about nothing! You ain't the fust gentleman wot's got a bit screwed. I was as drunk again as you are an hour ago; but I am an old hand, and knows how to set myself right in a jiffey."

"How? You'll do me a real service if you'll tell me," Gauntlet replied, in a thick, husky voice. "I would give a crown to feel as sober as when I entered this cursed den."

"I'll fetch you a remedy in a twinkling," said Black Lutterloh, with a grin; and he left the room.

It was singular the interest the beggar woman took in the poor fugitive.

As soon as the gipsy's back was turned, she raised her face, and looked eagerly towards him, but his heavy head was resting on his hands, and he saw her not.

"If I might dare rouse him," she muttered, anxiously, "but I much fear that the accursed drink has too much benumbed his senses for him to heed me."

"John, dear John!" she rapidly whispered, darting across the room, and laying a hand on his arm; "look up, dear! It is I, your Nelly."

And he did look up with a bewildered start.

But at the same moment she heard the returning footsteps of Lutterloh, and hastened back to her seat.

The gipsy brought in with him two sparkling glasses of ale.

"Here you are, my hearty," said he; "here's a cure, safe and certain. We'll drink together for luck."

And he set down one glass before his victim and raised the other to his lips.

But the half stupefied young farmer arrested his hand.

"First tell me," said he, in a strangely altered voice, "who—who was it called me?"

"When?"

"But a minute since. Who called 'John?'"

"John what?" the gipsy cunningly asked.

But the question seemed to rouse the other to a sense of the danger he ran in continuing the conversation.

"No matter, no matter," he muttered, passing his hand across his forehead.

And then he found his head was uncovered.

"Where's my cap?" he asked. "I must be going; where's my cap?"

"In the other room, I suppose. I'll

fetch it for you," said the obliging Lutterloh.

And again he left the room, leaving both full glasses on the table.

John Gauntlet's heavy head again sank on to his arms, and though the beggar woman called "John" again and again, he did not heed her.

But sudden thought prompted her to quick action.

She changed the position of the glasses, placing that which stood before the young farmer, where Lutterloh had placed his own, and *vice versa*.

Barely was this manœuvre executed when the gipsy returned.

"Here is your cap, old chap," said he, roughly shaking John Gauntlet by the shoulder; "now p'r'aps you'll be civil enough to swallow a glass of ale what I've bought and paid for for your good."

Without a reply, and as though now only anxious to get away without further delay, John Gauntlet placed the cap on his head, and snatching up the glass, drained off its contents, Lutterloh watching him meanwhile with devilish satisfaction.

"I think I'd lay down now a bit, my friend," he chuckled. "You may as well finish up comfortable after a dose like that. You're cured, there's no mistake about *that*. Here's wishing that you may avoid drinking habits in the future."

And he again took up his own glass.

Should she, the watchful beggar-woman, let him drink it?

Was it not his deserving, cold-blooded murderer as he was?

Maybe, but "murder for murder"

was no fair quittance in the eyes of God, and if it was a fatal draught and she let him drink it, she was a murderess!

The thought was terrible.

Anything rather.

Scarce knowing what she did, she sprang forward, just as Lutterloh raised the fatal glass to his lips, and the iron bar struck it down, shivering it into a thousand pieces, besides inflicting an ugly gash in the hand that held it.

The act was so sudden and unexpected, that for some moments the gipsy stood helpless in rage and amazement.

Then he recovered at once his speech and his inborn ferocity.

With a frightful oath, he sprang at the beggar-woman, and forced her backwards by the throat, raising his other great fist to deal her a cruel blow in the face.

But, as he did so, the shabby old bonnet and the veil slipped off, and a face, young and beautiful, though white as ashes, and distorted with terror, was revealed to him, while at the same time a piercing scream rang through the room.

"Help! John! help! It is I—your Nelly!"

No more stupefaction.

No more tipsy bewilderment and heaviness.

Swift as though the touch of an enchanter's wand had broken the spell that previously was on him, John Gauntlet became a sober man, and quick as lightning he responded to that pitiful cry.

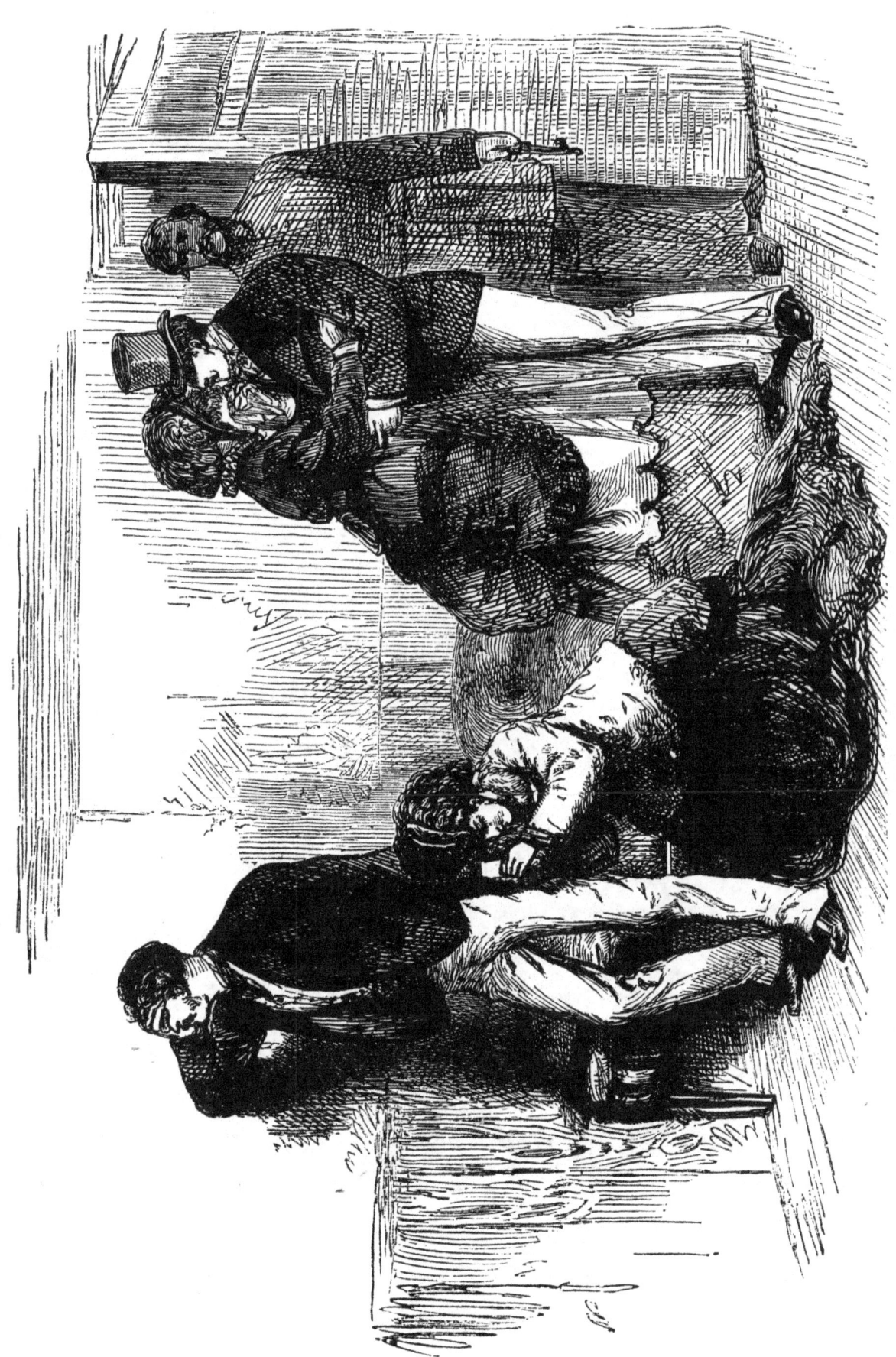

"WITH A GREAT CRY, HE REELED WITH HIS FACE TO THE WALL."—(See page 216.)

With the strength of three men, he seized the stalwart gipsy, and flung him with such force into the fireplace that the brittle cast-iron fender crashed in bits under his weight.

Then he caught in his trembling arms the fainting form of the faithful girl who had dared so much for his sake, and turned to stand at bay against the hideous crowd that, startled by the noise, came swarming out of the adjoining room.

The landlord was foremost, and seeing the predicament to which his excellent customer was reduced, he sprang towards John Gauntlet, with his fists vengefully clenched.

But John caught up the piece of iron the " beggar woman " had dropped, and handled it in a way that was a caution to rash belligerents.

" Let me out of this infernal den," he cried. " I ask no more. Stand clear all of you who have no wish for a broken head ! "

" But there's a score to settle yet, my man. Hi! gipsy, rouse up, my man ! He shan't escape ; wake up, and tell us what we shall do with him."

But Black Lutterloh was not asleep.

His violent fall had damaged his head somewhat, but this rough and ready blood-letting rather served to restore his senses than otherwise, and if he still lay where he had been thrown, it was only because he was all abroad as to what course to pursue.

What about the effect of the fatal drug that Mr. Phantom had provided him with ?

The grip with which the young farmer had grasped him was little like the grasp of one whose last hour was near. Had Mr. Phantom deceived him ?

In the midst of these bewildering reflections came the landlord's injunction for him to rouse up and say what vengeance should be dealt on his assailant.

By this time the room was quite filled with the noisy, drunken throng, who fully expected to see a glorious fight as soon as their friend the gipsy could be brought to the scratch.

Black Lutterloh, as he lay amid the wreck of the fender, had resolved that it would be better to quiet the uproar as speedily as possible.

" There ain't a-going to be no fight," he growled, as he scrambled to his feet ; " it was my own seeking, and I deserved what I got, so you can clear out as soon as you like."

" But —— me, Lutterloh ! you ain't such a cur as to let him off like that ?" said the amazed landlord.

" It was a fair stand-up fight, and— we won't say anything more about it."

He laid peculiar stress on the last words, glancing meaningly towards John Gauntlet the while.

And so he proceeded to slink out of the room, despite the taunts and jeers of the company.

" He deserves to be killed !" cried a voice in the mob—a shrill, piping voice—its owner could not be seen. " He deserves to be hanged ! Give him up to the police, somebody, and earn a hundred pounds."

" Aye !" " How's that ?" " Who is he ?" asked a dozen voices.

" John Gauntlet is his name, and he is wanted for the Monkshood murder !"

CHAPTER XXI.

AN UNWELCOME VISIT.

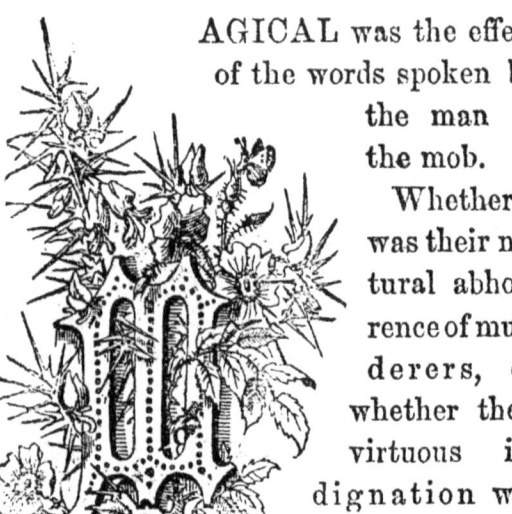

AGICAL was the effect of the words spoken by the man in the mob.

Whether it was their natural abhorrence of murderers, or whether their virtuous indignation was stimulated by visions of a hundred pounds reward, no man may say.

Anyhow, ere ten seconds had elapsed, John Gauntlet was beset and flung to the ground, and some tied his hands and legs, while others set off to find the police patrol.

Once only during that terrible scene had rash, heroic Nelly Blisset recovered her consciousness.

It was when the strange voice proclaimed aloud the fugitive's name, and the price that was set on his head.

Then, with a loud scream, she awoke, as it were, and flung her arms around him; but, on being torn from him, and rudely flung aside, she again relapsed into her former insensible condition.

But she was not entirely neglected.

Ere the two mounted constables the thirsters for blood money had fetched had dismounted at the door, a person in the crowd had taken compassion on helpless John Gauntlet's betrothed.

He had made friends with the landlord's wife (who, roused from her chamber by the tremendous uproar, came in with a dirty frilled nightcap on her head, and a greasy old dressing-gown slouched across her shoulders), and, drawing her aside, slipped a guinea into her hand.

"I'm a friend of the family—of *her* family, you understand, my dear madam," he whispered. "Wayward, infatuated young creature; she has run away from home to follow the fortunes of this scoundrel! Provide her a sleeping chamber, and—and keep her quite private and alone, you understand, for a day or two, and I will increase this little gift tenfold."

The woman replied with a grin of intelligence, and at once, assisted by her maid, bore unconscious Nelly Blisset away.

His voice was suspiciously like that which had proclaimed John Gauntlet a murderer.

And having seen his orders so far obeyed, he slunk away, chuckling to himself, and sawing his notched thumb-nail against his teeth.

*   *   *   *

Squire Reginald Vipert's London lodgings were at a fashionable hotel in St. James's Street.

Immediately after the occurrence of the murder of Joel Burke (on which swiftly followed Black Lutterloh's triumphant visit to the Hall), the Master of Monkshood hastened to town out of harm's way.

Not that he was a coward, physically speaking.

Lawless and unscrupulous as he was, when his wicked heart prompted, the blood of the bold Viperts ran in his veins, and in a matter of personal encounter he would give place to no man.

What he shrank from was the local scandal that common gossips would assuredly set afloat, and which his presence would only aggravate.

But he could not be but terribly anxious.

Deeper than ever he dived into the dissipations of the great city.

But neither wine nor dice could banish the forebodings that haunted him night and day.

Who was it that had murdered the gamekeeper?

If he was to believe popular rumour —nay, positive and undeniable evidence —the finger of guilt pointed straight at John Gauntlet, his enemy.

But the public, that was so unhesitating in the expression of its opinion against the man who had fled from justice, was not in the secret of Squire Vipert's bargain with Black Lutterloh.

Not that the gipsy ruffian had confessed to the deed.

The hundred pounds he had demanded and been paid, were not on account of any bargain he had made with the Master of Monkshood.

It was "hush money" on account of the "grey mask," and the terrible story that was attached to it.

Lutterloh insisted on this being distinctly understood when he accepted the money.

But in his heart, Reginald Vipert had no doubt as to who was the murderer, and this was his great dread and anxiety.

Should Gauntlet be taken and condemned to death, should he maintain silence to the end—the ghastly, dreadful end?

All day long he thought of this—of nights he dreamt of it.

Dreamt that the ghastly end was come, that the hangman's hand had drawn the bolt, and that John Gauntlet's dead and listless weight was swinging from the gallows.

Then he would wake in a sweat of terror, and resolve that, come what might, to-morrow he would take some step to rid his soul of the burden that tormented it.

But that "to-morrow" never came.

What step could he take that did not involve his own ruin?

Ruffian, thief, murderer, perhaps, as Lutterloh was, he, the handsome, gifted Master of Monkshood, did not dare to offend him.

Already he had discovered how unscrupulous the villain could be when provoked, and there could be no doubt that, if driven to it, he would turn and sting with all his might.

No; at present, at all events, Mr. Lutterloh must be let alone.

And was there nothing else that troubled Reginald Vipert?

Had the rude shock his vanity had received at the hands of the woman who had so strangely fascinated him, *quite* cured him of his unreasoning passion for her?

Could he have been asked the question, undoubtedly he would have replied "Yes;" adding, thanks to his lucky stars, that so abrupt and decided a termination had been put to his preposterous folly.

But this would have been only the testimony of his lips; his heart would have told a different story.

Her beauty, her gentleness, the tender beaming of her eyes, the thrilling touch of her hand—all were graven on his memory, and were not to be obliterated by the severe hands of policy and prudence.

She had despised him, struck him, and called him coward, but in this she had shown an amount of daring and audacity that in Reginald Vipert's eyes rather added to than diminished her attractions.

"Of course it is all over now," he repeated to himself a hundred times. "The gulf that hard fate has dug between us can never be bridged, and it would be madness to attempt to bridge it. But ah! what *might* have been? She could have saved me. I felt that she could, but she would not. Good God! was she mad to turn from a gentleman of blood and family—for that I am still, if nothing else, and cling to her devoted clodhopper? But she did it. She cast me off to drift down stream to the devil. I am a fool to waste a thought on her."

Nevertheless, he continued to think of her, and "what might have been;" which, of course, was very bad for John Gauntlet, and tended to harden the squire's heart's against him.

Such had been his unenviable condition of mind for a week or more, when one morning a visitor was announced, the servant handing in a card that bore an inscription, simple in itself, but which had an instantaneous and singular effect on the Master of Monkshood.

Lord Cecil Lavering!

Once, and once only before, had he made acquaintance with that name, and then in a manner less polite than on this occasion.

He had heard it bawled after him, as, wounded and faint, he sped away in the darkness of night on his good horse Fury.

"I'll hunt you down, as sure as my name is Lord Lavering!"

He had made no mention of that circumstance, even to the trustworthy Phantom, but he had never forgotten it.

"He has kept his word, it seems, curse him!" muttered Reginald Vipert through his white, close-set lips. "He's a rash man. What sort of a Daniel, I wonder, is he that ventures into the lion's den so unhesitatingly?"

Next moment Lord Lavering presented himself.

Squire Vipert uttered an involuntary sigh of relief as he beheld him.

On that dark night he had obtained but a dim and hasty view of his pursuer, and could form no idea of his size and appearance.

He had formed a conclusion from the

lord's bold threat, and pictured him in his mind as a broad-shouldered person, six feet high at least, and with a visage that bespoke stern determination.

When he beheld the stripling-like, almost effeminate young gentleman whose card had caused him such perturbation, his spirits revived.

Surely this could not be the emissary of anything very terrible?

"Mr. Reginald Vipert, I believe?" Lord Lavering remarked, bowing gracefully, but speaking in a tone that boded the serious nature of the business in hand.

"At Lord Lavering's service," replied Squire Vipert, returning the bow, and striving hard to appear quite unembarrassed and at his ease. "To what fortunate circumstance do I owe the honour of your lordship's visit?"

"To a series of circumstances, sir, that are not, I am afraid, altogether fortunate; that is to say, to all parties," said Lord Lavering, gravely. "You are recently from Monkshood, I believe, Mr. Vipert?"

"Exactly; and you?"

"From Newgate."

Squire Vipert started in genuine amazement, and regarded his visitor curiously.

The name of the grim prison sounded ominous in his ears, connected with that highway robbery business with which his mind was filled.

But he affected to make light of the matter.

"Not the most desirable of London abodes, my lord," said he, with a laugh. "Permit me to congratulate your lordship on your safe deliverance."

Lord Lavering's face flushed suddenly, and his blue eyes flashed angrily.

But he continued calmly, and without appearing to notice what the other said—

"From Newgate, Mr. Vipert, where lies, wrongfully accused of a heinous crime, as honest a fellow as ever lived."

Had not Reginald been so complete a master of himself, he must now have betrayed symptoms of his increasing alarm.

To what else could Lord Lavering allude except the highway robbery?

"I see plainly now how it is," the Master of Monkshood said to himself. "Some unfortunate wretch has been arrested for that precious business, and his lordship has found me out to redeem his threat. But the game is not played out yet."

Aloud, however, he remarked—

"Poor fellow! I'm sorry for him, but still, my dear lord, I am at a loss to understand how I am concerned in the fate of your interesting *protégé*. I hope that no one has misled you into believing that I am a philanthropist. I am ashamed to confess——"

"Mr. Vipert," interrupted Lord Lavering, his honest face glowing with indignation, "allow me to tell you that this levity, whether affected or real, is unbecoming a gentleman."

Squire Vipert drew himself up to his full height, and looked fierce, but the young lord fearlessly continued—

"Unbecoming a gentleman, I repeat; nay, I will go further, and say that your behaviour is unmanly and cruel, and disposes me to credit that which is laid to your charge, and which I hoped to find groundless."

Reginald Vipert's broad chest heaved, and his face turned deadly pale.

"Are you aware, sir, to whom and of what you are talking?" he exclaimed, rising from his chair, and gripping the back of it with both his hands, as though to hold them from doing mischief. "Are you quite sure, sir, that it was from a prison you came straight here, or was it from a madhouse?"

"Say from a madman, and you will be nigher the mark," returned Lord Lavering, bitterly. "I come from John Gauntlet, Mr. Vipert."

The sudden start that Reginald Vipert gave was real and not affected.

"From John Gauntlet!" he repeated; "from Newgate, and from John Gauntlet?"

"Surely it is not unknown to you that the poor fellow has been arrested, and lies there? You read the papers, I presume, sir?"

"Seldom, very seldom," returned the Master of Monkshood, his hectoring manner quite changed, and his voice agitated and subdued. "When —how was this?"

"Three days since. But it is not of him alone that I have come here to speak with you, but of another as well. Need I mention whom?"

"I am in ignorance until you inform me."

Lord Lavering shook his head incredulously.

"You play your part excellently well, Mr. Vipert," said he. "But let me tell you, knowing what I know, I must have some more substantial proof of your innocence than your bare denial to carry back to the heartbroken old couple, her parents. In a few words, where is Miss Ellen Blisset, Mr. Reginald Vipert?"

Magnificent, indeed, must have been the "acting" of the Master of Monkshood if the amazed face he now assumed was part of it.

"Miss Ellen Blisset!" he repeated. "I know not. In as few words, sir, as you ask the question, I answer it— upon my soul and conscience—I know not."

"You know not that she is missing from her home?"

"You have my answer, sir," replied Reginald Vipert, haughtily.

"I have heard your answer, Mr. Vipert; that is no answer," returned the young lord, resolutely. "You may not know the present hiding-place of the young lady, but your agent—the unscrupulous scoundrel in your pay—*he* knows. Is it upon your 'conscience?'"

And Lord Lavering eyed the other keenly.

"Is it upon your 'conscience' that you deny that, Mr. Vipert? Listen to me, sir.

"It was only since the disappearance of the young lady in question that I became acquainted with the story—the entire story of your unmanly behaviour —nay, your threatening gestures will not frighten me, Squire Vipert—your unmanly behaviour to the innocent girl who, in pure charity and gratitude, came to tend you in your sickness.

"This it was that aroused my suspicions that you might possibly be cognisant of her abduction, and set me on the right track for a clue to the mystery.

"That clue I have obtained, sir; and, on the word of a man, I will follow it to the end.

"You can assist me, and you *shall*. I have evidence—indisputable—that two days since your man, Phantom, caused her private removal in a coach at night from the wretched inn whither she had followed her unfortunate lover.

"Deny, if you can—once again on your 'conscience,' Mr. Vipert—that Mr. Phantom was thus acting in your service."

For several seconds Reginald Vipert was incapable of replying, so amazed was he at what he heard.

It sounded like a page from some extravagant romance.

Gauntlet in prison!

Nelly in the hands of Phantom!

He had not for three days heard from his faithful servant.

Then the intelligence was that "matters were in the same unsatisfactory condition."

What wonderful revolution had occurred so to change the whole aspect of affairs?

Lord Lavering, grown impatient at the other's prolonged silence, repeated his question.

"I ask you again, Mr. Vipert, do you deny that your man's dastardly behaviour, as regards Miss Blisset, was in accordance with your commands?"

"Since your own unprejudiced mind has settled the matter beforehand," sneered Mr. Vipert, "it is scarcely worth while to make you any answer; nevertheless, I may truthfully tell you that, supposing there to be any grounds for the monstrous story you bring me, I am no more concerned in it than yourself."

"You persist in denying that your confidential servant has not acted in this matter in your interest?"

This was a poser.

The strange news had fallen on the handsome young Master of Monkshood with such bewildering suddenness, that as yet he had not had a moment to resolve in his mind possibilities and motives, and this last question of Lord Lavering's opened his eyes.

What if Mr. Phantom—testy, eccentric, but devoted and ever faithful Joseph — *had* executed this daring manœuvre with the view of pleasing his master, whose feelings as regarded Nelly Blisset were, of course, no secret to him?

Such a movement was, undoubtedly, ill advised, preposterously rash, and full of danger, but if the stupid old fellow *had* done it in good faith, and with the unselfish motive of gratifying him, Squire Vipert, it would be too bad to betray and expose him.

At the same time it would never do for him to take such a villanous advantage of his man's unscrupulous doings.

Miss Blisset must be restored to her friends without delay.

Meanwhile, Lord Lavering, chafing with pent-up indignation, was awaiting an answer to his momentous question.

"Pray, sir," said he, "am I to interpret your silence as a confession of guilt ?"

"I have no desire to restrict your talent for interpretation, Lord Lavering," Reginald Vipert answered, coolly. "I can only say that it appears to me expedient to maintain for the present the silence I have observed as regards your last question. At least, you will admit that I am not answerable to *you* for my actions."

"Except so far as I may choose to call you to account for such of them as injure those who are my friends, and who are incapable of defending themselves," replied the brave little lord, his noble nature flashing in his honest blue eyes. "That, however, is a business to which that of greater importance must, for the time, give precedence."

"I shall not run away when your lordship does me the honour to call me out," returned Squire Vipert, his scornful eye taking measure of Lord Lavering's comparatively small stature.

"You decline, then, to give me any information concerning the matter that has brought me here ?"

"I have no information to give; that I solemnly swear, and I cannot help your incredulity," returned Reginald Vipert. "I promise you this, however," he presently continued; "I will cause inquiries to be made. As an

honourable man, I am bound so to do. If I find that my servant has really been guilty of this serious outrage, my best endeavours shall be used to remedy the wrong and secure his punishment. I wish you good morning, Lord Lavering."

"And when shall you set about making inquiries, may I ask, sir ?"

"Immediately. As soon as you leave me, I will at once write in such a way that Mr. Phantom will speedily get my letter, wherever he is."

"For the present, then, I will leave you, Mr. Vipert," replied Lord Lavering, sternly ; "but in twenty-four hours I will return here, to stay until I am satisfied."

And the young lord left the room.

As he approached the outer door, he saw a rough, flashily-dressed man, in angry altercation with the hall porter.

"My card ! What d'ye take me for ?" growled the hairy-faced fellow. "D'ye think I'm a shop-keepin' chap, wot's come to tout for orders ? Can't one gentleman wisit another without you pokin' your nose atween 'em ? I'm a-going up to him, I tell yer, and if yer likes yer can follow."

And up he went.

Possibly, had Lord Lavering known who he was, he would have prolonged his stay a little.

It was Mr. Richard Lutterloh !

CHAPTER XXII.

IN A SNARE.

DARING, desperate, love-crazed Mr. Phantom had made a venture, compared with which all he had hitherto done was mere trifling. A splendid opportunity had favoured him. That night, when, by a bold stroke of treachery, he secured the arrest of the man he hated more than anything else in the world, matters so tended that she for whom his miserable old heart yearned and ached so, fell into his power.

He could scarcely believe his rare luck.

He was in no way perplexed as to the miscarriage of his pretty poison scheme, the managing of which he had entrusted to Black Lutterloh.

He had heard the story of the "beggar woman" dashing out of the gipsy's hand the full ale-glass; and, though he was somewhat "fogged" as regards details, he shrewdly guessed how it came about that the potent pinch of white powder was wasted.

Not that he gave himself much trouble about that phase of the business.

It was sufficient for him that his chief enemy was in gaol, that his obliging though awkward-to-manage friend, Black Lutterloh, had taken himself off, and that his soul's idol was no longer unapproachable.

Sufficient! It was more than sufficient.

He reeled in the bewilderment of ecstasy as a man drunk with wine.

"Mine, mine, mine!" he almost cried aloud that night, or rather morning, as he walked away from the "Willow Weavers," after he had placed unconscious Nelly in the care of the hag attached to the establishment. "Mine, my captive! My sweet prisoner! I am her gaoler, ho, ho! her hard-hearted, relentless gaoler, and here is the key of her prison!"

And he drew from his pocket a well-filled purse, and for its precious sake, kissed it.

"I must walk, and keep on walking until I grow cool; until my brain ceases to throb so, and I may think, and design and plan," he continued, as, with his handkerchief, he wiped his perspiring brow (that was still adorned with Mr. Lutterloh's white hat). "Oh, Lord! it seems too good to be true! It's like one of those maddening dreams of her that have of late made my nights seasons of torture instead of rest. Mine! Mine to go back to this moment if I choose. Ha, ha, an old friend of the family ! An old gentleman whose heart is bowed in sorrow for the insane infatuation of the misguided young creature ! Yes, they would show me the room where they have placed her, and they would open her door ! Ho, ho ! different that, very different from crouching under a hedge like a homeless dog with no more comfort than the light in her window !"

How to take fullest advantage of his unexpected good fortune was the problem that occupied Mr. Phantom's teeming mind.

How to prolong to the farthest possible extent the bliss that had descended on him.

Could it be prolonged indefinitely ?

Ah ! that, indeed, would be a crowning glory !

"If I might only keep her in—well, in my power I suppose I might say, though it galls my heart even to *think* so harsh an expression against my tender darling ; if I might keep a hold on her as it were until it is all over— until this John Gauntlet sleeps in his quicklime bed within the gaol walls, then I might have more chance of winning her. Then she would be cast down ; ' broken-hearted' as fools say.

"She is a girl of spirit, and she would feel the shame of having been affianced to a fellow whose fit ending was the gallows. She would shun the scornful glances of all who knew her in the old time. She would be glad to flee to a strange land where her shame was unknown. Ah ! that would be my chance. Nelly and I, Mister and Mistress Phantom ! A new world, a

new life. A life of ceaseless, endless bliss !"

And so overpowering was the charming picture that Joseph Phantom gasped at the mere mental contemplation of it.

"It is keeping a hold on her until that fellow is disposed of that is the difficulty," he presently continued, with the manner of an injured man. "It may be weeks before he's condemned to death, curse him !

"If I could get over that difficulty all might go smoothly. I have money enough, and if I haven't, I know quite enough of my dear master's business to enable me to put the screw on him to the extent of a thousand or two. I'd do it. I'd make every sacrifice. I'll tell her so, and her dear heart shall be melted towards me in gratitude.

"I'll kneel at her feet and I'll say, ' others may slight and despise you, Miss Blisset, but in me you behold your devoted slave. My love for my country, my regard for the master I have served so long, all counts as nothing compared with my eagerness to serve you. I have money enough for the world's luxuries as well as its necessities. Then fly with me to foreign climes and pillow your aching head, your darling, your pretty curly head on this bosom."

And in his delirious enthusiasm the bow-shouldered, bow-shanked old dotard smote the said "bosom" with such reckless energy that an immediate and alarming fit of coughing was the result, causing him to lean panting and wheezing against the wall for ten minutes at least.

"THE FIGURE ON THE PRISON STEPS WAS THAT OF NELLY BLISSET."—(See page 225.)

True to his insane purpose, he was back at the "Willow Weavers" next morning, bright and early, more fully determined than ever on carrying it out.

But he encountered a check at the very threshold.

The young woman was ill, the landlady declared.

"We didn't fetch a doctor as we didn't know what your feelin's might be on that subject," said the old crone, with a profoundly respectful courtesy (the origin of which was that further sum of nine pounds that Mr. Phantom had promised).

Mr. Phantom was much agitated at the news.

"What are the symptoms that afflict the poor young creature?" he dolefully asked.

"Not good uns," replied the woman. "Queer in her head she seems, and feverish like."

"Not raving, I hope?"

"Oh, no; on the contrary; sort of dejected, don't-care-what-becomes-of-me fit she seems to have on her," replied the vulgar hag, with a knowing leer at her liberal customer; "but perhaps you mightn't feel so much alarmed at them there symptoms as— as a stranger."

Mr. Phantom looked at the woman with a startled, guilty face, and then answered, in some confusion—

"Not so much alarmed as a stranger! Exactly. Quite so. You mean to say, my dear madam, that being a friend of the family—a very old friend—I might have seen this sort of thing in the poor misguided young creature before? Well, yes, I have. As a medical man, many such cases have come under my notice, I assure you, ma'am."

"What's the treatment you prescribe for such cases when you meet with 'em, doctor?" the shrewd landlady of the "Willow Weavers" asked, with a grin that made Mr. Phantom feel anything but comfortable.

"Quiet, quiet, above all things," he replied, with a bland smile, that was intended to look professional, while all the time he was inwardly chafing at the woman's intrusive impudence.

"Yes, quiet; but not that above all things," she remarked, eyeing him steadily. "Shall I tell you what else you—as a medical man, of course—would prescribe for your pretty young patient?—and pretty she is, there is no mistake about that. I've seen a many beauties in my time; he! he! I was a beauty myself one time, doctor, though it would take more skill than you possess to discover a trace of it now. But I never met with a more charming——"

"Keep to the point, if you please, madam," Mr. Phantom interrupted, impatiently. "What else is it besides quiet that I would prescribe for the —the young person in whom I take a fatherly interest?"

"Seclusion!" answered the woman, boldly.

"Seclusion!" he repeated, quite taken off his guard by the chuckling old hag's shrewd guess, if guess it was.

"Aye, my good sir; am I wrong or right?" she asked, quietly.

Mr. Phantom was puzzled, not so much by the woman's words as by the peculiar meaning her utterance invested them with.

Could it be possible that she had an inkling of his real design?

If so, would she be willing to assist him?

Possibly.

"I should first like to know if you ask the question in idle curiosity or with any——"

"We do nothing in idle curiosity here," the crone interrupted him. "We are business people, doctor, and always ready to render a pound's worth of help for a pound. Now d'ye understand?"

"Not quite," Mr. Phantom replied, shaking his head, but with a gradually dawning perception of what was meant. "Say on."

"Before I say on, you must do two things."

"What are they?"

"Pay me the nine pounds you promised me. There's nothing like squaring accounts as we go."

Joseph Phantom placed in her hands a ten-pound note.

"What next?" he asked.

"You must answer the question I before put to you. Is seclusion one of the means of cure you would adopt towards your pretty patient?"

"What if I reply yes?"

"Perfect seclusion, where she will be safe from the worries of everybody, of her friends, of her parents, if she has any, eh, doctor dear?"

"Seclusion *is* seclusion, madam," answered Mr. Phantom, evasively.

"A nice, snug, quiet place, where nothing will happen to disturb her mind or distract her attention from the good counsels her kind doctor gives her?"

"Well! well! well!"

"Well, where will you find such a place?—*that's* the question."

And the hideous old crone chafed her hooked nose with the folded bank note, while her beady eyes twinkled wickedly.

Mr. Phantom found it difficult any longer to control his temper.

"Confound you and your 'questions!'" he exclaimed. "What's the use of 'em without answers?"

"The answer is not far off, doctor. Have a little patience. Recollect that you are not neglecting your patient while you are talking with me. We are holding a consultation for her good, eh, doctor?—for her good. I ask you where will you find such a place, and you can't tell me. But is that the end of it?"

"How?"

"Did I not tell you that we were people of business, and ever ready to render a pound's worth of service for a pound—to stretch a point, to serve a liberal paymaster?" the hag whispered meaningly, bringing her wrinkled face close to Mr. Phantom's, that he might not miss the important words.

He felt that he was on dangerous ground, and must proceed cautiously.

"You have not found me illiberal," said he.

"It is on that account that I deal with you so openly," the old woman replied. "Listen. Your patient, he, he!—we will call you 'doctor' and 'patient'—cannot stay here. We have no convenience for lady lodgers, more especially for lady lodgers who might grow dissatisfied with their lodging, and cry and make a fuss about being sent home. But I think I know of an abode that would be found suitable. It is far from here, six—eight miles. Not a mansion, but beautifully situated, not another house near it for half-a-mile. Just the place for a sick person, whose recovery depended on quiet and repose."

Mr. Phantom stared at the woman, too bewildered to speak.

Could it be true that such a wonderful and unexpected stroke of fortune could befall him?

If the days of the genii had returned, and he had sold his soul for the means of gratifying his basest wish, which was to have lovely Nelly Blisset to be his wife, he could hardly have asked for more favouring facilities.

"Who—who at present occupies the house you speak of?" he presently inquired, stammering with excitement.

"It is unoccupied, doctor dear, at present," replied the old woman, delighted to see that he was nibbling at the bait with a relish that betokened that he would presently swallow it; "but there is good furniture there, and fuel in store, and it might soon be made cosy and comfortable."

"But, if I accept your offer, and, for the poor lassie's sake, I am half resolved to," he replied, "I should require someone to be with her to watch and attend to her constantly. The house you speak of would not be of the least value to me without a house-keeper."

"Now we have got as far as talking about housekeepers, we must talk about wages," chuckled the ugly old witch. "I'll take the situation, if the pay is reasonable. How much, doctor dear—how much?"

"That would depend on much that cannot at present be considered," replied Joseph Phantom, who felt such a throbbing at the heart and brain as to be for the present quite unequal to bargain driving. "You will not find me a stingy employer if you serve me faithfully, and, before all, if you manage this delicate business in a manner that shall not in the least shock or offend the poor young lady, in whose welfare I am so deeply interested. That, of all things, must be guarded against, remember."

And Mr. Phantom laid his hand on the woman's arm impressively.

"I'll be as tender towards her as though she was my own baby," remarked the old woman, as her greedy eyes followed her strange customer's promising handling of his pocketbook.

"Here is another ten-pound note," said he, "and let me find her comfortably installed in the house you speak of by this time to-morrow. Let me hear from her own lips that your behaviour towards her has been in every way proper and respectful, and two other notes of like value shall be yours."

It is a bargain," replied the hideous old creature, snatching at the proffered bank note, and thrusting it, with the other, into the bosom of her gown. "Will you see her before you go now?"

Joseph Phantom reflected for a few moments.

The temptation was hard, indeed, to resist.

But then there was a chance that he might mar the pretty scheme that was so fraught with promise, and he conquered his fierce yearning.

"I think not," he made answer, with a sigh. "The sight of me—an old intimate of her home and family, my dear madam—might cause her distress, and just now she must be subjected to as little excitement as possible. Pray bear that in mind in removing her. I have not asked you how you propose accomplishing that difficult matter without causing her alarm, but I presume——"

"Set your mind easy on that score, my good sir," chuckled the beldam. "It is all planned and arranged in my mind, and its execution is as easy as fitting on an old glove. It shall be done so adroitly, that she shall know nothing about it until she wakes and finds herself there."

Then, after making careful note in his pocket-book as to the exact whereabouts of the low house to which hapless Nelly Blisset was to be conveyed, crafty Joseph Phantom took his departure.

Was he happy?

To judge from his strange antics, as he hurried down the road to catch the coach that would take him to Monkshood (where he had yet certain arrangements to make before he quitted for ever the home in which he had passed so many years of his adventurous life), one might have supposed so.

He chuckled until his hard, thin mouth widened like that of a hungry pike; he nibbled his notched nails, he snapped his fingers, he almost danced with the exultation that set his blood tingling so.

"Mine, mine, mine!" he repeated. "A splendid chance. Ha! ha! only that I know better, I might almost imagine that Providence had ordained it so. That our—Nelly's and mine—our marriage is one of those heaven-ordained affairs that one reads about in good books. But what matter *how* ordained, so long as it comes to pass—as it must, as it *shall!* What matters it to me if it be heaven-ordained or——"

And the infatuated old dotard, grinning like an ape, supplied the hiatus by snapping his fingers and thumb over his left shoulder.

"Now I can show her my real nature," he went on, muttering to himself. "I can overwhelm her with a sense of my generosity, my magnanimity, my honest, heartfelt passion. I can say to her, 'My angel, my love, my peerless little queen! we are here alone, and you are helpless in my hands. But my noble soul disdains to be satisfied with any arbitrary exactions. Still I am your kneeling slave, humbly suing for your compassion, for your pity—for just a little corner in your gentle heart, in which I may plant my love and tend it faithfully, constantly, until it grows so big that you must acknowledge it, and say, Joseph, my Joseph, I am thine; thine to love, honour and obey, as long as we both shall live!'

"We shall see! we shall see! To-morrow! Good Lord! what would I not give if I might strangle the intervening hours, and call to-morrow mine this moment!"

True to his promise, Lord Lavering waited on Reginald Vipert at the hour appointed.

He came not alone.

It was not a police-officer who accompanied him, but an individual no less formidable as regards intent and determination, though much more harmless in appearance.

Miss Nan Blisset!

No longer gay, laughing Nan of the old time, ere Mr. Phantom's black spite flapped its wings over the mill-house and the mill, but Nelly's staunch sister.

She had cried all her tears long ago, and there she was, dry-eyed, pale and resolute, with but one aim—the discovery of Nelly, and the punishment of those who had so cruelly wronged her.

Mr. Vipert was at home.

"The coward!" Nan had said. "We will go, but it will be our journey in vain. Expecting us, or rather you, Lord Lavering, he will not dare face us. He will seek safety in flight—join his confederate and agent, in all probability!"

And, as Nan uttered these last words, her eyes flashed, and she clenched her little fist in a way that would have made the cause of her emotion somewhat uncomfortable could he have beheld it.

But, to the surprise of Lord Lavering and his fair companion, Reginald Vipert had not taken flight.

He had just concluded breakfast when his visitors were ushered into his apartment, and he received them with cold politeness, and it was only by a momentary elevation of his eyebrows that his surprise at Miss Nan Blisset's appearance was made manifest.

Squire Vipert had not improved in personal appearance since the reader last beheld him.

Despite his desperate endeavour to appear possessed of that amount of ease and self-confidence that was common to him, it was, at a glance, evident that he wore the mask but with difficulty.

He was pale and haggard-looking, as is a man who has passed a long day of anxiety, followed by a sleepless night.

Such, indeed, had been the case.

As already intimated, his interview yesterday morning had been almost instantly followed by one with Black Lutterloh.

What was the exact nature of it need not here be discussed.

It was stormy.

The gipsy's great rough voice was heard by listening waiters; his mysterious threats and his big oaths; but, failing to find grounds for any other conclusion, they set it down that it was some prize-fighting ruffian, who had been hired to do some dirty work, and was dissatisfied with the terms of remuneration.

That, perhaps, was the reason why they left him a clear gangway, as, after the brief, hot altercation, he came striding down the stairs still muttering vengeance.

The fact is, Mr. Lutterloh had been not a little disappointed at his reception.

Full of the conviction that Mr. Phantom had put a trick on him, in the matter of the sleeping powder with which he had provided him to drop into unfortunate John Gauntlet's beer, he had, after due consideration, resolved to pay a visit to the Master of Monkshood (whose town lodgings he had made it his business to discover), with a view to seeking some explanation, and, perhaps, to " putting the screw on " as well, to the extent of fifty pounds or so.

To his amazement, however, he found the man he made so sure was at his mercy, fierce and defiant.

Lord Lavering's visit had roused the squire's anger to boiling point, and he did not hesitate, rash as the proceeding was, to give it vent at the earliest opportunity.

Before Lutterloh could open his mouth, the squire rose from his chair, white with fury, demanding how he, the big gipsy, dare dog him to his private lodgings, and bade him take himself off instantly, and remember that the servants would at once receive orders to thrust him out of doors should he think fit to venture on another visit.

And Lutterloh, waiting just long enough to blurt out a perplexing and inexplicable rigmarole about John Gauntlet and " the girl disguised as a tramp," and " that infernal scoundrel, Phantom, who was at the bottom of it all," took his departure, with a malicious shake of his enormous fist and a vague declaration that if he wasn't seen there again, he would very shortly be " heard of."

Squire Vipert had dispatched a hurried note by a mounted messenger to Monkshood; but he had returned with the strange intelligence that Mr Phantom had not been seen for two nights and a day.

No wonder, then, that he was ill at ease, that he felt disposed to defiance rather than conciliation.

" I need not remind you, sir, of the purport of my visit here," Lord Lavering remarked, calmly.

" I am fully aware of it, Lord Lavering, and of its disagreeable nature," returned the Master of Monkshood, peevishly. " We will get it over as speedily as possible, if you please; though I doubt if the assistance of a third party will materially tend to expedite matters."

And he savagely regarded Nan, who bit her lip and turned her face from him.

" At what point shall we begin, my lord ?"

" At the point at which we left off, sir. What have you done with this lady's sister ?"

" Before I reply I must make a stipulation."

Lord Lavering bowed.

" I am a gentleman, Lord Lavering, and my word is my bond of honour. You must accept my answer, brief and unsatisfactory as it may be, without presuming to doubt it, without subjecting me to the annoyance and indignity of cross-examination, such as it was your good taste to inflict on me on the occasion of your last visit."

Lord Lavering again bowed, but said nothing.

" Once for all, then, I know nothing of the lady in whom, it seems, in common with other members of her family "—here, with sneering polite-ness, he saluted Nan—"your lordship takes such kindly interest. I repeat that I know nothing of Miss Ellen Blisset's movements, or of the reasons that actuated her in leaving her father's house in the questionable manner she did. You would probably meet with better success if your lordship applied to that other object of your tender com-miseration, the man who is lying in Newgate, and who will probably be hanged for murdering a servant of mine."

In his irritable mood, he spoke the cruel words sneeringly and with spiteful emphasis.

But the next moment he had reason to repent his temerity.

The slender walking cane that Lord Lavering had brought in with him was lying on the table, and, goaded to fury at hearing her sister so lightly spoken of, Nan Blisset sprang at it, and before Lord Lavering could raise a hand to prevent her, she dealt at Reginald Vipert a stinging cut with it fair across his face.

"Miserable coward!" cried Nan; "highwayman in the cloak of a gentle-man! Let that make you remember when, in the presence of her sister, you dared sneer at the fair fame of a virtuous woman."

As for Lord Lavering, as soon as he recovered from his momentary amaze-ment, he gallantly stepped before Nelly's champion, and addressing the assaulted gentleman, exclaimed—

"Mr. Vipert, I regret that a lady should have so served you. I regret she should have been before me in administering that punishment you so justly merited. Will you kindly there-fore accept that livid mark of her dis-approbation as from me, and permit me to bear the consequences?"

A livid mark, indeed; a weal of greyish blue, extending from his eye to his chin, as the mirror on the wall plainly reflected; but he felt nothing of it.

He heard nothing of the latter part of Nan Blisset's remark to him, and he had but a confused idea of what it was that Lord Lavering said to him.

His faculties of hearing, of feeling, of speaking, seemed all to have been paralyzed and brought to a standstill by the words that Nelly Blisset's sister had given utterance to—"Highwayman in the cloak of a gentleman!"

Who had betrayed him?

Had anyone, or was this a mere random shaft shot by a passionate, sus-picious woman?

It struck home anyhow.

He felt his lips blanch, and his very knees tremble; still there was a chance —a small one, in his favour; anyhow, nothing would be lost by putting a bold face on the matter.

"This is no place for vulgar brawl-ing," said he, addressing Lord Laver-ing, in a quivering voice. "Did I choose to take up the gauntlet you have so chivalrously thrown down, I have strength enough, young gentleman, to fling you through the panels of yon door without the trouble of opening it; but I have self-respect enough to control the impulse, and will content myself with placing you before a police magis-trate. Will you voluntarily relieve me of your presence, and take this objectionable female with you, or shall I ring for assistance?"

"Ring, *if you dare*, Mr. Vipert," said Lord Lavering, coolly.

"If I dare!"

"Aye; you are very big and very strong, Squire Vipert," Nan exclaimed. "Making allowance for your still weak shoulder, your vaunting of being able to throw one through the door evinces that, however cowardly you may feel at liberty to act towards weak women, you think it judicious to display some courage towards your own sex. Or is it mere ruffianly bravado, Squire Vipert, such as enabled you so successfully to enact the part of highwayman and robber in Shrouder's Gap?"

There was no mistaking such language as this.

The bold face was a sad mockery now, and he was fain to turn it away in almost abject terror.

Nevertheless he essayed it.

"It is false," he exclaimed, furiously; "a base calumny! A monstrous outrage, of a piece with that you pair of conspirators have already inflicted on me. But you shall not make such villanous assertions with impunity, my Lord Lavering! You shall be put to the proof, if there is in England justice for a gentleman."

"Would you like me to produce proof, sir?" Lord Lavering asked, sternly. "Would you like to see it now and alone, or would you prefer to call up witnesses?"

"The proof! the proof!" exclaimed the Master of Monkshood, hoarsely. "Show it me."

"Do you know this?"

And, as he spoke, Lord Lavering produced and held up to Mr. Vipert's appalled gaze *the grey mask!*

"And do you recognise this, Squire Vipert?"

This time it was a piece of money.

The blood-stained crown piece that Reginald Vipert had given to Black Lutterloh on the night of the highway robbery, and which that cunning individual had so carefully preserved, first baking on it by his stable lantern the blood with which it was smeared.

He knew the piece of money again; Black Lutterloh had produced it for his edification on the occasion of his making his first demand for hush money.

It was terrible to see Mr. Vipert's face now.

For several seconds he stood speechless and ghastly pale, his handsome features distorted by passion, as well as by the cruel brand that Nan's avenging hand had set on them.

Then he broke into a loud, strange laugh.

"You have kept your word, Lord Lavering!" he bitterly exclaimed; "but I hope yet to escape the unpleasant termination to my existence that you promised me."

As he spoke, he rapidly unlocked a drawer and produced therefrom a pistol of elegant and perfect make.

At sight of it, Nan screamed, and clung to Lord Lavering, who, apprehending mischief, made a spring towards the Master of Monkshood.

"Nay," said he, with terrible calmness, "you need not fear; there is but one bullet in the barrel, and I am selfish enough to require its entire service. You will do no good in raising an out-cry, or in attempting to baulk me; you will only by a few minutes hurry my exit from a world I dare no longer face, and deprive me of the last satisfaction I shall ever experience. I wish you to take a message to Miss Blisset, where-ever you may find her, though where that may be, perhaps you will not be-lieve me when I say, I know no more than yourselves. Tell her that the mad folly of that night had its origin, neither in spite nor malice, but in love for her. Tell her that however much my acts may have led to her despising me, that on her account I have suffered such torments that even she would have spared me. Tell her, Lord Laver-ing, that I died saying, God bless her! and begging her forgiveness."

And having said so much, he made a hasty move towards his head with the capped and loaded pistol.

But Lord Lavering, active and agile, was too quick for him.

With a swift leap he cleared fully twelve feet of space that parted him from the would-be suicide, as Reginald Vipert's finger pressed the trigger, dashed the weapon aside, the bullet with which it was loaded ploughing a crimson skin mark along his temple, and then taking upward flight.

With a cry of affright, Nan fainted outright, while Reginald Vipert re-mained speechless and staring straight before him, stunned and stupefied.

"Thank God, rash man, for your life so miraculously spared," exclaimed Lord Lavering, sternly, as he wrenched the still smoking pistol from the other's grasp.

The words seemed to awaken Vipert to consciousness, and he made a des-perate endeavour to reach the drawer from which he had taken the weapon, and wherein in all probability its com-panion still reposed.

But again Lord Lavering was too quick for him.

By a dexterous movement he locked the drawer and secured the key.

"Rouse yourself from this madness," exclaimed Lord Lavering. "Why should you destroy your life that, at least, may be profitably saved, so that you may make amends for the wrong you have done? You declare that it was your rash, desperate love for this poor girl that induced you to act so outrageously. Prove it by your actions, Mr. Vipert. Listen. Your secret is safe with me—with us; I promise it. Aid us in rescuing her, and the past shall be forgotten. For *her* sake I beg —I implore you!"

Reginald Vipert answered not a word.

Like a man rescued unexpectedly from some deadly peril, he staggered to a chair, and hid his face in his open hands, while Lord Lavering busied himself in restoring Nan to conscious-ness.

At that critical moment there came a tap at the door, very much to Lord Lavering's embarrassment, as Nan Blisset, nearly restored, lay with her head on his shoulder, and his hand grasping hers in what at the very least deserved to be called brotherly solicitude.

Mr. Vipert was disturbed too.

"Who is there?" he asked.

"The post is just in, sir. Here is a letter for you."

Muttering impatiently, the Master of Monkshood opened the door, and took the letter from the man.

He glanced at the superscription, and in his amazement, exclaimed aloud—"From Mr. Phantom!"

CHAPTER XXIII.

A TERRIFYING PROPOSAL.

THE man with the notched nails was progressing to his heart's content with the desperately difficult affair he had been mad enough to engage in.

The hostess of the "Willow Weavers" had performed her part with a caution and fidelity that so pleased "the doctor," that an extra five pounds was placed in her hands in addition to the twenty pounds.

It was money easily earned.

Since her violent separation from poor John, after all she had dared and done in his behalf, Nelly's manner had strangely altered.

The hope that had warmed her heart seemed to have burnt out within her, black, brooding despair rising from its ashes.

She appeared crushed, utterly dejected, and heedless of what was passing around her.

The room to which the woman conveyed her was at the back part, and was at the top of the house, a meanly-furnished little place, and not particularly clean, but of these trivialities heart-broken Nelly Blisset seemed not even aware.

She did not even appear to be aware that she was a prisoner.

She had lost her love, and with him she had lost all the world, and what mattered to her where she sat and grieved?

So she passed the remainder of that terrible night, eating nothing, drinking nothing, and with no inclination for sleep, despite her long and tedious journey through the night, along the miry roads from Monkshood to that part of the country where the "Willow Weavers" stood.

All night she so sat, and through the greater part of the day following, and then came the old woman of the house, sympathetic and solicitous, with some mulled wine.

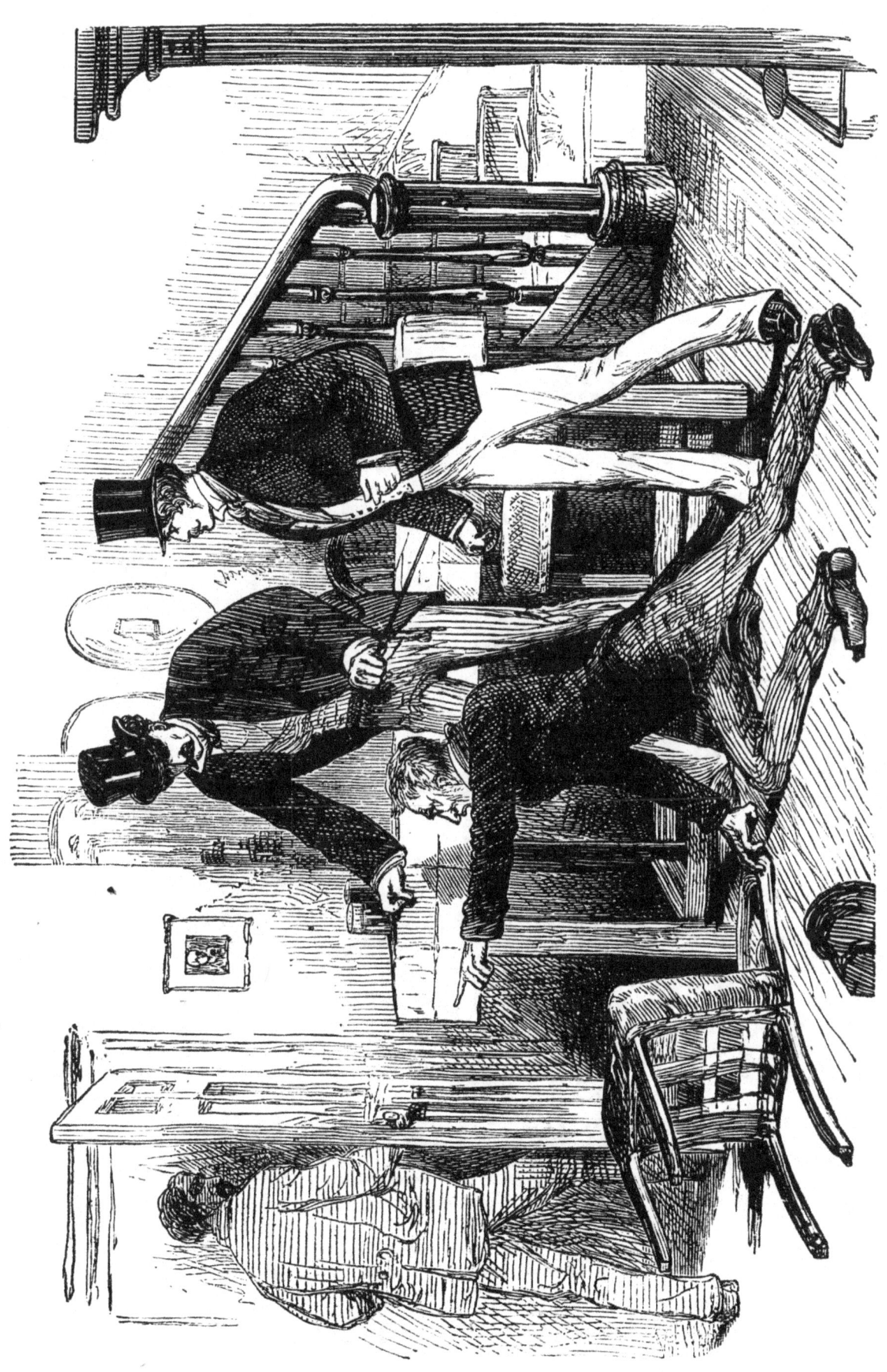

"POISONED."—(See page 245.)

"Take just a little, deary—just a sip for his sake, you know."

"For his sake? Is he coming here, then? Is he coming back? Did he say so?" inquired poor Nelly, passing her hand across her forehead in a bewildered, distraught way.

"Aye, did he, indeed. Be easy, child; take this sip of comfort, and then you will have heart to bear the good news I have come to tell you of him."

Almost mechanically Nelly Blisset took the proffered glass from the old woman, and drank of its warm and comforting contents.

Almost immediately she sank into a deep sleep.

When she awoke she could scarcely have been more amazed had she died and entered another world.

The bare walls on which she had closed her eyes had vanished.

The shabby old furniture had grown trim and neat, white curtains hung at the window—white almost as those of that dear little room over the porch at the mill-house—the window from which she had on that memorable night caught sight of her dear betrothed, footsore and weary, and utterly empty of heart, except for her.

She was lying, carefully covered over, on a comfortable couch, and in the grate a cheerful fire was burning.

Long as her sleep had been, she seemed not in the least refreshed, however. Her temples throbbed, and her eyes were heavy.

Her heart, too, was heavy, and her first act on returning to consciousness was to give way to an outburst of grief —helpless as that of a sick child.

Her nerves seemed benumbed, and her energies paralysed.

All she could do was to lie there sobbing, with her face to the pillow, crying—

"Lost! lost! lost!"

Suddenly she heard the door softly open, and, bearing in mind the old woman's promise, that "he was coming back," with her mind filled with thoughts of him and nothing else, she started up with a little scream, crying out his name—

"John, my darling! my——"

No more.

Not a syllable, or the least particle of one.

The endearing words seemed to freeze on her lips, and she could do no more than stare dumbly and aghast at the figure in the doorway.

It was not John Gauntlet.

It was Joseph Phantom!

She had not once seen him since she had made that last visit to the Hall in hopes of hearing news of her poor lost boy; for she could not banish from her mind the suspicion that Mr. Vipert's confidential man knew more than he chose to reveal.

But, as on every previous occasion, she came disconsolate away.

Mr. Phantom had as yet discovered nothing, despite his desperate anxiety to relieve the distress of his dear young friend, whose sobs and tears wrung his heart to its core!

And then the poor love-tortured death's-head squeezed her cold little hand in his own shaking, burning hot paw, and once again imprinted his fatherly kiss on her aching forehead.

Words are unequal to describe what the brave girl suffered in giving countenance to Mr. Phantom's displays of paternal solicitude.

But it was all for John's sake.

She would rather that Mr. Phantom had smote her on the forehead than kissed her there, but in hope that good to *him*, her lost, far away darling, might somehow come of the favour of the man with the notched nails, she had, with heroic resignation, submitted to the more painful infliction.

She had seen him since.

So entirely had her thoughts been occupied otherwise that she had scarcely once thought of him, and there he stood before her, in that strange place.

Joseph had done his best to make himself presentable to a lady.

He was attired in his very best suit of black, and his frilled shirt was spotless, and he wore between the frills diamond studs of a value that spoke highly of his " saving " propensities as a dependant.

Across the breast of his black waistcoat a magnificent gold watch chain was festooned, and on at least three of his bony, pale fingers glistened rings of worth.

Could he only have worn his head in some sort of bag or other covering, he might have passed muster as a respectable and eligible gentleman ; but there was his face, his hideous white face, wrinkled with years, and nervously twitching, despite the winning smile in which he essayed to wreath it; and, at sight of it, all the rest of the man was cast in the shade and forgotten.

Purring with his hands, and treading soft as the craftiest of mousers, Joseph stepped into the room, and closed the door behind him.

Nelly was the first to break the silence.

" Where am I ?" she indignantly inquired, as she rose from the couch and confronted him. " How dare you, sir, enter a room in which I am, unbidden ?"

Old Phantom made his meekest, his most humble bow.

" I must crave your pardon, Miss Blisset," said he, in a husky voice. " I am here, but *not* unbidden."

Instantly Nelly's manner changed.

If he was there not unbidden, who had bid him come ?

Who but John ?

And, with her eyes flashing in expectancy, she advanced towards him with her hand extended in welcome.

" It is I who should apologize," said she. " You were bidden to come. You bring me a message from him. Tell it me quick ! Tell me the glad news in one short word, if you can, in one little word ; say he is free."

But Joseph Phantom would rather the tip of his tongue were burnt off than utter any such cursed little word.

He compromised the matter, however, by taking her offered hand, and retaining it within his own.

" Not quite so, Miss Blisset, not *exactly* so, Ellen—Nelly—poor, sweet, suffering Nell ! Nay, start not at so simple a word of sympathy. It is in our contract of friendship, remember, that I—for old, *old* acquaintance sake " (he laid bitter stress on the word) " might call you Nelly. Have I since that time forfeited your esteem, Nelly? The Lord only knows what I have suffered to retain it; nay, to increase it!"

And earnest enough were the last words that the poor old dotard uttered.

Little beads of perspiration broke out on his bald pate at the bare recollection of his sufferings.

"You have not yet answered me," remarked Nelly, evasively, and with her heart sinking woefully to the depths of despair again; "who was it that sent you here, and what may be your purpose in coming?"

This was coming to the point with a vengeance.

Still holding her hand, Mr. Phantom cleared his husky throat, and moistened his dry lips ere he replied—

"You ask me two questions, Miss Blisset, and you couple them together as though they might both be answered in a breath; but that cannot be. Even the first one, had you the patience —the pity to listen, might well occupy a full hour in the answering. Who was it that sent me here? I must tell you, even though your scornful laughter should wither to death the feeble hope that burns within my bosom. Listen, Nelly, my angel, my goddess, my soul's torment, it is love that sent me here!"

And as he uttered the dreadful words his emotion bore him down to his knees before her; and he still held her hand.

Nelly answered not a word, but stood, her lips and cheeks blanching whiter each moment, her eyes flashing.

"Oh, pity me! pity me!" he moaned, bowing his grey head to her imprisoned hand. "I repeat it—it is love that sent me, that drove me here, that urged me here with stings and cruel pains that would have been unbearable but for the desperate—nay, I will admit the mad hope that the story of my anguish might excite your commiseration.

"It is true that I am no longer young; maybe I lack those fleeting and effervescent attractions of youth that captivate the giddy and inexperienced, but my heart is fresh and green, dear Nelly. It is an untried heart" (he regarded her narrowly. Had she ever heard the story of his passion for her mother?); "a heart that in its jealous retirement has been ripening and not withering. Ripening for you, sweet Nelly, ripening for you!"

Still she spoke not a word.

She shivered, but that may have been at the sound of the shrill wind blowing over the heath.

"I have wealth, sweet Nell," continued the anxious Joseph, warming with his suit, and venturing to press his lips against her imprisoned fingers.

"I have money enough to last us as long as I shall live, with enough left for you afterwards, ample, ample! I don't ask you to love me, at first, that is, I only ask you to take pity on me. We both have our sorrow, sweet Nelly, and in the peaceful retirement of a foreign land we would console each other. Say that you will be mine, darling Nell, my wife, my heart's delight. Say so, and let us fly to a more friendly shore, where the finger of scorn will not be levelled at the hapless victim of another's crime. Where——"

But he got no further.

Snatching her hand from him with a sudden impetuosity that nearly caused him to measure his length on the floor, Nelly passionately exclaimed—

"Treacherous, unmanly villain! How dare you address yourself to me in language that, for your life's sake, you would shrink from giving utterance to did you not deem me helpless to resent it?

"But you are mistaken in me, old man. Did I not already abhor, nay, loathe you, your dastardly insinuation against one for whose dear sake I would willingly give my life, would make me turn from you as from a venomous viper. Let me leave this place instantly. My terror for his safety has well-nigh bereft me of reason; but now I am fully alive to your dastardly machinations.

"I know not this place, to which you have caused me to be brought without my knowledge. I will not stay another moment. I will find my way to his prison, and beg and implore at its gate till they let me see him, that I may warn him against his worst enemy. Let me go, I say, Mr. Phantom, and beware that you drive not a desperate woman to madness."

It was no longer grief-stricken, weak Nelly Blisset who spoke.

What she could be when roused, has already been shown.

Very much indeed did Joseph Phantom resemble the venomous viper to which she had likened him, as he rose, shaking, and white with fury.

But with a prodigious effort he con-trived to speak with some degree of calmness.

"I am not surprised," he exclaimed, with a ghastly attempt at smiling, "I could scarcely hope that you would at once lend a willing ear to my humble appeal.

"You would have been lacking one of—one of the noble qualities for which my soul adores you, had you tamely yielded to me the treasure that has so long been in another's keeping. But I am not an impatient man, Miss Blisset, dear Nelly! more charming in your pretty fury than when you are passive; I am not an arbitrary man, and will make no harsh use of my power."

"Your power?"

"Aye, my maddening love for you, sweet Nelly, has instigated me to take such cautious means ere I ventured to lay siege to that obdurate citadel, your heart, that I am not likely to be scared by your outspoken simple denial of my suing. My sudden proposition has excited you, my soul's idol. I will leave you awhile, until you grow calmer. I can wait. Pray do not distress yourself by hurry. *You are perfectly secure here.*"

And as with emphasis he uttered these last words, his true devil nature peeped out from the mask of hypocrisy it was his study to wear.

Nelly's heart sank within her.

There was a bell-pull by the fireplace, and hurrying to it, she grasped it.

It fell soundless at her feet.

Rushing to the window, she essayed to raise it.

It was fast secured with big nails!

She looked outward, and the tops of the tall trees were below her.

It was Joseph Phantom's low, chuckling laugh that roused her from the stupor that these ominous discoveries caused her.

"Safely caged, you see, my pretty dove, safely caged," said he; "but only until such time as you promise not to fly away from me. It was the terrible dread that you might do so as soon as you heard my avowal that made me take such safe precautions.

"There is no other house within half a mile of this, and but one servant, who is in my pay. See now to what desperate measures pure, unselfish love drives a man! But my enchanter has the keys of her prison in her own keeping.

"She has but to say—'Joseph Phantom, I will promise to accept you as my husband,' and she is free. Free to go where she pleases. Free to command me, her abject, willing slave. Oh, Lord!" continued tortured Joseph, wringing his horny hands, and regarding her with eyes that fairly ached with admiration, "how readily she would say the little word if she knew my ardent, my consuming love for her!"

Down again on his knees went Joseph Phantom, whining and wiping tears from his eyes with his ever ready pocket-handkerchief.

Nelly's face too was covered.

As he commenced his insane rhapsody, she turned away her head, and pressed her hands before her eyes, as though to shut out the hateful spectacle he presented.

But she was not in tears.

His earnest, passionate words, his looks and gestures convinced her that he spoke truth when he assured her that she was so far in his power as to be cut off from all immediate help.

But, though a full sense of her imminent peril was revealed to her, it did not appal her.

She was of that temperament that grows cool and reflective under a crisis of great danger.

Not so much for her own sake as for his, whom she loved dearer than life.

What had best be done?

Nothing could possibly be gained by headstrong, violent resistance. Whatever her previous suspicions of the desperate, unscrupulous villany of the man before, they were now more than confirmed.

If she could gain a little time, but a single day, who knew what might happen?

While these rapidly succeeding thoughts held her silent, Joseph Phantom, with his heart oscillating at a tremendous rate between hope and fear, furtively regarded her from behind his pocket-handkerchief.

"Just the little word, the one little word!" Joseph ventured to murmur under his breath.

And lower still, under her breath, so that even his quick ears caught no sound, Nelly murmured to herself—

"For dear John's sake. It is my duty."

And she withdrew her hands from her face, and with her hesitating eyes regarded Mr. Phantom steadfastly, and with nothing of the scorn and hatred that flashed in them a few moments since.

It was splendid acting.

The blood rushed to the deluded old man's head, as the mercury rises in a thermometer that is held before the fire.

"The little word!" he murmured again; "the precious little word that means to me new life; to my adored liberty, wealth—everything!"

"No, no; it could not mean happiness," Nelly said, softly, while those eyes that had already made such sad havoc in his shrivelled-up old heart, were still fixed on him; "there can be no happiness for me while——"

"What? While what, my angel, my enchantress?" and, raised at a bound to the seventh heaven by her evident relenting, he sprang to his feet, and stood before her with his hands clasped together in an agony of expectancy. "Tell me, sweet Nelly, what is the obstacle, the hateful obstacle?"

"Not hateful," Nelly interrupted him hastily, and with a quivering lip that betrayed how desperately hard it was for her to continue to play the actress. "Should I ever forget him, his memory would fade from me in fond remembrance, and not in hatred. It is to John Gauntlet I allude, Mr. Phantom."

"Yes, yes, I knew that!" And the person addressed shut his mouth with a sound, as though he was grinding his teeth together.

"I repeat," said Nelly, slowly, "that, under any circumstances, there could be no happiness, no peace for us while——"

"While he is alive?" Mr. Phantom again interrupted, eagerly. "Then that need not long delay our——"

"Silence! While he is a prisoner, I would have said, while this terrible, unfounded charge hangs over his head, and he is doomed to suffer the ignominy that is another's just deserts."

Mr. Phantom's haggard brow again was overclouded, but as he paced the room to and fro, the cloud gradually faded and gave place to something like serenity.

"And you would not forget your promise if he were free?" said he.

"My promise!"

"Aye, the promise, the conditional promise, you would make me, dearest Nelly!"

"It could be nothing else than conditional, Mr. Phantom," returned the clever little actress, as she shook her head sadly.

"You would have me engage—supposing, of course, that I possessed any knowledge that would work to that end —to obtain the release of this—of John Gauntlet, as soon as the one desire of my existence was consummated?"

"Nay, before," returned Nelly Blisset, resolutely; "undoubtedly before."

Mr. Phantom's heart sank again, and he laughed a bitter laugh.

"Aye, before," he exclaimed, and savagely gnawing at the notched nail that was devoted to his hated enemy; "before, so that I may be mocked and laughed at for being so easily cajoled by a woman!"

Nelly Blisset, acting her part still, turned on him, with her eyes flashing with indignation.

"Are duplicity and false pretence among the ingredients of my 'noble nature' that you so much adore?" she asked scornfully. "Then we'll not prolong our conversation, sir. You have miscalculated, and will not find in me the valuable qualities mentioned."

The miserable old dotard was on his knees again in a twinkling.

"Pray pardon me," he continued, abjectly, "it was a sudden outburst, a rash and monstrous outburst, for which my distracted state of mind must be responsible. I know—I am convinced, that a soul capable of deception could not reside in a body so exquisitely perfect. I trust you, dear Miss Blisset; I implicitly, blindly trust you."

"And you will set him at liberty? It is in your power to do so," Nelly naïvely remarked, as a smile of such sudden radiance lit up her sorrowful face as nearly drove Joseph Phantom crazy.

"I—I said not so," he answered, in confusion.

Nelly's face grew angry again, and she turned her face from him impatiently.

"I said not so, that is, I can't positively, certainly make such a promise," he hastened to explain, fearful of again giving her offence. "I—I have some little power, some slight knowledge of certain circumstances that may be useful to those who would save him."

"For your happiness sake, Mr. Phantom, I trust that the said knowledge is not slight." And the bewitching eyes were again brought to bear on him.

"But one word more, my enchantress, simple and to the purpose," said Joseph Phantom, with painful earnestness. "If I do your bidding in this, you make me a sacred promise that you will be my wife—that you will wear the ring it shall be my blessed privilege to place on your finger, and none other?"

"When you are my husband," Nelly returned, demurely, "it will be for you to take care that nothing of the kind happens. See that you keep your promise, Joseph Phantom, and you shall have no reason to complain of injustice at my hands."

"I ask no more!" exclaimed the man of many notches, in enraptured tones. "It shall be done, if prompt action and desperate endeavour may accomplish it. Never fear, charming Nelly Blisset that now is, proud and happy Nelly Phantom that shall soon be, that I will waste so much as a moment. And now—may I ask it, may I beg and implore it?—just one kiss——"

But a look from Nelly at once scared him from the daring design.

"Well, well! it is but pleasure deferred—the sweet tantalization that sharpens the appetite," remarked the poor cadaverous old creature, grinning in ecstasies and rubbing his hands. "For a little while. Good bye, darling, good bye!"

And he hurried from the room.

"And now for an exchange of gaol birds. Curse him! I should like to have seen him hanged, but the god of love declares in his favour. Well, well, it must be a halter matter; it will fit that ruffian Lutterloh's neck as well, I'll be bound."

CHAPTER XXIV.

WHICH FOR OUR HEROINE IS A CHAPTER OF TRIALS, ENDING WITH A TRIUMPH.

T has been said that so high up in the desolate old house was the room in which Nelly Blisset was a prisoner, that, looking out at the window, she commanded a fair view over the tops of the tall trees that clustered thickly close to the ancient building, and in summer time completely hid it from view.

So close to the wall did one of these trees grow that its sturdy limbs were twisted in deformity through pressure against it.

Nesting time was long since over, and the birds had deserted the leafless boughs.

Nevertheless, had the hapless miller's daughter looked steadfastly among the branches of the tree in question, she would have discovered crouched there a "bird" of more evil omen than kite or raven.

A bird of prey as regards his nature; in his instincts, his tenacious sticking to the tracks of an enemy, and his relentless animosity—a bloodhound.

The reader will have little difficulty in recognising the individual in whose composition these unamiable qualities were blended—Mr. Richard Lutterloh.

He had neither forgiven nor forgotten the "trick" that Mr. Phantom had put on him as regards the tiny poison packet.

Of the changed glasses at the "Willow Weavers" he had not the least suspicion.

How should he?

There was no one present to change them, during the brief few moments he was away from the room to fetch John Gauntlet's cap, but she who was disguised as a beggar woman, and her behaviour on the memorable occasion was such that it was impossible to suspect her.

If she had intended to turn the tables on him by changing the ale-glasses and letting him drink up the poisoned draught, it was ridiculous to suppose, that after taking the all-important step towards revenge, she should herself, out of mere caprice, frustrate the design.

No.

The poison was a "trick" put on him by the old Monkshood steward.

A deadly trick he made no doubt, and one that somehow (he knew not how, but that mattered nothing) was meant to work his destruction.

A cowardly, treacherous trick; one that he could not let pass without first visiting the full weight of his wrath on the perpetrator.

With the view of discovering the traitor's whereabouts (for, as already stated, Mr. Phantom had vanished from the Hall), Black Lutterloh, had, as the reader is already aware, paid a visit to Mr. Reginald Vipert's town lodgings.

With what result has already appeared.

Baffled and enraged at Mr. Vipert's cool and defiant demeanour, Lutterloh's first act was to settle that spiteful score by causing to be secretly conveyed to Blisset's mill the grey mask and the blood-stained crown piece, together with an ill-spelt scrawl, without signature, explaining briefly the important history of the articles in question.

They were valuable articles to him, and well calculated to aid him in his leech-like designs on Squire Vipert's purse, but Lutterloh was not the man to consider self interest when his passion for revenge was roused.

His satisfaction, however, was but short lived.

He presently began to reflect on what a fool he had been to throw away, as it were, such useful weapons as the mask and the crown were; his fury against Mr. Phantom as the main and original cause of the sacrifice burning more furiously than ever.

" May the ——— take me afore my time," swore Lutterloh, " if I smoke another whiff of bacca till I have tracked him down and knocked his scheming old brains out !"

And there and then he set about the task with the dogged deliberation of a man who does not intend to spoil a pet design by undue haste.

How he contrived to trace his victim to the lone house among the trees need not be told.

There he was.

There he was in the wood that morning when the man with the notched nails urged his hideous love suit with his pretty grief-worn captive.

There he was when frightened Nelly rushed to the window and cast below that despairing, helpless glance.

He saw her.

He saw no more, but his crafty nature made it immediately clear to the gipsy that there was more behind.

That *he* was behind !

The man, the very thought of whom caused him to grin in hungry hate.

Lutterloh approached the house stealthily, to find that the shutters of the lower windows were adjusted as though the place was uninhabited.

This was good. His movements were not likely to be observed.

He had before marked the tree, the top of which appeared from below to be just on a level with the window at which the distressed face of the miller's daughter had been seen, and now he sprang into it, and by swift and agile exercise of his supple limbs quickly reached as high as he dare climb.

This was a stout, gnarled limb of the tree that clung to the wall just under the window.

True, he might have raised himself on this and looked into the room; but that would have been dangerous.

Besides, there was another, and a much safer course open to him, and which would perhaps serve his purpose equally well.

He laid his ear flat against the wall and listened.

Yes ; his arch enemy was there.

He was just in time to hear, though not very distinctly, Mr. Phantom assuring his helpless captive how vain was resistance in that house that was so far removed from any other, and inhabited by no one else except a servant who was in his pay.

He heard all!

Mr. Phantom's abject prayer for his victim's pity; the terrible, earnest, heart-wrung tones in which he implored her to have mercy on him, and not mock him.

As he listened, with his great flat ear pressed firmly against the wall, his hearing became so acute that he could even make out the sound of Mr. Phantom's falling down on his knees and his clasping his hands together.

But what had most interest for Black Lutterloh was the latter part of the strange interview.

That part of it where Nelly so artfully (the wily gipsy could see through the desperate girl's scheming, though love-blind Joseph Phantom could not) wormed out of him that he knew more of the mystery of the young farmer's complicity in the murder of the gamekeeper than he chose to reveal.

That part of it where Mr. Phantom promised that, for his true love's sake, "the guilty should be given up to justice, and the innocent restored to liberty."

When it came to that Black Lutterloh gripped the gnarled stem by which he held on in his great hairy fist and shook it as though it had been his enemy's throat.

"I shan't have to wait much longer for that pipe of bacca wot I put off smoking till a certain little job was done," he muttered through his set teeth. "It's only a bit of coarse bacca I've got, but what I've got to do to yarn it'll give it the flavour of Orinoky at the wery least. What a comfort it is that however many of his enemies a man knocks on the head, he has got only one life himself to lose!"

And even while Black Lutterloh was chuckling over his morsel of diabolical philosophy, he heard the hasty closing of a door below, and cautiously peering down, saw the object of the murderous job he was so eager to be at, equipped as for a journey, and hurrying towards the garden gate.

Lutterloh's first instinct was to hasten down the tree and go after him, and keep in sight until a fair opportunity presented itself for putting into execution his terrible design.

Indeed, he had descended at least ten feet, when he became suddenly inspired with a brilliant idea.

"Sudden death is too good for such a warmint as he is," he muttered. "A little torturing first would be more his deservin's. He talks about how it would wring his soul if he lost her, and, 'pon *my* soul, I believe that the old ape is in earnest. Werry good! I can wait for the settling of the big account, if heavy interest is a runnin' on meanwhile. His soul *shall* be wrung! Bust him! the treacherous thief! I'd wring it till the last frayed-out rag of it was torn from his lanky old carcase!"

And, after the expression of this amiable sentiment, Mr. Lutterloh spat his contempt in the direction in which the object of it had now vanished, and commenced his descent of the tree with deliberation.

He stealthily crossed the garden, and entered the wood from which he had recently emerged, and presently re-appeared, carrying, partly concealed by his smock frock, a bludgeon of formidable dimensions.

"Now for letting loose the 'dove,' as he calls her, and wot he thinks is so tightly caged. Not much of a dove, 'cording to my sperience of her," he continued, wincing, as he regarded a but partially-healed and jagged wound, extending nearly across the back of his left hand. "More like one of them Injun tiger cats, wot'll fight for their mates while they've got a tooth or a claw left 'em. But I don't bear her no malice for that. I like a gal with grit in her, even if she raspses me rather rough."

As he was so muttering to himself, he was treading cautiously over the neglected garden beds, trying the window fastenings in a manner that was quite "professional."

"I wonder what sort of a feller the one servant is," he continued; "a old feller, or a young feller; a big un, or a little un. P'r'aps the old humbug didn't speak the truth, and there are *two* instead of one. Well, wot odds? I'm a match for the pair of 'em, I'll wager, if they're the common sort."

And then, having at last discovered the window that presented the weakest point of attack, by means of his big, open clasp knife, he "sprung" the sash fastening, and, raising it fearlessly, applied his heavy shoulder to the closed shutter, snapping the iron fastening as though it had been mere twine, and causing it to fall with a loud crash into the room.

Lutterloh leapt in after it, his bludgeon ready poised in his strong grip.

"That ought to bring in the servants, I should think," he muttered coolly, and stood expectant at the door.

He had not long to wait.

He heard a hasty scrambling up the stairs, and then the key was turned in the lock, and there appeared not an ordinary servant and a stranger, but his old acquaintance, Mother Wheeler, the hostess of the "Willow Weavers!"

At sight of him the hag started back with a scream, while, in considerable amazement, he lowered his raised bludgeon.

"This here is a deeper game than I 'spected," he growled, savagely. "So *you* are the servant wot's in the 'pay' of the good gentleman wot lives here? Ha! ha! It was lucky that enough light came in at the window to let me see you, mother."

"Not lucky for *you!*" exclaimed the old beldam, rage rapidly taking the place of her first alarm.

"No; lucky for you, my old beauty. I should ha' knocked your wig over your eyes with this little plaything in another moment; which wouldn't ha' been pleasant atween friends."

"What do you want here?" exclaimed the old woman, quaking with fear of the ruffian before her. "Is robbery your purpose? Did the lonely appearance of the house tempt you to have a fling at it, bold Lutterloh? Ha! ha! as you say, this sort of thing, which in the way of business strangers must put up with, is *not* pleasant between friends. Be off, my lad, and I'll forgive you what it will cost me to have the shutter mended."

Lutterloh advanced towards the doorway in which the old woman stood.

"You can take the short cut, my lad," said she. "You can jump out as you jumped in. 'Twill save time."

The ruffian frowned as he put out his great hairy hand.

"Out of the way, mother. I've business to do."

"Business? Business here!"

"Aye, it won't take long, but it must be done. D'ye understand? It *must* be done," and he scowled in a way that was very intelligible.

"But—but who can you have business here with, my lad?" returned the old woman, stammering with fury, though somehow continuing to speak in tones of civility; "there is no one here except——"

"Except the party wot my business is with," Lutterloh interrupted unceremoniously. "Come, sharp's the word, mother. Show me the way to her room."

"Her room! You know that she is here then! What do you want with her?"

"I want to see how locks and bolts agree with her," replied Lutterloh, with a malicious grin.

"Well?"

"If she likes 'em, well and good; if she doesn't, then I'm a-goin' to abolish the inconwenience on the spot. No mistake, mother. I've come a purpose!"

And, pushing the furious old woman

on one side, the gipsy began to ascend the stairs.

For a few seconds the hag was speechless with passion.

She well knew the man and the desperate lengths he would go to attain his ends.

The unscrupulous remedies he was at all times prepared to apply to anything in the shape of opposition.

It went to the very core of her sordid soul to see "good money" slipping through her fingers so.

She already had tasted a substantial earnest of Mr. Phantom's generosity, and with a true scent and keen, foresaw that he would "bleed" freely yet.

There was but little time for reflection on the best course to pursue, but she made the most of that little.

She knew something of the undercurrents of the peculiar business in which she had become involved.

She would make the most of the said knowledge.

"Stay!" she called to Lutterloh, who already had nearly reached the second landing. "She is weak and ill; your sudden appearance in her room might so affect her as to frustrate the end you have in view. I don't care. It is on'y a matter of money to me, and I daresay her friends will pay as much for getting her back as t'other would for her being kept here. Let me go up, Lutterloh. I'll do your bidding, man. I will, as sure as I stand here a living woman!"

Lutterloh regarded her with suspicion while he chafed his ear reflectively.

"Very well; let's have it that way," he said; "p'r'aps it's better. On'y hear this, mother, I'm in earnest if ever I was in my life, and I'll cut your throat as freely as I'd snap a flower-stalk if you try to play 'possum with me. I'll give yer two minutes to bring her down. If yer ain't exact to time I shall come up arter yer; then yer know what'll happen!"

Without an instant's delay, the old woman sprang before him, and hurried up the stairs while he came slowly down.

She, however, did not make the ascent to the top of the house where was situated the chamber in which Nelly Blisset was a prisoner, without a stoppage.

She halted at a room door, and unlocking it, passed swiftly in and out again.

The object for which she had entered appeared in her hands in the shape of a pair of elegantly-finished pistols.

With these she hastened upstairs, and with a key of substantial proportions, opened the door of Nelly's room.

The picture the old woman presented did not tend to allay the terrors that already distracted the mind of the miller's daughter.

Her haste up the stairs had caused her to pant for breath.

Her face was ghastly pale, her grey hair in disorder, and in her hands were the deadly weapons before mentioned.

Nelly had heard something of the disturbance below, and now made sure that her last moments were near.

Falling on her knees, she clasped her hands together, and, in piteous accents, began to plead for her life, when the old woman hastily interrupted her.

"Quick!" said she; "your life depends on it. I came not to harm, but to save you. God forbid, my sweet chick, that I—one of your own sex, and old enough to be your mother's mother—should do you a mischief. But my life as well as yours is threatened."

"Threatened! By whom?" Nelly faltered.

"By your worst enemy—by the ruffian who would have basely poisoned your betrothed," the old woman whispered in her ear, "by the gipsy fellow Black Lutterloh!"

In an instant Nelly Blisset was up from her knees.

With tears of beseeching she could beg her own life, but this concerned one whose life was more precious to her than her own, and excited in her bosom a feeling before which tender emotions yielded.

"Lutterloh here!" she exclaimed, with her even white teeth set desperately together. "My dear boy's would-be assassin here?"

"Aye, and your would-be assassin and mine," replied the old woman, eagerly. "There is but one course left us. We are alone here, and he is bent on our destruction, hired, I suppose, by another of your enemies, my deary. I have but barely escaped his murderous clutches just now, and flew to you to warn—to arm you! Nerve yourself for the attempt as I shall. Recollect that life and liberty are the reward of success."

Liberty!

The mere utterance of the word seemed to convey to her not a little of its soul-inspiring influence.

Liberty !

Freedom from the net of terrible peril in which she had been so treacherously taken.

In which she was as yet helplessly involved.

Liberty to hasten to and comfort her dear persecuted lover, wherever he might be found.

With flashing eyes she eagerly grasped the pistol that the old woman held out to her.

That, at least, was some proof of the old hag's sincerity.

But she had no knowledge of the sort of human nature that inspires such creatures as the cunning old beldam of the "Willow Weavers," and their marvellous aptitude for prompt plot and contrivance.

"Lead the way," said Nelly Blisset, resolutely. "I will not flinch, believe me."

"You dare not flinch," returned the old woman. "It is his death or ours. He is armed with a terrible bludgeon, and, I have no doubt, is even now searching the house for us, so that he may put it to the murderous use designed. Come, girl, quick !"

"His blood be on his own head, then, if he stands in the way !" muttered Nelly. "I spared him once."

And they rapidly, though cautiously, descended the stairs.

All clear from the topmost flight to the last but one.

Then a heavy footstep and an impatient, growling voice was heard.

"He is there !" whispered Mother Wheeler, clutching Nelly's shoulder. "Mind, mind your promise, and

don't flinch. Life and liberty, remember !"

But, softly as she spoke, Lutterloh heard her, and, suspecting something wrong, came up the broad stairs, taking them three at a stride, and growling like an incensed bull.

In another moment, his repulsive, hairy visage, so well remembered by Nelly Blisset, appeared, and, as it seemed, brutally determined, if need be, on executing his sanguinary threat against Mrs. Wheeler, he had abandoned his bludgeon, and held in his fist his big, open clasp knife.

"Remember !" shrieked the hag.

And that was the signal for the miller's daughter to raise the pistol she held in her hand.

To take aim with and fire it, and, with a hideous oath, Black Lutterloh flung up his hands, and slipped and rolled down the stairs.

Instantly the old woman, with marvellous activity, sprang down after him.

"Quick ! he is not dead ! Let us secure him while he is still helpless."

And she flung open a cupboard, broad and deep, that opened out of the passage.

It was just close by where the wounded and insensible man had fallen, and peremptorily urged by the other, Nelly helped her push him in, on which the cunning beldam produced a key from a bunch at her side, and made the door fast.

"That is one trouble cleverly overcome; now for the second," said she.

"Aye, let us flee," replied Nelly, trembling now, and sick at heart at the terrible work just performed. "Let us hurry from this dreadful place and send some medical assistance to this poor wretch, whose life may yet be saved."

But the villanous hostess of the "Willow Weavers" chuckled mockingly.

"He will be well looked after, my dear; we take great care of everybody who falls into our hands. You have done a very pretty morning's work, my pretty one, and I dare say your kind guardian will be well pleased at it."

"My—my guardian! What do you mean, woman?"

And a terrible foreboding smote poor Nelly's heart.

"Only this, that the sooner you get back to your room, the better you will please me," returned the hag, with a scowl. "You won't find it to your interest to displease me. Up with you. I'm paid for keeping you fast, and 'tain't likely, you little fool, that I mean to let you go."

So unexpected—so bitterly cruel was the disappointment, that Nelly, for several seconds, stood dumbstricken and bewildered.

"I will die rather than return," said she, presently; "you, a woman, dare not—shall not compel me!"

"Is it so long since that you forget what a woman may do with a little toy such as this?" And Mother Wheeler significantly raised the pistol she held in her hand. "I have orders to use you tenderly, and I will, so long as you are grateful for it. Back to your room —quick!"

But in her overweening confidence in her own cleverness, Mrs. Wheeler had forgotten one circumstance.

The open window through which Black Lutterloh had effected an entry.

The door of the room in which the window was, was within a yard of where Nelly stood, and just the least bit ajar.

Nelly could see the open window through the chink.

In an instant she was resolved.

With a single leap, nimble as that of a hare, she bounded at the door, and swung it to with a slam, and in another instant, before the hag could recover from her amazement, she was out at the window, and lost amid the tall, neglected shrubs that grew in the garden, one entrance to which was the main road.

CHAPTER XXV.

COMMITTED FOR TRIAL.

URELY, could he have seen him, his most inveterate enemy must have been moved to compassion.

Three days had passed since John Gauntlet was thrown into prison.

But short work was made of his preliminary examination before a police magistrate.

Bruised in spirit and heart broken as he was, little did he dream of the terrible array of circumstantial evidence that was produced against him.

He had expected that his quarrel with the murdered man and the known animosity that existed between them, together with his hasty flight, would be brought against him, as substantial proof that his was the hand that was stained with the old gamekeeper's blood; but that was not all.

Before the horrified eyes of the court was produced the coat—*his* coat, with the great stone tied in the handkerchief —*his* handkerchief, in a pocket of it.

Torn at the breast and at the sleeve, as though the owner had last worn it during a deadly struggle with a man little less strong than himself, and still smirched with the dark crimson stains.

Stained and mildewed, and all befouled through lying in the black and stagnant pool into which unsuspicious Nelly Blisset and her sister had cast it at the instigation of cunning Lutterloh.

Of this last-mentioned circumstance, the amazed prisoner was not in the least aware until it was exhibited in the court before him.

And then, what could he do but shudder, and, with his hands, shut out the sickening sight?

What could be more convincing of his guilt than this voluntary act of a man conscience-stricken?

"Fully committed to take his trial for wilful murder!"

With these last terrible words of the magistrate reverberating in his ears like the harsh tones of a death bell, the hapless young farmer staggered out of the dock, and was conducted straight to Newgate by men who, used as they were to the ways of crime, shrank from him, and looked their detestation and horror for his coldblooded atrocity.

Through the remainder of that day, through the long, long night, John Gauntlet sat in his stone cell like a man entranced.

Heartless — hopeless — crushed, utterly miserable!

It was a mercy that the sources of his affliction were so numerous and conflicting; they prevented the concentration of his thoughts on the one main terrible calamity, which undoubtedly would have driven him mad.

Besides, it was impossible for him to think entirely of himself, and of his impending doom.

Where was Nelly?

As he last saw her so was the picture ever present to his eyes.

The cry she gave utterance to as the rough-handed ruffians at the " Willow Weavers " dragged them asunder still rang in his ears.

Where was she now?

Had she escaped scathless from that den of infamy, or had the revelation that she was not what she seemed—that, instead of a tattered old beggar-woman, she was a maiden, young and handsome—involved her in trouble that he knew not of? Perhaps might never know!

"And all for my sake!" moaned poor John. "Oh, Lord! it seems hard, indeed, that such pure, unselfish love should be mastered and mocked by villanous trickery. Bless her heart! A hundred thousand times, God bless her! So kind, so tender, so brave, and all—all for me!"

And conscience-stricken indeed must the gaoler listening at his door have supposed his prisoner committed for trial for wilful murder.

He was at liberty to communicate with his friends, he was informed.

"You'll want a lawyer, I suppose?" sneered the turnkey. "I shouldn't drive a hard bargain with him if I was you."

"Why?" John asked, apathetically.

"Because it will be money wasted, whatever he charges. You're 'booked' to a certainty. There can't be two opinions about *that*."

Nevertheless, poor John plucked up heart to send a few lines to Blisset's Mill, begging for some information, though never so slender a scrap, concerning his "brave, trusting darling."

Swift as was the messenger who conveyed the melancholy epistle, he was a laggard compared with the respondent to his appeal.

Dauntless, true-hearted young Lord Lavering.

His generous sympathy was the more worthy because it did not spring from any conviction of John Gauntlet's innocence, deduced from his personal consideration of the terrible and mysterious circumstances.

He was not gifted with a profound penetration for the unravelling of mysteries.

But he possessed the virtue of faith in an uncommon degree.

He had faith in Nan.

The seeds of it were sown on that memorable first night when, after his vain pursuit of the highwayman, he enjoyed the hospitality of the miller's abode, and when Nan Blisset embarrassed him so awfully by her decidedly motherly kindness in the matters of the slippers and the nightcap.

Day by day the said seeds had fructified and ripened, until his lordship's last faintest suspicion of "twap" had vanished, and he came to regard her as a perfect paragon of her sex, and a person entitled to his very highest respect and confidence.

At least, so in his unpractised heart's simplicity, he interpreted the feelings and emotions her society engendered within him.

Once, and once only, had he, after a sleepless night, sought a solution to a question that lay uncomfortably on his susceptibilities.

"Miss Nancy, you remarked at the commencement of our—of our——"

"Acquaintance," Nan suggested, archly.

"Exactly; I was about to say intimacy, but yours is the more appropriate word undoubtedly. On that occasion, you will perhaps remember that you remarked that you always wished for a brother to pet and spoil."

"I think that was among the foolish things I gave utterance to, Mr. Cecil."

He insisted still on being called "Mr. Cecil" at the mill-house.

"And—and do you think that you have made any advance towards that wish since that memorable evening? As regards myself, I mean, Miss—I mean Miss Nancy."

And his modest young lordship blushed as though he had just confessed to setting fire to his neighbour's house, at the very least.

"As regards yourself, Mr. Cecil," returned downright, honest Nan, "I can never hold but one opinion, since our wide-apart positions render it impossible for me to regard you as a brother, and your sterling goodness of heart puts 'spoiling' you quite out of the question."

A bolder and more confident man would possibly have pursued the argument from the vantage-ground thus gained, but Lord Lavering, blushing still more, indeed until his very ears shone crimson amid his curly side locks, first stammered his entire concurrence in Nan's sentiments, and then blundered an apology for his self-conceit, and finally, quitted the subject not in the least degree wiser than when he approached it.

Not the least wiser, perhaps, but more profoundly than ever impressed by her sterling honesty and sound common sense.

He had consulted her as to John Gauntlet's complicity in the murder of Joel Burke, and since she had unhesitatingly declared her absolute belief in his perfect innocence, from that moment that, too, was Lord Lavering's belief, and he was prepared to stand by it to the last extremity of his courage and the last guinea in his purse, defiant of a world but too apt to be rashly censorious.

So it came about that as soon as John's sorrowful letter was received at the mill, straight ensued the momentous question—

"Who will go?"

Lord Lavering said, with a promptness that caused Nan's tearful eyes to flash with admiration—

"I will!"

And he did go; but he had little to explain for the poor fellow's consolation.

Her flitting from home that night, when the footweary young farmer came to thrust a comforting letter under the mill-house door, and broke down so woefully under the porch, was discovered next morning by a brief note she had written and left on her dressing table.

"My dear Parents,—*A life dearer than all the world to me calls me to its succour. I do no wrong, therefore I will not say forgive me. Pity me that my poor fellow should be so cruelly used, and pray for us both. He came to me under my window last night, stealthily, and to leave me a letter; but I saw him looking, ah! so weary of living and heartbroken, that I dare not let him go away alone.*"

Lord Lavering brought this pitiful little tear-stained paper scrap with him, but he could tell nothing beyond concerning Nelly.

He informed him of his visit to Reginald Vipert—his first visit, that is to say, and how hopeless, at present, was the prospect of gaining any information in that direction.

"But do you think that *he* is cognizant of her hiding-place?"

And it was terrible to behold the expression of the young farmer's face as he rose up suddenly from his prison bench, and confronted Lord Lavering with his muscles quivering, and his fists clenched.

"He insists that he is a gentleman," replied Lord Lavering, evasively; "and as such his simple denial—and he makes it emphatically—should be sufficient to exculpate him."

After this he dare not reveal what he had heard respecting Nelly's mysterious abduction by Phantom from the "Willow Weavers."

No good could by any possibility ensue from further torturing the poor fellow.

Besides, the information was derived from a not entirely reliable source, and needed consideration.

Then came that second interview, at which Nan was present, between Lord Lavering and the Master of Monkshood, when the latter was saved from self-murder by the prompt hand of the former.

The interview at which Reginald Vipert's eyes were opened to the villany of his confidential agent, Joseph Phantom, as well as to his own wickedness and folly.

Straight from the hotel in St. James's Street, accompanied by Nan, kind-hearted Lord Lavering once again visited the miserable prisoner awaiting his time of trial.

He was under a promise.

"When next you come, you will bring her with you, or tell me all you know of her! You promise me that—solemnly, sacredly promise it?"

"I do."

These were the concluding words of the first interview between Lord Lavering and the young farmer, and now, however bitter was the task, he was bound to redeem his word of honour.

It would be too painful to describe the meeting.

Hearing the rustling of a woman's attire, the poor captive had sprung to the door of his cell, and when the gaoler opened it, there he was with his white face radiant and his arms extended wide!

Ah! what a blight fell on that face; how hopelessly, woefully, those arms drooped to his side when his disappointment was made manifest.

And still there was no comfort in

Nan's face—nothing but a confirmation of his worst fears.

"Don't say the word," he whispered, hoarsely, as he staggered back to his seat; "I can say it, but it would kill me to hear it from your lips. Don't even say 'No;' just nod your head when I ask the question, and I shall understand. Is my Nelly dead?"

"No, no, no!" cried Nan, earnestly; "that anguish at least is spared you, dear John; she is, thank God, still alive, but——"

"But *what?*"

They did not understand him quite, it seemed.

Was there anything that could happen to his darling compared with which death would be the lesser evil?

Look on the man, on his clenched hands, on his staring eyes, and his bloodless lips for an answer!

"But what? but what? Tell me quick, for God's sake!"

What could they do but tell him?

And he listened, still standing upright, with his blank, stony face fairly before them.

Listen, as might a man risen from the grave to learn a true account of what would not let him rest there.

What he would do when the terrible narrative was concluded, seemed impossible to say.

Of all things it appeared likely that he would fall flat down on his face like an image of wood from which the supports are taken, and save the judge and the jury and all the rest of the law's myrmidons further trouble.

But beneficent Providence otherwise willed.

Even while Lord Lavering, anticipating the worst, was lingering in his story, a small distant noise was heard in the outer prison stillness, at sound of which John Gauntlet started and shook.

"I am mad! I am mad!" he muttered. "My ears hear voices that are far away. I——"

"Oh, Heaven help you, kind sir! But for you they would have kept me from him."

No madness this; unless both Lord Lavering and Nan are mad.

No voice "far away," but close at hand. Closer and closer still.

Nelly's voice! Nelly's self!

Haggard, travel-stained, with only one shoe, and a little foot cut and bleeding—Nelly Blisset!

Thus the cell door, once more swung open, reveals her.

And John Gauntlet, with the vacant gaze of a somnambulist, again spreads wide his arms, and essays to speak.

But his lips have forgotten their function, and move dumbly. With a great cry, he reels, with his face to the wall, with one hand before his eyes, and the other held out behind him.

"I am afraid! I am afraid!" he gasps. "It is not real; it is but my brain's mad fancy. Let her touch me if she has hands to grasp, lips to kiss; but I dare not look! She will vanish if I look!"

But she does *not* vanish!

Down on her knees is she ere the words have left his lips, choking with sobs, and grasping and kissing the outstretched hands, while Nan, as yet too much amazed to believe it real, clings for support to Lord Lavering.

CHAPTER XXVI.

A MEETING.

JOHN! John! look at me—speak to me. It is I, your Nelly. Say that you are not angry with me for coming here," cried Nelly, passionately.

Angry with her!

Convinced at last that it was no cruel delusion that was tormenting him, but his veritable darling, in fleshly reality, with a cry that was unintelligible to all but her, John Gauntlet turned swiftly about, and raising the kneeling Nelly, clasped her to his bosom.

"Once again! once again!" This was all he could say.

And then, as these two sorrowing hearts yearned to each other after their cruel estrangement closer and closer still, there ensued a silence that was more eloquent than words most passionately uttered.

"Once again, though it should be the last time, the very last!" cried the young farmer, his voice trembling with emotion. "Now death may come, if it must; it has no longer any terrors for me."

"No, no; life, not death!" the poor girl replied, as she clung convulsively to him; "or if death it must be, then let it be for both of us. Swift death, my darling! I would rather it were so, than that I should be left lingering."

"Nay, there are years and years of life for you, poor birdie," and as her face reclined against his breast, he caressed her wind-tangled locks with his heavy hand; "what you have lived to struggle through may be taken as a surety that you will conquer at last. Oh, my Nell! I have heard of your perils, and they caused me a keener heartache, a thousand times, than mine own."

"Aye, and such perils!" Nelly softly responded, as she shudderingly crept yet closer to him.

"I know, I know. I have heard all, or, if not all, more than enough, from this right noble gentleman——"

And then, for the first time, such had been the all engrossing object of her errand, she was aware of the presence of Lord Lavering and her sister Nan.

A few words of gratitude to the one, and a hasty embrace to the other, was all the recognition that Nelly could afford to bestow just at present, so that it was fortunate that the now by no means "cherry-cheeked party" found a supporter, as well as a consoler, in her true-hearted companion.

"Such perils, **my poor darling,**"

continued the miller's daughter, as she crept back to his side, as he sat on the rough prison boards, and laid her head on his willing shoulder, "as would have driven you mad, had you so much as dreamt of them. But they are past now, and here I am, bruised a little and faint, and very, very tired through my long, weary journey over the strange, rough road; but no matter for that, it is all forgotten, as a terrible night's dream, and this is my bright morning."

And the upward look she gave him could scarcely have expressed more of content and rest from pain and weariness.

But the atmosphere of a prison is not congenial to the outgushing of the heart's affections.

Nothing as yet had been explained.

True, here was Nelly, but how had she escaped the perils that seemed to encompass her so inextricably?

It has been stated that, at the termination of that momentous interview between Nan and Lord Lavering and Reginald, in the breakfast-room of the latter at the hotel in St. James's Street, a letter was received from Mr. Phantom.

In it the writer daringly renounced at once and for ever his service in the Vipert family.

Such was the old dotard's infatuation, that he did not scruple to state his case with an amount of effrontery and insolence that opened the eyes of the Master of Monkshood to the volcano on the brink of which he had been unsuspiciously treading.

Certain "family secrets," the worthy steward said, were in his keeping, secrets that were worth money, did he choose to part with them—a good round sum of money—two thousand pounds say.

Would Mr. Vipert stop the sale of them by immediately forwarding a draft for the sum named?

Mr. Phantom required the money immediately, so the letter said, as he was on the eve of going abroad.

"Not alone, however. I take with me such precious worth, in the shape of a lovely woman—need I mention her name?—that the wealth of all the world would to me be but a poor equivalent. She is mine! A love that is a hundred times stronger and purer than any that her farmer swain, or even your gentlemanly self, ever felt towards her attracts me to her, and she is mine, I tell you. I have her in my custody, my worthy late master, and I will hold her—aye, though I grappled with death, for I would still hold her, and go down with her to the grave?"

How had she, a weak, defenceless maiden, contrived to break away from a hold that was so reckless and villanous?

Still nestling to her betrothed, and with Nan and Lord Lavering close and attentive listeners, she briefly told them.

How that she had been drugged by the wicked old hag at the "Willow Weavers," and conveyed, by her agency, insensible, to the lone house in the plantation, where Mr. Phantom was.

How that, in order to make a little precious time, she had affected to make terms with the hideous old steward, though her heart loathed and sickened against him all the time.

How that Black Lutterloh had suddenly appeared on the scene, bent, as the beldam who kept the house assured her, on her destruction; how that the woman had placed a pistol in her hands, and she had shot him; and how that the old woman had at once revealed to her that her assumed friendliness was but a convenient sham, and insisted on retaining her a prisoner; together with her daring method of escape by the window.

That was many hours since.

How she had discovered her way she could not tell, nor how she had lost a shoe.

Indeed, though her foot was all bloody, she was unaware of this minor misfortune until it was made known to her.

Such was the beginning and the end of the strange, incomprehensible story that Nelly Blisset had to tell, to which her hearers listened in wide-eyed amazement and wonder.

The coolest and most self-possessed of the party was, of course, Lord Lavering, and he was altogether bewildered by it.

It was Lutterloh's prominency in the business that perplexed him.

Hitherto, although he had heard mention made of the person in question, he had attached no importance to him in connection with the calamity that had fallen on the family at the mill-house.

True, he had been secretly informed by the sisters of Black Lutterloh's inopportune appearance at the scene of the murder in the wood, as well as of the advice he had given them as to the disposal of the torn and bloodstained coat in the pool; but he had set it down as just the sort of advice a thick-headed, though kindly-intentioned person might give under like circumstances, and resolved to take no steps as regarded the gipsy until he instructed a lawyer for John Gauntlet's defence.

But lo! here was the paw of Black Lutterloh thrust out, and visible in the most unexpected places.

In the "dosing" of John Gauntlet's beer at the "Willow Weavers."

In his apparently murderous visit to the lone house hired by Mr. Phantom.

But most important was what Nelly had said as regards Mr. Phantom's almost promise that he would use the secret knowledge he possessed to attach the penalty of guilt to him whose ruthless hands had earned it, and set free the man who had been so cruelly, unjustly arrested.

"He mentioned no name?" Lord Lavering inquired.

"No name, neither did he make any promise, except one that was conditional," Nelly replied, with her arms still locked about John's neck. "My consenting to marry him—him with his terrible face and his heart of malice—was the terms on which he agreed to save my dear boy's life. And, oh!" she cried, as the sudden alarm seized on her, "what if the rash step I have taken should make me as well as yourself his deadly enemy, my dear one, and he should hold his peace and you should——"

"Ah! that would be terrible, terrible," Nan interrupted her, shudderingly, as she covered her face with her hands.

"There must be no delay. Thank Heaven! we have, at least, one staunch friend, whose noble, unselfish heart will strive its utmost for you, John. God be good to him! It seems as though kind Providence sent him to us just on the eve of our cruel adversity."

And Nan took Lord Lavering's hand and kissed it with a fervour that brought tears in his lordship's blue eyes.

"I have not the least doubt that such was the case, Miss Blisset," said he, with a desperate attempt to instil a little cheerfulness into the woeful party. "And this you may safely rely on—that Providence never leaves its work half finished, or raises up an instrument in wanton mockery. We will all do our best, as I trust we have from the beginning. But, as Miss Nancy says, no time must be lost. Phantom and Lutterloh should be secured with all speed, as well as the wicked old wretch who contrived the abduction of Miss Nelly. Trust to me to take instant measures for ensuring their arrest, or at all events the destruction of all their power to do mischief. More perhaps may be done by means of diplomacy than open hostility."

At this moment, a gaoler announced that the time for excluding visitors and shutting up the prison for the night was rapidly approaching.

"Farewell, then, till to-morrow," said Lord Lavering, pressing both the poor prisoner's hands heartily. "We must not be over-confident; but who knows but that the gleam of sunshine, all unexpectedly enlivening your cell this afternoon, may speedily expand to livelong daylight and liberty!"

Too deeply moved to reply, or, perhaps, grudging to speech the few remaining moments that he might enjoy her dear presence, John still held Nelly to him, and kissed, and still kissed her.

"We will return to Monkshood tonight," continued Lord Lavering, "and you will have at least, the blessed satisfaction of knowing that she is restored, and safe under her father's roof, and that her mother and her sister are with her to comfort her."

"And that you are there to protect them," said John huskily. "Don't, pray don't think, Lord Lavering, that because my words to you are few that my gratitude is scanty. Were my heart less full of thankfulness, my tongue would be freer of speech. If it should be my unjust doom never again to be restored to the dear old home, my last thoughts will be of you; but if it should please kind Providence to make my innocence clear and set me free, then I may be able to show you that I am not the man who deals in empty words."

The gaoler at the door rattled his keys, as a gentle hint.

Then one close embrace, a fervent kiss, and an earnest good-bye, and John Gauntlet was again alone.

He must have been a young gaoler who had the custody of the young farmer's cell, or, at least, a man with a heart susceptible of pity; for just to spare the poor young creature, who went away so helplessly leaning on the arms of the other two, the anguish of hearing the harsh grating of the key in the great lock of the cell door, he made pretence to linger until they were out of earshot before accomplishing that duty.

CHAPTER XXVII.

DISAPPOINTED AND DESPERATE.

EANWHILE, how fared it with that most daring of schemers and plotters, Mr. Joseph Phantom?

Hard, hard, cruelly, excruciatingly hard.

A terrible time has he had of it since the reader last set eyes on him, which, as will be remembered, was when, exultant and jubilant as a man on the eve of becoming a bridegroom, he set forth from the house in which his pretty dove was caged.

There was now only one step wanted to the consummation of his soul's delight, and that was the sending of a man to the gallows.

"Nothing will be easier," mused Mr. Phantom, as he jauntily picked his way to the coach office. "I will have nothing to do with hunting the villain up myself. I will put the matter in the hands of the police.

"Not the surburban police, I know too well what a jolter-headed, rapacious lot they are. I will run up to London —to Scotland Yard, and lay my information there; and give them perfectly to understand that I shall expect the hundred pounds that are offered as a reward for the murderer's apprehension.

"A hundred pounds is a nice neat sum. A handy sum for a man who is about to be married. A useful sum, swiftly and sweetly earned. Ha! ha! I'll buy my pretty little maid a necklace of pearls with it, and it will serve her afterwards as a pleasant reminder of how faithfully I kept my promise.

"I can kill two birds with one stone," he continued, as he snapped his fingers at the very thought.

"I can go first to Scotland Yard, and then to Doctors' Commons. No humdrum, tedious formality of 'banns' for me.

"A special license will be the thing. It won't cost above ten pounds. Perhaps I might be able to pick up a second-hand pearl necklace that she won't know from new, and then that neat little hundred pounds might pay for both.

"Ha, ha! it would seem as a funny joke between my little maid and myself, that the money that brought a murderer to the halter, procured also the means for me to put my head in the matrimonial noose.

"Ha, ha! I'm in high spirits this morning. I'd like to have a good hearty laugh, only I'm afraid of that confounded cough that is sure to come on if I excite myself."

Three hours afterwards virtuous Joseph Phantom, the enemy of evil-doers, the stern denouncer of breakers of the law, turned out of Whitehall and into the arched way that is the entrance to the headquarters of the metropolitan police.

To the attentive ear of a chief of the department, he confided his belief that the murderer of Joel Burke, the Monks-hood gamekeeper, was still at large, and urged such satisfactory reasons for the belief, and withal gave his testimony in so gentlemanly and straightforward a manner, that it was decided that immediate steps should be taken for the arrest of Mr. Richard Lutterloh.

This pleasant little business satisfactorily accomplished, Mr. Phantom was so elated that he indulged in the unwonted luxuries of a cigar and a hansom cab, giving orders to the driver to proceed with all speed to Doctors' Commons, from the grim portals of which he in due time emerged beaming with delight, and with his hand fondly pressed against the pocket that contained the precious document that was to convert "Miss Ellen Blisset, spinster," into Mrs. Joseph Phantom.

He had used such expedition that the coach that was to convey him home did not yet start for fully two hours.

"It is not often that I find myself in London, and in a jovial mood, too!" said Mr. Phantom; "I'll enjoy myself till it is time for me to start. I will go and have a look at Newgate, where lies my unfortunate friend the Monkshood clodhopper. He, he! It is cruel to give the beggar his liberty only that he may witness the perfidy of that little puss who, I'll be bound, hundreds of times has sworn eternal devotion to him. It would be a much greater charity to let him end his romantic career in company with the chaplain and Mr. Ketch."

And humming a pleasant tune, the man of the notched nails passed by St. Sepulchre's church, and turned into the Old Bailey.

It was waning towards evening now, and in the heart of the City it is dusk always half an hour while it is yet daylight in the country.

Mr. Phantom was an economical smoker, and the stump of the cigar he had purchased an hour and a half since still adorned his lantern jaws.

"Ah! this is the debtors' door, as they call it," he mused, as he paused at the iron-studded wicket in question— "the door at which many a bold villain has emerged on his way to pay his last debt.

"Where are you, brave Lutterloh? He, he! You are boozing and swaggering in some roadside beershop, I'll be bound. Good Lord! how your unhandsome crop of coal black hair would stand on end if you only knew how soon this door will open for you!"

And, chuckling pleasantly, he passed on until he came to the next door in the prison wall.

"And this," said he, "is the door of the governor's residence! A fine door, with a brass knocker. Debtors may knock at this door and go away satisfied, for the governor has a warm berth of it. I think that I should like to be a prison governor. It must be very nice to——Hallo! there is a woman on the steps! She can't be a debtor—more like a beggar. What, in the name of all that's comical, could induce the silly creature to come a-begging of the governor of Newgate! I've half a mind to——"

What?

To enact the part of a man suddenly stricken with palsy?

So, indeed, it seemed by the sudden extinguishment of his pleasant vein, and the dropping of the cigar from his gaping jaws, and his shaking and trembling.

What was it that Mr. Phantom had half a mind to do, and never accomplished?

What was it that made him clutch at the uneven stones of the prison wall to prevent him falling down on the pavement?

The female figure, half kneeling, and half crouching on the steps before him.

It was as amazing as though the earth had opened and yielded to his sight, alive and in the flesh, one dead and buried years and years ago.

The figure on the prison steps was that of Nelly Blisset!

It was impossible that he could mistake her.

Dress-stuffs there are of a pattern, and mantles, and so far the similarity might for the moment impose on him.

But her hair!

Those glorious tresses of chestnut colour, that were like no other woman's that his enraptured eyes had ever feasted on; there they were, escaped from their riband, and tumbling about the poor little head so sorrowfully bowed.

Yes, it was Nelly.

The "pretty dove" whom he thought so safely caged in the lone house at Oakenfield, distant from London fully fifteen miles.

His bride.

The adored creature of his heart's desire, his wife by promise, she for whom he had risked so much—nay, had sacrificed *all*, *here!* Here, at the threshold of the prison that held his hated rival!

He could not move or speak. He felt his heart pulsing weaker and weaker, while the blood that deserted it, and rushed upwards to his brain, caused his temples to throb with a heat that was torture.

How had she escaped?

With his own hands Mr. Phantom had tested the strength of the bolts that secured the door of her room; the nails with which the window sash was made fast were driven home, stem and head, into the massive frame.

Had Mother Wheeler betrayed him?

That could hardly be.

He knew that unless he was outbid, he was safe in this respect, and who was there to outbid him?

And in the midst of these tormenting cogitations the door was opened, and as she rose to her feet, uttering words of earnest thanks, he caught a glimpse of her face by the light of a street lamp at that moment kindled—he heard her voice, and the last faint doubt as to her identity vanished from his distracted mind.

She had already entreated admission, it seemed (little did Mr. Phantom know how touchingly and repeatedly), for the door opening, she entered the prison at once, and the closing of the heavy portal was, to the ears of the man with the notched nails, like the harsh grating of the stone that in Eastern countries closes the gaping mouth of the vault in which the dear dead are sepulchred.

Mr. Phantom needed no telling what was the mission that had brought her to the prison.

What but to seek an interview with John Gauntlet?

Why, she was with him at that very moment, in all probability!

While he, mocked, cheated, laughed at, was swearing in impotent fury outside those grim walls of stone, she was within —with *him!* In his arms!

In his mad mood, Mr. Phantom pictured the passionate embrace, the up-turned face, the kisses that fell even faster than the great, glad tears, the fond, sob-broken words of ecstasy; and in his agony he groaned aloud, and clawed at the senseless wall with a vengeance that would have seriously damaged his cherished finger nails had he not at the time worn his black cotton gloves.

What could he do?

Nothing, absolutely.

Nothing, but wait until she came out.

It would be dark then.

She should not get off so easily as she imagined.

He would speak to her; he would have an explanation that should satisfy him, or it should go hard with her— hard with *him*, too!

But then it flashed with cruel vivid-

ness to Mr. Phantom's mind that the steps he had already taken deprived him completely of the devilish power he had previously wielded.

The visit to Scotland Yard had done the business!

There, as already stated, he had made such revelations as went very far towards showing that the man whom he hated, whom he would most cheerfully have hanged with his own hand, was guilt-less, and might presently demand his liberty.

It was as though the whole community of fates was leagued against him.

As he stood there in the black shadow of Newgate wall, with his white face aghast in despair and bitter, bitter dis-appointment, his worst enemy might have pitied him.

But his malevolence was not in the least blunted by his affliction.

"Baffled, baffled!" he muttered, as his breath went and came quick; "but not yet beaten. If cursing her would kill her, even though my soul's ever-lasting perdition were the penalty I paid for the sweet privilege, I would strike her dead now, *now* as she lies folded in his arms. That would, indeed, be precious revenge; but I must be content with a common and more vulgar sort, but quite as effective. Quite, quite! I'll wager my life on that!"

And the recess in which he stood concealing him from observation, with murder in his bloodshot eyes, he spread out the fingers of his huge hands and grinned devilishly, as he slowly, and with every sinew at tension, closed them again tight.

"I'll wait! I'll wait!" he repeated

determinedly. "It will be dark when she comes out; and the ampleness of my vengeance will repay the waiting. So I am to be sold, mocked, and laughed at! He is to take her to church, while the bells in the old steeple ring their rejoicing and my derision! Well, well—we shall see.

"I should have known it," he broke out again, passionately, after a few moments' pause; "it is in the blood. Like mother, like daughter! Oh, curse 'em, curse 'em every one!"

So brooding in his increasing malice, Mr. Phantom waited in the shadow of the wall for fully an hour.

Then a man came out of the prison, and in a few minutes returned with a hackney coach.

"That's for her; something seems to tell me that it is so, and she'll escape me now if I am not careful," he muttered, new alarm seizing him, "but I won't be baulked. I'll hang on behind the coach. Aha! now I have it! If the coach is for her, I'll hang on behind, and when we get to a dark part of the road, I'll cut a hole in the leather work with my knife, and stab her while her back is to me."

And with his excited brain swimming with his diabolical design, he drew himself close against the black wall, and watched.

He had not long to wait.

Again, the prison door opened, and Nelly Blisset appeared—but not alone.

By the light of the lamp over the door, Mr. Phantom distinctly made out who her friends were—Lord Lavering and her sister.

So unexpected was this foil to his villanous plot that he could not stir or utter a sound. He could do nothing but crouch and screen himself from view, while he fairly gnawed his notched nails in rage and mortification.

He watched them enter the vehicle, and especially noted that Nelly and her sister sat with their backs to the horses, Lord Lavering facing them.

"It would be sheer madness to adopt the plan I last thought of," he muttered savagely; "they are too strong for me. I must let them go just now. It is a bitter, cruel disappointment, but there is no help for it. But she shan't escape; with the devil's help I'll yet be quits with her. Make the most of your brief triumph, my pretty mocking bird. Nothing shall save you. Nothing, nothing!"

CHAPTER XXVIII.

A SURPRISE.

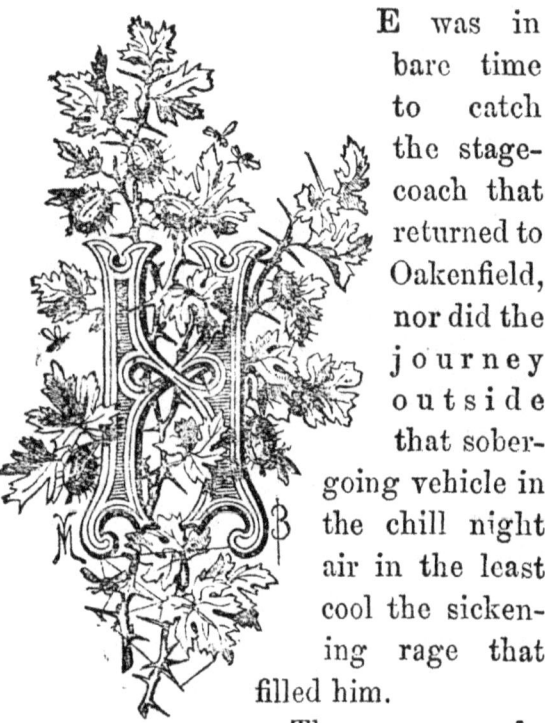

E was in bare time to catch the stage-coach that returned to Oakenfield, nor did the journey outside that sober-going vehicle in the chill night air in the least cool the sickening rage that filled him.

There was only one course for him to pursue.

To return to the lone house and endeavour to ascertain from his treacherous confederate, the old hag of the "Willow Weavers," the particulars of the escape of the girl his heart was now set against with all the rancour of love turned to hate.

It was a long walk from the place of alighting to the place in question, and as he strode swiftly along the dark road, Mr. Phantom's mind was busy with cunning schemes and devices for compelling Mother Wheeler to disclose all that she knew, however much, at first, she might be averse to doing so.

"I'll spend my last guinea to compass my revenge," he muttered. "Money is of no value to me now; life itself is as naught. Penalties have no terror for me. I only live for the achievement of one object, for the attainment of which I would sell my very soul."

Somehow it had not since occurred to him that his confederate might have abandoned the solitary house at the same time that her charge either slipped from her hold, or, by her connivance, made good her escape.

Great was his astonishment, therefore, on making for the rear of the premises by which he had hitherto gained access, to find the windows shrouded in darkness.

"She has decamped, curse her!" was Mr. Phantom's mental ejaculation. "She has taken the bribe, and returned to her villanous husband, making sure that I shall not dare follow her there. But she's mistaken. I'm not the same meek and mild person she has been accustomed to deal with. There's as much difference between the Joseph Phantom of yesterday and to-day, as between a tame, purring cat and a wild cat of the forest.

"Hang 'em all! I wish that, like a cat, I had nine lives. I wish that *she*, the viper, the sweet-faced trickster, who has so villanously cheated me, had nine lives. I'd take 'em all! I'd crush them out all at once. I wouldn't leave her so much as a minute of the very last one to say a last prayer in."

But he had yet another surprise in store for him.

Not in the least expecting but that the door was as fast as bolts and bars could make it, Mr. Phantom laid his hand against it, and it yielded to the slight touch, and swung well open.

His hopes revived.

It was clear that Mother Wheeler had not gone.

His acquaintance with her was of no long standing, but he knew enough of her to be aware how extremely unlikely it was that she would run away and leave her valuable goods to the mercy of any tramp who might chance to come that way.

He entered the house and called aloud. There was no response.

It was pitchy dark, and he had not the least idea in what part of the establishment might be discovered materials for making a light.

He ventured to advance a yard or so further, and again called out and listened for a reply.

Did his ears deceive him?

Was it a human voice that responded?

Not in spoken words, but by a muffled moaning sound that was frightful in the black stillness.

Mr. Phantom was by no means a man of courage.

Still he was desperately circumstanced.

If it was a human voice, it must be that of Mother Wheeler.

Where was she?

Stealthily and on tiptoe he made yet further way into the house, and finding that all was still, he again ventured to call out.

"If it is you, Mrs. Wheeler, say where you are. It is I, Mr. Phantom."

But the next instant he repented his rashness.

As though it was against his very back, all in the darkness he heard a scratching accompanied by a groan, that was even more dismal than the one that preceded it.

Mechanically stretching out his hands, Mr. Phantom's fingers came in contact with what unmistakably was the lock of a door.

Of the cupboard door in which Black Lutterloh's insensible body had been bundled many hours before.

If fright had not held such complete mastery over Mr. Phantom, there can be no doubt that he would at once have made speedy exit from a place fraught with such horror and mystery.

But his legs declined to second the urgent prompting of his coward nature, and would make no movement at all, except in the way of trembling.

"Who—who is it?" he gasped, still holding on by the lock of the cupboard from whence the awful sound proceeded.

A dolorous groan was the only response.

"Is it you, Mrs. Wheeler?"

Another groan, accompanied by a feeble shaking of the fast-secured door.

"I see it all now!" Mr. Phantom muttered savagely to himself; "the pretty, tender creature, on whom I was fearful that the wind might blow too roughly, has been at her pranks here! There has been a struggle between the two women, that is evident, and the young virago has conquered and made her antagonist a prisoner while she effected her escape."

Then, in a more conciliatory voice, he called out—

"I would let you out, my poor woman, if I could, but I can't find a light, and I don't know how to open the door without a key. Can't you speak just a few words and tell me where the matches and candles are kept? There, I will place my ear at the keyhole; now I shall be able to hear the merest whisper, if you will make the effort."

Mr. Phantom's hearing was singularly keen, and what he heard was an awful imprecation involving the eternal ruin of someone's eyes and limbs, but uttered in a low, growling tone, as by a person in great pain.

"She wishes that she had hold of her, I think she says," the man of the notched nails whispered to himself. "So do I, the heartless vixen! Who knows? Maybe this desperate and enraged woman, if she is not too badly hurt, might be disposed to assist me in my revenge. I might be glad of the assistance of her friends, even; I wish I had a light."

Another groan, and an impatient rattling at the inner side of the door, made the wish all the more urgent.

Opportunely, it flashed to Mr. Phantom's mind that, when at the height of his felicity, a few hours since, he had indulged in the rare luxury of a cigar, he had likewise purchased a box of cigar lights. They were in his pocket still, and he hastily struck one.

The first glaring glimmer of its blue and sulphureous flame, however, did not reassure him.

It showed him blood on the ground!

Blood from the door to the foot of the stairs, a yard or so distant (indeed, the cupboard was under the stairs), all bedraggled and smeared, making it evident that the wounded person had been dragged that distance.

The blue light, however, showed him something that was more to his purpose.

A broad-bladed clasp knife.

The implement with which Mr. Lutterloh had forced back the catch of the window, when he effected an entry into the solitary house, and which had dropped from his wounded hand when Nelly Blisset's shot brought him down.

Picking up the knife, Mr. Phantom struck a second fusee, and by the light of it essayed to shoot back the bolt of the lock, all the time uttering words of comfort and consolation to unfortunate "Mrs. Wheeler" within, and begging her to bear up until he could effect her release.

He, however, was not expert at lock picking, and another and still another light was struck—when, lo! just as he had kindled a fifth, with a shock like that of sudden thunder, the door flew open with a crash, and with such force as to send him spinning against the opposite wall. But that was not the most startling part of the calamity.

The fusee was at the height of its lurid blaze as the door was projected open so unexpectedly, and there was revealed to his appalled gaze, not a bleeding, faint, and prostrate woman, but the ghastly figure of Black Lutterloh!

Of but brief duration was the light, but it revealed enough to make Mr. Phantom utter a scream of terror.

Black Lutterloh, with his face deadly white, where it was not smirched red, and with his black, gipsy eyes gleaming with devilish ferocity.

Another instant, and all was black darkness, and he was pinned and felt himself caught by the throat and flung to the ground.

"If you say a word, if you utter so much as a single syllable till I give yer leave, I'll strangle yer as I would a thievin' cat," Lutterloh growled in his ear. "Are you alone?"

He could tell by the descending movement of his victim's lower jaw on his knuckles that he had nodded his head affirmatively.

"Where is she?"

As he asked the question, he slightly relaxed his murderous grip, and enabled Mr. Phantom to make feeble answer.

"She! Mrs. Wheeler? I don't know. Oh, Lord forgive me, I never thought——"

"Not she — t'other?" fiercely demanded the ruffian, giving the prostrate man such a shake as a great dog gives a lesser. "The gal, curse her! Where is she?"

With a prodigious effort Mr. Phantom contrived to ejaculate—

"I echo that; though it be with my last breath, I, too, say curse her! Curse her now and for ever! But why —why should you, my friend—my dear, kind friend, who——"

"Why should I curse her?" Lutterloh fiercely interrupted him. "Why— because I hate her; aye, almost as

much as I hate you. Can I put it stronger than that, eh? Tell me, Mr. P'isoner, can I?"

Mr. Phantom felt the knuckles again indenting his windpipe, and hastened to acquiesce.

"No, no, my good Lutterloh, certainly not; or so I daresay it seems to you just at present; but only give me a chance, and I will convince you of the cruel injustice you do me. It is sheer madness for us to lie here grappling each other in the dark. Release me, I say, and give me a chance in the light of proving to you that since we so cordially hate an enemy, we should love and help one another."

But it wasn't a light that Mr. Phantom wanted to prove what was the quality of his regard for the man who had him by the throat.

All that he required was liberty for his right hand!

The hand that still grasped the broad, sharp clasp knife!

At present he could not use it, as he had been flung down with his right arm under him, and Lutterloh's enormous weight kept it there.

He felt that his life hung on a thread; that unless he got the upper hand of the desperate gipsy, he had but a little longer to live.

But he had to deal with one whose cunning was at least equal to his own.

"Yes, we'll have a light; but not afore I find my knife will I let you go, you old snake! I heard you tinkering at the lock with it; whereabouts did you drop it? Turn over; p'r'aps it's under yer."

There was a moment when, had Mr.

Phantom possessed the courage, he might have used the formidable implement, but the opportunity required such prompt embracing that his courage bungled over it and it was lost.

His fingers relaxed their grip on its handle, and he pushed it a little away.

"Yes, it is under me, I can feel it," said he, innocently; "just under the small of my back."

Then he was permitted to rise.

"Go afore me, and keep on striking them lights till we find whereabouts the kitchen is," Lutterloh growled, authoritatively.

Not daring to disobey, Mr. Phantom led the way, and now that the way was lit, easily enough succeeded in finding the room.

From the ceiling of the kitchen an oil lamp was suspended, and after a little difficulty, Mr. Phantom succeeded in igniting it.

Then, for the first time, he had an opportunity of noting the appearance of his enemy.

He presented a terrible spectacle.

He wore a sort of smock of a whitish colour, and the lower side of it, under his left arm, was as though it had been dipped in crimson dye.

His hands, too, were stained in the same sickening manner, and even his jet black hair was smirched as though the wounded man in his despair had torn at it with his wet hand.

He could not fail to observe the effect of these ghastly signs on Mr. Phantom.

There was a deal of horror in the glance of the man with the notched nails; but there was something else besides in his expression that seemed to say—

"If it came to the worst, I think I might get the mastery in a struggle with a man wounded as desperately as this one is."

Cunning Lutterloh read the glance so, at all events.

"Don't make rash kalkilashuns," said he, with a ghastly grin, "I ain't hurt nothing to speak of. If you had lost so much blood out of your withered old carcase, it 'ud ha' drained you dry. It's on'y a flesh wound, I tell yer, and the bullet passed cut. It stings, it's true, and I like it for that. I've got work of a sort afore me that a man needs spurring up to."

And he scowled and nodded in a way that made Mr. Phantom's heart quake.

"The bullet!" he faintly ejaculated. "What bullet!"

"The one as she, your dove, your delikit angel—may the devil tame her!—the bullet that she, egged on by that other beldam, shot at me—at me," continued Lutterloh, shaking both his clenched, hairy fists, "whose on'y object was to do her a good turn. Faugh! Whereabouts is kep' the brandy, or the beer, or summat? It makes me sicker than my hurt does when I think on it."

And, favoured by fortune, he spied on the dresser a bottle containing the identical liquor in requisition, and greedily drank it.

There was not very much in the enraged ruffian's last observations, but to Mr. Phantom's shrewd ears, it furnished a clue almost to the entire mystery.

Nor, indeed, was he long kept in any

sort of doubt, for, with his chilled blood excited by the brandy, Lutterloh at once launched into a furious account of his injury from first to last—including his great inciting grievance, the "trick" that Mr. Phantom intended to put on him in the manner of the poison that was given to him to dose John Gauntlet's ale.

"But it is all as one!" exclaimed Black Lutterloh, with a diabolical grin, as he took another pull at the brandy bottle. "I began to be afraid that luck was dead agin me, and that I should be done out of the treat wot I've long promised myself. I s'pose it don't make no difference to you how soon it comes off?"

"What—what do you mean?" Mr. Phantom asked, aghast. "What treat?"

"The treat of seeing you kick the bucket," Lutterloh coolly replied. "S'pose we see about it at once? I feels as though I wanted a livener after being so long boxed up in that confounded hole under the stairs. Come, I'll be more generous to you than you would have been to me. I'll give you a choice; shall I cut your throat——"

Mr. Phantom gasped out a cry of terror as he clutched at the edge of the dresser for support.

"Or would you prefer the more gentlemanly process of hanging?" continued the now more than half-drunken gipsy, his maliciously twinkling eyes showing how much in earnest he was. "If so, here is a handy bit o' hemp, and with that there hook in the beam overhead, we are set up with all the tools wot are necessary to complete the job neat and 'spectable!"

In despair Mr. Phantom's eyes eagerly sought the door, observing which Black Lutterloh took a few leisurely steps across the kitchen and locked the door, and put the key in his pocket.

"I'll give you half a minit to make up your mind," said he; "a pious creeter like you, wot attends his chapel reg'lar, can't want longer. You oughter be grateful to anybody wot'll give you a lift out of a world wot's so full of wickedness."

And the ruffian chuckled at his own wild sarcasm, as he proceeded with great care to make a running noose in a length of clothes' line that was lying handy.

"Or," he remarked sneeringly, as he suddenly desisted in the operation, "maybe you'd like to die genteeler still. What about that pisen stuff? Was it all used up that time when you thought to play me a trick, or have you got any left?"

All the time that the reckless villain was speaking, Joseph Phantom had stood trembling in mortal dread.

It was terrible, after all his pains and trouble and scheming and money spending, to be murdered in cold blood, as though his life was of no more account than that of a rat!

"Lutterloh!" he exclaimed, with a desperate endeavour to speak calmly, "we are wasting time, precious time in this mad talk; let us converse like reasonable men—as men who have lives to save as well as revenges to gratify. You have drunk too much brandy now, and it blinds you to your own interest."

But Lutterloh, as, with the air of a

connoisseur, he tried the strength of the slip-noose he had just completed, laughed his ugly laugh.

"A man's interest is to get all the walue he can out of his feller creeters," said he. "Wot I'm goin' to get out o' you is your life. I would rather have it than a hundred pounds, told down!"

"Or five hundred?" Mr. Phantom suggested, quakingly.

Mr. Lutterloh coolly nodded assent, as he leapt on to a table and attached the cord to the hook before mentioned.

"Or a thousand!" urged wretched Joseph Phantom, "a thousand pounds, paid down, all in gold. Paid down on the spot and counted, I repeat," he continued, eagerly, perceiving that Mr. Lutterloh paused in his job of gallows-making. "Hah! I thought you would grow more reasonable presently, my dear friend. You don't like me; why, then, should you make a sacrifice in my favour?"

"I don't mind to; you get on with sayin' your prayers, and don't trouble yourself on that score."

"But, dear Mr. Lutterloh, you are doing so," now persisted agonized Joseph; "if you'll just desist from—from what you are so busy about, I'll prove it in half a minute. You may take my life away from me, but you can't take it in wear to eke out your own. You can't hoard it up, and spend it for your pleasure; but how is it with a thousand pounds—a thousand pounds, I mean, that you take from your enemy, leaving him penniless—a hungry beggar, whose only resource is to beg his bread? Think, good Lutterloh, what a blessed feeling

it must bring a man to know that the man he hates is begging his bread—tramping the country, barefoot and ragged! An old man such as I am, used to little luxuries and comforts, reduced to beggary and rags, and sleeping of winter nights in barns and outhouses."

Lutterloh listened to desperate Mr. Phantom's extraordinary argument with disbelief in his eyes, though, at the same time, with a puzzled air, as though, against his inclination, he saw something in the case as Mr. Phantom put it.

"Where's the thousand pounds?" he asked.

"This piece of paper represents it," returned the man of the notched nails, inwardly rejoicing at the prospect of escape from death.

And, as he spoke, in a mighty hurry he took from an inner pocket his pocket-book, and unclasped it.

As he did so, and hastily groped amongst its contents, a tiny folded paper slipped from between two other papers, and fell unheeded to the ground.

Lutterloh observed it, and as he leapt from the table, placed his foot on it and kept it there.

"Here is the thousand pounds," said Phantom, unfolding a cheque for the amount; "all I have in the world, I swear, and already signed and ready for presentation at the bank. I had prepared it so because I thought to have a hasty use for it," he continued, with a savage contortion of his white face. "Well, it is yours. Take it and let me go."

Lutterloh regarded him attentively.

"Not I," said he, with a cunning laugh; "if I take it, I shall hold you fast till I prove the value of it. I've heard of such a thing as stopping cheques afore now. Mind yer," he continued, "I don't say as I have altered my mind. Like as not, when I have had a good think about it, I may pay you a visit in the night and settle up in a hurry. I shouldn't go to sleep if I was you. But come, we've had jawing enough; now let's get to roost for a little while. I shall be glad of an hour's snooze myself; there's a heavy day's work to-morrow for me."

"Yes, yes, let us get to bed," remarked Mr. Phantom, eagerly, and with his mind occupied with but one idea—escape; "don't trouble about me. I can find my way in the dark to the room I have before slept in. Good night, my dear friend."

And he moved towards the door.

Lutterloh grinned.

"It ain't no trouble at all," said he; "I'd let you sleep alone with great pleasure only I know what a nervous old genelman you are. You'd be havin' bad dreams, and jumpin' out o' winder or summat. We'll sleep together, and I'll watch over you like a guardgin angel."

There was nothing but for Mr. Phantom to submit, and, taking the light, he led the way, Lutterloh following closely behind.

To the consternation of the man of the notched nails, Black Lutterloh, as though in obedience to an afterthought, had turned back at the kitchen door to secure the cord, in which he had so very ingeniously contrived a running noose.

"Lay you down there!" exclaimed the gipsy ruffian, pushing Mr. Phantom roughly towards the bed.

With a quaking eye on the rope, the latter obeyed.

"Put this round your cussed old neck."

And Mr. Lutterloh extended the noose.

"Mercy! mercy! my dear friend—my good friend. You promised——"

"I'm a-goin' to keep my promise," the gipsy interrupted him with a brutal laugh. "I'm a-goin' to hold you fast while I make up my mind. Put your head through, I tell yer. That's the sort. Now, don't yer see, I shall be able to let you know. If I should decide agin yer, I can let you know it without wastin' of words. You'll feel a sort of a tightening about your gullet, and there'll be an end on it."

Sweating with fright and rage, Mr. Phantom was compelled to do as the ruffian bade him, and when the cord was adjusted to Black Lutterloh's satisfaction, he flung his burly figure, his blood-stained garments, and his great unclean clout boots on the dainty white counterpane, and wound his end of the cord round and round his hand.

"That's comfortable," said he, as he made the line fast so taut that the least movement of his victim would be made known to him. "Now you can go to sleep, and dream that yer mother is rocking yer in the cradle."

CHAPTER XXIX.

POISONED !

IVID as was the imagination of Mr. Phantom, it was scarcely equal to the task Black Lutterloh had imposed on it.

The cradle of his childhood must have been a thorny one indeed if it in the least resembled the couch he so unwillingly shared with his tormentor.

For a little while Lutterloh was restless, groaning and muttering as though with the pain caused him by the bullet wound in his side, but gradually the fumes of the brandy he had drunk overcame him, and Mr. Phantom's anxious ears were greeted by the sounds of snoring.

Was there no means of escape ?

It was horrible to lay there like an animal tied in the shambles awaiting the pleasure of the slaughterman.

The room door was ajar.

So confident was the gipsy in his method of securing his prisoner that he had not thought it worth while to adjust the fastening.

Oh, for a knife ! For that knife that reposed idly in Black Lutterloh's pocket not a foot distant from his hand, but which for his life sake he dare not touch. Could he untie the knot ?

Cautiously, and an inch at a time, he raised his hand and essayed the task, but Lutterloh was an old hand at setting traps and snares, and it would have been more easy to have untwisted welded wire.

His teeth were yet good—would it be possible to gnaw the cord through ?

Stealthily he wriggled his head lower on the pillow, so as to get the line in his mouth ; but at that instant, Lutterloh started in his sleep, and gave it a jerk so sudden, that Mr. Phantom's eyeballs felt like starting out of his head. No, no, it was of no use.

He must lie there, living an hour of torture in each moment, until the ruffian who had him so completely at his mercy awoke and decided his fate.

The suspense was terrible.

There was a church at some distance, and Mr. Phantom could hear its chimes tolling the weary hours, one o'clock, two, three, until day began to dawn.

Then his quick hearing detected a strange sound.

That of horses' hoofs on the highway.

They must have been far away indeed when he first heard them, for it seemed half-an-hour at the very least ere they came quite close.

There was more than one horse.

Two at least.

Clearer and louder came the sharp click, click of the hoofs, until they could not have been more than fifty yards distant.

"They will pass, and I shall presently hear the sounds dying away in the distance," groaned the miserable wretch. "Ah! if I could only call out and make them understand the peril I am in. No doubt they are honest yeomen, who would instantly halt and render me assistance, if I might call out and let them know the peril I am in through this devil. But I dare not! Ere my voice was heard, the villain would wake and tighten the cord, and I should be a dead man."

But Mr. Phantom was mistaken in his doleful forebodings.

The horsemen, whoever they were, did *not* pass the lone house.

His anxious ears could make out that they drew rein while still at some little distance, and that, walking their steeds, they came to a standstill by the gate of the garden.

What did the strange visit betoken?

Who were the horsemen?

And again, were they friends or enemies? Friends!

The mere thought of the word caused Mr. Phantom to set his teeth together bitterly.

He had no friend; no, not one in all the wide world.

Who, then, were his enemies?

The curtained window was within easy hand reach of where he laid, and commanded a view of the garden and the road beyond.

Could he peep out?

He tried the daring experiment, and instantly repented.

The deadly noose tightened about his throat with a jerk, and Black Lutterloh started upright on the bed.

"What, you would slip your leash, eh?" growled the still half-asleep ruffian. "Come closer, curse you, and lay quiet."

And, unceremoniously as though Mr. Phantom was a restive dog, Lutterloh hauled at the cord.

"No, no! Look—look out at the window! They are there," was all that his wretched victim could gasp.

"They! Who?"

Black Lutterloh was quite awake now and off the bed (still with the string of Mr. Phantom's hempen collar in his grasp), an peeping out at the window cautiously, and with a corner of the curtain raised.

Joseph Phantom had but one desperate hope, and that was that the horsemen might turn out to be police officers.

Had he not given information concerning his suspicions of Lutterloh's complicity in the murder of Joel Burke?

What was more reasonable than that the police had tracked the desperate gipsy as far as the "Willow Weavers," and there obtained from Mr. Wheeler information that enabled them to continue the pursuit?

If this were so, he had nothing to fear.

Nothing—except that Black Lutterloh might suspect him, Mr. Phantom, of having a hand in giving him up.

But at that instant, the gipsy himself solved the all-important problem.

"I can't quite make 'em out—it ain't light enough," he growled; "but there's two of 'em."

"What, constables—mounted constables?" Mr. Phantom asked, with rash eagerness.

"Why? D'ye expect constables? You ask arter 'em as though you would be disappointed if they didn't come."

And with suspicion gathering in his savage eyes, Lutterloh eyed the other keenly, still with a hard grip on the cord.

Mr. Phantom at once saw his danger.

"My dear Lutterloh," he hastened to explain, at the same time affecting to be much terrified, "you misunderstand me. Do *I* want constables here? Is it likely? If you knew all, you wouldn't ask so preposterous a question. I—I am in as much dread of constables as—as even you can be. Let us keep 'em out, good Lutterloh; you and I. Two against two, we're a match for 'em."

At this moment a loud rapping at the door at the rear of the house was heard.

Lutterloh's face twitched nervously as he again cautiously peered out at the window.

"They ain't constables," said he. "I can see the horses at the gate, and the saddles and bridles on 'em, and there's nothing of the mounted police in the cut of 'em. They're gentlemen's horses, and—eh!"

And as the gipsy uttered the startled exclamation, he raised the curtain higher and looked out more boldly.

"What—what is it?" Joseph Phantom asked eagerly, new terrors seizing him.

"I knows one of them horses," Lutterloh answered, through his set teeth; "I oughter know him, since many a score times I've groomed him; it is Fury!"

"What, the squire's horse—Squire Reginald's horse?"

"Aye, and it is Squire Reginald, and a curse on him and all his dealings, who is at the door now," growled Lutterloh, furiously, as with a single jerk he brought Mr. Phantom close to him; "your master, you whey-faced old dog, and a friend of his. What do they want here? Is it you or is it me? Who set 'em on the track, eh?"

And he gave the cord that still encircled Mr. Phantom's neck a twist round his great fist, causing Mr. Phantom's eyes to start unpleasantly from his head.

"Not I, not I," gasped the poor wretch. "I swear, though it is my last moment, and the salvation of my soul depends upon it, that I have no hand in their coming here. Don't, don't for God's sake, man, squeeze so hard; let me speak! I swear that Vipert is my enemy no less than yours, and that I will help you, willingly help you kill him, him and his friend, whoever he may be."

Hypocrite as the gipsy knew him to be, there was that in his tone that bespoke Mr. Phantom's desperate earnestness.

Besides, might there not be some truth in the old man's assertion?

Had not the Master of Monkshood, that morning when he defied and as good as turned him out of the room in the London hotel, exclaimed—

"Be off! Hang Mr. Phantom and you, too! I wash my hands of you all as rogues of the same feather."

Meanwhile the beating at the outer door with the whipstocks of the horsemen grew louder than ever.

"You'll stand by me?" Lutterloh asked, doubtfully.

"To the last—to the very last," rejoined Phantom, eagerly.

"They've come armed, we may safely reckon on that," spoke Lutterloh, as he released the other's neck of the halter. "We shan't have much of a chance unless we are armed too."

"There's a pistol in that trunk," the man of the notched nails answered readily, as he pointed to a new leather portmanteau, his private property.

"It is already loaded. But the key. Let me consider, where is the key?"

"Here, that'll do just as well," said the gipsy, making a heavy lunge at the lock of the trunk with his iron-shod boot, and causing it to fly open in an instant.

"Only one! Well, you take that, you'll do better with it than with this little tool," continued Lutterloh, unclasping his great knife. "Our safest way is through that blessed door they're hammerin' at."

"Why not by the front?" Mr. Phantom asked.

But Lutterloh shook his head cunningly.

"The fox is as knowing as the fox-hunter," said he; "these two, may the

—— burn 'em! haven't come alone; it isn't in human natur' for two men to find pluck enough. They've got the traps with 'em, and they're lurking in the front, while clever Squire Vipert and his friend are beating us up at the back. It is because they think that escape will be attempted at the front, that I shall try the back. 'Sides, since somebody's got to be knocked on the head, it may as well be one wot you hold a grudge agin."

"To be sure, to be sure," remarked Mr. Phantom, readily enough, but with a sinister expression in his eyes, that boded no good for Lutterloh.

"You know how to use a pistol?" the latter asked.

"Trust me; I'm not good at long shots, but at a few paces I'm a certain aim, my dear friend."

And, being now in possession of the weapon, almost a grin overspread Mr. Phantom's ghastly face.

"You go first; I'll keep close behind you," he said.

"We'll go down as we came up, if it's all the same to you. It ain't polite to walk afore a gentleman," sneered Lutterloh.

Mr. Phantom bit his lip; but, with affected alacrity, stepped in front, and commenced the descent of the dark stairs. As before remarked, he was a rapid as well as a subtle thinker.

If this was the Master of Monkshood at the door, who was it with him?

Perhaps the man whom, in his coward heart, he feared more than the ruffian close behind him.

What if the second was John Gauntlet?

John, released from Newgate through the communication he, Joseph Phantom, had made at Scotland Yard, and now bound on a mission of vengeance !

The impatient hammering at the rearward door still continued, and Mr. Phantom could almost persuade himself that he could recognise John Gauntlet's fiercer knocking from the other.

His only chance was to make a little favour somewhere.

Black Lutterloh was his late master's most dangerous enemy.

Might he not earn some claim to merciful consideration if he put the reckless gipsy past making mischief ?

This was his thought, and the source of the sudden light of satisfaction that lit his cadaverous countenance when Lutterloh handed him the pistol.

He would have shot him from behind and as he was descending the stairs, had not the other been too cunning for him.

He, however, was only baulked, and not beaten, in his villanous intention.

But he was altogether at fault when he supposed that Lutterloh was not to the full as cunning as himself.

Not a movement or a glance escaped the watchful gipsy's observation.

The door at which the two horsemen were knocking led directly into the front kitchen—the kitchen in which Lutterloh had made such deliberate preparations for hanging Mr. Phantom on a meat-hook.

As they softly entered the place, the eyes of the latter rested on the hook and the beam, and he gripped his pistol vengefully.

Softly as they trod, however, those without, who listened, heard them.

"Open the door ! Whoever is within there, open quickly, or be prepared for the consequences of further refusal !"

It was not Squire Vipert's voice.

It was not John Gauntlet's.

Mr. Phantom heard it, and at once recognized it.

It was Lord Lavering's !

This was better.

It gave him an infinitely better chance than if it had been the young farmer.

"You stand o' this side, and I'll stand o' that," whispered Lutterloh ; "and I'll lift the bar, so that the next time they press against the door, they'll come tumbling in. Then a stab and the touch of a trigger will do the business."

"To be sure, the touch of a trigger !" responded Mr. Phantom, nerving himself for the desperate deed he meditated.

"Are you ready ?"

"Quite."

Lutterloh stooped to lift the bolt, but a slight noise behind him caught his vigilant ear, and, turning about swiftly, he caught Mr. Phantom in the act of taking aim.

In an instant, however, his arm dropped.

"I—I—am ready, quite ready," said Phantom, in a fright ; "undo the bar, man, quick."

Lutterloh stood regarding him for several seconds with an expression of countenance that is indescribable.

"You look like a man who is ready," said he ; "why, you are quaking like a partridge under a hawk. You want a stimulant. It's lucky that there's a drink of brandy left in the bottle. Put the pistol down a minute, and reach it down off the dresser."

Afraid for his life to disobey, and being not at all averse to a drop of the fiery liquid to sustain his courage, Phantom did as he was desired.

But, as he turned his back, Lutterloh swiftly withdrew from his pocket a little packet.

That which the evening before had unsuspectedly dropped from Mr. Phantom's pocket-book, and was secured unobserved by the cunning gipsy.

He swiftly undid the folds of the packet, and held it open in the hollow of his hand.

"Give it here," said he, stretching out his other hand towards the bottle. "I'll have first drink, and leave you the rest."

Before he handed it back, however, he dexterously slipped into the black bottle the powder out of the paper.

All unsuspiciously, Mr. Phantom gulped down the contents of the bottle to the last drop.

"That's nice! That's invigorating!" he exclaimed, with savage satisfaction, as he repossessed himself of the pistol. "Now I shan't flinch, bold Lutterloh! Unbar the door. Quick, before I——"

Lutterloh made no move towards unbarring the door.

With the same devilish expression of countenance as before mentioned, he stood regarding his victim.

"Before you what? Speak up. You ain't drunk, you know, and it's no use your shamming it!" said he, with a villanous grin.

Mr. Phantom looked like a drunken man, at all events.

His white face flushed purple, his hair reeked with sudden sweat, and he seemed to be fast losing power over the muscles of his mouth.

"I—I don't know," he faltered, staring before him wildly; "it was such a little drop that it could not have overcome—have overcome—I don't understand——"

And his failing knees compelled him to sink down into a chair, the loaded pistol falling idly from his hand.

"P'r'aps I can help you to understand," cried Lutterloh, his swarthy face fairly alight with devilish glee. "Can you read? Can you read anythink in a paper wot ain't got no reading on it? Can you read *this?*"

And as the savage ruffian spoke, he impaled the blue paper that had contained the white powder on the point of his clasp knife, and held it within a few inches of Phantom's eyes.

The effect was instantaneous and terrible.

With a piercing shriek Joseph Phantom threw up his hands.

"Ha! ha!" Lutterloh laughed, "you're a scholard in every lesson wot may be learnt in the devil's school, read it; read it out and tell a hignorant man wot it ses."

"Poisoned! poisoned! poisoned!" shrieked Joseph Phantom, slipping from the chair and writhing on the floor. "Oh, curse you, curse you! Help, without there! Break the door! Burst it in! He shall not escape—thus shall——"

And in his agonised writhing, his hand encountered the fallen pistol, and he would have grasped it had not Lutterloh stamped it out of his weakening hand with his heavy foot.

Then he made for the door, which, at that moment, was violently burst in, and Mr. Vipert, with Lord Lavering, rushed into the room.

They passed by the gipsy standing close by the wall, and hastened to Mr. Phantom, who roused sufficiently to raise himself on his elbow, while the Master of Monkshood leant over him.

But it was too late for aid now.

All that Phantom could do was to fix his fast glazing eyes on Lutterloh, and, as he pointed at him with his extended finger, feebly gasp the single word—"Poisoned!"

But ere the two gentlemen could take any action towards securing the murderer, he had cleared the threshold at a bound, and was off and away.

When Reginald Vipert and Lord Lavering looked down again, all that remained of subtle, wily Joseph Phantom, was his distorted and huddled-up dead body.

CHAPTER XXX.

NELLY IN DANGER.

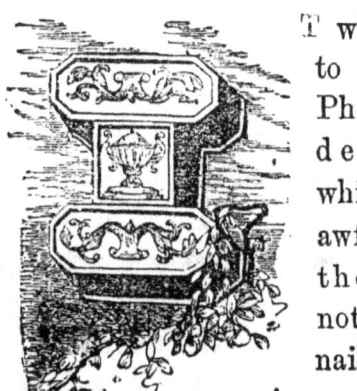

T was impossible to leave Joseph Phantom's murdered body, which lay so awfully still—the impotent notched finger nails showing conspicuous in the pallor of death—without taking some steps towards making it at once clear to the legal authorities how his untimely end was consummated.

Black Lutterloh was mistaken in his calculations that no two private gentlemen would venture alone and unaided to face the possible danger to be encountered at the lone house.

Thanks to the information furnished by Nelly, Lord Lavering was able to comprehend, with tolerable certainty, the situation of the place to which the unconscious miller's daughter had been inveigled.

Beyond this, however, as to the ruffian whom Nelly had shot being dead or alive—as to what had become of Phantom—of the iniquitous Mother Wheeler, all was vague conjecture.

As soon, therefore, as Lord Lavering had safely bestowed his double charge—Nan and her sister—he hastened with all speed to Reginald Vipert, and frankly confided to that penitent gentleman his difficulty.

The advice that the impetuous Master of Monkshood gave was prompt and to the point.

"Let us hurry to the abominable den you speak of at once, my lord," said he; "if we find those we seek there, why, so much the worse for them, and the better for those whose cause you have so generously espoused. If the whole brood of evil birds have taken flight except the poor villain shut in the cupboard, we may find life enough yet remaining in him to enable him to give us valuable information. As for myself," he continued, pressing Lord Lavering's hand, "I am humbly, gratefully at your lordship's service, and will stand by you to the last, heart and soul."

These were the simple terms of compact between the men who, but so short a time since, were bitter enemies; and in a few minutes they were galloping in hot haste to the scene that already has been described.

It was fully two miles from the solitary house at Oakenfield to the nearest town, and thither, while Reginald Vipert watched, Lord Lavering hastened on Bay Dolphin, and in less than an hour returned with a couple of constables and a medical man.

The latter, however, merely for form sake.

So virulent was the poison Mr. Phantom had swallowed, that, as the doctor averred, had he been in the room with him at the time, it would have been impossible to have saved him.

Hurried, however, as had been their movements, the morning was far advanced before Lord Lavering and Mr. Vipert found themselves at liberty to consider what steps should next be taken.

The ruffianly Lutterloh, who, it appeared, had added another to his previous crimes, they had no doubt would soon be in safe hands.

The information that Joseph Phantom had lodged at Scotland Yard had already been transmitted to those police stations that were near the neighbourhood the desperate gipsy was known to haunt, and ere the day was at an end the hue and cry would be fairly raised, and he would be fairly tracked down.

"Were it not too grave a matter for wagering on, one might pretty safely bet that he will be found in no house," Mr. Vipert remarked; "almost every park and wood and forest for miles round hereabout are familiar to the rascal; he'll be found quaking and trembling in some copse or hollow tree, you may depend."

But they hardly knew the man they were speaking of.

His time for quaking and trembling had not arrived yet.

"Shall we return to London and acquaint poor Gauntlet with what has happened?" Squire Vipert suggested.

"That would seem the proper course," returned Lord Lavering, thoughtfully; "but, altogether against my reasoning, I seem drawn the other way."

"The other way?"

"Aye, towards Monkshood. I don't know how it is. This sort of excitement is new to me, and I suppose my nervous system is disturbed," returned his handsome young lordship, half laughing, though still looking anxious. "I feel that we are wanted at Monkshood somehow."

"I much doubt if I have any title to be included in your lordship's presentiment," responded Reginald Vipert, with something like a sigh; "but whichever way you go, I am with you."

And they turned their horses' heads and pricked hard with the spurs.

Not too hard.

Not too hard, though the sensitive sides of Fury and Bay Dolphin spurt a tiny jet of crimson at each cruel goad.

Not too hard, though those mettlesome creatures are urged to such desperate speed, that in the end they lie prone on the highway with their dead tongues moistening the dust.

Human life is more precious than horse life, and now, if ever it was, human life is in danger.

It is said of lions and tigers that the taste of blood, though it may appease their hunger, increases their appetite for more blood, and that they will spill it for the mere savage delight of seeing it flow.

Lutterloh had tasted blood—the blood of revenge, that is so much more precious than any other; and there was a deal of the tiger in Lutterloh's nature.

He had seen the man who, according to his erring, brutish instinct, had meditated a deadly "trick" against him, writhing in death agony at his feet, and the spectacle had stirred his evil passions to their lowest depths.

"That's one game won, and I'll play high for the next—high as the topmost round of the gallows ladder."

The "next game" was to be played against Nelly Blisset.

The grudge he held against her was all the more bitter because, as it seemed to him, she had acted the part of a traitor towards him.

He was bent on serving her at the very moment when she aimed at him the treacherous bullet that had caused him such unceasing pain since the moment when it ploughed its way through the fleshy part of his side.

That pricked him more at every step, and stimulated his thirst for vengeance.

A long eight miles parted Oakenfield from Monkshood, but from the moment when Lutterloh made his escape from the place where lay his first victim, he fearlessly faced it.

"I'd better keep on while I'm warm to the work," said he to himself; "it won't do to grow cool; hell-broth should be sipped hot, or it loses its real flavour. I'm tired; I've lost such a lot of blood through that infernal shot, or I shouldn't feel it; but I'll push on. Dinner's a-waitin' !Ha! ha! Breakfast at Oakenfield, and dinner at Blisset's Mill. Dinner's a-waitin'! Afore I get there, I'll find a stone, and give my carvin' knife a whet on it."

And so, now grating his teeth with the pain his wound caused him, and now indulging in ruffianly pleasantry by way of keeping up his courage, Black Lutterloh made so light of the eight miles, that by nine o'clock in the morning, he had reached the plantation that skirted the hill atop of which stood Blisset's Mill.

But how in broad daylight to reach the mill-house was the difficulty.

The proverb, however, that declares that Satan is never at a loss to provide his children with a means of doing wickedness was verified in Black Lutterloh's case.

Even while he was pondering the puzzle, there came lumbering along the road the miller's waggon that was drawn by jog-trot old Dobbin, and driven by the redoubtable Peter.

The waggon was empty, except for a heap of sacks, and when Peter approached the foot of the hill, he climbed down out of the vehicle and took his place at Dobbin's head.

It was a desperate venture, but Lutterloh's chances were desperate, and he had firm reliance in his luck.

Allowing the waggon to pass his hiding-place, he crept out, and, nimble as a hare, was up into the vehicle behind, and under the sacks, while innocent Peter never for a moment paused in the tune he was whistling.

Up the hill and to the mill-house!

In at the gate where the watch-dog was yawning in his kennel, and, for a minute or so pausing at the very house-door, in at which Peter turned with some message for the miller.

Peeping from under the sacks, Lutterloh could see the porch and the window just over the porch.

Her window!

He knew it of old.

Ah! if he was only in the room beyond!

It might be done if he dared.

Done! Aye, as easily as ascending a ladder.

From the waggon rail to the porch top it was not more than three feet, and the window was not two feet above that.

What a splendid chance to lose!

And it must be lost, for here came that beastly Peter!

"Here, Peter! what did old Gummidge say about the lost meal sack?"

"Why, I'll tell you, master."

And in went Peter again.

Now for it!

One, two, three!

He is on the waggon rail, and up on the porch.

Four, five, six!

He has lifted the sash; he has vanished, and the sash is closed again.

Lutterloh could hardly believe in his wonderful luck.

The room was empty, but it was evident, from the appearance of the bed, that it had been occupied last night.

"I knew I was right," the ruffian muttered to himself; "when she escaped from the house, she made straight for home, as a matter of course. Ha! ha! If she was to come up now, she'd think it was the ghost of the man wot she shot come arter her. But she'd soon find her mistake. Ghosts ain't got a fist like this to squeedge a wind-pipe, nor a blade like this to slit one!"

And with a diabolical grin he surveyed his black muzzle in Nelly's dainty looking-glass.

There was a clothes closet in the room, tall and deep enough to contain his huge bulk.

"I'll hide in here," said Lutterloh. "When she comes up, as she's sure to in a little while, I'll put her past squeaking before she can open her lips."

Nothing is so patient as hatred that is sure of its victim, and Lutterloh waited and waited until more than two hours had passed.

Not, however, without comfort for his malicious heart.

He could hear Nelly's voice, and Nan's voice, and the voices of the old miller and his wife, and though he could but indistinctly make out their conversation, he could hear plainly enough to understand that he formed a prominent feature of the discourse.

He grinned as he laid a hairy hand to his ear and listened.

It was perfectly clear now who had committed the Monkshood murder.

John Gauntlet's release was certain; indeed, his detention at Newgate was now but a merely formal matter.

He would be home and amongst them again in two days' time at latest, and all would be well.

"I'd like to have the catching of that villain Lutterloh," spoke stout old Blisset. "I am an old man, and he's a lion in strength and a wolf in temper, so they tell us, but, hang me, but I'd tackle him if he came within my reach."

The old miller sat in the room beneath, and had a rule been placed atop of his bald head, the distance between it and the feet of the villain in question would have been found something less than a couple of yards.

Black Lutterloh grinned, and felt the edge of the open knife in his pocket.

Another half-hour passed, and the old miller went about his work, and soon after Lutterloh pricked up his ears at sound of a footstep ascending the stairs.

He grasped the door by an inner button, and settled his mind to the sanguinary business before him.

But, to his disappointment and disgust, it was not Nelly Blisset, but her sister Nan.

Nan had come up to set the room in order, and when that was done, she came to the looking-glass in which so shortly before, Lutterloh had contemplated his villanous visage, and proceeded to brush and arrange her rich brown tresses.

Black Lutterloh had a fair view of her through a chink in the closet door, and presently saw her desist from her hair brushing, and gaze earnestly out of the window through which he had entered.

"It is he!" he heard her softly exclaim to herself, with her hands clasped, and her face suddenly beaming. "God bless him for his true heart! it is he, but who is it riding with him? What news do they bring, that they come galloping here at so rapid a pace?"

Lutterloh in the closet heard her words, with a savage quickening of his pulse.

He heard more, too—the rapid galloping that Nan Blisset had alluded to.

Who were the rapid riders, and what was their mission at the mill?

As to who they were, he was quickly informed.

"'Tis the Squire!—Squire Vipert!" Nan continued, in amazement, now that she got a fairer view of the horsemen. "Squire Vipert and Lord Lavering riding in company! That is strange, indeed. Nelly! Nelly! come up here, dear?"

And instantly responding, up came Nelly, wondering at her sister's urgent call. And, with his eyes glaring with the hatred that burned within him, Lutterloh saw her.

"Squire Vipert!" Nelly ejaculated, as she looked in the direction in which Nan eagerly pointed, "and coming *here*. I must not see him, Nan."

"Aye, but you need not fear him in the good company he is," Nan replied, in tones that would have gone straight to the chivalrous young lord's heart had he heard them; "he brings nothing but good with him; never, never."

"But I would rather not see Mr. Vipert," pleaded Nelly; "remember, my sister, we have not met since that unhappy day when——"

"Well, well, have your own way, dear," Nan interrupted, kissing her. "I must run away, for they are at the door. Stay you up here, Nell, until I come to you again."

"I'll never call out again about my luck failin' me," the ruffian in the closet grinned to himself, as he heard the last welcome words that Nan uttered as she prepared to go below to receive the honoured guests.

"Aye, stay you up here, my pretty wild cat!" he mused, as, with eyes still fixed on her, he gave the edge of his knife a finishing touch on his heavy palm. "Stay you up here and get your deservings. I hope she'll like the appearance of you when she does come up again."

And hearing the horsemen at that moment draw up before the mill-house door, Nan sprang down the stairs, leaving Nelly Blisset alone in the power of the bloodthirsty villain, crouched like a beast of prey, and ready for a spring.

Nelly came to the window.

Nothing could better have served the murderer's purpose!

The window was not three paces from the closet.

In three seconds the blow might be struck and exit made from the window, and off and away before even an alarm was raised.

He opened the closet door just a little.

Her back was towards him, and she sat, her fair cheek resting on her hand, thinking of John, and of the bliss of again greeting him a free, happy man.

A quick step behind her, a muttered imprecation, and a savage lunge of the clasp knife over her shoulder aimed true at her heart!

Followed by what?

By a shriek of death agony, and the fall of her bleeding, lifeless form to the ground?

No; the gods be thanked! Such a sanguinary tragedy was not to sully that bright, sunny morning.

Black Lutterloh's knife struck home as he aimed it, but a talisman turned its cruel point aside.

A charm, a precious relic, that had been poor Nelly's close companion, her daily, her nightly consolation since her dear boy's incarceration.

Her lover's miniature in its massy gold setting.

About her neck was its ordinary place, but, since it had become so very, very sacred, Nelly had worn it just where her heart beat against it, and, true as the stalwart original, had he been standing by her side, it had saved his life.

Foiled, baffled, and wounded too (for the sharp blade, meeting with the staunch impediment, had closed on his clenched knuckles), Lutterloh uttered a fierce oath, and prepared to renew the attack.

But Nelly's piercing cry of affright had been heard in the little parlour below, and, ere five might be counted, Lord Lavering and Reginald Vipert were in view of the appalling spectacle—Nelly Blisset lying like one dead upon the ground, and Black Lutterloh with his red knife and his red fist glaring at them like a panther brought to bay.

With that indomitable pluck that possessed him, little Lord Lavering was about to spring on the villain, when the Master of Monkshood courteously put him aside.

"Let that be my task, my lord," said he. "I am stronger and better able to cope with this ruffian than are you."

And, with his riding-whip still in his hand, thong in hand, and heavy butt end swinging, he dashed at the gipsy.

But, wounded as he was, in the side as well as the hand, Black Lutterloh still retained a prodigious amount of his bull strength.

Throwing down his knife, he caught the loaded whip-stock as it descended, and with it the hand of the squire; and then, quick as lightning, his own other disengaged hand grasped him by the throat.

"You're a strong man, squire," cried the ruffian, "but you should think twice before you handle a bear of *my*

breed. Only that moments is precious, I'd squeeze your windpipe as flat as a bit o' tape. Lay there, —— you!"

And, with no great apparent effort, he flung tall Squire Vipert from him with a force that sent him staggering against the opposite wall.

Then, without waiting to open it, he dashed headlong through the window on to the porch just beneath, and with a yell of savage defiance, leaped from it down into the garden, and so away.

But he had not yet escaped.

Ere Squire Vipert could recover from the bewildering effect of his unexpected defeat, Lord Lavering, fearless as though he bore a charmed life, bounded through the shattered sash, and with a leap light as that of a greyhound, reached the ground, and was instantly in hot pursuit.

But Lutterloh had a start of several seconds, and, for a fellow of his bulk and stature, was an excellent runner.

Besides, he was a man running for his life.

The hill on which the mill stood was skirted by a dense wood, and it evidently was the gipsy's intention to gain its cover as quickly as possible.

It was not until he had nearly attained his object that he was conscious that he was being pursued.

When he for a moment made the discovery, and saw who it was, panting and almost breathless as he was, he could scarcely forbear a loud laugh of derision.

CHAPTER XXXI.

BRAVE LORD LAVERING.

HIS is a new state o' things," said Black Lutterloh, scornfully, as he saw Lord Lavering dashing after him, "the hare hunting the hound 'stead of t'other way It seems a pity to spile the face of such a pretty genelman, but I certainly shall have to do it if he is so rash as to follow me out of the open and into the thicket. But I don't think he dare."

No question of that.

He underrated the sterling mettle of the individual who was now pursuing him.

He came dashing on, peremptorily calling on the other to stop.

Scarcely twenty yards parted them when Lutterloh leapt the hedge that separated the pasture land from the gloomy wood, and as he did so, with a vengeful shake of his great fist, he cried out to Lord Lavering to think better of following him any further.

He might as well have addressed the wind, and expected it to obey him.

Lord Lavering's only reply was a

defiant shout, and such an increase of speed that ere fifty yards of the wood were penetrated, pursuer and pursued were at arm's length.

"In the king's name I arrest you as a murderer !''

And next moment the delicate and jewelled hand audaciously grasped the villain's rough collar.

Lutterloh could scarcely believe his senses.

It seemed to him pretty much as though a silky-coated spaniel had dared attack a full-bred bulldog.

Foaming with rage, with a jerk he tore away the collar of his smock from Lord Lavering's grasp, and faced him with an ominous scowl.

"I told yer what would happen if yer *would* come arter me," he cried, viciously. " Since you wouldn't take sound advice, you must take the consequences."

And, with all his strength, he aimed his great clenched fist full at the young lord's face.

Quick as thought the blow was parried, and Lutterloh received under his left ear a blow which, but for his enormous strength, must have brought him to the ground.

The effect on Black Lutterloh was only to sting him to greater fury.

He placed himself in attitude.

" I'll make sure this time," he exclaimed, through his clenched teeth.

But though of slender stature, Lord Lavering was a perfect model as regards muscle and sinew, and the British art of boxing was an accomplishment to which he had given special attention.

With masterly dexterity he parried the vicious blows, and in return delivered his own white fists, hard as ivory, against Mr. Lutterloh's visage.

Bright lights for an instant danced before the big gipsy's eyes as he was sent staggering backwards.

He had never reckoned on his gentlemanly antagonist possessing such strength as well as skill; but he was not so blinded by passion as to lose sight of prudence.

Rough and tough as a bull, there could be no doubt that in the end a trial of fists must end in his favour.

But Lutterloh had no time for experiments.

He had reckoned on being able with one smashing blow to bring his pursuer, senseless and bleeding, to the earth.

Failing in that, his cunning immediately suggested another project.

" I'll lure him to'rds the chalk pit," he thought to himself. " I'll bring him to the very edge of it, and then I'll treat him to a fall of sixty good feet as easy as I would cast a baby down."

And taking advantage of his woodcraft, quick as a hare he darted round a great tree, and was off again ere Lord Lavering suspected his design.

" You great hulking coward, you shan't escape me !"

And, in an instant, the chase was renewed.

But Lutterloh was at home among the trees, and wound in and out among them in a manner that made his capture impossible.

Suddenly, however, he came to a standstill, and with a sudden backward dash, seized Lord Lavering by the arms.

" You cursed fool !" he exclaimed, panting for breath. " I'd ha' let you off with a smashed face if you'd ha' let me; now I'll show you a trick that won't leave a whole bone in your carcase."

And, exercising his prodigious strength, he fairly lifted his young antagonist off his feet, and swung him round.

The sight that, at that instant, greeted Lord Lavering's eyes, was one that would have daunted many a bigger man.

They were on the brink of a chasm, the sheer depth of which was enough to make one giddy to contemplate.

An ancient chalk pit, long since abandoned and unprotected, except for the stunted bushes that fringed the verge of it.

But the murderous feat that Lutterloh had promised himself would be so easy of accomplishment was not yet performed.

A sense of his peril endowed the lithe young lord with twice his ordinary strength; and at the school where he had been trained, wrestling had been regarded as inseparable from a perfect knowledge of boxing.

In an instant his legs were wound about those of Lutterloh in so scientific a fashion, that, had they been linked together with iron fetters, he could not have been held more helpless.

Thus, dead locked together, the two men swayed to and fro for several seconds, and then both came to the ground.

Up again, and on their legs in an instant; and, with glaring eyes, and teeth firmly set with devilish purpose, the gipsy again sprang forward, to make a second hold, but science again showed itself superior to brute strength.

Dexterously dropping on one knee, Lord Lavering caught his man by the hips as he came on, and next moment Lutterloh came crashing down on his back amongst the briars.

But here his cunning served him.

He did not rise to his feet.

He rolled swiftly over, and, before Lord Lavering could regain his feet, Lutterloh had him in his arms.

Neither spoke a word.

Within three yards was the edge of the terrible precipice, and with a tremendous effort, the gipsy contrived to roll himself and his antagonist over yet once again, and Lutterloh was uppermost, and now not two feet parted them from the brink of the terrible gulf.

Fortune seemed suddenly to have turned her back on the most worthy.

About his waist, Lord Lavering wore over his riding-coat a broad strap, such as in those days horsemen sometimes wore, for the convenient carrying of a pair of pistols.

Lutterloh made a sure grip on the belt, and this gave him an immense advantage in manœuvring his victim to the edge of the pit.

But at that instant was heard the sound of swift footsteps treading through the fallen leaves and forest litter, and then a piercing shriek rent the air.

So sudden and thrilling was the sound, that Lutterloh was startled, and looked up and about him, and then came Lord Lavering's desperate chance.

With a strength that seemed almost impossible in one of such slender build, he arched his back and drew up his knees with a violent jerk, and next instant Black Lutterloh was over the edge of the precipice.

Over the edge, but he had not fallen.

He kept his grip on the leather belt, and only that a thorn bush gave Lord Lavering some sort of anchorage for his hands, they must instantly have launched together into the awful abyss.

"I ain't goin' alone!" gasped Lutterloh, his devilish malice not deserting him even at this terrible moment. "I ain't much afore my time, and arter all, it's sweeter to die this 'ere way than on the gallows. Ha! ha! the bush is a-breakin'! I never thought to kick the bucket in such 'spectable company."

The bush was not breaking; it was surely, though slowly, tearing up by the roots, and then——!

"Help! help! Quicker, for God's sake!"

And the piercing shriek was repeated till the woods rang.

It was Nan Blisset.

With her hair dishevelled, and her face pale with affright, she came bounding on, calling on Reginald Vipert, whom she had outstripped, to hurry.

Another moment and she is at the verge of the pit, and she sees the men in deadly grapple, the yielding bush—all!

No more shrieking, or wasting so much as a single word.

"Hold on but for another little minute," she exclaimed in a whisper that sounded scarcely like her own voice. "Hold on, Lord Lavering, and with Heaven's help, I may save you yet."

Altered, however, as was her terrified voice, he at once recognised it.

In a moment he opened wide his eyes that had been closed as though to shut out the terrible doom that seemed inevitable, and their glances met.

"God bless you, Nan Blisset!" he exclaimed, with difficulty. "It is at least some consolation to know that ——"

"Hush! your very words seem to make the yielding bush strain the more. Quick! Give me your hand!"

And, planting her feet firmly, she seized his hand that clutched the slender stem of briar so nervously, and with her other hand somehow contrived to loosen the buckle of the waist strap from its holding.

With a fearful cry, and still grasping the belt in his fist, Black Lutterloh plunged headlong into the abyss, and Lord Lavering (thanks in part to Reginald Vipert's assisting hand) was saved.

And now that the horrible peril was at an end, heroic Nan's fortitude forsook her, and she sank, well-nigh fainting, to the ground.

She would have fallen entirely, had not Lord Lavering's arm been so ready to catch and support her.

"Courage, courage, my brave darling!" he exclaimed, pressing her to his heart. "It would have been hard to die in so dreadful a way, but crueller than all to have met my death, and you never to have known how long, how ardently I have loved you!"

There was miraculous reviving in

this sudden out-gushing of the heart's pent-up purest essence.

She had heard his words, and she needed but to look into his honest, bright eyes, moist with tenderness and gratitude, to be assured to the full of their sincerity.

And when he read what was in her eyes so plainly written, and bent his face to kiss her, the arms that were suddenly clasped about his neck relieved his sensitive mind of fear lest he had given offence.

* * * * *

Nigh seventy feet below lay Black Lutterloh. Was he dead?

Reginald Vipert, shading his eyes, looked down into the dark depths of the old pit, and fancied that he saw a faint movement of the dim white mass below.

Then his keen ears detected a feeble moaning.

"I believe that there is life left in the ruffian yet," said he. "I shall be glad, indeed, to find it so."

"Glad!" Lord Lavering exclaimed in amazement.

"Aye, my friends; it is better to have a wounded than a dead man to account for. Stay here, if you please; I will be back in a very little while."

And he darted away towards the high road.

Nor, as good fortune willed it, had he far to go for assistance.

As before stated, the information that Black Lutterloh was "wanted," had gone the round of the constabulary, and the hue and cry was general.

Having got scent of him, two officers were proceeding along the road, and Squire Vipert overtook them.

A few words served to induce them to turn back, and, by a circuitous path, Lord Lavering and Nan accompanying them, the bottom of the old chalk pit was reached.

Lutterloh was still alive, though his terribly lamed and mangled condition made it evident that his hours—nay, his very minutes were numbered.

He roused and opened his eyes at the sound of their approaching footsteps.

One of the constables, with excessive zeal, produced a pair of handcuffs from his pocket, and advanced towards the poor, crushed and helpless wretch to fix them on his wrists.

"There's no 'casion; the bones is broke," Lutterloh feebly remarked, with a ghastly attempt at a grin. "Don't touch me; I shall fall all to bits if you move me from where I am lyin'."

Squire Vipert knelt by him, and made a hasty examination of his injuries.

"You are right, man," said he, solemnly; "death must speedily ensue on such terrible hurts as you have received. Nay, snatch not your hand away from mine. I am no longer your enemy. Make your peace with God while you may."

Lutterloh's face grew yet more livid, and great beads of sweat bedewed his forehead.

"Must—must I die?" he feebly ejaculated.

Reginald Vipert shook his head.

"I ain't a pauper; I can afford summat better—better than a parish doctor," he gasped abjectly. "I've—I've got a thousand pounds in my pocket. It's true, quite true; he—Phantom—gave it to me. I'll give half of it—all of it to a doctor who can—can patch me up for just a little while."

Those that stood about him listened incredulously.

They thought that the man was simply raving.

"All the wealth in the world would not save you, unhappy man," spoke Reginald Vipert. "Let me implore you to make what reparation you can by making confession——"

"Aye, aye, a confession! Oh, Lord! I—I can feel that I am a-goin'. Yes, I will confess. Fetch—fetch a parson, some of yer."

There was no bully bravado in Lutterloh now.

For the first time, probably, since he was a little child, his cheeks were wet with tears.

"You had best not wait for that," urged Mr. Vipert; "we are gentlemen, and——"

"Isn't there a woman with you? Didn't I see a woman?" the poor wretch faintly, though eagerly inquired.

Nan stepped forward.

Lutterloh's glazing eyes at once recognised her.

"It was you who—who pitched me down here," he said, feebly; "but I forgive you. You're a noble gal. Yes,

I'll confess to you; you'll pray for me, eh, same as a parson would, eh? You won't have the heart to cuss a poor feller when he's dead?"

"No, no, indeed; you shall have my prayers, my long, earnest prayers if you will clear away the stain of crime that falsely rests on an innocent man," Nan returned, dauntlessly kneeling by the dying man. "Tell me, quickly, before these witnesses, that it was not John Gauntlet who——"

"No, no; it was I," Lutterloh interrupted. "I murdered him. I never meant it, but poor Joel Burke roused the devil in me, and I killed him at a blow, with the stone in the hankycher! It was all me; and the unborn baby is not more innocent than John Gauntlet. It was I who hid and saw him—saw him take off his coat when he came across the poor body, and, takin' pity on it, took it up to carry. It was I who took up the coat when he was gone, and tore it and stained it with blood and placed the stone and the hankycher in the pocket. It was I who did all this, I solemnly—solemnly—Oh, God! I — I ! — you'll recollect to — to pray——"

And then an inarticulate rattling in his great throat, and Black Lutterloh was a dead man.

CHAPTER XXXII.

A HAPPY END AT LAST.

HE bells of the belfry in the church at Monkshood were unwontedly busy in the course of the fortnight that ensued on the terrible tragedy narrated in the foregoing chapter.

It was not all cheerful business, however.

In the first place, their sad and shameful duty was to toll out the news that two individuals, the one a murderer, and the other very little better, claimed a corner of the churchyard of the parish on which they had legitimate claim.

Since it was impossible to refute the said claim, the matter was compromised by providing one grave for the two, Joseph Phantom and Black Lutterloh, in a remote corner.

An event soon happened to dispel the gloom occasioned by these proceedings.

Nay—a double event!

A brace of events, each of which demanded of the Monkshood bells a service of a nature very different from that which they had last performed.

A wedding peal!

The Monkshood bellringers were in a quandary.

Here were to be two weddings in one morning, and a perfect joy peal was due to each, and each peal would be wanted at exactly the same time, and there was only one set of bells!

It made it all the more difficult because of the two couples who were chiefly implicated in the forthcoming ceremony one was respected exactly as much as the other, and to give either the preference was quite out of the question.

At last one of the Monkshood churchwardens made a suggestion of so happy a nature, that its adoption was immediately resolved on.

It was true that there was but one peal of joy bells, but, in consideration of double pay and extra beer, the bellringers manfully promised that the best music that had hitherto been got out of their brazen clappers was not half that which should be rung out of them on the present occasion.

Never, within the memory of the oldest Monkshood inhabitant, was heard such a tuneful clatter.

And in the midst of the merry welcome (it was a blue sky, with sunshine so bright that the vane on the old steeple shone as though it had been newly gilt), while the parishioners to a man, woman, and child, turned out in their holiday best, and the beadle wore his Sunday coat, with a bouquet at his breast, and even the lame old pew-opener sported a new cap, with cherry-coloured ribbons, the old fashioned state carriage of the Viperts dashed up to the gates, followed by other carriages, all bright and sparkling, and with white favours bestrewing them—in the coachmen's buttonholes, on the horses' head gear, as plentifully as snowdrops in a spring meadow.

The Vipert state carriage!

But a Vipert is not about to be married.

It is Squire Reginald himself who leaps out of the carriage, and offers his assisting arm, firstly to Nelly Blisset, and immediately after there descends an individual at sight of whom the crowd assembled set up such a tremendous shout, that even the bells seemed to hear it, and to be stimulated to still more desperate efforts.

It is John Gauntlet!

There is scarcely anyone there who has set eyes on the young farmer since he was last among them, cheerful and happy, so that it cannot but occur to them that he is thinner than of yore, and that his cheeks have lost some of their pure country bloom.

But no one there ever saw him looking more radiant and supremely happy.

No one yet saw him holding his head more proudly erect, or marked more of the pride of manliness in his bright eyes.

"Huzza! huzza! huzza!" and they would have broken on to the flower-strewn path in scores to have shaken him by the hand, had not the second bride and bridegroom appeared on the scene.

Could this be Nan Blisset?

Nan, the buxom, the fearless, the ready-handed miller's daughter.

As such in her homely garb she appeared a beauty, but not the splendid lady the Monkshood populace now beheld.

As the bride of a lord, sumptuous was her attire, magnificent her decorations of diamond and pearl; but she bore her grandeur with maiden modesty, and clung to the arm of him who was so soon to be her husband—brave, true-hearted Lord Lavering—as though, of all her jewels, she was the most precious and adorable, while he, with his handsome face beaming with happiness, gracefully acknowledged the blessings and good wishes that moved every tongue.

Then the gay throng (including prim Dame Blisset in her antique dress of lavender silk, and old Bob, the miller, the happy father of both brides, and who was in a perfect bewilderment of bliss) crossed the sacred threshold.

Then came the altar scene (which, as newspaper reporters say, is "too well known to need description"), and the chief actors in the performance emerged—Mr. and Mrs. Gauntlet and Lord and Lady Lavering.

Was that the end of it?

Not quite.

One person conspicuous in this story had yet a duty to perform.

This was Reginald Vipert.

Within an hour of the consummation

of the marriage ceremony, to their great amazement, he appeared before them equipped for an immediate journey.

He had striven hard all along to appear at his ease and cheerful, but a feeling of sadness was at his heart, and the endeavour was not altogether successful.

"You are not about to leave us?" Lord Lavering exclaimed, while all the rest looked their surprise.

"It is in accordance with a previously fixed resolution that I do so," returned the Master of Monkshood, with a sober smile. "I have imposed on myself for my sins the penalty of self banishment from my native land for a few years. 'Twere better so. Better for myself—for us all."

And as he uttered these last words, his glance for an instant wandered towards fair Nelly.

"The preparations for my journey were made long since," he continued, with more briskness in his voice, "and I start immediately. First, however, permit me to confer on those my folly has so imperilled some substantial token of my remorse. The holding, with the farm and the pasture you have hitherto rented of me, John Gauntlet, will in future, by free gift from me, be yours absolutely; and the mill, my good friend Blisset, and all about it within your fence, is now your own freehold."

Their voices would have been raised in remonstrance, but he silenced them.

"It is too late now, my friends, to object," said he, laughing his old laugh. "The deed is done these nine days past, and my lawyer will settle all that needs settling. And now, I bid you all good-bye, and God bless you!"

And in another moment he was gone.

They never saw him afterwards, but his generous gift endured with them, and increased and flourished.

As for Lord and Lady Lavering, though it was necessary that they should have a town house, at least two-thirds of the year were spent by them in the handsome little mansion his lordship had built within a mile of Gauntlet Farm.

And it is Gauntlet Farm still; and though two generations of Gauntlets, hale and handsome lads and lasses, dwell upon the place, a hearty old fellow, with white hair, and shoulders somewhat bent, may be seen serenely wending his way to church on Sunday mornings, arm-and-arm with a lady whose face still bears ample traces of the remarkable beauty that once was hers.

"And how are you, Mr. Gauntlet?" the minister asks, as he cordially shakes hands with the patriarch; "and how is your good lady?"

"Hearty as for myself, thank ye kindly," replies John Gauntlet; "and as for the mistress, she's as well, and, I do think, as happy as she was years ago, Bless Her Heart!"

THE END

LONDON:

KELLY AND CO.,

15, GATE STREET, LINCOLN'S INN FIELDS.